MRS. BLAKE IN ALBION

Folding her wings, Kate Blake emerged from the timestream into 1791, to find her cottage, London, and England—

—gone.

Instead there was Albion, an empire of Greek-speaking Isis worshipers ruled by . . . William Blake's lover, Mary Wollstonecraft! Naked "dancers" coupled on holographic TV, jet aircraft linked holy cities—and ICBM-launched warheads filled with plague across the Atlantic.

Because Albion was in a genocidal war with Oothoon —the white-hating tyranny whose living god, the winged serpent Quetzalcoatl, flew down from the sky to address patriotic rallies; where Aztecs kept castrated, impoverished whites on reservations . . .

Outrage quickly gave way to horror as Kate realized that William had made good his threat. He and the Zoas had tampered with Time. They'd destroyed Rome, France, Britain, America. They'd destroyed Jehovah, Christ, and Allah.

William Blake had murdered God.

And made a world in which his wife had never been born.

RAY FARADAY NELSON

TIMEQUEST

A TOM DOHERTY ASSOCIATES BOOK

TIMEQUEST

First printing: November 1985

A TOR Book

Published by Tom Doherty Associates
49 West 24 Street
New York, N.Y. 10010

Cover art by Don Brautigan

ISBN: 0-812-54650-4
CAN. ED.: 0-812-54651-2

Printed in the United States of America

To Kirsten,
my beloved wife and companion
in a thousand adventures.

Hear the voice of the Bard!
Who Present, Past and Future sees.
—William Blake
Songs of Experience

1

NUDE BUT FOR WINGS, the Zoas swarmed from century to century, savoring of each age its unique bouquet. In tunic, toga and sandals, with shortsword and dagger at the ready, they mingled with the Roman crowd, heard the hysterical ovation as Nero passed, then, as the rain came, watched the blood of Jewish gladiators turn the earth to brick-red mud.

In doublet and hose they rode in procession awhile with a king and stole a royal kiss from a princess, a lean, wide-eyed lass with a taste for commoners.

In airtight silver suit and fishbowl helmet they walked the desert of Mars.

In monkish robes they watched armored knights crash together on horseback and then, when one knight fell, continue the fight on foot, panting, grunting, weeping.

In glowing fog of energy like a second skin, they stood at a wide oval porthole and watched the triple star Capella recede, turn red, and fade into blackness as the rest of the sky crowded in on it.

In hairy, dirty animal skins they ran barefoot through tall grass, howling at a shaggy, bellowing mastodon that fled before them toward a trap through a steamy afternoon.

Then at last, weary and laughing and nude once more, they rested on a cliff overlooking a swamp that would someday be London, gazing down at a torpid, gigantic, mottled-brown diplodocus that lazily chewed leaves and waded while a gray overcast moved sluggishly overhead.

The Zoas, some male, some female, unstrapped their

wings and laid them among the ferns, white feathers among the gray-green feathery fronds.

The diplodocus swung its little head in their direction, neck graceful and swanlike, tiny eyes glittering like wet ebon pebbles, but made no move to harm the Zoas or to flee.

Many of the Zoas wandered, in twos and threes, away from the swamp, toward a distant grove of giant redwoods, gathering samples of ferns, palmlike cycads, tasting the fruit of the ginkgos.

Two Zoas remained at the cliff's edge, reclining on the natural lawn of fern that grew there.

Tharmas, who in the century of his birth had been King of Atlantis, smiled; dark bearded, ruddy, handsome. "I told you it would be wonderful, my friend."

His companion did not speak at once, but when he did his tone was somber. "Wonderful? I saw only madness. I never realized before how much of history consists of meaningless violence, of stupidity, of blind passion." His white beard bespoke age, but his athletic body seemed to indicate youth, and from his face jutted a large, prominent nose.

Tharmas laughed, white teeth glowing in the unnatural light. "Exactly! As a drama, it lacks nothing!"

"It lacks one thing."

"One thing?"

"Reason." His voice was grim.

"You crave reason? Ah, my poor friend, you've come to the wrong planet. Must everything submit itself for judgment to your reason?"

"How else can I judge?"

"Don't judge at all. Enjoy!"

"I could as soon not judge as not breathe. The brain, like the lungs, stops only in death."

King Tharmas mockingly placed his hand on his friend's head. "Let that be your name then, at least among us Zoas. I hereby dub you, 'Your Reason.' "

"Your Reason? Your reason?" He spoke faster. "Urizen! I like it! Yes, I accept the name."

"Welcome to the League of Zoas, Urizen," said the king, and kissed Urizen on the lips.

Urizen pulled away, rubbing his lips with the back of his wrist. "In my century men do not kiss men like that."

Tharmas roared with laughter. "One century among so many, and a hardhearted century at that. To enjoy the gift of time-voyaging you've just discovered, you must transcend the prejudices, the narrow folkways, the tribal taboos of your parents, transcend them or find the taste of other times and other places bitter in your mouth. Everything changes, Urizen. Everything!"

"Not everything."

"Oh?"

"Reason does not change."

The king laughed again. "You disappoint me. After what you've just seen, certainly your reason must see reason's limitations. Certainly you noticed how, at certain branching forks in history, the meaning of everything, including what is meant by reason, shifts. Going down one branch, reason means one thing. Going down the other, reason means another. Ah, but never mind. You'll understand after a while. When we've rested you can come with me as I check here and there in the timestream to make sure we haven't in some way changed history."

Urizen spoke with anger. "And if we did change it, who would care? Who would even know, except ourselves? Any change would be an improvement. You saw the hate, the war, the ignorance, the injustice! What's so sacred about that? Why should we take such care to avoid changing one bloodstained minute?"

Some of the nearer Zoas turned toward the two, sensing a good argument developing. Men and women who have seen so much may settle nothing in their discussions, but when they argue they range far and argue brilliantly.

King Tharmas responded indignantly, "We don't know what would happen if . . ."

Urizen broke in. "So much the better! I say break the chain of history and see what happens! I say take the risk. I say step in and make changes deliberately."

"Once we start, where would we stop?"

Urizen leaned forward, his harsh voice rising. "We stop when we have created a perfect society, joy without pain, stability without fluctuation. We stop when mankind lives under perfect laws of peace, of love, of pity, compassion, forgiveness. . . . One command, one king, one God, one law! It's worth a little risk!"

"Ah Urizen, you know so little. Soon experience will temper your dreams of power."

"Dreams?" Urizen sprang up. "Power is no dream if you use it!"

Urizen picked up wings and began strapping them on. Tharmas too stood up and touched him on the forearm, saying softly, "Urizen, my friend . . ."

Urizen turned and pushed Tharmas away. Still the king, taking it for good-natured horseplay, repeated with a grin, "Urizen . . ."

But, abruptly, Urizen vanished.

The Atlantian king hesitated only an instant. "Comrades! Zoas!" he shouted, and they, hearing the urgency in his voice, came running from all around.

"Listen, all of you," Tharmas cried. "Our new friend . . . we must find him and stop him."

"What's he going to do?" came the voice of one of the women as she struggled into her wings.

Tharmas answered angrily, "I doubt if even he has any clear idea."

Moments later the cliff again stood vacant. The diplodocus noted this fact with monumental indifference. . . .

. . . but in eighteenth century London a redheaded, blue-eyed boy awoke to glimpse, peering in at his window, a bearded, winged naked man. The boy screamed. The man flew up across the bright disk of the full moon.

2

THE BOROUGH OF BATTERSEA LAY shrouded in fog on the right bank of the Thames, opposite Chelsea. Even on those rare days when the sun shone, Battersea remained a drab, gray place; no tourist from the continent visiting London would waste his time on its ordinary, sagging, half-timbered little homes crowded together, its ordinary dusty little shops, its ordinary little market-gardens.

Kate Boucher, however, loved this drabness. In her twenty-one years of life she had never seen better, indeed never left London for even one day. She saw a gentle human beauty in her city, and her vision transformed everything into God's goodness, not only for herself, but for those around her.

Now, as she rode beside her father on a rattling vegetable wagon down a narrow cobblestone street, soot-blackened chimneysweeps, bearded streetvendors, and ragged barefoot child prostitutes turned to watch her, amazed not only by her costume, an antique bridal gown, all white from head to toe, not only by the glow of youth and health that burned in her slender body, not only by the classic Grecian elegance of her face—framed in curly light brown hair—but above all amazed by her strange eyes that seemed to look through this world into some magical world beyond.

Her father, dressed in his Sunday best—black coat, waistcoat and kneebreeches with a puff of white muslin at the throat—smiled at her from time to time, saying nothing to break the enchantment. In the wagon behind them rode Kate's mother, sisters, and brothers, likewise all scrubbed

and brushed and dressed-up for the occasion, and they too
spoke not a word. All knew better than to try to talk to
Kate when she was in her dream.

The wagon rounded a corner, entering a larger, grayer
street, and up ahead Kate could see the modest neighborhood church of St. Mary, a veritable cathedral to her.

On the church steps a small group clustered, waiting.

''William,'' she breathed.

For there he stood, her future husband.

William Blake's family crowded close around him, but
her eyes focused only on him, on his stocky twenty-five-
year-old body and unkempt carrot-orange hair, on his large
strange eyes that seemed to mirror her own, as if they
might be brother and sister instead of bride and groom.

William's mother and sister hovered a bit apart from his
father and brothers. All dressed neatly and respectably,
save William. Even at his own wedding William wore
frayed kneebreeches and soiled cuffs.

His mother and sister also bore the name of Catherine,
the same as Kate. Now there would be three Kate Blakes.

Kate noticed a frown on William's father's lean, weary
features. The old man had opposed the marriage all along.
Perhaps he still did, though he knew no way to prevent it.
William made enough with his commercial engraving to
support her, so parental threats to ''cut Bill off without
sixpence'' carried no weight at all. Still she could not help
wondering what Mr. Blake objected to. She thought the
man liked her well enough: in fact he seemed almost trying
to warn her, to hint of something dreadful about young
William that could not be mentioned openly. Time and
again he'd touched her arm when they were alone for a
moment and been on the point of speaking, only to lapse
into a miserable silence.

The vegetable wagon reined up at the foot of the church
stairs and William came running to help her down. How
gallant he was, but not in a studied way like a gentleman!
No, he was all impulse with no thought for propriety.

She laughed delightedly as he lowered her to the walkway.

How strong he was!

Hand in hand they ascended the steps and entered the

dim church vestibule. Out of the corner of her eye she studied his profile, so calm and noble even now. How strange that a man so free and impulsive never laughed!

After the ceremony, the lean, balding sexton stepped from the shadows. "Will you be good enough to sign the church register, Madam?"

Kate drew back from the extended hand holding the goose-quill pen. "Why no, I'm sorry but . . ."

The sexton persisted, "Your husband signed. The law requires it, young lady."

"I can't." Her voice was barely audible. "I can't spell, you see."

William's father turned away from the guests and regarded her with a raised eyebrow. In a moment all eyes were upon her.

William stepped to her side protectively. "Is it absolutely necessary?" he demanded.

"Absolutely," the sexton replied primly. "However, sir, the law will be satisfied if the bride draws an X on the proper line."

She haltingly drew her X, pausing between the two strokes with a pensive frown, then returned the pen to the sexton.

"Very good, very good," the sexton muttered, nodding with satisfaction. "And now could you tell me your maiden name?"

"Boucher," she answered him shyly.

The sexton bent over the register, pursing his lips, then glanced at Kate's father. "Could you give me the correct spelling for that, please?"

Now Mr. Boucher too showed considerable embarrassment. "B . . . U . . ."

"Yes, yes, go on."

"T . . . C . . . H . . . E . . . R." He pronounced the last letter with vast relief.

The sexton looked up, annoyed. "Heavens, man. That's not Boucher, that's Butcher!"

Mr. Boucher drew himself up with dignity. "Beggin' your pardon, sir, but is it my fault the Good Lord didn't give me nor me daughter the high position in life what opens the door to the world of book learnin'?''

The sexton carefully blotted the ink. "Of course not, Mr. Boucher. I understand. I understand perfectly."

William put in, "Perhaps you can change it."

The sexton shook his head firmly. "No, now I've blotted the ink. Butcher it is and Butcher it stays."

Kate felt ill. Everything in the marriage ceremony had gone off perfectly, and now this had to happen! Such a little thing, but it brought to light other things not so little, things she'd brushed aside as unimportant but which now forced themselves into her mind and demanded her attention.

Her husband's profession was the making of illustrations for books, and worse, his hobby was the writing of poetry. How could she, who could neither read nor write, fit into this world of words? She glanced at the graven inscriptions on the walls, inscriptions in English she had seen almost every Sunday of her life, but which remained as enigmatic as Egyptian hieroglyphs. A vast despair drifted over her, obscuring her bridal joy.

Thus as they left the church and descended the broad marble staircase, Kate clung hard to William's arm as if, having seen her shortcomings exposed in such a humiliating way before his well-educated family, he might cast her off and leave her forever.

A fine carriage waited at the curb.

"How elegant!" she cried, recovering her spirits.

William remarked soberly, "Enjoy the ride, Mrs. Blake. We won't take many. My father rented the carriage. He can afford it. I can't."

He helped her in, acting the role of gentleman with a self-mocking air.

The coachman gave the horses a cluck of the tongue and the carriage lurched into motion. Kate looked back over her shoulder to watch her family climb into the old vegetable wagon. Her father waved to her, shameless tears running down his cheeks, and as she waved back she thought, *He's as fine a Christian gentleman as anyone else, even if he ain't been to school.*

"Where to, sir?" the coachman rumbled with dignity.

"Twenty-three Green Street, Leicester Fields."

"Very good, sir."

They rounded a corner and Kate's family was lost to view. She missed them already.

William quietly closed the door behind him.

"Well, here's your new lodgings, Mrs. Blake."

"I like that!" Kate said.

"Like what?"

"I like to have you call me Mrs. Blake. Sounds so homelike, don't you know. Mrs. Blake." She laughed and he smiled slightly.

She wandered about touching things as he looked on. Two small rented rooms on the second floor; she had had more space at home and less formality, less sense of intimidating propriety. Here the curtains seemed too white, the comforters on the bed too well-stuffed, the pitcher and washbasin on the dresser too finely made, too delicate, too fragile. And those candlesticks on the mantel . . . were they really made of gold? She took one down and examined it. No, only lead covered with gilt. That made her feel better somehow.

"Quite a nice place, Mr. Blake. I believe I'll stay."

"I knew you'd like it, Mrs. Blake."

A long uncomfortable silence.

"Would you like a fire, Mrs. Blake?"

She turned to stare out the window. She could not see the sky, only a dirty brick wall a short distance away, but by the ruddy glow on the wall she knew the sun was setting. Already a faint chill set her to hugging herself and rubbing her arms vigorously.

"Indeed yes, Mr. Blake. A cold night's comin', I expect."

She could hear him moving around, arranging the wood in the fireplace. The red glow outside faded and a vague uneasiness crept over her. But what could possibly be wrong? She had just done what every respectable girl dreamed of doing. She'd married, and somewhat above her station. Then, abruptly, it came to her. Since they'd entered the flat, William had not once touched her.

"Mr. Blake?"

"Yes?"

"Be you ashamed of me now?"

"Good heavens no."

"I ain't so well-learned as some."

She had remembered Polly Wood. William had been in love with Polly Wood, so in love he'd gotten sick from it. Polly had had brains, education, breeding, but had not loved William. Kate was William's second choice, not his first, and she knew it.

Kate had met William while he stayed with the Boucher family in Battersea, trying to forget Polly, and Kate well remembered their first conversation. He'd told her of his hopeless love, of Polly's cruelties, Polly's infidelities, and then he'd asked, "Kate, do you pity me?"

She'd answered truthfully, "Yes, I surely do!"

Then he'd said softly, "Then I *love* you!"

But now William knelt behind her in front of the fireplace, saying, "Education's not important."

She whirled from the window to face him. "Promise me something, Mr. Blake."

"Anything you like."

"Promise me you'll teach me reading and writing."

"I told you that wasn't important."

"It is! It is! Promise me! Swear you'll teach me!"

He gazed up at her, a look of surprise on his broad features. "Very well, girl, if it'll make you happy."

For a moment she was indeed happy, wonderfully happy, then she realized Polly knew more than simply how to read and write.

"Mr. Blake, promise to teach me everything you know! How to draw, how to paint, how to talk big words and think bigger thoughts. Me mum always said I was a clever one. I can learn anything. You'll see!" Her words tumbled over each other in her eagerness. "I'll surprise you, Mr. Blake, I will!"

He grew even more serious than usual. "I can teach you some things, but not everything. Certain matters must remain . . ."

Panic swept over her and a terrible despair, for it seemed to her he had built a little shrine within himself where he would forever worship the divine Polly, the saintly Polly, the wise Polly, the all-knowing Polly, and at that shrine there would be no place for an ignorant, common farm girl, not even as a co-worshipper.

"No, no, Mr. Blake! Everything! Do you think men so much cleverer than women?" In her desperation she snatched at his pride in being an advanced thinker, a man who had often preached to her about freedom and equality for all, even women.

"It's not that, Mrs. Blake." He shook his head slowly, sadly. The room had grown quite dark, but the flickering glow of the fireplace illuminated William's face in a way that transformed it into a mask of moving light and shadow, made it look almost demonic. "It's nothing to do with men and women. Certain things I know I could not teach to anyone, male or female."

"Mr. Blake, what are you talking about?"

He sighed and stood up. "I can not . . . I must not tell you."

For a moment she stared at him, speechless, then she noticed he was looking past her, his eyes focused on something behind her, something that moved. Out of the corner of her eye she seemed to glimpse the blurred outline of a human figure. She whirled to look, but saw no one.

"Good God, Mr. Blake," she whispered, terrified.

Later, with the fireplace in the next room the only illumination, Kate and William lay side by side in bed, under voluminous comforters, not touching each other. For some time the gentle crackle of the fire had been the only sound, then Kate murmured, "Are you asleep, Mr. Blake?"

"No." His voice sounded calm, distant.

"I never took you for the shy sort, Mr. Blake. Is this how young gentlemen of your class generally spend their wedding nights?"

After a moment he reluctantly admitted, "I suppose not."

"I can tell you for sure, sir, 'tis not the way things go in my part of town. From me own brother I'd have got at least a kiss goodnight."

"I thought we had more between us than that."

"Than what, pray tell?"

"Than the simple lusts of the flesh."

She sat up abruptly. "The simple lusts of the flesh! In case you've failed to notice, we're husband and wife, man! What goes between husband and wife ain't no sin! I don't understand you, Mr. Blake. No, not at all. You always had the gift of gab, sir, so you could make everything clear to a poor girl. Turn over and explain."

"There is nothing to explain."

"At least sit up and face me. I want to see what's in your eyes. They say a man's soul peeps out from behind his eyes, you know, so you can glimpse what he's really like."

Slowly he sat up and faced her, but his features were so shadowed she could not make out his expression. His voice, when he spoke, had the same deep, grave tone as ever. "Please, Mrs. Blake, don't plague me so."

"Then tell me what gnaws on you, my man. I'm sure there's something. You've oft preached to me about how a true marriage rests on honesty, so let's see a little honesty now. What is that business you was talking about? That business you can't teach anyone?"

"You mustn't ask me."

"I do ask you. Tell me true. I'm a brave girl. Would you rather Polly lay here beside you instead of me? Tell me true, for your own sake as well as mine." Tears began to trickle down her cheeks.

"No, Mrs. Blake. I never think of Polly now. That's all past."

She believed him. He sounded so truthful, so dignified, like a minister praying. But she had to go on, to ask, "Mr. Blake, do you love me?"

"Oh yes, Kate, yes, with all my heart!" But still he did not touch her.

"Then why . . . then why do you not take me in your arms like a natural man?"

"I must keep pure."

"Keep pure? Keep pure? For what?"

"So I won't lose . . ." She saw he felt he had said too much.

"Won't lose what?" she fairly screamed.

"The gift."

"What gift, Mr. Blake?"

His face contorted with anguish, but he did not answer.

"What gift!" She grabbed him by the shoulders and shook him.

"I can't answer that," he said, but his calm had begun to crack.

"You will answer, Mr. Blake, or I shall pack up and go home this very night." Her own words frightened her, but she could not take them back. He stared at her silently out of his large, agonized eyes. She pitied him, wanted to let him keep his secret, wanted to simply stay with him and his mystery, living like brother and sister if that was what he wanted. She wanted to touch his cheek and tell him it didn't matter, that everything was all right, that she didn't care. Oh God, those eyes! She could see them now in the dim flickering firelight, so full of pain!

But she didn't move or speak.

When at last his answer came he whispered it so softly she could scarce be sure she heard him correctly. "I have visions, Mrs. Blake."

"Visions, Mr. Blake?" She too spoke in a hushed voice, as if in a cathedral.

"Since the age of four I've seen things nobody else could see."

"What . . . what kind of things?"

"Angels. Demons. The distant past and distant future. Ghosts. The face of God."

"The face of God?"

He suddenly turned his back to her. "No more, Mrs. Blake! No more! For the sake of your own sanity, ask no more!"

And she did not ask any more questions that night; but later, as she listened to his gentle snores, she lay awake for hours mute with fear as multitudes of invisible beings seemed to move and shift in the waning firelight, to swirl about the room in clouds, evil, monstrous, ancient and infinitely powerful, and it seemed to her they had already destroyed her happiness and her marriage, and that they would not rest content until they'd also destroyed her mind and taken her life and borne her away to where, among the sullen embers, sinners scream and writhe and thrash, loins ablaze with eternal unquenchable lust.

William had made several close friends in his art student days, and now Kate found herself required to entertain them, to play the hostess for them, a role she performed at first with pleasure, but soon with resentment, for they were educated, well-informed, sophisticated, and witty, and she was not.

John Flaxman came by the most often. Hardly an evening passed without a visit from this odd young man, with his disproportionately large head, his powerful but hunched, bent body, and his sidelong awkward gait. Typical of many another night was the time he brought with him his recent bride, Nancy, a remarkably beautiful young woman to be coupled with the ugly Flaxman.

"Come in, come in," cried William. "Kate will set out some ale for you."

Kate hastened to comply.

"Ah, William," said the visitor. "We missed you at the meeting at Rev. Mathew's." He threw himself into a chair at the dining room table while his Nancy slipped demurely into another chair beside him. "Mrs. Mathew feels you're slighting us."

"I don't go to meetings much any more," said William.

"You mustn't let marriage make you a hermit."

"I like to stay home with Kate."

"Unhealthy! Unhealthy! Bring your Kate along. My Nancy goes along with me."

"Kate doesn't fit in there."

"Nancy fits in!" He smiled at her fondly, like a gargoyle in love. "Of course it doesn't hurt that she speaks not only elegant English, but fluent French, Italian, and Greek. One has to have a certain level of accomplishment to converse with the sort of people who inhabit the Mathew drawing room, people like Hester Chapone, author, artist, and virtuoso singer, or Hannah More the poetess, or the

elegant Elizabeth Montagu. Nothing common about them.''
He glanced at Kate with cruel amusement.

Kate waited for William to defend her, but as usual he did not.

Nancy Flaxman bit her lip, embarrassed. "You make too much of me, dear." Kate could tell Nancy knew how such remarks cut into her soul, but Nancy was not the kind of wife who contradicted or criticized her husband.

When William spoke up, it was to declare, "No, no, Nancy! We can't let you hide your virtues behind the veil of modesty. I always say my prints are not finished until they have passed the test of your informed and tasteful judgment." He turned in his chair and called out, "Come, Kate! Where's that ale for my friends?"

Kate served the drinks in silence.

After a pensive sip, the gargoyle continued relentlessly, "Artists and writers have always sought the company of their own kind, William my lad. Only through the stimulation of the group can the individual genius flourish! I tell you, behind every seemingly isolated man of brilliance we find a brilliant little group. The challenge of the group brings out the best in us, and the critical judgment of the group weeds out the mediocre. You know, before women attained their present high place in society, the home and the group waged eternal war on one another. Shortly after I married, that old bachelor artist Joshua Reynolds said to me, 'So Flaxman, I'm told you're married. If so, sir, I tell you you're ruined as an artist!' " He chuckled and again gazed fondly at his spouse. "He didn't know the modern woman is different."

"You're too kind," said Nancy in a pained voice, looking at Kate.

To Kate, however, Nancy's pity hurt more than John's contempt. She fled to the kitchen but William called her back. "Come out and talk to us, Mrs. Blake. Don't be so thin-skinned. John means no harm."

Dutifully Kate returned and sat down beside William, expressionless as a china doll.

"That's right," said their guest, smiling blandly. "We mean no criticism of you. You only imagine it. And if we do take a little dig at you now and then, it's all in fun. Why, without a bit of criticism, how could we ever improve?''

"He's right, you know," said William earnestly.

So Kate sat with them a while, listening to their light-hearted talk of art, poetry, Druidic magic, and the visions of Emanuel Swedenborg, though most of it might as well have been in a foreign language. Indeed, the Flaxmans, like others in William's circle, thought nothing of quoting whole paragraphs of French, Latin, Italian, or Greek.

As soon as she decently could, Kate broke away with the excuse that she had housework to do.

Later, in bed, she said, "Teach me, Mr. Blake. You promised to teach me. Teach me now."

He yawned before replying, "Teach you what?"

"Teach me to spell my own name."

With that, in the darkness with this man who would not act the man with her, she began what she came to call "The Learning," the endless project of self-education.

The following Sunday afternoon William and Kate went boating on the Thames, he at the oars, she reclining on cushions in the stern under a frilly parasol that preserved her fashionably pale complexion against the ravages of the August sun. She dressed in white, from her ankle-length skirt, through her shaped bodice, to her little bonnet, looking quite like some grand royal personage, partly because the fashion favored royal personages trying to look like commoners, but mainly because of her own other-worldly dignity, her natural nobility that made other boaters whisper among themselves about foreign princesses "traveling incognito."

Her half-closed eyes gazed fondly on her husband, and she smiled, remembering the first time she'd seen him. She'd known instantly they'd marry, had in fact almost fainted with excitement. Now, in spite of his strangeness, she felt as at home with him as if they'd been married before, as some pagan Hindu might say, in a previous incarnation.

His garb, on the other hand, bespoke his station in life,

that of a simple tradesman, with his black buckle shoes, tight gray stockings, brown knickers, white shirt with puff sleeves, and long brown brass-buttoned vest; his unsmiling face bespoke his temperament.

They drifted with the tide downstream past the Tower of London and the forest of masts where sailing ships from all over the world lay at anchor, continued almost to the Isle of Dogs, then, when the tide reversed, drifted back again while the shadows lengthened and a faint haze gathered.

She let her fingertips dabble in the cool water and listened to the distant cries of fishmongers, the creak of ships sluggishly rocking, the barking of dogs, and the cries of the wheeling gulls. Over all drifted the pungent but pleasant aroma of sea water, decaying fish and woodsmoke.

Through most of the afternoon they hardly spoke, yet at last she fell to speculating on what thoughts might lurk concealed behind those large grave blue eyes of his, what secrets might hide there, known to him alone.

Finally she broke the silence.

"Mr. Blake, when will you teach me?"

He rested on his oars, answering calmly, "I've taught you some already . . . how to spell your name, how to spell mine."

"I mean about the other things."

His serious features grew more serious. "Other things?"

"About your visions, as you call them. About angels, demons, ghosts, and the face of God."

He sighed before answering, "I suppose your soul will give you no peace until I tell you everything, now that I've so foolishly pricked your curiosity."

She sat up and gazed at him intently. "Have you really seen the face of God?"

He nodded. "I have."

"But no man sees the face of God and lives. I heard that straight from the pulpit!"

"I saw Him. When I was four, God peered in at my window, then flew off across the face of the moon. I ran screaming to my mother with fear."

Kate frowned, puzzled. "With fear? But God's our

gentle Father, Mr. Blake. We don't have nothin' to fear
from Him, at least if we've done no wrong. That couldn't
have been God you saw, but it might have been that other
fellow . . . you know who.''

"It was God. No one else could look so wise, so
all-knowing. If you'd seen Him . . .''

"What did He look like?''

"Bearded, muscular, naked . . .''

"Naked? And was He flapping about in public without a
stitch on?''

"Yes.'' William still spoke with a calm, reasonable
tone.

"Now I *know* 'twas the other fellow!''

"No, God and His angels never wear clothes.''

"How do you know?''

"I saw them naked with my own eyes, walking among
the hay-makers in a field one summer morning, I swear it,
and I saw them naked again when I walked through the
fields hard by Peckham Rye, all up in a tree with their
bright wings shining among the boughs like stained-glass
windows.''

"All naked?''

"All! But one day in those same fields I met the prophet
Ezekiel. My mother whipped me when I told her.''

Kate, dumbfounded, could only go on questioning. "You
told your parents?''

"Oh, yes. They thought I lied, but when I kept it up
they began to worry.''

"I'm not surprised.''

"Because of that they didn't send me to school, but
taught me at home as I'm teaching you. Now at last I think
they've come to understand that my visions are a gift from
God, but they showed wisdom in keeping me from school.
The other children would only have laughed at me. When
the time arrived for me to learn a trade, my parents
apprenticed me to an engraver named Ryland, but I wouldn't
go.''

With a growing panic she laid her hand on his arm.
"Why not?'' Now William had begun, she had to hear it
all.

"I had a vision," he murmured, gazing off across the water. "I seemed to see Ryland hanging by the neck, and later, sure enough, he *was* hanged exactly as in my vision, for forgery. Now do you understand why I didn't want to tell you these things?"

Slowly she nodded, mastering her fear, keeping her voice from betraying her. "Yes, I think I do, and I understand another thing too."

"What's that, Kate?"

"I understand why your father did not want you to marry."

Once started, William's monologue flowed on as endlessly as the Thames on which they drifted. The air turned cold. The sky turned red. The other small pleasure boats turned toward shore. Still he talked on. He told her of his vision of Gwin, King of Norway, and King Edward the Third and King Edward the Fourth and a woman in medieval times named Fair Elenor who was handed her husband's head in a bloody cloth and died of shock, events from every time and place he swore he'd seen with his own eyes.

The sun set.

The fog rolled in.

At last they returned their boat to a grumbling boatman and walked slowly arm in arm up the dimly glistening cobblestone street toward home in the flickering lamplight from windows where normal people, with laughter and much clattering of plates, ate their normal suppers. Now at last William was silent, trudging along, shoulders hunched, not looking at her.

She glanced at him, seeing a dark massive silhouette against a window where children thronged around a table, and her lips set into a firm determined line. She came from a huge family, with an army of aunts, uncles, cousins, nephews, and all the rest; a family that had its share of drunks, wife beaters, woman chasers and even out-and-out criminals, but in all that vast family she had never heard of a single divorce, nor had she heard anyone speak of divorce among her motley ancestors, though she'd certainly heard many another scandal of rascally great-grandfathers

and wanton great-grandmothers. She did not know how to
go about getting a divorce, or even if a woman could get
one at all. What God hath joined, let no man put asunder!
Marriage was a woman's profession and her only profession. To fail at marriage was to fail at everything.

Kate did not intend to fail at anything.

She thought, *If he be mad and I stay with him, we'll not
be really married unless I share even his madness. Whatever it is he sees, I will learn to see too. I will!*

She smiled, content with her decision.

William, looking at her at last, glimpsed the smile in the
lamplight and asked, "Ah, Kate, what fancy brings that
strange levity to your lips?"

The smile broadened. "You men may have your visions, Mr. Blake. We women can see a bit of the future
ourselves."

"Don't mock me, Kate."

"I mock you not, you serious man, but I believe we all,
men or women, can see the future when we make that
future ourselves."

3

KATE REMAINED A VIRGIN after five years of marriage.

It no longer seemed strange to her—soothing rather, and peaceful, with the kind of peace that comes, with the vow of chastity, to a nun. She felt, to make the semblance complete, she'd somehow—she couldn't exactly remember when—taken a vow of poverty also, and her vow kept her from complaining when her William fell short as a good provider.

William's father died; her own parents never visited her. She knew in their eyes she had risen above their own humble station in life, so they could come only if summoned by the man of the house, and William never summoned them. For this she came to be grateful, for she did not want her family to guess the shameful strangeness of her marriage. The few artists and writers who dropped by took their cue from the snobbish Flaxman and spoke to William but not to her. Had she unknowingly taken a vow of silence as well? She rarely thought about it, for she had undertaken a project that seemed to have no end, her self-education, what she called "The Learning."

She began with reading.

William started her; after that she continued on her own, consuming books with an omnivorous passion. William's profession, that of engraver, provided her with a steady supply of the most advanced writing, often before publication, especially since one of William's clients was the radical Joseph Johnson, editor and publisher of the influential magazine *The Analytical Review*.

Flaxman's departure to direct the Wedgewood Studio in Rome changed nothing; she remained an all-but-invisible presence in William's world, reading, reading, reading, but never speaking. The Learning filled all the spaces left in her life by the coldness of her husband, the absence of relatives and friends, her lack of children. (This last drew arch comments from the women in William's circle, most of whom had adopted the theory and practice of motherhood as if it were a new religion.) In place of all else Kate had The Learning, and counted as wasted any day in which she did not learn at least one new thing.

Her awe of William's friends faded as The Learning progressed. From demigods they shrank, by degrees, to the rank of shallow fools, concealing ignorance behind a mask of brilliant wordiness. Only a few retained her respect, those few who, in some way, had embarked on the same sort of self-education project she had. She listened to them all talk and judged them, condemning those who were content with themselves and taking courage from the little triumphs of those who struggled for improvement, never once revealing herself to them by one incautious word.

When Thomas Paine, the American revolutionary, arrived in England to promote a wild scheme to build a single-arch bridge across the wide Schuykill River near Philadelphia, the publisher Johnson entertained him at a small supper gathering in his home which included some of the most controversial authors of the time and also obscure associates of his publishing company. Among these latter were Mr. and Mrs. William Blake.

The ladies and gentlemen adjourned to the drawing room to partake of smoking tobacco, a delightfully sinful practice imported from the American colonies; Kate joined her husband in the circle, sitting slightly behind him as if to use his stocky body as a shield.

Paine, of course, held center stage, acting like a lord among commoners, in spite of his democratic ideals. He had a thin, oval face, a large nose and a sly smile, and his gestures had that loose, uncontrolled enthusiasm that set apart the Yankee from the more restrained Englishman.

He gave his clay pipe a vigorous puff and said, "I called my little pamphlet *Common Sense* and common sense, I am persuaded, is all a man needs to get him through this life. That, and the courage to use it. No divine revelations for me. No stone tablets, no Bibles. Common sense does the job."

William Godwin, at thirty-two the intellectual leader of this little coven of freethinkers, leaned back pensively as the others awaited his comments somewhat as Catholics await the latest pronouncement of the Pope. Godwin, a gaunt, rigid man with an even larger nose than Paine's, usually dominated the conversation with his abrasive voice and ready flow of words.

"Reason, I agree," he said, "is Man's highest faculty. King and commoner alike should submit to it for the betterment of all." He coughed on the smoke that had begun to hang thick in the air, ebbing and flowing in slow phantom eddies.

Paine answered with a chuckle. "They should, sir, but do they? On every hand, madness sits enthroned and tyrants understand but one argument, the fiery rhetoric of the flintlock pistol."

Godwin sniffed haughtily. "You show too much faith in violence, Mr. Paine, which can easily turn against reason. True revolution takes place not on the battlefield, but in the mind, where the present grows from the past as naturally as a plant grows from a seed. Education, not war, is reason's tool."

Johnson chimed in. "If the government hears you've been educating the working class, they'll make you a gift of a one-way ticket to Botany Bay." His remark solicited no more than a polite ripple of laughter.

Paine returned to his point, drawing himself up primly. "Guns first, then education. You can't teach much with the threat of deportation hanging over your head."

"Hear, hear!" seconded the other American, Aaron Burr.

"Revolution is serious business," Paine added. "It's not women's work."

At this a woman in her late twenties, who had been listening intently but without comment, sat bolt upright and said, with an angry edge to her voice, "Not women's work?"

"Ah," said Johnson, amused. "I see we are about to hear a few words from the spirited Miss Mary Wollstonecraft."

Mary Wollstonecraft had been sitting next to Kate, and Kate had been studying the woman out of the corner of her eye. Never had Kate seen such beauty wedded to such a keen eye and intelligent expression. Miss Wollstonecraft dressed like an American, without any constricting bodice, in a cream-colored chemise dress of gauze with a very plunging neckline and a pale blue sash below the breasts, and her long dark hair fell in disarray over her delicate shoulders.

"You quite mistake yourself, sir," said Mary evenly but with passion. "Revolution is, if anything, more a woman's job than a man's. Because women in England are taught to be either slaves or useless, depending on their social class, men suppose we ladies to be either drudges or drones by nature. Foolish prejudice, gentlemen! Foolish prejudice! Let women be educated the same as men, to think, to command, to plan, then women will easily do all that men do. When you speak of liberty and equality, don't forget that the feminine half of humanity remains in bondage to the masculine half."

Paine chuckled indulgently. "Nature, not politics, has created that tyranny, my dear."

William Godwin attempted to regain the floor. "Allow me to defend the lady's position. You see . . ."

Mary cut him off. "I'll defend my own position!" The whole circle gasped, for she had done the unthinkable, had interrupted the Immortal Godwin. She continued, allowing no room for others to comment, condemning monarchy in one breath and democracy in the next, wild-eyed, nostrils flared like a fistfighter in the ring. All existing systems of government fell short of her exacting specifications, it seemed, particularly in their treatment of women; she pinned her hopes to another system which as yet existed only in her head.

Kate was impressed and, she noticed, so was Paine.

And now William too was nodding agreement in his ponderous way. Mary looked his way and smiled.

Again Godwin attempted to break in. "May I say, my dear . . ."

"You may not!" she fairly shouted. "And don't call me your dear unless you plan to make yourself my lover! You talk all the time, sir. Let others have a chance. Our friend the engraver, for example, has not said a word tonight. In a so-called democratic group like ours, should not the voice of the working man be heard?"

Godwin flushed brick red with anger.

Mary continued coaxingly, "Come, Mr. Blake. That is your name, isn't it? Should we or should we not accept the rule of reason?"

William hesitated and Johnson, in a patronizing tone, answered for him. "Bill's a religious man. He wants us to accept the rule of faith."

At that William blurted out awkwardly, "No, not faith. Not reason either." Kate touched his arm, painfully aware of his shyness.

"What, then?" Mary pressed him.

William answered in an odd, dreamy voice. "You know, I discussed this very question with Socrates just a few days ago." The guests exchanged uneasy glances. Kate tried not to show her embarrassment, even managing a wan smile. "Socrates placed neither faith nor reason in the primary place, but vision. In his philosophy all imperfect things in our world reflect perfect things in some other, higher one, and only the visionary can glimpse this higher world. I asked him the source of the things in the perfect world and he grew quite impatient with me. 'Perfect things are eternal!' he told me with considerable heat but, as those who know me might guess, that failed to satisfy me. I always seek the source and can't rest until I find it. Vision may be closer to the source than reason and faith, but it's not the source itself, nor are the things the vision-ary sees, however perfect.''

"What then, pray tell?" Mary demanded teasingly. "Don't keep us all in suspense!"

"Imagination," Blake intoned, his shyness and ner-vousness rapidly evaporating. "Before the chair I sit in could exist, the designer had to imagine it. Before this house could exist, the architect had to imagine it." He warmed to his subject. "Before the clothes I wear could exist, the tailor had to imagine them. Before the very words we speak could exist, our ancestors had to imagine them. As below, so above. Before the things in the perfect world could exist, someone had to imagine them. Faith loves the past, reason loves the present, but the future belongs to imagination. Only imagination soars forward beyond what was and what is to what might be.''

Paine asked slyly, "Is imagination God, then?"

William answered without hesitation. "Imagination comes before God, sir!''

"Upon my word!" exclaimed Burr, amused. "A new heresy!''

Godwin said incredulously, "Must even God be imag-ined before He can exist?''

"Even God," replied William gravely. "Look." He held up his hand. "I imagine my hand opening and lo, it opens." He suited the action to the word. "I imagine my hand closing and lo, it closes. Always, always, always the same. First imagination, then reality. That's how the uni-verse works, my friends, and if we wish a better life, if we seek a real revolution and not a mere changing of the guard, let us enthrone imagination as our emperor and let reason and faith be his faithful servants.''

"Preposterous!" Godwin exploded.

Burr asked maliciously, "Ah, Mr. Blake, sir. Are you sure you did not imagine this Socrates you claim you spoke to?''

William turned on him a gaze of pitiless contempt. "Socrates is a real person, Mr. Burr. Have you read no history?''

At this everyone burst into laughter. Everyone, that is,

but William, who looked around puzzled, as if he had not intended to make a joke, and Kate, who stared at her husband with anguish, embarrassment, and pity.

At 27 Broad Street, next door to his parents' home where he'd been born, William opened a printshop. It soon failed.

With the help of the patronizing Rev. Mathew, he had a book of his adolescent poems published, but perhaps as a result of the Reverend's lukewarm introduction, few people read it when given it as a gift, and nobody bought it.

William exhibited two watercolor paintings inspired by the American Revolution at the Royal Academy: nobody noticed.

His friends tried to raise money to send William to Rome to finish his art education; nothing ever came of it.

In the autumn of 1785 they moved again, to 28 Poland Street, around the corner to the north, a fairly substantial house with three stories and an attic, where they remained for nearly five years.

A few doors away, at number 22, stood the Old King's Arms Tavern where William began to spend an increasingly large part of his time, becoming leader of a group of eccentric occultists who claimed to be a survival of the ancient Druidic priesthood. Kate never dared venture into this male stronghold, though William brought her many a disquieting tale of pagan rituals performed in a spirit part serious, part mocking, and altogether drunken.

"Who did you see there?" she would ask him when he came home around midnight.

Like as not he'd reply, to her dismay, something like, "The Great Horned One."

He did, however, permit her to accompany him to meetings of another occult group, the New Jerusalem Church, a sect inspired by the writings of visionary mystic Emanuel Swedenborg, who, his followers claimed, conversed with ghosts, and had visions of distant events. The congregation numbered about sixty at best, but in their declaration of thirty-two resolutions, adopted unanimously, they defiantly proclaimed that "The Old Church" (meaning all other churches) was dead, and with awesome persistence they did mental exercises to develop their powers of spirit communication and clairvoyance. She felt no regret when William dropped out. The cold fanaticism of the Swedenborgians frightened her, though no more than her husband's claim that "Whatever they claim to do, I do actually."

All the while she continued with The Learning.

It was in the evening she went to school, with William as her one and only teacher, and it was then, more than at any other time, that she felt close to him. Slowly, patiently, never once losing his temper, never once laughing, he guided her reading, taught her in addition how to draw, how to paint with watercolors, how to cut the copper engravings with which he made his modest living—illustrations (most copied, but some original) for books full of fencing, history, sentimental poetry, and second rate lovesongs.

Her style in drawing, painting and engraving kept at first so close to his own that they themselves could not tell, where both of them had worked on the same picture, who had done what. Then, without a break, her work gradually became more flowing, freer, less dependent on the imitation of old masters. He, in turn, began to learn from her, and the stiffness of his early work all but vanished, though he never quite caught up with her steadily increasing skill.

Night after night she would lay down her graver and turn to him, gazing into his large round eyes in the candlelight, and ask, "Is that done proper, Mr. Blake?"

And he would answer, "That's capital, Mrs. Blake."

He was a good teacher.

She was a good student.

But try as he might one thing remained he could not teach her. He could not teach her to see his visions.

At least once a month they sat side by side in two worn rocking chairs before the glowing embers in the fireplace.

"First," he would tell her, "let us make sure you're ready."

"Ready as I'll ever be, Mr. Blake."

Though he called her "Kate" at times, she never called him anything but "Mr. Blake."

"Have you abstained from strong drink? Not even coffee or tea?"

"Not a drop."

"Have you abstained from the lusts of the flesh? Leonardo da Vinci, you know, could never have seen what he saw if he'd indulged in the lusts of the flesh."

"Have no fear, Mr. Blake. I'm a good girl, I am."

"Have you taken any drugs or medicine?"

"What would I do that for? I ain't sick."

"Then let us begin. Look into the fire. Relax. Let your soul lie quiet."

"Like this, Mr. Blake?"

"Like that, Mrs. Blake. Now watch and wait. Don't force it, but if you see something, tell me."

A long silence might then follow.

"What am I supposed to see, Mr. Blake?"

"A face. A human form. An animal. A landscape perhaps. Some unfamiliar scene from, for example, Biblical times, ancient Egypt or Rome."

"I don't see nothing."

"Patience. Relax. You will."

But she didn't.

That was how they spent their evenings, but now and then such a strange evening preceded a still stranger night. Kate would awake sometime between midnight and dawn and discover William was not beside her. She would rise, put on her robe, and go into the other room.

There she would find William sitting in his usual chair, staring into the darkness and sometimes—and this really frightened her—he would speak to people she could not see.

"Gaius Caesar! Good to see you again!" he'd say, or "Moses! May I ask you something?" and he'd lapse into Latin, Hebrew, or Greek. Or perhaps his unseen guest had a name totally unfamiliar to her. "Well, hello, Prime Minister Churchill," or "Good day, President Kennedy!"

When the spectral conversation had finished William

would go to his worktable, shuffling like a sleepwalker, and begin writing as if unaware she was in the room.

One night, after he'd been talking with someone, he came over to her and handed her a short metal tube, round at one end and with glass at the other, that she could have sworn had appeared in his fingers by magic.

"By all that's holy, Mr. Blake, what have you there?"

"Push the little button on the side."

"Oh! It lights up. Is there fire in it?"

"No, don't worry."

"But it shines so."

"There's lightning trapped in it."

"Where did you get it?"

"From the future, Kate. They call it a flashlight."

"Good heavens!" She set it on the table quickly, as if it were hot.

Days, evenings, nights; they drifted by, unreal, dreamlike, until the night William's brother died.

The boy Robert Blake, like his elder brother, drew, painted, and wrote poetry. Pale, slender, never quite well, he had long delighted in painting watercolors of faeries, elves, and gnomes which William claimed the boy actually saw. Wise Robert neither confirmed nor denied such claims, contenting himself with smiling and saying nothing, escaping the ridicule heaped upon bold William.

Now Robert lay in bed, still wearing his sphinxlike smile, tired, thin, and enigmatic, while Kate and William nursed him. He lay motionless in the dim flickering candlelight, so motionless Kate more than once checked his pulse to be sure he still lived, only to see his wistful eyes, so like her own, open and gaze up at her with an odd pity, as if he felt compassion for her vigorous health, her firm grip on life.

When, now and then, Robert spoke, William leaned close to catch every word, unnaturally alert though he'd hardly slept for days. There was one time in particular.

"William," the boy whispered.

"Yes?"

"I want you to be rich."

"We have enough to get by."

"You deserve more. You have such talent. You work so hard. Some day museums will pay fortunes for the least of your sketches."

"I doubt that."

"They will, they will!" Kate heard fever in the boy's voice and tried to sooth him by stroking his hot forehead. "I have seen it. I have been to the future and seen it."

Kate shuddered. Two madmen in the family! But William only nodded, saying, "I don't know. I never tried to find out . . ."

"Rich!" Robert clutched William's arm. "Why should you not share the wealth your skill creates? Why should you wear threadbare pants while fat stupid dealers who cannot draw a half-moon buy whole wardrobes of the richest garments . . . fat stupid fools who can buy and sell art but cannot see as we see."

William replied gravely, "To see as we see is payment enough. We have no cause for complaint. No one need feel sorry for us."

Robert began to cry. "We poor artists. We poor idiot artists."

William said, "Save your compassion for the man who has nothing but money, who must humiliate himself by buying from us the visions he cannot see himself."

Robert had become barely audible. "But they exploit us so."

William shook his head. "We exploit *them,* Robert. By taking hold of them by their greed, we force them to pass on our visions to the world."

Robert closed his eyes. Kate, alarmed, took his pulse yet again, and again those strange eyes opened.

Robert whispered, "I will rescue you, William. I will rescue you from poverty."

Kate murmured, "Hush now. Save your strength."

Robert's voice rose. "Up ahead, in the future, they have more than we do. They have fantastic inventions. I've seen them!"

William answered quietly, "I've seen them too. Never mind . . ."

Robert struggled to sit up. "I will go into the future. I will steal one of their secrets and bring it back to you."

"Robert! Lie down!" cried out Kate, thoroughly alarmed. "Please, Robert!"

"Rich!" he screamed. "I'll make you rich!"

Then he fell back on his pillow, eyes wide. His skin began to turn a ghastly blue-gray. Kate did not need to take his pulse to know he had died, but she did anyway.

"He has gone," she said. "Gone to Heaven."

William shook his head firmly. "Not to Heaven, Mrs. Blake. Not yet. I saw him leave his body and fly up through the ceiling, clapping his hands for joy. You heard what he said. He's up ahead somewhere, in another century, stealing the fire of the gods for us, and mark you, he'll be back. My brother is a man of his word. He'll be back."

She turned on him. "You madman!"

Calmly he replied, "Now, now, you're upset."

She ran from the house and walked the streets until dawn. Returning, she found William sprawled face-down on the bed. For an awful moment she feared he too had died, but then she saw his back move slightly. He slept continuously for three days while Kate made all the arrangements for Robert's burial in nearby Bunhill Fields, kept house, and did two original engravings for Joseph Johnson.

Upon delivery, Johnson exclaimed, "Ah, my compliments to your husband. These are a good deal better than his usual, and I've always admired his work."

She smiled, keeping her secret. "The artist thrives on praise, good sir."

She was roused from a deep sleep by William shaking her by the shoulders. "Kate, Kate, I've just spoken to Robert!"

"Your brother?" She rubbed her eyes resentfully. "Your brother's dead, Mr. Blake."

William's eyes glowed like blue pearls in the light of the candle he held in his hand. "Get up! Don't you want to hear what he said?"

"What he said? What he said? You're dreaming. Go back to sleep and dream some more."

"In dreams the dead speak to us more clearly than ever, Kate. Listen!"

"Oh, very well." Without anger she swung her feet to the floor. Since her outburst on the night of Robert's death she had resolved to simply accept everything William said or did, however insane.

"You know, Mrs. Blake, how unsuccessful my book of poems was?" He led her into the other room, candle held high. Their shadows danced and capered along the walls like demented ghosts.

She nodded sleepily. "We still have almost every copy." She glanced at a dimly-visible shelf lined with twenty identical copies of the slender volume.

"Robert told me how we can succeed with my next book!"

"You don't say." She sat down in her favorite rocking chair before the fireplace while William vigorously poked up the flames.

"It's so simple, really. I should have thought of it myself." He seated himself in the rocker next to her. "We don't make much money with our engraving even in the best of times. You can't deny that, Kate."

"I don't complain, Mr. Blake."

"No, no, you're a perfect angel about money, but certainly someone makes money in the book business, someone other than the writer or illustrator or book vendor. Who, Mrs. Blake, who?"

"How should I know?" She followed her question with a yawn.

"The publisher, Kate! You see those men when you deliver my work to them, how they dress, the homes they live in. How clearly I see everything, now that Robert explained it."

"Robert is dead, Mr. Blake," she told him again, without emotion.

"Only his body! His spirit went into the future, just as he promised, and brought back something that will forever liberate us from the poverty that now imprisons us. Mrs.

Blake, he showed me how you and I can ourselves become publishers!''

"You and me?'' Her hand flew to her throat.

"You and I. He showed me a new printing process used by the people of the future, a process combining text and illustration in one and the same plate.''

"We have no press.'' To herself she thought, *Thank God*.

"We don't need a press. With this process we can, if we like, simply hold the paper against the inked plate and rub it with the back of a spoon.'' He mimed the motions of the technique with his stubby fingers, then rocked forward to tap her on the knee with his forefinger. "If we want color, we just dab it in.''

"Oh no, Mr. Blake. No!'' She needed no supernatural powers to prophesy that it would be she who would do most of the dabbing.

"Yes, Kate, yes! We'll make a fortune with limited editions illustrated by the author.''

"I don't recognize you, Mr. Blake. You never used to carry on so about money. Why, you acted like 'twas a sin to want it!''

"I was so selfish, thinking only of my own simple needs, but you . . . you shouldn't have to go on living like this.''

"Did Robert tell you that, too?''

"Yes, he took pity on you. That's why he gave me this process, to rescue you from poverty.''

"Upon my word, that's strange. In life he never liked me. How is it that now he's dead he thinks of nothing but my welfare?''

"He repented!''

"Even so, we can't . . .''

"We can't reject this gift. That would break his heart.'' She sighed. "If you put it that way . . .''

She knew she would go along with this as she went along with everything else, but she thought, *Robert, me boy, you always did have a vile sense of humor.*

*   *   *

Every Tuesday night the little coterie surrounding William Godwin (they called themselves the Tuesday's Children) would gather for dinner and conversation at the home of their mutual publisher, Joseph Johnson, at 72 St. Paul's Churchyard. The dining room was a narrow, upstairs room, irregularly shaped, but the food was good and the thought revolutionary.

Little by little Mary Wollstonecraft broke through Kate Blake's wall of reserve. Mary talked well and Kate listened well, so they made an excellent pair, and soon Mary began dropping around to the Blakes' kitchen during the afternoon to recount, like some scandalous serial, all the gossip of the Godwin circle, and in particular all her own (to her) fascinating exploits. Mary would sit at the kitchen table, chattering away, while Kate went on with household chores. Sometimes Miss Wollstonecraft's opinions struck Kate as unbelievably strange, as for example when the beautiful young lady burst in and delightedly exclaimed, "I'm in love, Kate!"

"Do sit a bit and have a spot of tea, Mary," said Kate, preparing to be amused.

Mary threw herself down at the table. "I feel so wonderful!"

Kate poured her a cupfull. "How nice for you, dear. Can you tell me the gentleman's name?"

"Henry Fuseli!" She pronounced the name with pride.

Kate felt, as she had often felt before with Mary, an uneasy thrill, half attraction, half shock. "But Mary dear, don't you know Mr. Fuseli's a recently and happily married man?" Fuseli, a tiny chap seventeen years older than William, had been an irregular member of the Tuesday's Children for some time. A painter, offspring of a family of painters, Fuseli specialized in fantasy and dream pictures such as "The Nightmare," which depicted an insane, ghostly, glowing white horse leering down at a bed containing a cringing, just-awakened woman.

"Of course I know he's married," Miss Wollstonecraft replied impatiently. "Do you take me for a dunce?"

"I would think it cause for despair, not celebration, to be in love with a married man. They say many a poor woman in your situation has thrown herself in the Thames and drowned.''

"Oh, fear not, Kate! I know better. Aren't we all believers in freedom and reason, Henry, his Sophie, and me? We shall simply sit down around the table, we three, and work out a reasonable arrangement whereby we can all live together in love and harmony.''

"Under one roof?'' Kate paused in her bread mixing to stare at her companion in amazement.

"Of course! Sophie, as you know, was his model before their marriage. He painted her, I'm sure, in that costume we all wear at the moment of birth, so his manly lust was raised to the point of frenzy and he had to possess her, even at the cost of his liberty. I understand men, Kate. They are more like animals than we women, poor things. Henry and I have quite a different sort of love, a higher, more spiritual love, you might say.''

"Like brother and sister?'' Kate prompted, thinking of her own curiously ascetic marriage.

"Well, not quite like brother and sister.'' A mischievous smile played a moment about Mary's lips. "Our love has had, I confess, what one might vulgarly term a physical expression, but in essence it remains spiritual and pure. I would compare my feelings to those of some of the more devout female saints, as their thoughts dwell upon the form of their savior.''

At this Kate exclaimed, "Oh, for shame, Mary! To even think such thoughts risks your immortal soul!''

"To give my immortal soul for one kiss from Henry's pretty lips . . . I say the price is right!''

"Thank God Mr. Blake didn't hear that. He can't abide blasphemy.'' Kate glanced around nervously.

Mary continued with childlike glee. "Sophie can minister to Henry's animal nature, while I minister unto his spirit, and I'll content myself with that except on those days of the month when she is indisposed or when illness prevents her from performing her marital duties.''

"Heavens, child!''

"Yes, Sophie shall be his physical wife and I his spiritual wife. If she truly loves him as she claims, how can she deny him those higher joys I can provide him which she, poor earth-bound soul, cannot? I can play some role in the household that will conceal our true relationship. Perhaps I will masquerade as his chambermaid! Certainly he'll take no more liberties with me than many another respectable gentleman takes with the domestics.''

"Oh Mary!" cried Kate, impulsively clutching the young woman's arm. "I know this world has its temptations, but we must resist . . .''

Mary stood up, determined. "Must we? We're Tuesday's Children, not smallminded Irish fishwives. We talk freedom on Tuesdays the way Christians talk love on Sundays: will we, like them, leave the rest of the week to the whims of fortune? Henry and Sophie and I will turn talk into action, unlike the rest of you. We shall enjoy a nonpossessive love, without jealousy, while the rest of you merely maunder on about perfect societies of the future. You will talk about the Earthly Paradise; we shall live in it!''

With that Mary strode from the room, head high, almost bumping into William as he entered.

"Poor woman," said Kate, shaking her head sadly, anxiously.

"Poor woman?" echoed William as the front door slammed. "I've never seen such happiness on a human face!''

Kate said softly, "We've all been dreaming. Mary will be the first of us to wake up.''

Try as he might, William could get no further word of explanation from her.

Kate Blake was worried.

Before, William had dabbled with his own artistic projects only during slack periods when he had no paying work to do, but now he was beginning to put the paying work to one side and devote himself more and more to what he called his "Illuminated Printing.''

First fruit of this labor was a print based on a drawing of Robert's entitled "The Approach of Doom.'' Then he began making plates for a collection of his own philosophical sayings under the working title *There Is No Natural Religion*.

One afternoon she confronted him with, "Well, Mr. Blake, you should have finished today the frontispiece for John Casper Lavater's *Aphorisms on Man*. Where is it, I'd like to know?"

He waved her aside. "I'll do it tomorrow. Publishers expect to wait a day or two past the deadline. They respect a work the more the longer it takes."

"But you've never been late before."

"I have my own aphorisms to illustrate. This Lavater is a mealy-mouthed humbug, anyway. When my book comes out, you and everyone else will join me in forgetting all about him."

"In the meantime we have to eat."

"Oh, woman, the Bible says 'Man does not live by bread alone.' "

That night she served him, for the first time but not the last, a supper consisting of empty plates.

And that night she first heard him mention the name "Urizen."

They had completed one more unsuccessful attempt to get Kate to see something, anything, in the fire, and now sat side by side in their rocking chairs, staring at the embers.

She began, "You've seen more than usual lately, have you not, Mr. Blake?"

He nodded soberly. "The gift, like a muscle, grows stronger with exercise. I can live for days in another time."

"But you never seem to leave."

"I always return to the same time I leave from."

"Where have you visited?" She had come to accept his time voyages, to speak of them as if they were outings to the seashore.

"To the future, where men will build cities on planets that circle distant stars; to the past, where a land vaster than England sank beneath the Atlantic." She noticed uneasiness in his voice. "I've taught myself Latin, Greek, and Hebrew, but I've gone to centuries where those languages, and the King's English, are forgotten or not yet thought of.'' He hesitated.

''Is something wrong?''

He glanced at her with furrowed brows. ''I saw a man. I think it was a man.''

''A man?'' she prompted.

''I thought I alone, among living men, could move through time the way the dead do, but then I saw . . . him. I saw him in the future, then I saw him in the past.''

''Are you sure it was the same man?''

''I spoke to him! There could be no mistake. I introduced myself to him, shook hands with him. He seemed familiar, as if I'd met him before somewhere, and he seemed to know me, too. In the future we stood and talked while riding in a flying machine that forever circles the Earth without falling, then in the past we spoke together again in the few minutes before the earthquakes began, the earthquakes that destroyed the Atlantic Continent, called Aztlan Tiki by its people.''

''Did this man tell you his name?''

William pronounced it with awe. ''Urizen.''

''What did he look like?''

''He had a huge nose, and he was tall, white-bearded, naked.''

''But that's what you told me God looked like!''

William stared at her. ''That's right! You don't suppose . . . yes, now I remember! That face I saw at my window as a child! It was Urizen!''

''Then you shook hands with God?'' At last she could not keep a hint of disbelief from her voice.

''I don't know. He chatted like a man, passed the time of day like a neighbor I might meet in the street,'' William said, bewildered. ''Is that how God acts?''

''Tell me what he said.''

''He welcomed me to some kind of exclusive club, open only to that one person in a billion who can escape the bondage of his own time and place. He invited me to travel with him, to voyage forever and never return to my own time, to share some great work with him. I . . . I refused.''

She touched his hand, thinking, *He refused because of me. He could not bring himself to leave me.*

But then he said, "I refused because of fear, Kate."

"Fear? Fear of some daft naked man running around?"

"Man? Or God? Or what? You might be right about him, don't you see? He might be . . . the 'other Fellow.' "

4

KATE READ THE BIBLE all the way through, then attacked the classics, reading in manuscript translations and commentaries done by William's scholarly friend Thomas Taylor, who had rejected Christianity in order to embrace the worship of the ancient Greek family of gods, some of whom he claimed had been reincarnated among the multitude of cats that infested his little house in Walworth.

Taylor, a one-time bank clerk, had quit his job to devote full time to preaching the pagan gospel and, lacking the proper formal education to teach at a university, had contented himself with delivering a series of twelve lectures in the Flaxman living room to a small group drawn mostly from the Godwin coterie. Kate and William attended, and William immediately began incorporating Taylor's brand of "Platonism" in his own work after Taylor had admitted to him privately that his understanding had come in the form of a "mystical vision."

Taylor was a typical "Tuesday's Child," writing for this small group of kindred souls who met regularly in private homes to read aloud to each other various works-in-progress; not writing for the outside world, yet somehow blundering into print and a modest measure of success.

Kate, aided by the gossip mongering of Mary Wollstonecraft, followed the doings of the Tuesday's Children with fascination—the romances, the occasional marriages, the arguments and ingroup power struggles—but took no active part. She only watched and listened and learned,

49

gradually realizing the measure of truth in Flaxman's belief that working with such a group could bring out the best in a writer or artist, spur him on to heights he never could have attained alone.

Certainly the Tuesday's Children helped Kate more than they could possibly know in her long, hard "Learning," filling her head with wild, strange, advanced ideas she had never heard of before, that few outside the circle had ever heard of before, giving her an education as complete as that of any professor, though free of the quibbling pedantry of formal schooling.

Yet for William, the Tuesday's Children proved a mixed blessing, stimulating his mind to new brilliance on the one hand, but on the other hand encouraging him to turn more and more away from the commercial art by which he made his modest living, instead devoting himself to work no one outside the Tuesday's Children ever saw. At last, to Kate's humiliation, William drifted into the habit of living off money from his more successful relatives.

He did just one commercial job in 1789, three engravings for John Casper Lavater's *Essays on Physiognomy*, including a small tailpiece, and this job he finished late.

Kate delivered the plates, and relayed to William the publisher's objections.

"He didn't like your little vignette, Mr. Blake."

"And why not?"

"It should have shown a hand holding up a candle."

"And so it did!"

"But you added some moths flying into the flame."

"The design needed something to make it unusual."

"And he didn't like waiting a week past the deadline."

"A week? That long?"

"Yes indeed, Mr. Blake."

"I hope you told him what I said to tell him."

"That you had other more important work to do? Thank God I didn't need to tell him anything at all. He didn't press me. It goes against me nature to lie, it does." Her speech still occasionally reflected the Cockney of her childhood, try though she might to ape the sophisticated conversation of the Tuesday's Children, and in spite of her vocabulary, which had become immense, though studded with words she mispronounced, words she'd read but never heard spoken.

William angrily turned back to the plate he was preparing for his own book of poetry, *The Songs of Innocence*. Eventually there would be thirty-one of these plates, each prepared by the same slow painstaking process originally outlined by William's ghostly brother.

Singing all the while tunes of his own composition, William wrote and drew in etcher's ground on a sheet of paper which he had previously soaked in a solution of gum arabic and allowed to dry. He then spread the paper, face down, on a heated copper plate and, like some fanatically laboring gnome, rubbed the paper with the back of a spoon; then, still singing lustily, he submerged the plate, paper and all, in a pan of water until the gum softened and the paper floated free, leaving the design, in reverse, adhering to the copper.

After an eight-hour bath in nitric acid, the drawing stood out in high relief above the surrounding eaten-away areas. Oh, how Kate hated this part of the process, not only because of the danger of the acid, but even more because of the stench.

However, she shared his pride when at last he washed the plate, inked it against a blank plate pressed against it, and rubbed the first proofsheet of bookpaper against the design with his ever-handy spoon, producing, as a magician produces a perfect rose from a hat, a remarkably attractive picture with a softer, more painterly quality than any ordinary engraving.

As he worked and sang Kate watched a while, then picked up that odd souvenir of the future, the flashlight, and idly switched it on and off a few times.

"Mr. Blake, you can pick up something in one time and carry it back with you into another, can you not?"

"Quite so, Mrs. Blake." He went on with his work, not looking at her.

"Tell me then, could you go back to yesterday and get that set of engravings you did for the Lavater book?"

"I suppose I could."

"Could you take those plates back a week and hand them in on time?"

"How can you plague me with such trivial matters? Can't you see I have more important things to do?"

"No, wait. Could you go back to when you were cutting the plate of the hand holding the candle and tell yourself to leave out the moths?"

"What? Go back in time and meet my own self?" He frowned and looked at her resentfully.

"Well, why not, I ask you?"

"Don't you see? We'd create a whole new world. The world with the plate with the moths on it would vanish and a new world would appear containing a plate with no moths on it."

"No harm in that!"

"I might change something else as well . . . who can say what? No, no, too dangerous!"

"Such a little thing . . . and you and your friend Urizen go back and forth in time like a shuttlecock anyway."

"But we never interfere. The spirits travel in time too, but since they can't touch anything, that causes no problems. The flesh-and-blood time voyager tries to act as much as possible like a ghost."

"Were you a ghost when you took this thing?" She held up the flashlight.

"Urizen gave it to me."

"I didn't see him do it."

"I left, visited the future, and saw Urizen, then returned to the same instant I'd departed from. Thus it seemed to you, no doubt, that the flashlight appeared by magic."

"Lord help us!" She rolled her eyes Heavenward.

"But even that small thing made the others angry."

"What others?" She had heard of no others.

"Urizen and I are not the only time travelers. I've met quite a few others, but they stay mostly in the far future. They call themselves the League of Zoas. Zoa is an ancient Greek word meaning 'beast,' like the symbolic beasts the Biblical prophets saw. These Zoas argue and struggle with each other. Urizen changes the past in some small way and King Tharmas goes back and changes it again, back to what it was.''

"Well now, if Urizen changes the past like you say, so can you.''

"No, you don't understand. Urizen makes no major changes, and King Tharmas and his helpers always correct whatever he does.''

"But this flashlight!'' She held it up, certain now she'd win the argument. For a fraction of a second she glimpsed a hand closing on it, then it vanished. She screamed.

"You see?'' His smile radiated sweet reasonableness.

She stared in terror at her empty hand as William, humming another of his folksong-like tunes, continued his work.

"What a spiteful woman!'' exclaimed Mary Wollstonecraft, seated at the kitchen table.

"Because she wouldn't share her man with you?'' Kate demanded, half-turning as she pumped water into a large pan with a small handpump.

"*Her* man? *Her* man?'' cried the beautiful young lady. "Oh, my dear, I see the Queen's English needs reform before being used among us freehearts, if indeed we be as free in action as we are in words, we Tuesday's Children. How can we use possessive forms such as 'my,' 'his,' or 'hers' with human beings? Are we objects, like tables and chairs, that we can be owned? You should have heard Sophie speak of 'My Henry,' as if he had not existed before their wedding, as if she had formed him like a pot on a potter's wheel! I did not ask to take him from her, only to serve him, to be a humble part of their lives, like a daughter.''

Kate put the water on the coal stove to heat. "Not a daughter, surely, unless you mean to add incest to your list of sins.'' Kate's tone was kindly, amused, but she wanted Mary to know she did not condone her words or her actions.

Tears appeared in Mary's eyes. "Oh, Kate! Would that I could go back in time and find the man—for it must have been a man, not a woman—who invented marriage, the most universal form of slavery and the model for all the others! You know I am a pacifist, that I abide by the sixth commandment if no other, but this man I would kill with joy. In the name of justice I would stone him to death, Kate, as so many poor women have been stoned to death for adultery. Adultery! If God is love, how can love be a sin? If God is infinite, how can love be contained within the tiny cage of human law? Love blows where it wills, like the wind, and falls where it wills, upon whom it wills, like the rain!" And like rain, tears streamed down Mary's cheeks.

Kate suddenly caught sight of William standing in the doorway, listening with an expression of great interest on his broad features.

Mary, who had not yet noticed William, continued her lament. "Sophie was so heartless! She ordered me from her house and forbade me ever to return . . . I, who only wanted to help her, to share her burdens like a sister."

Kate shook her head in wonderment. "First a daughter, now a sister. Catch a husband of your own, dear, for certainly your head is full of families."

"And you should have seen Henry!" went on the unfortunate girl. "He stood by and said nothing, letting her mistreat me, and said nothing, and on his pretty face I saw such a sheepish grin, as if he were a boy caught with his hand in the cookie jar. What happened to that fine flow of words I'd heard from him before? Can a man only say great and wonderful things with his trousers off?"

"You poor creature!" Kate embraced her, and though she seldom spoke in company, broke through her natural shyness in a torrent of words that oddly mixed the Cockney of her childhood with her new language of books. "In Heaven, the Bible says, there is no marriage. Soon enough we'll leave this imperfect world and go on to one more like our dreams, a world where love ain't fenced or hindered. Even here below we can love each other free as angels if we love in the spirit, but in the flesh burn painful passions we can't lightly ignore. Jealousy! A thousand ballads justify murder in its name. Fear of abandonment! Ah, there's a child in each of us that does not want to lose its mum and dad. If you and I were strong, we wouldn't need to own our men, nor be owned by them. We could say goodbye with the same light laugh we say hello, but we're not strong. We're weak and afeared, under sentence of death one and all, and we huddle together like children in a haunted house in a storm, thinkin' if we don't hang tight to the hand we hold, we'll lose it and never find another. Contain your soul in patience, Mary Wollstonecraft, and sooner than you'd like you'll set sail for a land where you and Sophie and your darlin' Henry can forever live united."

At this William spoke for the first time, startling Mary so she twisted in her chair and stared up at him wide-eyed. "Nonsense," he said firmly.

"You don't believe that?" Kate demanded, bewildered. She had thought, from many a midnight philosophic discussion, that his views and hers were the same. Indeed, it was he who had taught her, or so she thought, half the contents of her mind.

"I used to. No more," he said.

"Well then," said Kate, "what do you believe now?" She had noticed subtle changes in her husband since first he'd mentioned Urizen, but never before had he announced an actual recantation. She feared the change, sensed in it a danger to their marriage, yet uneasily welcomed a chance to find out where he stood, and where she stood with him.

He said softly, "We must take what we want from life." He extended his hand and touched Mary on the cheek. "We must take it now."

This gesture of human warmth was so uncharacteristic of William that the women exchanged a worried glance.

He went on, voice quavering with restrained emotion. "Better to nourish a serpent in your bosom than an unsatisfied desire."

Kate saw how he looked at Mary, with the sharp-edged beginning of lust, the way most men look at most women sometimes, and she felt two conflicting emotions at once. She felt jealousy, yes, and wondered with anguish, *Why couldn't he have looked at me like that at least once in all our time together?* But also she felt a wild surge of hope.

If William could want Mary in that way, if indeed he could have his will with the girl, could he not then turn to his own wife? Could the death of William the Monk be the birth of William the Husband? She thought, *Take her, William, take her! Bed her as she wants to be bedded, then come to me.*

William gazed at Mary with a slow, rising hunger.

Kate gazed at Mary with gratitude.

Mary gazed at one, then the other, first with surprise, then with fear, at last with understanding as wordlessly the three concluded an agreement none of them dared acknowledge aloud.

Mary smiled.

That evening Kate sat in her rocker studying her husband as he sat in his own rocker next to her. William seemed so bland, so impassive, so masked. Was he thinking of Mary? Was he planning how to catch her? Was he talking to Mary in his mind, in his powerful imagination, telling her secrets he'd never told his lawful wife? At this thought she felt a sudden terrible pain in her chest.

When a man says he loves you, do you ever know who he's thinking of?

She didn't mind him bedding the girl. She wanted that. But she could hardly bear to contemplate the conversation the two might have before and after, a wise, worldly, witty conversation between two intellectuals, between two writers. What would they talk about? Art? Poetry? Religion? Politics? Of course! All those things! And would they talk about Kate? Would they perhaps share a condescending laugh at an ignorant farmgirl's expense?

Kate turned her gaze to the fire crackling so merrily in the grate. If she could see his visions, she would be close to him, closer than anyone else. She tried one more time. Still she saw nothing.

"Mr. Blake, will I ever see them?"

"Who, Kate?"

"The Zoas. You visit with 'um near every day, but I never see nothing." When she complained, her Cockney got worse. "It's a man's world, right enough."

"Perhaps you are the lucky one." His voice had become more than usually somber.

"How can you say that? Your life has ever so much more adventure in it than mine."

"What good is experience without understanding? I tell you, Mrs. Blake, the more I see, the less I understand. I thought for a while—yes, I'm serious—I thought Urizen might be Satan, but now I see he shares power with two others, Tharmas, called the Lord of Sex, and Luvah, called the Lord of Love. I know not what to think! Have you ever heard of three Satans?"

"One's quite enough, I should think."

"I talk to these Zoas. I shake hands with them. But what are they, Kate? Are they angels? Sometimes they wear wings like angels. Are they demons? None seem really evil, not even Urizen, though the others warn me against him. Urizen's sin, if sin it be, is a passion for reason. He must know the why of everything. I think he'd like to take apart the universe to see how it works."

"And if he couldn't put it back together again?"

"That wouldn't matter a jot to him. Once he and I stood at dawn in the fields outside Jerusalem in 30 B.C. and watched a shepherd tending sheep. Urizen saw a sheep straying toward us and I thought he'd give the sign for us to slip away, but instead he knelt before the sheep and whispered to it, 'Who made you?' As if a sheep could talk!"

Kate said, "Well, the Good Lord made the sheep and everything else. I hope you told Urizen that."

William sighed. "I wrote a song about it and tried to sing it to him, but he wouldn't listen."

"I'll listen, Mr. Blake."

William cleared his throat and began to sing, rocking in his chair in time to the music. The melody was his own, but as usual it had the quality of an old English folk ballad.

"Little lamb, who made thee?
Dost thou know who made thee?
Gave thee life and bade thee feed
By the stream and over the mead;

Gave thee clothing, wooly, bright;
Gave thee such a tender voice
Making all the vales rejoice?
Little lamb who made thee?
Dost thou know who made thee?

Little lamb, I'll tell thee;
Little lamb, I'll tell thee;
He is called by thy name
For he calls himself a lamb.
He is meek and he is mild.
He became a little child.
We are called by his name
I a child and thou a lamb.
Little lamb, God bless thee.
Little lamb, God bless thee."

After a long silence Kate's rocker creaked as she leaned toward him to say softly, "Very pretty, Mr. Blake."

But William replied, "Urizen smiled at me with that faint mocking smile he has, and said, 'After all you've seen, does the word God still mean anything to you?' "

A week later Kate had been dreaming of lambs and herself as a shepherdess when she heard a sound like a soft footstep. She opened her eyes, at the same time reaching beside her to awaken William. William's side of the bed was empty.

"William?" she called out.

No one answered.

With that sure instinct all women have, she knew he was with Mary, but all she could think of at first was, *He'll lose the gift.* Along with his virginity, his ritual purity, William would lose his ability to see visions. *But,* she thought, *I won't lose mine, if I have any.*

Then she heard another soft footfall.

"Who's there?" she demanded of the darkness.

There was no reply.

Slowly, numbly, she became aware of a tall, motionless

figure standing at the foot of the bed, just beyond the bedstead.

"Oh my God," she murmured, clutching the bedclothes to her chin.

The figure loomed naked, muscular, bearded. The beard, long and white, seemed to glow faintly, or perhaps the feeble light filtering in from some unseen moon shone upon it.

"Urizen?" she called out.

The figure did not speak.

"Urizen, sir," she said, trying not to show fear. "Good to see you, sir. My William speaks of you often. I almost feel I know you already, and I'm certainly glad to make your acquaintance." She sat up, still clutching the bedclothes to her throat with one hand while extending the other for a handshake.

The figure, however, neither moved nor spoke.

Kate stared at the naked body and thought, *Maybe I'll lose my own ritual purity tonight*. Her fear faded ever so slightly, to be replaced by a curious anticipation. *I'll struggle, I will,* she thought without conviction. *I'm a good girl!* She continued to sit there, hand extended stupidly.

"Urizen!" She called his name again. "Don't take advantage . . ."

The man chuckled softly and slowly faded away to nothing.

She lay awake until, shortly before dawn, she heard William come in, instantly identifying his way of walking, his way of clearing his throat. As he entered the bedroom, she said triumphantly, "I saw him!"

William began immediately, "I'm sorry, Kate. Oh Lord, I'm sorry. I couldn't help myself. She tempted me so. Can you ever forgive . . ."

"Mr. Blake! I saw him!"

"If you hadn't been so cold to me, I wouldn't have . . ."

Kate lost patience at last and screamed at him, "Will you shut up about your silly little sin and listen to me? I tell you I saw him! I saw him!"

"What?" he blurted, bewildered. "Who?"

"I saw Urizen, right where you're standing now. I can

see your visions! I can share your madness! I can really be your wife at last!"

William sat down on the bedside and took her hand. She felt sweat in his palm and his touch was cold. "You saw Urizen? Then he saw you!"

Now it was Kate's turn to be bewildered. "Where's the harm in that? He's your friend, isn't he?"

"I don't know. I never told him exactly what time and place I came from because I wanted to be sure first that . . . that he wouldn't hurt you."

"But . . . I've done him no ill. Why would he hurt me?"

"I don't know, Kate, but I do know this. Now he can appear whenever he likes and do whatever he likes to us, and no one in the world can protect us or catch him. If he feels like it, he can even go back into the past and do some little thing and we, you and I, will cease to exist!"

Kate looked at him, speechless. Why did he not take her in his arms, if not from lust, at least in simple protectiveness? She had seen his vision. He had had his woman. Why then had not his distant soul come closer? Why was everything still the same, or worse?

A week passed, and Kate changed.

With new desperation she asked herself the hardest question the mortal mind can form. "What do I really want?" Because William had never acted as a man was expected to, not even now, after all that had happened, she had been forced to face this question most women never face, this question law and custom answers for them.

Part of The Learning had been, for some time, devoted to working up to this question, to exploring around it. She had read the answers given by various classical and modern authors, had heard the answers given by Godwin and his circle but, unsatisfied, had increasingly turned to her own vague longings and impulses for some response. The Godwinites eternally debated the nature of Utopia, and Mary Wollstonecraft even tried, however unsuccessfully, to test their theories in the relentless laboratory of daily life, but only Kate adopted the groping, uncertain method of trying to read her own heart.

Her longings told her Utopia was a place where people touched each other often, embraced each other, kissed each other, stroked each other. Yes, whatever might be their political system, whatever might be their religious beliefs and rituals, whatever their philosophy, they must sit on each other's laps, put their arms around each other, not merely talk, like William and his friends, like all Englishmen. Perhaps from time to time all this touching would lead to sex, not always between married couples. There would then be the pain of jealousy, the fear of separation—Kate now knew from her own reaction to William's brief affair that the pain was not unbearable. She knew she, like Mary, was prepared to pay this price.

Kate also knew Utopia must be green.

Regardless of philosophy, religion or political organization, Utopia must have trees in it, and flowers, and grass, not like metropolitan London, where sooty brick and stone and iron hid the earth and for blocks not even a weed could be seen.

And there must be water!

Kate was sure of that.

There must be pure, clean, flowing water where bright fish darted in the deeps, not like the Thames, that open sewer, that long festering wound.

And the air—the air must be pure and clean too, not filled with soot and dust like London.

Should Utopia be a democracy, a monarchy, an oligarchy, an aristocracy? Something else, as yet unheard of? Kate, reading her own heart, neither knew nor cared, but she was certain it must be a place where people could breathe the air, drink the water, sit under a tree, and touch.

She, who once had loved London, knowing nothing better, now longed for a new London, a London that satisfied her heart's yearnings, and it seemed to her she could have it if only she could somehow awaken others to the same yearnings, simple yearnings that must lie slumbering in every human heart, and which people could actually satisfy in reality if only they followed their feelings. How easy it would be! One couple would open up to each other, begin to really talk for the first time, to ask for what they wanted instead of what they were supposed to want, and when they came to an agreement they would begin to tear up cobblestones, begin to plant things. Then another couple would join them, or perhaps men and women would come one by one, or by threes where a man had both wife and mistress, as many secretly did. Utopia would grow and grow, a green circle spreading steadily outward.

How clearly she saw it in her imagination! Heaven on Earth! The New Jerusalem! The Body of Christ! The Kingdom of Love! It would be so easy, so easy! Her eyes filled with tears of joy when she thought of it.

Then she would look at William, the man who never laughed, and she would despair. Utopia would never happen because William wouldn't let it.

William the Monk had not become William the Husband, but William the Possessed. His sin, so small in Kate's eyes, loomed fearsomely large in his own, and fearsome too was the arrival of Urizen in his own bedchamber. Like some anguished medieval flagellant he drove himself into his work, as if work could bring him absolution, as if work could bring him at least the illusion of safety. As he had expected, his loss of ritual purity had been followed by a loss of his gifts for time-voyaging and vision-seeing, but this, he told Kate, he counted more blessing than curse.

Upon finishing the engraving and printing of a few copies of *The Songs of Innocence,* he made no attempt to sell the thing, but immediately started a new project entitled *The Book of Thel,* often staying up most of the night to labor on it.

Kate read what he had written and commented, "Well, Mr. Blake, you've certainly changed your tone since that lamb poem I liked so well."

"My lamb poem? Sentimental garbage!"

"Garbage, you say?" She was somewhat taken aback.

"I don't see the world like that anymore. Behind the mask of smiling religion I see a skull."

"A skull, Mr. Blake? Surely not!" How could he speak of skulls while bright morning sunlight filled the room?

William turned haunted eyes toward her, eyes no longer calm and dignified. "Does the Bible explain who and what Urizen is?"

"No, but . . ."

"Does the Bible tell us what to do about him?"

"No," she admitted, frowning and biting the tip of her forefinger.

"Then what good is it?"

She took a moment to answer. "Perhaps the Good Lord don't mean us to know such things."

He snorted with disgust and turned his back on her.

This interchange pointed up a difference in their attitudes toward religion, there in the beginning, but now increasing. Before meeting William, Kate had never read the Bible, but had gone to church every Sunday morning. He, on the other hand, had entered the church building just twice, once when baptized and once when married. She still attended without fail and now that she could read she regularly read the Bible, though without any systematic plan. William read it again and again, as he had since childhood, each time starting at the beginning and doggedly continuing to the end, though lately with an attitude of sneering disdain. He now read it, he told her, in the "infernal sense," making all the heroes into villains and all the villains into heroes, turning all the morals on their heads so all the wrongs became rights and all the rights wrongs.

She picked up the manuscript and reread the last few lines.

"A grim business you've written here, Mr. Blake. You have a girl named Thel wandering about asking a flower, a cloud, a worm, and a dirt clod, 'What's the meaning of life?' Well, I understand that, right enough, but then this girl, if I follow you, visits the Land of the Dead, and there she finds her own grave."

"Exactly, Mrs. Blake."

"And a ghostly voice asks, 'Why cannot the ear be closed to its own destruction?' "

"Yes."

"And then this girl runs screaming back to the Land of the Living."

"Correct."

"A grim business indeed, if you'll pardon me saying so. Not like you at all. Can you explain the symbolic meaning to me? There's always a symbolic meaning to a poem, an upliftin' moral of some kind."

"Not in this one. It means what it says and nothing more."

"This Thel is not just a girl, is she? Isn't she a symbol for something or other? Curiosity? Youth? Innocence?" She hesitated, then lowered her voice. "Virginity?"

"No, nothing like that."

"Come along there! Who is she really?"

"If you must know, she is me." He glared at her from under his thick brows.

"You? But you ain't no young lady! At least not unless you been fooling me all these years." She laughed but he didn't. He never laughed.

Instead he quoted, " 'A prophet is not without honor, save in his own country, and among his own kin, and in his own house.' "

"So now you're a prophet, are you?"

"I have seen the future."

That silenced her, but she did understand the symbolic meaning now. William had visited the past, dwelling place of the dead, and returned terrified because someone had spoken to him there and invited him to stay.

And then had followed him home.

Writing the poem brought William no relief. As the weeks passed with no more sign of Urizen, Kate watched her ordinarily calm and self-possessed husband grow more and more distraught.

If he sang, it was, "Why art thou silent and invisible, Father of Jealousy?" seeming to confuse Urizen at one moment with Jehovah, at another with Satan. In the evenings, instead of teaching her, he muttered endlessly about how Urizen might be "The Spectre of my sin."

His sin! How Kate wished he would forget his little sin,

would forgive himself, absolve himself. It was not his sin that tortured her, but his repentance. Would he never be done with his damned repentance?

And more and more often he would gaze at her out of his vacant blue eyes and demand, "Kate, am I insane?"

Her answer was always the same.

"No, Mr. Blake. *I saw him too!*"

5

IN 1791 JOSEPH JOHNSON PUBLISHED Mary Wollstonecraft's slender volume *Vindication of the Rights of Women*, and Mary became famous.

Idolized by the Godwin circle, still she did not shun her old friends, and Kate still welcomed her in the Blake kitchen. Their shared unspoken secret drew them together at the same time as it formed a wall of embarrassment between Mary and the guilt-ridden William. If he and she happened to meet, Mary would call out a hearty hello that would do justice to an Alpine mountaineer, but William would turn red and look at his feet, so that Mary came to take a malicious pleasure in trying to tease some word from him.

Still, earlier in the same year William had engraved six illustrations for another of Mary's books, also published by Johnson, *Original Stories from Real Life*, and had taken special pains with the work, doing ten drawings where only six were needed, and had also, with the same loving care done sixteen of the fifty-one plates (from designs by the eminently forgettable Chodowieki) for Mary's translation of Salzmann's pompous *Elements of Morality, for the Use of Children, with an introductory Address to Parents*, a tome Mary cheerfully described to Kate as "utter rot."

William also wrote, though he never showed it to her, a poem entitled "Mary," in praise of her honesty and outspokenness. Kate found the odd little verse one day while dusting, but thought it best to pretend she had never seen it, though she hated pretense and resented having to keep silent.

And sometimes, when Mary had been visiting Kate, Kate would catch sight of William standing at the front window, wistfully watching Mary until she passed from view.

At such times Kate would think with anguish, *If he loves her, why doesn't he go with her? Why must he eternally torment me with his faithfulness? Must I kill myself so he can feel free to go with her?*

Yet anguish and torment began to do the work kindness and patience had failed at. Kate, gradually at first and then more and more, began to see visions.

Her Learning had begun again, and Kate and William sat in their rockers night after night, gazing into the glowing embers. He wanted to give it up, to stop these experiments which had become as frustrating to him as to her, but she had made a vow to learn this, his last secret skill, now that she could write and draw and engrave, now that her skill as an artist had actually surpassed his. Now and then, quite clearly, she had begun to see faces in the dim redness, mad ogre faces that leered up at her mindlessly, mocking her, sneering at her, seeming to laugh without a trace of pity at her futile search for education, vision and love. How she hated those faces, yet she could not stop looking at them, could hardly wait, when one night's watching was done, to see them again the following night.

And now it was William who saw nothing, William the Unclean, William the Adulterer, William, Satan's Friend.

There were other faces, impossibly beautiful yet filled with demonic delight and a cruelty that terrified her; yet others that looked at her with concern, kind faces that seemed worried about her. Some resembled Mary Wollstonecraft, others Polly Wood.

She described them to William and whispered, "Who are they, Mr. Blake?"

"Ghosts, I suppose."

"But so many?"

"Sometimes they cluster around an important event in history."

"Why?"

"To watch."

"But this is no important historical event. We're not important."

"Perhaps we are. Speak to them, Kate. Ask them what they're watching for."

A swarm of monstrous, disfigured faces swirled before her. "What do you want here?" she demanded. They did not answer, only went on moving and changing, like fog. "What do you want?" she repeated. They never answered.

She saw scenes sometimes, bleak landscapes with crumbling castles at dusk, the wind-sculpted dunes of unknown deserts under unwinking stars, forests where the trees glowed in the night blue and green and violet and moved languid fleshy limbs like the arms of women, silver vessels that swam the void like schools of fish from star to star. No sounds came from the visions, though sometimes they spread by slow degrees out from the fireplace to surround her, completely replacing her familiar home. She might have lost herself in them but for William's voice coming to her from empty space in the visionary sky, saying excitedly, as if from a great distance, "What do you see? Tell me what you see!"

She'd reach out her hand and he'd take it in his, so she felt safe enough to continue, whether it went well or badly.

She'd been walking one day down the cobblestone street, on her way to market, when the ghosts gradually appeared all around her, transparent bodies like a reflection in a window, where one scene is superimposed on another. A cloud of them swarmed, beelike, about her head, regarding her curiously, and for an instant they clustered so thickly she could no longer find her way and had to halt and stand motionless while they swooped in on her, coming so close she could feel their cold long hair brush her cheeks like spiderwebs.

A coachman had shouted a warning and, as she jumped to avoid the horse's hooves, the ghosts had faded quickly away.

Later, at home, she'd told William about it, but his only

comment was, "Good! You're progressing splendidly." She didn't like the ironic edge to his voice.

Yes, it was then she'd at last wanted to end her Learning of visions, but she remembered her vow and told herself firmly, "One more night."

So here she sat again in her rocking chair, a shawl around her shoulders, gazing fixedly into the coals while William spoke quietly. "Relax, Mrs. Blake. Relax and tell me what you see."

The formerly impossible had become all too easy. The room grew vague, drew back, while the red glow expanded to fill her entire field of vision, and now she quickly began seeing images in the redness, moving images.

"Mr. Blake, I see your brother Robert."

"Yes?"

"He seems worried. He has raised his hand as if to warn me to go back."

"Speak to him."

"Too late. He vanished. I see the other men now, men I don't know. Who . . .?" She felt a sudden fear. "Who are they?"

"I don't know, Kate. I see nothing at all. I've lost the gift. I've lost it forever. Oh, Kate, forgive me. . . ."

"They too raise their hands in warning."

"Perhaps you should heed them. I sense something myself, even with my dead, befouled spirit. A dirtiness . . ."

"No! I have worked so hard, so long! I must go on!" She startled herself with her own determination, her own anger at William's timidity.

"Kate!" William's cry came to her out of a universe of pulsing red light, light that seemed to dim and brighten in time with her own heartbeat. She could barely hear him, he seemed so distant, so unreal. She grew lighter herself, and suddenly could no longer feel her chair beneath her. She drifted forward, touching nothing, slowly at first, then more rapidly, passing without resistance into the body of one of the warning figures, then out through his back.

A red-lit plain spread out below her, empty and lifeless. Ahead, crouching on the horizon, waited a city unlike any she'd ever seen, a city gigantic and inhuman, made of immense black blocks of lava leaning together.

Weightless as thistledown, she floated up and over the city walls.

"William!" she screamed.

His answer came so faintly she could not say with certainty she'd heard it.

The citizens of this sinister and forbidding metropolis were not human, but some sort of huge loathsome toads or lizards that, like mocking caricatures of humanity imagined in some drug-induced nightmare, walked upright and wore rich, luxurious silks, satins, lace, and black leather studded with twinkling, multicolored jewels, monsters armed with wondrous curving swords and daggers inscribed with characters in some unknown alphabet. Alien and damp with slime as they were, they had a certain grace, a seductiveness that seemed to rouse in her some slumbering, nameless lust, an urge to submit to degradations she could not even imagine, yet groped toward, longed for, with a painful yearning intensity.

She saw them but an instant, then they vanished, to be replaced by clouds of ghosts who streamed past in a blur as if she were falling through them at an ever-increasing velocity.

"Mr. Blake, where am I going?"

No answer.

Something loomed ahead of her, something huge, dark, and formless. She screamed and closed her eyes.

"Are you all right, Kate?"

She opened her eyes, saw William leaning over her, concerned, anxious. The fireplace in front of her looked reassuringly normal.

"I think so." She laughed nervously, then sat bolt upright. "When I left, the fireplace was painted white!"

"White?" William sounded puzzled.

"Mr. Blake, it was white, I swear, but now it has a plain wood varnish finish. It's brown, Mr. Blake!"

"It always has been brown."

"No, it was white! I know it was white!"

A deep harsh voice came from the shadow to the right

of the fireplace. "You must get used to things like that, Mrs. Blake."

Urizen stepped into the firelight.

"I hope I didn't startle you, my dear," said the powerfully-built, white-bearded, naked man. He bent to kiss her lightly on the forehead, and it seemed to her he reminded her of someone else, someone she knew well.

Urizen stood on her right, William on her left. What would they do now? Urizen extended his hands, one to William, one to Kate.

"Congratulations, my friends," said Urizen softly. "Don't look so surprised. Smile! Laugh! Today you have found the success you sought so long. Today you graduate!"

She hesitated, then took Urizen's hand, a hard muscular hand but certainly a human hand, for all his strangeness. "Well, thank you, Mr. Urizen. I'm pleased to meet you, I'm sure."

He had both Blakes by the hand, drawing them toward him. She half-fearfully allowed him to pull her to her feet. He said, "Come, my dear. You too, William."

"Urizen . . ." William protested.

"No arguments, either of you. We must celebrate. Allow me the liberty of inviting you to my home."

Kate tried to pull free, but Urizen held her easily.

William tried an excuse. "I can't. I lost the gift."

Urizen laughed contemptuously.

The room dissolved.

The ghosts reappeared, but now she could not only see them, but hear and feel them. They howled with endless dismay as they streamed past, a swirl of distorted, anguished faces and twisted bodies, and as they brushed against her they felt like a cold damp wind that passes through the skin to freeze the bone. Images flashed in and out of focus, each lasting only a fraction of a second. Buildings. Mountains. People moving at impossible speeds. Darkness and light alternating faster than the mind could register.

And she had, all the while, the horrible feeling of falling.

This time, however, she could see William, hand still

grasped in Urizen's other hand. William called to her, "Don't let it frighten you, Kate." His own face looked rather pale.

The fall slowed, then stopped.

Kate, William, and Urizen stood on a parched white desert. The sky blazed white, too bright to look into. Nearby lay a jumble of bleached ruins.

"Where are we?" Kate demanded, when she could speak.

Urizen answered, amused. "London, or rather the place where London was many a million years ago. This is, you might say, the End of Time, if time can be said to have an end."

She tried to pull free. "You can let go of my hand now, sir."

Urizen laughed. "Not so fast, my dear lady. As long as I touch you two, you share in the energy fields that protect me and carry me through time. The moment I let you go, you die. How long would you last without air, under a sun hot enough to smelt iron? And soon that sun will explode and end this world, end the whole solar system." He tugged on their hands. "Come."

They trudged over the baked earth toward the ruins.

A portal came into view, a passageway leading down into the ground. Urizen paused before they entered and said with mocking formality, "Welcome to Golgonooza, Kingdom of Perfection!"

Golgonooza was an underground city, or better, an underground cathedral, for its high stone ceilings and vast endless echoing passageways clearly suggested the majesty of the great medieval churches, as did its tall, brilliantly-lit stained-glass windows.

Urizen explained, "You see sunlight behind those colored windows, my friends, but sunlight filtered and tamed by a long journey from the surface. The sun gives us the only light we have and the only light we need."

William asked, "Even at night?"

"We know no night in Golgonooza, sir. The Earth keeps always the same face toward the sun. Look here!"

A muscular forefinger pointed toward one of the windows. "I particularly like the design of the windows in this chamber. Don't you?"

The one he indicated, in the artistic style of ancient Egypt, depicted a smiling young woman bending over an agonized old man. The woman's headdress suggested the horns of a bull, or a half-moon on its side.

"Isis," William whispered.

"Ah, you recognize the tale." Urizen grinned.

"Indeed so."

"Isis has just poisoned her father, the god Ra. She won't give him the antidote until he tells her his secret name. When she knows his secret name he will have to obey her every command."

By his tone Kate gathered Urizen found some moral in the story, but Kate could see no virtue in poisoning one's parents. As the three walked on across the wide flagstones, Urizen released his grip on them, and though she could breathe the air in the room she snatched at William's hand as if he, not their muscular host, had the power to hold the elements at bay.

William glanced up at the next window. "And that's Prometheus, isn't it?" The stained glass showed a proud young man chained to a rock and trying to beat off an attacking eagle.

"Right again, sir! A great hero, according to the Greeks. He stole fire from Heaven for humanity. As punishment the gods chained him to a rock to be tormented by that eagle for all eternity." He paused theatrically, then added with a sly smile, "But humanity, of course, didn't have to give back the fire."

As he spoke they came to another window, and this one Kate recognized. "Why, that's Adam and Eve by the Tree of Knowledge!"

Urizen corrected her with a schoolmasterly air. "The Tree of Knowledge of Good and Evil. Not just knowledge, my dear, but knowledge of Good and Evil. If you forget the last part of the phrase you miss the point of the story. And notice how attentively they listen to their friend, the Serpent."

"Their friend?" Kate drew back.

Urizen nodded. "One might even say their Savior. The Serpent gave them freedom, and would have given them eternal life if he'd been allowed to. But come; there's more."

The next window showed a desert at dawn, hazy pinks, yellows and blues in the background and in the foreground a powerful black-bearded man wrestling violently with what appeared to be an angel. The style suggested da Vinci.

"My favorite." Urizen gazed up at it with intense, glittering eyes. "Orthodox Christians would identify that as Jacob wrestling with an angel, but you and I, Mr. Blake, and all those who read the Bible for themselves without the mealy-mouthed interpretation of some priest, know no angel is mentioned. Jacob wrestles with none other than Jehovah God in person, and wins! Am I right, Mr. Blake? Am I right?"

Much to Kate's alarm, William nodded slowly, his face pale but calm. If ever a man knew his Bible, it was William, yet how could this be?

The penultimate window depicted a tall thin man with short hair in a yellow robe raising his hand in blessing over a circle of similarly-clad men and women who appeared to be singing.

"I knew all the others," said William, "but not this one."

"This one shows the future, my friend. Or better, one of many possible futures." Urizen spoke with undisguised admiration. "The man's name is Newton McClintok, Pope of Etnroa, Kingdom of Singers. The woman at his side . . . that's Holly, who represents Power as Newton represents Vision. Listen to their slogan: 'If we could share this world below we'd need no world above.' What do you think of that, eh?"

William did not answer, though Kate prayed silently he would.

The last window in the chamber appeared unfinished. Peering up at it, Kate recognized the face in the center of the composition, though everything around it was vague or simply blank. "Mr. Urizen! That's you!"

Urizen bowed. "And an excellent likeness, wouldn't you agree?"

"But why isn't it finished?" put in William.

Urizen drew himself up to his full height. "Because *I* am not finished."

"Unfortunately." This last was a voice from the next chamber, a voice Kate had never heard before.

As the word died away in echoes, Kate turned to see two tall, bearded men walk toward her with a stately, measured tread. As they approached they passed alternately through darkness and patterned colored light from the stained glass windows, so at no time could she clearly see their faces.

"Ah!" Urizen spread his arms as if to embrace the newcomers. "My good friends Luvah and Tharmas. You know Mr. Blake, of course, but this time he has brought his lovely wife, Kate. Allow me to introduce you."

"I am King Tharmas," said the first. He kissed her hand. "In my own time, I am Lord of Atlantis."

In his left hand, apparently as a badge of his office, he carried a brass shepherd's crook studded with many-colored gems and settings of gold, and his helmet was a huge seashell, the only item of clothing he wore on his slender youthful body. His dark beard was curly and his features vaguely Negroid, but his skin was red: not the red of sunburn or too much wine, but a fine, natural red that covered his whole body evenly except for his palms, which were markedly paler. All in all, he was one of the handsomest men Kate had ever seen, though the anger in his features made Kate step back from him uneasily, and that same anger gave his voice an unpleasant harshness.

"And this is Luvah," said Urizen, gesturing toward the other man.

Luvah stared at her in motionless silence.

Luvah too was handsome, even beautiful, his thick black beard a disturbing contrast to the rounded feminine curves of his breasts and buttocks. He could have been a monster, a bearded lady in some circus sideshow, if it were not for his immense and stately dignity. He wore a crown of silver thorns that, together with his soft, straight beard, made him greatly resemble some of the more effeminate representations of Jesus, and on his left arm he carried a silver lyre that, with the slightest motion, tinkled faint half-formed fragments of melody. Beneath his long eyelashes his dark eyes glowed with fury, and the softness of his naked body could not conceal the rigidity of anger.

Urizen added, by way of explanation, "Behold the end-product of science! In his century, far, far in your future, they know how to make themselves hermaphrodites, like Adam before the separation of Eve. The best of both sexes, they like to think, but I'll let you judge that for yourself, Mrs. Blake." Urizen had noticed the look of revulsion on Kate's face. "Luvah may look like a shrinking violet, but I assure you in his own century he rules a galactic empire, human and nonhuman, of over a thousand stars, a small but respectable slice of the Orion arm of the Milky Way. They call him The Unapproachable, the Warmaker, the Lord of Hate. He has been known to exterminate the populations of entire planets out of spite, but don't let him intimidate you, my dear. At heart he is the gentlest of souls. As he would tell you, if he deigned to speak to you at all, everything he does he does for love."

King Tharmas broke in: "Mr. and Mrs. Blake, Luvah and I share with Urizen the rule of Golgonooza and of the League of Zoas. May we speak to you? Alone?"

"He means without me around," Urizen told Kate dryly, then faced the two rulers and said with cold formality, "The Blakes are my guests, Your Majesties. We have certain rules . . ."

Tharmas thumped the flagstones with the butt of his brass staff, setting the echoes ringing. "Rules? How dare you, of all people, speak of rules!" With a slender hand whose red fingernails resembled claws, the silent Luvah touched the monarch's arm restrainingly.

William spoke haltingly. "Urizen is . . . my friend."

Kate shot him a glance of alarm.

Urizen was delighted. "You see, Tharmas? You see, Luvah? The Blakes are with me!"

The king shook his head sadly. "I hope that is not true; by whatever gods there be I pray it is not true. The gift of time-voyaging is granted to few. Of all the billions on all the Earths, only a handful have the talent and fewer still the training for it. All, sooner or later, settle down and join the League of Zoas, content to merely observe the vast drama of history. All but Urizen! Only he, like some rowdy in a theater, insists on jumping up on the stage and disrupting the performance. He's not satisfied to watch history. He wants to change it!"

Luvah stood at the king's elbow, motionless, his lips, cheeks, and eyelids colored with cosmetics that hid all trace of expression except for that fearsome glitter in his eyes. His womanly face might have been an ancient Greek mask, its very immobility conveying an unmistakable suggestion of menace.

William stood firm. "I don't understand this dispute between you Zoas, but I know one thing. Urizen, not you, sought me out and spoke to me, made himself my teacher and guide when I needed a teacher and guide to save my sanity."

"Only to recruit you!" Tharmas protested. Luvah nodded agreement.

"Whatever his motives, he came when I needed him. He gave me his help. When I had almost convinced myself that my gift was but a terrible sickness of the mind, he came to me. Where were you then?" William demanded.

The Atlantian replied, "We in the League do not impose ourselves and our ideas on people. We wait. Those who have the gift find us soon enough. If they then have questions, we have answers."

Urizen spoke with contempt. "Answers? You have no answers. Answers come from experience. None of us have enough of that. We must first experiment, then . . ."

Tharmas cut him off. "We have certain self-evident truths—"

"Self-evident?" boomed Urizen. "One of these being, I

suppose, that you will lose the gift through sexual intercourse?''

"Well, yes . . .''

"Fool! I have disported myself for weeks in the bordellos of Imperial Rome!'' cried Urizen. "And I see as clearly as ever and fly as far. You lose the gift as you gain it, through belief. What egotists you are to think Eternity cares any more what you do with your genitals than what you do with your earlobes!''

William had turned pale. "You mean I haven't lost the gift?''

Urizen clapped him on the shoulder. "Not unless you think you have!''

William turned on Tharmas. "You lied to me!''

"No! It's not true!'' Tharmas protested.

"Try it!'' shouted Urizen. "Try it for yourself, William!''

Kate began to open her mouth to speak to William, to advise caution, but her lips had scarcely parted when he vanished.

Urizen laughed triumphantly, but his laugh broke off abruptly and he too was gone.

After a moment of paralyzed silence Tharmas turned to Kate, his tone pleading for forgiveness. "We didn't know, Mrs. Blake.''

"Where have they gone?'' Kate demanded.

"We don't know.''

At that she fairly screamed, "What *do* you know, then?'' Tharmas could not answer.

"Find them!'' cried Kate.

With a helpless gesture Tharmas vanished too, and an instant later Luvah followed.

As they vanished, William and Urizen reappeared, laughing delightedly. William had grown a beard.

"Where have you been?'' cried Kate.

William, slightly dazed, took an unsteady step toward her. "To Etnroa, Kate.''

"Etnroa?'' She remembered the stained glass window, the thin man in the yellow robe.

"Oh, Kate, somewhere up ahead in our future there's a new religion, a religion of life for art's sake, a religion that makes life itself an art and the world a work of art. Would you believe they remember me and celebrate my birthday and call me their forerunner, the First Etnroan? My statue stands in city squares, amid strange buildings all glass on their south face, buildings heated entirely by the sun even in winter so they never need burn a lump of coal or a stick of wood. Because of that the air there is clear and clean and pure, not like here. And Kate, green things grow everywhere, indoors and out!''

In his excitement he grasped her hand, and because he so seldom touched her, she almost drew back from surprise.

He babbled on: ''Like me they make books by hand in limited editions, often only one copy, where they combine drawing and writing in a single work, books where they reveal their innermost thoughts and feelings without fear. Like me they participate in little groups of creative friends— these groups replace the family as the building blocks of civilization. And, oh, Kate, like me they sing, they sing songs of their own composing. You've never heard such singing! Solos, duets, trios, massed choirs! The harmony is richer than anything you've ever heard, the counterpoint more complex, the rhythm more compelling. You can't help but dance! Our own composers would weep with envy if they could hear it!''

''A dream . . .'' Kate tried to calm him down. ''It's just a dream.''

''We can go there, Kate! We can go there and never return, go there and live out our lives in a land where every man and woman is a poet.''

She tugged at his hand. ''If everyone's a poet, then who washes the dishes?''

''The poets!'' William answered in ecstasy. ''Singing all the while! They live as simply as the red Indians in the colonies, yet know more than the wisest professors at our universities. They own almost nothing yet live better than our kings by sharing the inheritance of thousands of years of progress, the combined thought of all the races and nations on Earth. They have no marriage, for they see no one can own a person, that all of us, men and women alike, must be independent and autonomous, interacting with other free people in a constant swift, subtle negotiation. They have no money and thus no economic classes, no nations and thus no armies, no war. Oh, if you could have seen them, Kate, walking naked in the afternoons in the streets without shame, laughing, singing, embracing!''

''Naked? Embracing in the streets? Good heavens!'' But to herself she thought, *In such a world could William finally really love me?*

Urizen broke in, amused. ''Certainly you two could go to Etnroa and stay there, but why? You have all of time and space to chose from—past, present, and future. Why settle in any one place?''

William said, ''Yes, yes, why indeed? Kate, we went into our past, too. I met King Arthur, the real King Arthur, who lived hundreds of years before the birth of Christ. What an age of glory, Kate! What an age of courage! You should have seen the calm virgin girls walking unafraid to their deaths as human sacrifices!''

''To their *deaths*?'' Kate released his hand. ''Human sacrifices?''

''They stepped into a roaring fire as you and I might step into a bathtub,'' said William with awe. ''And even as their flesh turned black, they smiled like trusting babes.''

''And had you lost the gift?'' Urizen prompted him.

''No, sir! Not a bit!''

Urizen patted him on the back. ''So much for the Eternal Laws of right and wrong. What say you, Mr. and Mrs. Blake? Will you let Tharmas and Luvah imprison you within their narrow prejudices, or will you throw in with me and be free?''

''With you!'' cried William. He spoke for both of them, though he had not bothered to consult Kate, to ask her opinion. She wanted to ask for time, time to think. Something, she felt, was wrong, but she couldn't quite put her finger on it.

''Come then,'' said Urizen. ''Let's try our wings!''

He meant this quite literally, helping the Blakes to slip into the broad, white-feathered wings the Zoas used in their trips through time. ''The wings,'' Urizen explained, ''serve to guide you, not support your weight. The force that propels you and holds you aloft is the energy of the timestream itself. Temporal energy can also form a forceshield that protects you even in the void of outer space."

William asked, "Where's the machine that converts all that energy?"

Urizen, for answer, solemnly pointed to his own forehead.

"And another thing, Urizen. Does it do any harm to tap out so much energy?"

Urizen smiled with charming frankness. "I must confess, sir, I haven't the vaguest notion."

And with that the trio plunged into the space outside of time, winging their way hand in hand back and forth through the centuries, chattering, joking, pausing to glimpse some particularly freakish folly of humans or laugh at some particularly outlandish turn of fashion. Kate would never have believed men could admire some of the more grotesque women's costumes from the more obscure ages of history if she had not seen them for herself.

"Look there!" cried Urizen. "The natives call that the miniskirt!"

"Indecent!" Kate exclaimed, but she was not really shocked.

And in another century they paused near an elevated bikeway that separated two communities of radically different architecture. One community seemed built to resemble something from the American continent of the 1920s; the other looked like Ancient Egypt. "Beware this era," Urizen cautioned. "This is the civilization of the Mims, neighborhoods that each mimic a different historical period. You could lose yourself here, delude yourself into thinking you were in the wrong place, in the wrong century. Come!"

He led them in flight at dazzling speed across the Atlantic, hurtling like a meteor through the stratosphere. In minutes they found themselves hovering above the west coast of the American continent. Below them, on an elevated bikeway, a lone, gaunt cyclist pedaled doggedly through the chilly damp air of morning.

"That's Newton McClintok," Urizen said.

"The man on the stained glass window?" asked Kate. "The Pope of that cult of Life for Art's Sake?"

"Yes, but here he is no Pope, just a poor fool pedalling from one community to another, looking for one where he fits in. You see how infinite are the branching forks of choice? In one reality you rule the world; in another you cannot in all that world find a place. Nothing is inevitable. We are blinded by the illusion that society makes us do this, duty makes us do that, fate makes us do the other thing. Looking at the timestream from the outside, you realize nothing makes you do anything. At every instant you choose what you do. At every instant you choose what you are. At every instant you answer the question, 'What do I really want?' Always, always you choose. Always, always the only rule is the iron tyranny of whim.''

Thus they flew at hazard through time and space like bees that sample blossoms from random fields, until abruptly Urizen announced, "Here we are!''

Kate looked around.

She recognized London, but a London subtly changed.

William said, "We've overshot. This is the city as it looked in my childhood.''

Yes, Kate recognized the costumes of the people who passed the mouth of the alley where they stood as those of her mother's day.

"Perhaps we should have worn something more in the fashion of the time,'' said William, frowning. Kate and William's garb appeared only slightly odd, while Urizen's nudity would have been freakish in almost any era.

"We'll leave in a few minutes,'' Urizen said as he unslung a large leather bag from his shoulders. The object in the bag seemed long, slender, and heavy.

Kate glanced around nervously. If someone should catch them standing here in these white wings . . .

"Ah,'' breathed Urizen, his voice dropping to a whisper, "here she comes now.''

Kate followed his line of vision, then gasped.

Her mother came toward them down the cobblestone street, but her mother as a young woman, no older than Kate herself. No one could mistake the family resemblance.

Urizen smiled.

Kate gazed at her mother as if in a trance, and the noise of wagons and braying mules and shouting peddlers faded away, the stench of smoke and manure. All she could see was that youthful, beautiful face that she had known as old and wrinkled. How few and how slight the changes that separate lovely youth from ugly agedness!

"May I speak to her?" Kate whispered.

"If you like," Urizen answered softly.

Kate slipped off her wings and stepped from the alley. "Mother?"

The woman, who had been lost in reverie, looked up sharply. "Do I know you, girl?"

"I'm your daughter."

"I have no daughter. Upon my faith, lass, I ain't even married."

"But you will marry."

"Gor, I hope so."

"And you'll have a daughter named Kate."

"Be you a gypsy witch? I'll not give you sixpence, though you speak ever so true."

"Gypsy witch? No, I . . ." But how could she explain? A thousand thoughts thronged her mind, begging for utterance. Warnings! Advice! Questions! She did indeed know her mother's future, and could tell her what pitfalls to avoid, what safeguards to adopt against misfortune. So many choices lay ahead, and to Kate it seemed her mother would make a dozen wrong choices for every right unless saved by Kate's marvelous hindsight.

But now her mother looked past her, eyes widening with horror. Had she seen Urizen? Kate turned. Urizen had indeed stepped from the alley, flintlock pistol in hand.

"Urizen, what . . ." Kate began.

Urizen took aim and pulled the trigger. A click, an instant's faint sizzle, and the weapon discharged with an earsplitting bang, belching forth a cloud of blue smoke.

Kate screamed as her mother fell sprawling, face down, on the cobblestones.

"I don't understand," Kate said, too stunned to weep.

"I don't understand." She knelt by the corpse. "I don't understand."

Urizen said coldly, "Get up, Mrs. Blake. You can't help her. No one can."

People started toward them from the other side of the street. William angrily grabbed Urizen's arm.

"Let me go, you fool," Urizen snapped. "I can set things right if we get out of here."

"How?" William demanded.

"Come. I'll show you."

He snatched up the wings Kate had shed and, with a rush, they found themselves again in the shadow world outside of time. A brief blur of phantom faces, then she saw again the alley she had just left, but without her mother's body. They had gone backward in time, but not far.

Urizen seated himself on a barrel and, humming softly, began filling his flintlock pistol with gunpowder.

"My mother," Kate murmured. "Is she really dead?"

"Quite dead," Urizen replied, tamping in the powder with a short ramrod drawn from the underside of the gun.

"But that means," she continued falteringly, "I never was born."

"Does it?" Urizen asked.

William's face clouded with anger. "Urizen, you said you could set things right."

"And so I can, sir." Urizen neatly plopped a steel ball down the muzzle, then tamped in a bit of wadding. "Patience, William, patience."

He had finished loading the weapon, and now cocked it. "My theory, for what it's worth, is that when we step outside the stream of time we break the chain of cause and effect. Things change in the ordinary world of space and time, but not in that other place. In a moment you'll see. Ah, here they come!"

Kate heard a woman's voice, strangely familiar, cry out in surprise. She whirled. Not three feet away stood a second Urizen, a second William and . . . a second Kate. Kate had seen herself in a mirror many times, but not like this. The other Kate lived and breathed as an independent being, not a reflection, and looked back at her. As she fell back a step, Kate noticed, from the corner of her eye, that Urizen had again aimed his pistol.

The second Urizen tensed.

The first Urizen fired.

The second Urizen fell.

Her ears ringing from the shot, she saw, with a supernatural clarity such as comes with fever, the second Kate and the second William bend over, take hold of the second Urizen, and all three vanish. There remained no sign of them but a spot of blood in the dust.

"How could you do it?" Kate asked in a strangled whisper.

"He let me," Urizen explained placidly. "He lowered his mental shields for me, as I'd planned."

"No, I mean how could you bring yourself . . ."

"I wanted to see what would happen."

"But my mother . . ."

"Why don't you go to the mouth of the alley and have a look?"

With William close behind, she did as Urizen suggested.

Yes, her mother was there, coming down the street, preoccupied with her own affairs, paying no attention to the people she passed who looked with curiosity toward the alley, wondering, no doubt, about the shot they'd just heard.

Kate let her pass, remaining in the shadows. She had so much to say to her, the same as before, but now it was all washed away in a wave of gratitude simply that the woman was alive. Thank God she was alive!

Kate, still unsteady on her feet, blurted out, "But . . . but where did the second Urizen, Kate, and William go?"

"I must confess," Urizen answered lightly, "I haven't the least notion."

William looked shocked. "You mean you perform experiments involving murder, and you don't know what you're doing?"

Unperturbed, Urizen replied, "It is by performing such experiments, my dear sir, that we find out what we're doing." He returned the pistol, still smoking, to his leather

bag. "And now we must depart before the local citizenry
arrive to inquire about that shot." She could indeed hear
the murmur of voices and the sound of footsteps beyond
the alley.

Was it her imagination or did she see, among the ghosts
who swarmed around them as they returned to Golgonooza,
the tortured faces of Urizen and Kate's mother?

The Blakes met other Zoas, not only humans from
various ages of history, but creatures from other planets,
from other levels of reality. Dragon-men, eagle-men, lion-
people who seemed made of blazing fire.

But William most delighted in taking Kate to Etnroa, to
what he called "The Age of Song." She never forgot her
first visit, when, hand in hand, she and William materialized at dawn in a canyon in the mountains near the west
coast of the North American continent, dressed in the garb
of their own period.

"Won't they think us strange?" whispered Kate in the
stillness of morning. "We won't look like them."

"Never mind," William answered. "Urizen taught me
what to say."

They started up a broad paved highway. A few bicycles
and a three-wheeler passed, the cyclists paying them no
attention, and Kate relaxed.

Ahead, partially obscured by mist, towered a building
fronted by a sheer expanse of glass at least twenty stories
high. The building leaned back as if resting against the
cliff behind it.

"That's the city of Cliffside, a whole town in one
building," William explained. "It faces south to catch the
sun's rays, and is tilted so that in summer, when the sun
rides high in the sky, the rays don't penetrate very far
inside, while in winter, when the heat is needed and the
sun rides low, the rays penetrate to the backmost walls
where the warmth is stored in the mass of the cliff itself.
In summer the citizens are cool, in winter warm, and all
without the burning of a single lump of coal or stick of
wood."

Walking briskly, they topped a rise and another part of

Cliffside came in view, a sort of glassed-over foot extending outward from the base of the tilting façade. "Greenhouses," William explained. "The Etnroans do all their farming indoors, where they can conserve water and protect the crops from weather and insects."

Kate found herself panting in the thin, cold mountain air. "Not so fast, Mr. Blake. I'm fair winded."

Reluctantly he slowed his pace. "The Etnroans love the mountains. The thin air adds years to their lives."

"Not to mine," she panted.

Now they came in sight of a red marble statue, twice life size, of a thin, ascetic-looking old man. In the pedestal she read the words, graven on a bronze plaque, "Paolo Soleri, architect of Utopia."

William explained, "Paolo Soleri invented the basic architectural style of Etnroa, the principle of the two suns. He demonstrated how a city could be built to be completely self-sufficient. The citizens of Cliffside have everything they need here. They don't need to import or export anything. Such cities are called, they tell me, arcologies."

The Blakes passed the statue and came to a flight of broad stone steps rising to a semicircular entrance like half a cup on its side. "Almost all the materials Cliffside is made of come from close by," he said.

They started up the stairs.

At the head of the stairs a small, slim woman in her twenties watched their approach. She wore no makeup and her light hair was cropped short, but she was perhaps the most beautiful woman Kate had ever seen. Her eyes were like glowing emeralds, full of alert intelligence, and her simple yellow tunic, decorated only with an orange metal sundisk pin on the center of the chest, draped a figure at once athletic and delicately sexual. She raised a slender hand in greeting. "Welcome to Cliffside, strangers. Are you expected?"

"No," said William.

"Then perhaps you will give me delight and breakfast with me."

"Gladly, and thank you," said William.

Kate looked on as he ceremoniously touched fingertips

with the woman, then when they looked at her expectantly, she also performed the ritual, though a bit self-consciously.

"I am Aleetha, a harpist." She led them inside through a small door next to the larger, heavier one, which was elaborately carved with intertwined flowers and nude human figures.

"I am William Blake, an artist, and this is my wife Kate."

Aleetha laughed. "William Blake? I understand. You are anachronists, role-players who take on the identities of famous people from the past. I hear such role-playing is a great fad in the valley and out on the coast. Here in Cliffside we think more about the future than the past." She gave them a quick but intent glance, her movements like those of a small bird. "You do indeed look like the original William and Kate. Is it plastic surgery or only typecasting?"

William was puzzled. "Plastic surgery? Typecasting?"

Aleetha laughed again. "But of course you can't let on you know what those words mean. That would break character. I have studied the Blakes and their coterie—William Godwin, philosopher of reason and freedom, his wife Mary Wollstonecraft, the first feminist, his daughter Mary Shelley, who wrote *Frankenstein*, his other daughter, Claire Claremont, who was Lord Byron's mistress and mother of his daughter, his son-in-law the poet Percy Shelley, and all their friends and lovers. Many historians call that group the first Etnroan Circle, the seed of what has become our present dominant civilization, but of course you must know all that from researching your roles."

"Oh, yes," said William quickly. "We know those people as well as if they'd been our personal friends."

Kate restrained a smile.

"Come," said Aleetha. "We must hurry or we'll be late for the morning songs."

They broke into a trot up a long, gently-sloping corridor. The walls on either side were translucent up to slightly above eye level, where they became transparent, and were pierced at regular intervals by doors that were gold-colored glass mirrors. Every detail had clearly been planned to make maximum use of the sunlight that now streamed throughout the interior at a steep low angle. The strangeness of everything worried Kate. So far Aleetha had accepted everything they had said at face value, and had even covered up for them when they made a slip, but sooner or later they would be bound to make a slip nobody could cover up. Then what would happen? They would have to explain somehow that they were time-voyagers from the past, or they would have to flee. Kate did not want to leave, not yet. There was an atmosphere of peace here such as she had never experienced before, a timeless fairy tale quality that reminded her of stories she'd heard as a girl about people kidnapped to the Kingdom of the Faeries, where a hundred years passed as if it was a minute. Etnroa was strange, yes, but familiar at the same time.

From behind one of the mirrored doors Kate heard the murmur of voices. Aleetha pushed open the door and led them inside. The delicious aroma of frying fish filled Kate's nostrils and she felt suddenly hungry. The room appeared to be a kind of restaurant or mess hall, with tan, wood, rectangular tables where yellow-robed Etnroans of both sexes and all ages sat in twos, threes, and fours eating, laughing, and gossiping. The far wall was a floor-to-ceiling window through which Kate got an excellent view of the mountains.

The side walls rose to slightly above eye-level and were transparent aquaria where swam all manner of fresh-water fish.

"Pick a fish," Aleetha instructed. "I'll take that one." She pointed to a fat trout drifting lazily to and fro. A muscular young man standing on a platform leaned over the top of the open tank and adroitly netted the trout, beheaded it with a quick blow of his meat cleaver on a chopping-block pillar, and gave it to her. The Blakes followed Aleetha's example.

"We like our fish fresh," Aleetha commented.

She handed hers to one of a gang of cooks laboring vigorously at the center of the room over a battery of gas stoves. Kate could not understand everything. It was all so new to her. Yet the way they prepared the fish, so quickly, so easily, with no wasted energy, seemed to epitomize the whole Etnroan approach to life, an approach that expressed itself in every detail of food, clothing, and shelter. Nothing was taken for granted. Each moment seemed shaped by art, by the search for the best way of doing things, the easy right way, by the search for grace and simple beauty, and though she knew almost nothing about these people, Kate was struck dumb with awe by the way they moved, as unconsciously lithe as cats, by the way they talked, in a kind of half-song, and by their bodies. The Etnroans seemed drawn from every race and mixture of races on Earth, but none of them was fat or underweight, none showed any trace of either vice or illness. Aleetha, who had seemed a goddess of beauty a moment before, now had become only one deity among many.

Their trays loaded with fish, potatoes, beans and fruit, Aleetha and the Blakes sat down at a table next to the door and commenced their meal. Never had Kate tasted such food, and when she remarked on it, Aleetha said proudly, "Here at Cliffside we honor cooking as an art, the equal of painting and music. Everything is fresh, grown within walking distance of where it is consumed. Everything is prepared by taste, with love and knowledge. Each element in every meal is the end result of countless small changes in genetic engineering."

Kate had no idea what was meant by "genetic engineering," but carefully concealed her ignorance.

Someone began humming a simple tune.

Another voice joined the first, following in harmony. A third voice joined in, in counterpoint. A fourth voice began, a fifth, a sixth, no two melodies the same, yet all blending harmoniously in great organlike chord progressions. Kate leaned toward Aleetha and whispered, "How do they remember all those tunes?"

Aleetha looked at her in surprise. "Why, they don't remember the tunes at all. They're improvising, of course, making up everything as they go along."

"But it all fits together!" Kate blurted stupidly.

"Of course." Now at last Aleetha was suspicious. "Are you really a role-player, Kate? A role-player would know that. A role-player improvises the same way."

"I am Kate Blake."

Aleetha continued to stare at her.

Now individuals began to sing words which Kate realized must also be improvised. The soloists took turns, surrendering the floor to each other by a code of nods and smiles, and when the lyrics took a witty turn, a ripple of laughter flowed through the crowd without stopping the smooth shifting of the hummed harmonies. Kate dimly understood that this too, this spontaneous singing, exemplified the whole Etnroan attitude. The group existed not for itself but to provide a background, a framework, a support for the individual, to bring the individual to a height of accomplishment impossible in isolation.

But now to her dismay Kate saw Aleetha glaring at her, demanding, "Who are you, Kate? Who are you really?"

William stood up. "We are William and Kate Blake."

Aleetha persisted. "Yes, yes, those are your role names. Tell me your real names. Tell me your real home."

William, pale, answered firmly, "William and Kate Blake, from London." Kate too stood up.

Heads turned toward the Blakes. The singing died.

Aleetha said, "We are kind to strangers, but if you know us at all, you must know we can be cruel too, more cruel than the coastal or valley people, to those who betray our hospitality, who lie to us or spy on us."

"Run, Kate," William whispered, and they fled.

In a moment they reached the hall, and before their pursuers could follow them they leaped out of the timestream and into the shadow world; but as they rushed through the shifting grayness Kate felt not that she was escaping from an alien and dangerous era, but that she was leaving a home, a home she had not realized was hers, and she was homesick already.

In the halls of Golgonooza at the end of time, naked Urizen led William and Kate through the cathedral-like chamber of windows, and his voice echoed when he spoke to them. "I will show you a staircase you have never seen before, a staircase to the lower levels, my friends. Someone awaits you there, someone who wishes to meet you."

"Indeed?" said William. "Who?"

"Vala." Urizen's voice took on a curious timbre, an uncharacteristic tenderness, so that Kate thought the bearded Zoa must love this Vala, whoever Vala might be.

"And who is Vala?" William persisted.

Urizen replied pensively. "Some say she is the daughter of Luvah, the galactic emperor. But is Luvah mother or father? Biologically he can play the role of either sex, you know. I myself think he only adopted her. She doesn't look at all like him, fortunately."

They started down a winding white marble staircase.

"Why does she want to meet us?" William asked.

Urizen's smile was even more enigmatic than usual. "She thinks her fate intertwined with yours somehow. You know the fancies women have."

They reached the foot of the stairs. The light on this floor was noticeably dimmer than on the floor above. Urizen glanced at Kate with an ironic expression that made her decidedly uneasy. Clearly Urizen was enjoying some sort of unsavory private joke at her expense.

The Zoa stepped to a curtained doorway. "I leave you here. Go in. Introduce yourselves."

Kate asked nervously, "Won't you come in with us?"

Urizen slowly shook his head. "No. I find I cannot look at her without pain, and I do not like pain."

"Pain?" Kate glanced with apprehension at the doorway.

Urizen chuckled. "Oh, she's no monster, if that's what you think. Ordinarily I'd call her beautiful, but she is . . ." He hesitated, then his tone turned to anger. "She's pregnant!"

He strode away.

Hesitantly William called out, "Miss Vala? Or should I call you Mrs. Vala?"

"Miss will do just fine," came a voice from beyond the curtain, a world-weary feminine voice that Kate found tantalizingly familiar. "You are William Blake, are you not?"

"I am."

"Come in, come in."

William pulled aside the curtain and stepped within, closely followed by Kate.

Kate gasped, her hand flying to her mouth.

Vala, except for her long black hair, looked exactly like Mary Wollstonecraft.

William, also stunned, murmured, "Mary."

His features, in the dim reddish light, were drawn.

Vala raised a painted eyebrow. "Do I resemble someone you know?"

"Mary," William repeated.

Vala smiled with orange-painted lips. "This Mary must have made quite an impression on you, judging from your expression." She reclined on a couch upholstered with orange velvet, fingering a necklace of rubies. Her long, translucent, crimson robes rustled as she changed position.

Kate spoke sharply. "Don't toy with us, Mary!"

"I am Vala. If ever I was someone named Mary, it was in another incarnation, or another level of reality, or another branch of the timestream. From here that place can never be more than a fantasy, a fading dream. Such an ordinary name! Hardly suitable for a galactic princess."

William said uncertainly, "Mary is a radical philosopher, an important intellectual leader."

"Really?" Vala mocked. "Intellectuals do not lead. Rulers lead. Kings. Queens. Dictators. Presidents. Rulers act. Intellectuals write excuses for their actions."

"No, no," said William. "Philosophers provide the ideas that rulers put into practice, when the people demand . . ."

Vala laughed outright. "The people demand? By the gods, are you really a Zoa? Have you really traveled the centuries? A timebound man might speak as you do, but not a Zoa! From a Zoa one expects a certain weary detachment, a wise disillusionment."

William said stubbornly, "I will not abandon my dreams."

Vala reached up and touched his cheek. "Darling child, keep your dreams. Reality has nothing to offer that compares with them. As Newton McClintok once put it, 'A fool's paradise is better than none.' In reality's apples we always find a worm. Only dream apples are perfect, always sweet. In all the branching forks of time, people meet again and again. Sometimes to love, sometimes to hate, sometimes to pass each other, indifferent. Of course like everyone else, I seek a way to be together with someone. Don't you? You and I, like everyone else, want unconditional love, to be loved no matter what we do. Everyone wants that gift, but no one has the strength to give it. The basic tragedy! The one constant of all human relations through all the branching forks! Pain! An anguished hunger of the heart that only illusion can satisfy! Keep your dreams, my darling fool, keep them.''

Through all this long tirade Kate felt the pain Vala spoke of, felt it as a tightness in the chest, a constriction of the throat. When Vala touched William's cheek and called him darling, Kate tasted Hell. Between William and Vala there seemed to be a unique bond, though they had just met. Of course! Every relationship between two people is unique, yet Kate longed to be Vala to William, to be Mary to William, to be Polly Wood to William, or failing that, to find an abandoned corner of time where she and William could live out their lives alone, with no other people at all.

Then Kate remembered Urizen's refusal to visit Vala; Urizen too had spoken of pain. Kate spoke to Vala bluntly now, with a familiarity she would have used with Mary, as if Vala were Mary, as she seemed. "Why does Urizen hate you?"

Vala smiled archly. "Ah, Kate, who do you think I carry in my womb?"

"How would I know?" Yet a terrible suspicion leaped into her mind.

"Urizen," said Vala smugly, confirming that suspicion. "Urizen rides within me, awaiting birth, so Urizen is jealous. He is jealous of the father. He is jealous of himself. As a babe he knows safety and calm. As a man he knows the same pain we all do, multiplied by the paradoxes of time. We Zoas know pains the timebound cannot imagine. With the coin of pain we pay our fares on our voyages through the centuries. Yet we have our consolations.''

"Consolations?" Kate echoed.

"How lucky for me, my dear, to see my unborn babe fullgrown, to know in advance how handsome a man he will become."

She took Kate and William by the hands and drew them to her, saying, "Kiss me on the cheeks, my pretty comrades, and go. I wanted so to see you, and I have seen you. I wanted to puzzle you, and I have puzzled you, and so goodbye."

Vala's perfume, when Kate kissed her, was Mary's perfume . . . or was it?

Urizen impatiently awaited the Blakes in the hall of stained-glass windows beneath the unfinished window of Urizen's face. "You said, my friends, that when you had enough information you would choose between the other Zoas and me, between their way and mine. I can teach you no more. I have told you all I know and shown you all my tricks and taken you down a representative sample of the branching forks. Now you must choose."

"We're ready," said William firmly.

"No, we're not!" contradicted Kate.

"Trouble in the family?" Urizen raised an eyebrow. "I would not wish to come between husband and wife."

"Mr. Urizen, sir," Kate began, "it wouldn't be fair if we made our choice here in Golgonooza. You've quite dazzled us with all your wonders, and we must have a clear head for such an important decision."

"What do you propose, woman?" Urizen spoke coldly.

"Let us go home to London, to our own century, to our own home. There we'll see things in a more normal light."

William turned on her, face livid with anger. "Golgonooza is our home now, Kate! And all the branching forks from beginning to end. I can no more go back than a butterfly can squeeze back into his cocoon. We belong here with our friend and guide, Urizen."

Urizen smiled.

Kate shook her head vigorously. "No, no, Mr. Blake.

You're so easily influenced. I'm sorry, but it's true. You always get carried away by every new fancy, with no distinction between the false and the true. Indeed, I think the more false the idea, the more eagerly you pounce upon it.''

"Mrs. Blake!" William drew himself up indignantly.

"You won't admit I'm right, but I could give you an example or three. Now you're my husband, right?''

"Yes," he admitted with suspicion.

"And you love me, don't you? Or at least you once did.''

"I'll always love you. You can't say I've given you reason to think otherwise.''

"Then to make me happy—you do want to make me happy, don't you?—come back with me.''

"Kate." He wavered.

"Please," she pleaded.

"Oh, very well.''

He would do it, she could see, but he'd find ways to make her regret asking him to do it. That was a man's way. Only a woman, she thought, can do an unselfish thing without resentment.

Urizen, though annoyed, managed to maintain his façade of politeness. "You decide not to decide. Very well. I will wait a bit longer, but you must understand something.''

The Blakes turned toward him expectantly.

Urizen no longer smiled. "I and the other Zoas disagree on many things, but on one thing we agree completely. We cannot allow anyone not a member of the League to enjoy the power of time-voyaging.''

"I understand," Kate said softly.

"Good!" Urizen's habitual smile returned. "Then take your wings and go, with my blessing. I'll drop in on you from time to time to see if you've changed your minds.''

"You've traveled into our future already, haven't you?" William demanded. "You already know what we'll decide.''

Urizen, for the first time, seemed really puzzled. "I've tried to see it, yes, but whenever I look the stream has shifted to another branch and your decision is different, with all that implies for the future. No decision in all time has more far-reaching implications.''

"And another thing." Kate took courage from Urizen's uncertainty. "Vala says she is your mother. Is that true?"

Urizen laughed outright. "Now that's a very interesting question! A more important question for you than you might think. I'll tell you the answer myself if and when you become one of us.''

William, with Kate's help, printed a book, using his own process.

During the months of its preparation he not once turned his hand to the production of anything that would put bread on the table, though Kate, now a skillful engraver, cut a good dozen illustrations that met with increasing approval not only with Johnson but with several publishers of advertising catalogs. She told them William did the work; they wouldn't have liked the idea of a woman engraver, but she smiled when they commented on a new freeness of line and, more important, a new promptness of delivery.

William printed his book, his strange little book, in a limited edition, each page rubbed against the inked plate with the back of a spoon. A limited edition? Ten copies, no more.

And Kate dared not suggest these ten copies be offered for sale. Once printed they all, save one, were locked in a trunk, to be taken out occasionally so that one illustration or another could be hand-painted with watercolors.

The copy not locked away William delighted in reading aloud again and again to Kate, and though Kate hated every word of this book, she let him read, listening at first, then later, when she'd involuntarily memorized it, pretending to listen.

She endured it all because of the look on his face, the look that seemed to say, "You took eternity away from me; can't I keep my harmless little hobby?"

He entitled the book *The Marriage of Heaven and Hell,* in satirical imitation of Emmanuel Swedenborg's spiritual travelog *Heaven and Hell*. William did not sign the work

—perhaps, Kate suspected, because the thoughts were as much Urizen's as his own.

Though she knew the entire book by heart, certain passages lingered with her:

> As I was walking among the fires of hell, delighted with the enjoyments of genius, which to angels look like torment and insanity, I collected some of their proverbs, thinking that the sayings used in the nation show the nature of infernal wisdom better than any description of buildings or garments.
>
> Let us look at some of these infernal proverbs.
>
> The road of excess leads to the palace of wisdom.
>
> He who desires but acts not, breeds pestilence.
>
> What is now proved was once only imagined.
>
> Everything possible to be believed is an image of the truth.
>
> You never know what is enough unless you know what is more than enough.
>
> As the caterpillar choses the fairest leaves to lay her eggs on, so the priest lays his curse on the fairest joys.
>
> Sooner murder an infant in its cradle than nurse unacted desires.

And this last, which William took special pleasure in reading to her:

> Let man wear the fell of the lion, woman the fleece of the sheep.

Kate understood the constant emphasis on the need to act on desire, even forbidden desire. In this he screamed a defense against the relentless prosecution of his own conscience, before which, in the court of his soul, he stood trial for adultery. In this he howled out the torments of his personal Hell, attempting to transform them into poetry, into the "enjoyments of genius."

And she also understood another part of his book, the story of an angel who, swayed by William's arguments, became a devil.

"This angel, who is now become a devil, is my particular friend; we often read the Bible together, in its infernal sense, which the world shall have if they behave well. I also have the Bible of Hell, which the world shall have whether they will or no."

Kate bore it all patiently, but finally could keep silent no longer. They sat in the kitchen on either side of the table, as they so often did. William had just finished reading once again the phrase, "This angel, who is now become a devil, is my particular friend." He gazed at her expectantly, the candlelight dancing on his face, revealing an expression she did not recognize as his own.

She began hesitantly, "This angel who has become a devil . . . that's Urizen, isn't it?"

William slapped his palm exultantly on the tabletop. "Ah ha! So you comprehend! I'd begun to think I was reading to a stuffed owl!"

She laid down her graver and the illustration she'd been cutting, regarding him seriously. "And Urizen, you say, is your particular friend?"

"What else can I call someone who offers me, as a gift, absolute freedom?" In his voice, as in his eyes, there lurked a madness she had not noticed before, or had managed to ignore.

"I thought it was I, Mr. Blake, who was your particular friend."

"You're my wife."

"It's the same thing."

"Not at all! One loves one's friends because one wishes to. One loves one's wife because one must."

The hardness in his tone hurt more than the words, though they were bad enough. For a moment pain constricted her chest so she could not speak. Fighting back tears, she said, "Clever talk, Mr. Blake, but I doubt you'd say such things if we was close, like other married folk."

"Close? What do you mean?"

"You know, Mr. Blake. In bed."

William leaped to his feet. "In bed? Are you telling me that after all these years you finally want to offer up your virginity to me?"

"Mr. Blake! I was always willing. It was you what didn't want to!"

"I can't believe it! Kate Blake, who goes to church every Sunday, leaving me at home, never missing a day. She's a common whore after all, selling her body like any bawd on a streetcorner!"

"A whore, Mr. Blake? That's a lie!"

"Who are you then, Mrs. Blake? Are you Helen of Troy? Are you Cleopatra? Who are you that I should trade the world and all eternity for your fat arse? You're a whore, I said, and I say it again, but much too expensive a whore for a poor man like myself."

He turned and strode from the room.

She did not cry. The time for tears had passed, the time when tears would have sufficed to fight the raging flames of pain. Instead she sat motionless for a long time, then picked up her illustration and graver and tried to work.

She had to give it up.

Her hands shook too much.

6

THE PUBLISHERS LIKED KATE'S ENGRAVINGS much more than William's, though she continued to pretend he did them. The Blakes celebrated a newfound prosperity by moving to better lodgings at 13 Hercules Buildings, Lambeth, in Surrey. The Hercules Buildings were clean, pretty terrace houses on the east side of the street: the Blakes rented ten large rooms and a small backyard garden overgrown with unpruned grape vines that concealed a cozy arbor beneath the shade of a clump of poplars.

It was a paradoxical neighborhood.

In times past the rich had frequented its scattered luxurious gardens and parks: the Temple of Flora, the Apollo Gardens, the Flora Tea Gardens, and a mile down York Place, Vauxhall.

But now the fickle rich had departed for other more fashionable settings, leaving the green parks to prostitutes, thieves, and mobs of foreigners who shouted drunken incomprehensible obscenities in the night. Nearby stood a grim building called the Royal Asylum for Female Orphans, actually a workhouse, a prison for children whose only crime was poverty.

Thus the neighborhood reflected the internal world within the Blake family: a façade of flowers and greenery concealing violence, suffering, and hate.

William's one customer, an admiring and humble government clerk named Thomas Butts, bought an average of one drawing or print a week, with such titles as "Elohim

Creating Adam," "God Judging Adam," and "Nebuchadnezzer." This was William's entire output.

William also tried his hand at teaching art to the sons and daughters of the few old well-to-do families remaining in the area, but, lacking either the will or the ability to tolerate mediocrity, he soon fell from favor.

No, it was Kate who brought home the bacon, and Kate also who fried it. Without her the Blake family would have had to move to a workhouse. (London provided such places for adults as well as children.) If some editor asked her why she did not sign her work, she lightheartedly lectured him on her dear William's modesty.

In company, as when they took tea with the Butts family, the Blakes presented a flawless image of domesticity; at home, with no one to see them, they lapsed into the habit of silence. Better silence than words which, if spoken aloud, would have ended their marriage!

They began to go out as never before, visiting someone almost every night, as if the lives of others might fill up the emptiness of their own. The Godwin coterie, surprised by their new gregariousness, welcomed them, and more than ever Mary Wollstonecraft became Kate's friend, talking to her and subtly teaching her to talk, and the ambivalence of Kate's feelings for Mary increased—she almost loved her, yet could not see her speak to William without feeling some anguish.

Thus when Mary took ship for France, either (as she said in public at Johnson's weekly supper) to view the French Revolution firsthand or (as she told Kate in private) to get away from the embarrassed Fusili, Kate missed her greatly, missed her only close friend, her rival, her teacher. Did William miss her too? He did not say, but sometimes he stood at the window a long time, as if he had been watching someone who, a moment before, had passed from sight around a corner.

The dinners at Johnson's continued, enlivened by the radical tirades of the American, Thomas Paine.

One evening Kate and William treated themselves to a ride to the supper in a hansom cab, and as they rattled along behind the clip-clopping horse, Kate studied William's sober face in the shifting light. He was moody again, and sullen, as he had so often been of late. She couldn't talk to him. Whatever she said, he took it wrong, so sometimes she found herself saying one thing one moment and the opposite the next in hopes of hitting on something that would please him, and then he would accuse her of "yes-but-noing" him. She was sure that if only they could talk, they would find themselves in agreement on most things, both practical and philosophical, and where differences existed, they could reach some rational compromise, yet William wouldn't have it.

"Have you been with Urizen again?" she ventured, fearful of his coldness, his hidden hatred.

"And what if I have?"

"Why didn't you tell me?"

"You don't like him."

"I never said that. I like to think he's a friend to both of us, a friend of the family."

"He's only your friend because of me."

"Oh, Mr. Blake, what a cruel thing to say!"

"You can't always have kindness and truth at the same time."

They fell into a painful silence. Kate couldn't stand it. She had to speak.

"Well, what did he say, Mr. Blake?"

"He gave me a choice. I can change history or let a great man die."

"What great man?"

"Tom Paine."

"What on earth do you mean?"

"I can't tell you. That would take the choice out of my hands."

She wanted to question him more, but their cab had pulled up outside Johnson's place and the driver now jumped down to let them out. She paid; she had more and more taken upon herself the duties of family treasurer, along with everything else. In the lamplight William's face was a grim mask. She could well believe he was torn by some fearsome issue of morality.

Upstairs the food had not yet been served, but the

conversation was in full swing behind a blue cloud of tobacco smoke. Paine, the celebrity, was there, and the irrationally rational Godwin, and Fusili and his Sophie, and four or five lesser torchbearers of liberty. Johnson, pipe in hand, beamed and hobnobbed, delighted with them all, as if they were his prized possessions.

"Have you read Tom's book, William?" demanded Fusili. He never spoke to Kate, only to William.

"No, but I intend to," William responded.

"He calls it *The Rights of Man*," said Fusili. "And if you've read Mary's essay of the same title, you may have noticed our Tommy's little plagiarism." Mary Wollstonecraft, Kate knew, had written a sharply reasoned answer to the conservative Gladstone under that title a year earlier. Paine's book, though intended as a refutation not of Gladstone but of Burke, was indeed remarkably similar.

Paine broke in good-naturedly, "I'll gladly admit the influence of our unfortunately absent friend, but I believe I've added at least a few phrases of my own, as the lady would be happy to confirm if she were here. I venture to say anyone in this room could have written either of our tracts. We've helped ourselves so often to each other's souls we're less human individuals than some kind of collective octopus, a quill pen in each tentacle."

Fusili persisted, "Are you saying, sir, that we practice conformity in our nonconformity, orthodoxy in our unorthodoxy?"

Paine chuckled. "I feel I can borrow a good idea when I hear one and still remain my own man."

This soft answer failed to turn away Fusili's wrath. "Some of us, it seems to me, do all the producing of those good ideas, while others of us do all the borrowing. In our circle I count three original minds. The rest of us are, at best, clever parrots."

Paine was no longer amused. "I suppose you include yourself among the three?"

"I do, sir," said Fusili. "I am the first person in history to base my philosophy on dreams."

Paine demanded coldly, "And who, pray tell, are the other two original minds?"

"William Blake here." He clapped William on the shoulder. "The first person in history to base his philosophy on madness."

"And the third?"

"Our dear friend Mary, the first person in history to base her philosophy on the facts of a woman's life. If our little gang is remembered for anything, it will be for the thoughts of these three genuine pioneers, William, Mary, and myself. Out of of our most casual remarks whole literary, artistic, and philosophical movements will someday arise. Men and women who never heard of us will repeat our words as their own."

Fusili's Sophie broke in. "You make altogether too much of that lady, dear. She has a way with a pen perhaps, but she can't sew a straight seam and her cooking . . ." She rolled her eyes heavenward. "Absolutely inedible!"

Fusili glared at her a moment, then softened. He could never stay angry at a beautiful woman, let alone his own Sophie. He patted her cheek indulgently and murmured, "You're right, of course."

Kate found something annoying in his manner. He patronized his wife, as he might patronize a child or a mental defective, never paying her the compliment of a good argument, but Sophie never noticed. Sophie, in fact, never noticed much of anything, but her husband seemed to enjoy listening to her prattle with a vague smile and half-closed eyes, as if it were dinner music.

Paine, however, was disappointed. As Kate well knew, he loved argument and had just been marshaling his thoughts for a good one, only to see it evaporate.

Kate intuitively understood his feelings and filled the awkward gap in the conversation. "I've heard, Mr. Paine, you gave a brilliant speech at that public meeting last night." She had known of the meeting, but had actually not heard anything about it, one way or the other.

The American brightened. "Really?"

"Everyone's talking about it," she added, feeling a little guilty already at her own dishonesty.

Paine grinned. "I did indeed wax eloquent, if I do say so myself."

"What did you say?" asked the genial Johnson, between puffs on his trusty pipe.

Paine drew himself up in a somewhat self-satirical pose, finger raised heavenward. "I spoke thus: My country is the world, and my religion is to do good."

"Hear! Hear!" called out Fusili, with a hint of mockery, but only a hint. The artist seemed in a benevolent mood.

Paine continued, "Man is not the enemy of man but through the medium of government."

"Amen to that," said the anarchistic Godwin, applauding politely.

"Society is produced by our wants and government by our wickedness!" Paine warmed to his subject.

"Bravo, Mr. Paine," said Godwin.

"The monk and the monarch will molder together. Neither has a place in the world of tomorrow."

Abruptly Blake interrupted: "You must not go home tonight."

Paine turned to face him, more than somewhat taken aback. "What's that you say?"

William repeated, "You must not go home tonight. If you do, you're a dead man."

The subdued babble of Johnson's guests ceased. Only Sophie could be heard in the silence saying to a woman novelist, "The servant girl was so cheeky I had to discharge her. You know how . . ." Then, looking around her, Sophie too stopped talking in mid-sentence.

"What do you mean, Mr. Blake?" Paine demanded.

"The King is not moldering yet, Mr. Paine. He has sent his troops to arrest you, and if you go with them you will not return alive."

Paine paled. "How do you know?"

"I have word," said Blake. "From a trustworthy source. I cannot give you his name."

Johnson put in, "Mr. Blake would not speak lightly on such matters. From things he's said before, I'd almost credit him with the power to tell fortunes."

"I believe you, sir," said Paine to Blake. "I have long feared such a thing myself, not from any power to tell fortunes but from the simple ability to tell which way the winds of politics are blowing."

"I have a coach and four that brought some of our guests," said Johnson. "If I mistake not, the horses are still in harness, and rested. If you left now you could just make the next sailing from Dover, given a spot of luck, and I'll write you letters of introduction to my friends in Paris." The publisher was already reaching for his quill pen.

"I'll ride with you as far as the docks," said William.

"And I too," added Kate.

"Aren't you afraid you'll be arrested along with me?" Paine demanded.

"It would be an honor, sir," William replied crisply.

Minutes later Paine and the Blakes were clambering into the waiting coach, Paine without luggage save for the letters Johnson had hastily scrawled for him.

"The Dover pier, and hurry," Johnson called up to the driver. A crack of the whip and they were on their way, clattering and bounding down the dark cobblestone street. Kate, glancing back, saw the dim figures of mounted soldiers appearing from a distant sidestreet.

"Look!" she cried.

"They'll go to Johnson's, and Johnson will delay them as long as he can," said Paine.

"But not forever," said William. "Can't we go any faster?"

Paine replied grimly, "The coachman must spare the horses somewhat or they won't last until Dover. We can't go at a gallop the whole way, you know, but neither can our pursuers. A ridden horse can outrun a coach horse in a short stretch, but over a long stretch like this we'll make better average time and have more endurance, particularly over hard cobblestones. A horse works hard with a fat redcoat on his back."

Kate, seated next to William, was thrown against him, then against the side of the coach. She thought, *Assuming, of course, that we don't break a wheel*. The horses had settled into an even trot, but the road, in no better repair than it ever was, still jolted the coach with bumps and potholes. Here and there they passed through major puddles, sending cascades of dirty water to either side. In one way fortune favored them: few other travelers ventured out at this late hour, so the way was mostly clear. If some solitary wagon appeared out of the gloom, wending its way homeward from market with a drunken driver nodding at the reins, the coach easily evaded it, and as the houses grew fewer and farther between, fortune favored them again. The overcast lifted and a full moon lit their way over a deserted stretch where otherwise darkness would have slowed them to a walk.

"Thank you, sir," said Thomas Paine. "I may well owe you my life. Who knows what would have happened if the King's bully boys had collared me?"

"What would have happened?" William's face was unreal, ghostly, in the moonlight. "You would have been arrested, tried, convicted, and executed for high treason."

Paine laughed. "What luck you came along!"

"Luck?" William stared at him with large haunted eyes. "In dying you would have become a martyr to freedom, and in your name the British people would have revolted and unseated the King, ending the monarchy here and eventually on the continent as well. The resulting democracy would have united with the American Colonies to rule the world in peace and prosperity for two hundred years. Your name would have echoed eternally down the corridors of history."

Though obviously skeptical, Paine asked, "And what will happen now, if you can indeed read the future?"

Blake raised his voice to make himself heard over the din of drumming hooves and clattering wheels. "In France you will write a book attacking the Bible which will turn all mankind against you, and when you return to America, it will be to die in ostracism and poverty. The British Royal Family will rule with steadily dwindling power into the Twenty-first Century, and they and their European relatives will preside over two world wars, followed by an armed truce that threatens universal extinction."

Paine glanced at him sharply. "I am indeed planning such a book. How did you know?"

"I know. I cannot tell you how."

"Are you telling me not to write it?"

"You will do what you will do, regardless of my advice. I can only warn you of the cost."

"The cost? But you claim to know the cost of saving me, yet you did it anyway. Why?"

"I know you. I like you. I could not stand by and let you die. I should have, but I couldn't."

Through the remainder of the trip no word was spoken until the coachman shouted down, "We're comin' to the docks, m'lords, and the ship's still in port."

They clambered from the coach and Paine embraced the Blakes and thanked them, then sprinted up the gangplank moments before it was raised.

As the ship glided away into the night with a great shouting of commands and ringing of bells, Kate heard distant hoofbeats and the rattle of sabers and, as William drew her back into the shadows, a squad of redcoats came down the quay at full gallop.

"Stop that ship! Stop that ship!" the officer shouted, but it was too late. The ship was French and would not have turned back even if signaled.

The soldiers questioned William, Kate, and the coachman, but lacking a warrant, did not arrest them, though the officer looked William intently in the face, as if memorizing every feature, and said with soft menace, "I'll remember you, Billy boy."

When he had nothing to do, which was increasingly often, William went for long walks, and on returning would say he'd been down to the intersection of Barley Street and Hercules Road and from there perhaps had crossed the Thames by way of Westminster Bridge to wander about in Chelsea, or perhaps he said he'd gone out the other way to visit some unnamed friend.

She knew and did not know, both at the same time, that he lied.

And she also knew and did not know that he'd actually visited Golgonooza.

To know something and not know it . . . every wife learns the trick, sooner or later.

To do it she had to avoid reading what he wrote, because she already knew (and did not know) what she would find.

To do it she had to look away from his drawings, because she knew (and did not know) they showed things he could not have seen in either Lambeth or Chelsea.

The Blakes hired a maid.

"Kate, will you help me seduce her?" William demanded. William who did not even smile, let alone joke.

"Seduce her?" Kate cried in dismay.

"If you really loved me, you'd not begrudge me this little pleasure."

"I begrudge you nothing, but . . ." She could not go on. Her William could not say such things. This was Urizen talking through William's lips, William's dear lips that could only speak to her kindly and lovingly.

Kate wept.

William fired the maid, but put the blame on Kate's jealousy.

And then, not long after, he forced Kate to join him in sitting naked in the grape arbor in broad daylight while he read to her mockingly from *Paradise Lost*, and when the good Thomas Butts accidentally walked in on them there, William called out, "Come in! We're only Adam and Eve, you know!"

William began a long poem glorifying the French Revolution, but even though Kate found a publisher for it, he did not finish the manuscript, shouting at her that he'd outgrown the ideas in it.

One day, at last, he grew careless, or perhaps he wanted finally to free himself from his own lies. He returned from a one hour walk with three days' growth of beard.

He stood a moment in the front doorway, a shaggy silhouette before the bright noonday sky. (For once the sun was shining.) Then as he saw her staring at him from the other end of the dim hallway, he entered slowly and shut the door behind him.

"You've been with Urizen." She put it as a statement of fact, not a question.

"Yes, Kate. I've been with Urizen." His voice was the calm, kind voice he'd had so long ago, before he'd become her husband.

She leaned her broom against the wall. "We must talk, Mr. Blake. Come along now."

She led him into the living room. They seated themselves in the comfortable overstuffed chairs her work had bought.

She asked him quietly, "Why did you have to lie?"

"If I'd told you, you would have forbade me."

Kate nodded. That, at least, was true. "So you went behind my back. A gentleman would have told me."

"I did not want to fight with you. I did not want to part from you."

"You see it as a choice between him and me?"

"Isn't it?"

"And you chose him."

William was obviously miserable. "I didn't want to choose at all. I wanted to keep on with you as long as I could, but the temptation . . . Oh, Kate, believe me, I love you. I never wanted to hurt you."

"I believe you. Yes, I do. But tell me, among the Zoas, which side are you on?"

"I am with Urizen."

"I needn't have asked. He made you the best offer, didn't he?" Her tone, which had been flat and tired, now had an edge on it.

His voice changed in response, grew hard and angry. "Yes, he did. A better offer than the other Zoas. A better offer than you."

"We've a good home here, Mr. Blake, and you've had rather an easy time of it of late, doing whatever you like all the time. My father would envy you, he would."

"A pretty prison, but a prison all the same."

She wanted to stop there, to say no more, to leave it alone, but her mouth, as if it had a life of its own, went on talking. "A prison you say? What are you? A wild animal? Prowling, prowling all the time, but I notice you always come home for meals."

His face flushed as red as his hair. "I won't be spoken to like that in my own house."

"Your house? When have you last chipped in for the rent?"

"I paid in advance."

"Paid in advance? And how do you figure that, Mr. Blake?"

"I taught you to read and write, to draw and engrave and paint. Though you were a woman, I taught you more than a man would learn at a great university about art, history, language, religion, philosophy. Thanks to me you're not an ignorant fool like Sophie Fusili, or a sentimental idiot like those woman novelists at Johnson's. Thanks to me you're the superior of all those women, and of most of the men."

Kate asked softly, "The superior of Mary Wollstonecraft?"

He hesitated, and that hesitation hurt her more than anything he might have said, then he answered, "Her equal, certainly."

She wanted to cry out to him to teach her just a little bit longer, just a little bit more, to teach her something, anything, that Mary didn't know. Instead she said coldly, "Thank you, Mr. Blake, but I don't believe I would have enrolled at your school if I'd known the tuition was so high."

"But you do owe me, Mrs. Blake. You owe me your life."

"My life?" That startled her.

"Your life. If I wanted to I could go into the past and change something so you wouldn't exist."

"You wouldn't do that."

"I could!" He was triumphant. "I could, but I didn't."

She wanted to speak now, but couldn't. It seemed to her that William had gone into the future and someone else had come back in his place, a changeling, a monster. Did she really want to share her life with this creature who looked like her husband, but who sat there and threatened her life?

At last she managed to speak. "I never thought I'd fear you, Mr. Blake. You was always so kind, so patient with me, teaching me things, helping me. Never thought I'd fear you, but I do. You do what you like, my friend. I won't stop you."

He stood up. "That's my good old girl, Kate." He smiled down at her, reached out to pat her arm. She shrugged off his hand.

"So that's how it is, eh?" he said.

"That's how it is."

He turned and walked slowly toward the hall. She wanted to call him back. Perhaps if she did, he would come! What could she lose? But before she could open her mouth, another thought came. She thought of Vala.

"William?"

"Yes?" He paused in the doorway.

"When you go to Golgonooza, do you visit Mary?"

"Mary?" He frowned, puzzled.

"I mean Vala, if that's what she calls herself."

"I see her from time to time." His voice was strained.

He saw her, all right. He probably saw her constantly, laughed with her, talked with her, gazed at her as if she were a goddess, gave her all the faithfulness and loyalty and closeness he had never given his lawful wedded wife.

"Go to her then," said Kate. "Go to her. She's the one you love, isn't she?"

"We're just friends."

Kate leaped to her feet and screamed, "Go to her! Go to her! She's waiting for you! Go to her!"

William backed out of the room.

"Go to her!" Kate screamed again at the empty doorway.

She heard him speak to someone in a low voice, heard a rustle of wings, then abruptly knew she was alone in the house, though the front door had not opened.

She slept alone for nine nights, tossing and turning, weeping, talking to herself, praying. During the day she went on as if nothing had happened, and if anyone asked about William, she would say, "He's gone to visit relatives."

She drew; and her drawings took on a dark intensity, a wild freedom, they had lacked before. In drawing she could forget, could lose herself in worlds of her own imagining. What if the gods she drew did wear William's face? What if the demons did too? In the line, in the color, she could become almost a deity herself, could shape things to suit her heart's desire. The real world never obeyed her. The real world never did what she expected, let alone what she wanted. She would have settled for simple predictability, if goodness was too much to ask.

Sitting up in bed on the tenth night, one of her sketches resting on her knees, she said softly, "It doesn't matter what he does. Even if he doesn't love me, I can still love him. Even if he is unfaithful to me, I can be faithful to him. Nobody, not even him, can change my feelings against my will. Nobody, not even him, can make me despair. I will not despair then! I will not! Whether he wants me or not, I will follow him. Whether he needs me or not, I will serve him, I am what I am. I feel what I feel. I will always be Mrs. William Blake until the day I die."

She put down the drawing, dressed herself for travel in a long skirt, a blouse with puff sleeves, and riding boots, and, after a last fond tour of the house, she sprang into the dark swirling place outside of time and headed for the future, her heart light, a song on her lips. She had been complicated, at war with herself. Now she was simple, of one mind, and at peace. She had been floundering in the currents of uncertainty, washed from one state of mind to another without control. Now, amazingly, she had found her footing. Now she stood firm, knowing who she was, knowing what she wanted. She might win. She might lose. But within she would always be grounded in a profound contentment.

The phantoms that streamed past her screamed out their usual warnings, but she paid no attention. The worst had already happened, and she had survived it.

Still smiling, she arrived in Golgonooza and made her way to the Hall of Windows. At any moment she expected to see William, but the room was deserted. She went downstairs to Vala's chamber, but found no one. She wandered at random, exploring portions of the city she had never known existed.

How easy to get lost in such a place!

There seemed to be four gates to the city, yet instead of leading to some other place, they led into each other, defying the laws of space.

From tablets of bronze she read the directions: the western gate was surmounted by statues of four cherubs, one of iron, one of stone, one of clay, and one of many mingled metals.

The northern gate was surmounted by groups of four bulls, four groups in all. One group was called Generation and was of iron, a second group was called Ulro, with bulls of enameled clay, a third group of bulls was in mixed metals, and a fourth also in mixed metals.

The eastern gate also bore four statues, each of seven figures, representing respectively Generative Forms, War, Disease, and Death. This last seemed made of ice, and portrayed the sevenfold form of death.

The southern gate bore four groups of four lions each, and one of the groups seemed not to be statues at all, but living animals.

No matter how she turned, she always found herself returning to what seemed to be the center of the maze, a palace under a dome inscribed *Cathedron: Los's Palace* and surrounded by an eternally burning moat of fire.

Los? She had not heard that name before, yet by the looks of the castle he must be the king of the Zoas.

She found an abandoned stone table covered with plates full of partially-eaten food. She sat down and ate. It was still warm, yet she saw no sign of the other guests at the banquet.

She continued on.

Near the eastern gate she found a rock of crystal, odorous with wild thyme, and on it, incongruously enough, a lark's nest where a living bird greeted her with song. A fountain there divided into two streams that flowed through a simulated forest. One stream she followed easily enough to the western wall. The other poured through an opening that seemed to lead to the void of outer space, though the whole city was underground.

For the fifth time she found herself approaching the burning moat around Cathedron, gazing up at its towers and pinnacles, and this time she noticed a strange gate inscribed *The Gate of Luban*. For a moment she could not say what the curious opening reminded her of, with its subtle, organic curves, then suddenly she realized it represented an immense vagina, at least three stories tall.

"Beautiful, isn't it?" came a voice from behind her.

She whirled, startled.

There, not far away, stood Luvah, lovely and monstrous at the same time, with his thick black beard and rounded feminine breasts and buttocks, wearing the silver crown of thorns that made him look like some parody of Jesus Christ. On his left arm he carried a silver lyre that seemed softly to play bits of melody all by itself, without waiting for the fingers of the musician. Luvah's voice was deep and gentle: it could have been either a woman's or a man's.

"You didn't speak to me before," said Kate uncertainly.

"Before?"

"When Urizen introduced us."

"Urizen never introduced us."

"You don't remember?"

"That Luvah you met must have been me at some future time. I am Luvah as a young person. You must have met Luvah as an old person. But now we have met. Who are you?"

"I am Kate Blake, from London, from the past."

"The past is a large thing, much larger, I fear, than the future. And this is London, you see." He gestured at the surrounding hall. "Golgonooza is London, a London grown large enough to cover all the British Isles, knit together by gateways through which you can pass to far places without crossing the distance in between. And tell me, pray, what brings you here to the City at the End of Time?"

"I'm looking for my husband."

"Your husband?" The hermaphrodite was puzzled.

"I forgot you haven't met him yet. His name is William Blake, but of course you wouldn't know him."

"But I do know him!"

"You do?" Hope sprang to life within her.

"Of course! He is the ruler of Golgonooza! We call him Los, the Mighty, Lord of the Imagination. It was by his instruction that all this vast metropolis was built."

Impulsively she strode forward to grasp the strange being's delicate hand. "You must help me find him!"

Luvah said softly, "Are you sure you want to find him?"

"Yes, yes!"

"He may have changed."

"I don't care."

Luvah pointed with a long graceful finger. "I think I saw him going into the Garden of Vala, about a half mile in that direction."

"The Garden of Vala?" She did not bother to conceal her anger.

"Beware Vala's Garden, Kate Blake. It is a realm of waking dreams, where impressions of despair and hope forever vegetate in flowers, fruits, fishes, birds, and clouds, a land of doubts and shadows, sweet delusions and unformed desires. It does not seem to occupy any physical space, as seen from the outside, yet from the inside it appears as vast as a whole planet. If Lord Los is there, with Vala, he may wish to remain there. He may forget any other place exists. Even if you find him, he may not recognize you."

"Thank you kindly, sir, for your warnings and your directions." She started off briskly in the direction Luvah had indicated.

Soon she found herself standing before a wide opening identified by a bronze plaque as *The Gates of Dark Urthona.* Beyond, as Luvah had promised, lay a strange dreamlike landscape, constantly shifting and changing, under a reddish dim sun. It would indeed be difficult to find anyone there, but very easy to get lost oneself.

Behind her she heard footsteps and glanced over her shoulder. Luvah was following her, but taking his time.

"Please reconsider," called the woman-man. "The danger . . ."

She turned her attention again to the land beyond the gateway. Suddenly she thought she caught a glimpse of William in the distance.

Without hesitation she ran forward.

Behind her the entrance vanished; ahead of her the figure of William shifted and changed. As she ran breathlessly toward it, she saw it was only a curiously humanoid treetrunk.

She stopped, looked around.

In Urizen's company she had several times passed near the garden, but this was the first time she had actually entered. Now she saw on all sides beautiful alien vegetation: vines, flowers, treetrunks and a kind of translucent grass, and it was all in constant motion, blooming and dying as rapidly as normal Earth plants might have done if their life processes had been greatly accelerated.

Fighting back panic, she seated herself on a stone, only to leap up again with a little scream. The stone too was alive and moving only a little slower than the plants.

A pale, low-hanging slow-moving fog, full of shimmering iridescent lights, obscured the sky ahead of her. She saw that it would soon also obscure the dim sun, destroying her last method of judging direction. In the brief time since she'd entered, the landmarks in the garden had so greatly transformed themselves they were no help at all in guiding her back in the direction from which she'd come.

"Luvah!" she called, but there was, for answer, only the whispering of the plants, which seemed constantly to be gossiping together in some unknown language.

A narcotic aroma drifted on the sluggish breeze, a sweetish heavy odor that coaxed her not so much to sleep as to waking dreams, to aimless somnambulistic wanderings.

She fought to keep her mind clear.

"William," she shouted. "Mr. Blake!"

The drugged air softened the edges of her panic. She threw herself down on the translucent grass. For a long time she could not remember what she was doing there, then her eye was caught by the colors in the wings of a huge beetle, about the size of a full-grown cat, that walked toward her with a show of infinite dignity.

She touched its hard smooth back.

"You are a handsome gentleman, you are," she told the creature in a faraway voice.

The beetle replied with a low growl.

"Handsome, yes, but no gentleman." She drew back her hand.

The nature of her mission drifted back into her mind. She called out, "William! Luvah! Urizen!" At this moment she would have accepted help even from the evil Urizen . . . evil as she thought of him, anyway.

The beetle fled.

But she heard a distant voice. "I'm coming."

The figure of a man—or was it a woman?—seemed to materialize out of the tangle of moving vegetation. With effortless grace the figure approached and stood looking down at Kate, but she no longer remembered calling. "Who are you?" she demanded.

"I am Luvah."

"What are you doing here?"

"You called my name, Kate Blake."

She thought she might have met this Luvah somewhere, but couldn't remember where. He reminded her, as if reading her mind, "Urizen introduced us."

"Urizen?" The name sounded familiar.

"Are you looking for your husband?"

"My husband?"

"William Blake."

She frowned, trying to connect the name with a face. "You told me he was . . . here, didn't you?"

"Not I, but it might have been me as a youth."

"Could you explain . . . ?"

Luvah laughed a soft musical laugh. "When I think of what you have waiting for you, I almost believe I should leave you here, as an act of kindness. Perhaps that is what my younger self thought. Perhaps that is why he sent you here. But . . . ." He bent over and took her hand. ". . . you have work to do." He pulled her to her feet.

"William. Where is he?" Her voice sounded like that of a baby asking where the world comes from.

"He went with his court back in time."

"His court?"

"Oh yes. He rules us now, he and his prime minister Urizen."

"Back in time?"

"To the Battle of Actium in 31 B.C., when the fleets of Octavian Augustus Caesar fought the fleets of Cleopatra for the throne of the Roman Empire. You might not recognize your William. He calls himself Lord Los now, and travels always with Urizen on his right hand and Vala on his left."

"Vala?" Suddenly her mind cleared. "Mr. Blake is with Vala?"

Luvah's red lips parted in a slow smile. "Yes."

"I might have known!" Kate snapped. "Well, we'll put a stop to that, won't we?"

"We, Mrs. Blake? I will not accompany you."

"King Tharmas will help me."

"No, my poor woman, we have voted a new policy. No more struggling against Lord Los and Urizen. Let them have their way. They're so sure they're in the right, and we have never been sure of anything. Perhaps they know things we do not, as they claim."

"No, Luvah!"

Luvah nodded. "Yes, my dear, you may do what you will and can against them, but we will remain here in Vala's Garden, Tharmas and I and all the others, until the sun explodes. That will be soon, you know. We will remain here, forgetting, dreaming . . . the air here heals us, soothes us, relaxes us, helps us to let go of the universe, to let go of life, easily and effortlessly. We will not suffer."

"Then I will go alone," said Kate.

"As you wish." Luvah took her hand in his long, pale fingers and led her languidly to the exit from the garden, then kissed her cheek softly, just once, before she departed.

Once outside the garden, Kate looked back. She thought

for a moment she could see Luvah waving to her, but no, it was just a tangle of vines swaying in the breeze.

Blue. Blue. Blue.

The blazing blue of the cloudless Mediterranean sky burned into the eyes of the young, sickly Octavian, making everything shimmer, while the deck rose and fell, rose and fell, with the ocean swells. Leaning against a gunwale to keep his balance, he wiped sweat from his pinched features with the back of a bony hand, listening to the unreal murmur of the oarsmen trading obscene jokes among themselves in Greek to ease the tension. He squinted up at the sun, now almost at the zenith. "It's noon," he shouted in his high cracked voice to the ship's captain. "Why doesn't she attack?"

"Patience, my lord," answered the old seaman. "She will."

Cleopatra would commit her fleet, and in doing so would reveal her plan so that Octavian could counter it. At least that was the theory of Octavian's top strategist, the cunning Vipsanius Agrippa, and over the years Octavian had come to regard the faithful Agrippa as almost an oracle.

Octavian had no shelter on his ship, no shade, not even what fitful shade might come from a raised sail. Not only the sails, but the very mainmasts had been left behind on land to make way for archers' towers, catapults, ballistas, grapplers, and sharp-beaked boarding gangplanks. On the more than four hundred ships that stretched out in a rough line from Octavian's galley on the south to Agrippa's galley on the north, not so much as one small square steering sail could be seen.

To the east, half-hidden by a shimmering haze, Cleopatra's fleet, a roughly equal force, also drifted and waited, the green shoreline at their back, and the narrow channel from which they'd come.

Octavian, seasick, dazed, shielded his eyes with his hand and studied the enemy ships, as if he might, even at this distance, catch a glimpse of the traitor and adulterer Mark Antony and his Greek-Egyptian witch, Queen

Cleopatra Ptolemy. Witch she must indeed be, as the superstitious oarsmen whispered, to cast a spell that would make a Roman forget Rome! Could she be, as her followers boasted, not a mere mortal, but the goddess Isis incarnate? The ancient Egyptians had always believed their rulers to be gods and goddesses. The Greeks, behind their cynical façades, believed it too, and so did the Jews. With parched lips Octavian whispered, "I can fight a man, or if need be a woman, but a goddess?"

"The wind, sir," called the old sea captain.

Octavian could feel it, the welcome sudden cool breeze on his cheek, his sunburned cheek. He smiled crookedly and thanked the gods under his breath, but then he saw the gust had started to turn his light ship, exposing its vulnerable side to the enemy. His ships were drifting together, bunching up.

The wind obeyed Cleopatra!

When the captain spoke again, it was with a touch of anxiety in his voice. "Here they come, my lord Octavian."

With the breeze behind them Cleopatra's ships began their fearsome advance, and Octavian, downwind from them, could hear her oarsmen begin singing in time with their oarstrokes, hear the heartbeat boom of the oarmasters' drums. Louder and softer by turns, as the wind rose and fell, he could hear the terrifying sound of forty thousand men singing in unison, voices harsh with exhilaration, singing in a barbarous alien mode and a barbarous alien language of which he could understand only the name they bellowed out at the end of each stanza.

"Isis!"

Octavian thought, *She is a goddess. She is!*

"Give the command, sir!" called the sea captain.

Octavian opened his mouth, but nothing came out.

"We're ready, sir," the captain prompted.

Still Octavian could say nothing.

With a curse the captain gave the command for him. "Attack!"

A great shout rolled down the line of Octavian's own ships, and his own oarsmen struck up a familiar battle song as the ship lunged forward.

The captain came to Octavian, his lined dark face anxious. "I had to give the command. I know you could have my head for it, but I had to do it."

Octavian swayed. "Never mind. Never mind. Thank you. I'm not well, not at all well." His voice trailed off, the final words lost in the thump and splash of the waves under the prow.

But as the breeze cooled his fever his sickness faded and the battle-lust of his troops began to infect his own hesitant spirit. Aware of the eyes upon him, he forced a smile and snatched his shortsword from its scabbard, brandishing it above his head.

"We will win," he told himself. "We will win anyway." He laughed out loud.

Then he raised his eyes skyward and the laughter died.

There, where an instant before he had seen only wheeling gulls, three winged human figures had appeared, gliding toward him as if leading Cleopatra's fleet into combat. First came a redheaded man in a brown coat and knee-breeches, then a powerful naked man with a white beard that thrashed in the wind, and last a woman in flowing red gowns.

A cry of dismay went up from Octavian's rowers, ending their song in mid-phrase, as the three glided down in a great spiral to alight on the foredeck of Octavian's galley.

"Who . . . who are you?" cried out the would-be emperor.

The redhead answered in strangely-accented Greek, "Tremble, mortal, for we are the ancient and terrible deities of Egypt: Osiris, Isis, and Horus, rulers of the Land of the Dead."

"But what do you want . . . from me?"

"Your sword," boomed the white-beard.

When Octavian hesitated, the redhead, unsmiling, stepped forward and snatched it with a curt, "We need it."

"What for?"

The woman spoke for the first time. "A gift to Cleopatra Ptolemy, from this day forward Empress of the World!"

With that the three took to the air.

As his fleet milled in confusion Octavian sat down on

the deck, all his woes narrowing down at last to one anguished moan. "How will I ever break the news to Mama?"

So high above she might pass for a gull, Kate Blake watched the three winged figures deliver the sword to Cleopatra's flagship. Even at this distance the symbolism was as clear to her as to the opposing armies below. What had William done? And why? And what effect would this action have on history? Should she intervene? And if so, how? What could she do that wouldn't only make things worse?

She needed time to think, and a little peace, the kind of peace she felt only in the safety of her own little home. With the skill born of long experience she launched herself uptime toward the London of 1791 and 13 Hercules Buildings.

She materialized in the street.

The smile that had begun to form on her lips died aborning, and for a moment she thought she must have made some mistake, yet that could not be. She had long ago learned how to measure her journeys down to the minute or, if need be, to the second.

All the same, there before her under a bright midafternoon sun stood what appeared to be a small café or tearoom exactly where her house should be, an atrractive structure in a half-timber style that suggested Tudor. A sign in Greek characters swung gently above the front door. William had taught her some Greek, yet she found she could not read the sign at all.

Dazed, she pushed open the door, noting in passing a carving in the door that apparently portrayed the Virgin Mary and the Baby Jesus.

It was indeed a tea room! The dim interior, the murmur of conversation, the clink of dishes and silverware, the occasional polite laughter; all were exactly what she would have expected in a small suburban tearoom.

Then she began noticing things that were not as they should be.

First, the costumes of the customers resembled nothing

she'd seen in any of the time periods she'd visited. Both men and women wore long flowing garments of some heavy silklike material. Were they Arabs? No, they were bareheaded and no Arab ever wove such fine clinging cloth. Some glanced at Kate curiously; doubtlessly her long skirt, puff sleeves, and boots were equally puzzling to them.

Second, a soft music filled the room from some source Kate could not at first locate. The timbres had a harsh oriental edge to them and the rhythms were complex and percussive, not at all proper British tearoom music, even played, as it was, softly enough not to disturb conversation. But where did this music come from? She could see no musicians.

Then came a shock.

The music came from a television set mounted high on the wall. No one watched the TV screen where, in color and three dimensions, nude women and men were dancing. Everyone, it would appear, took this for granted, yet Kate knew there should not be any TV here. Television was an invention of the twentieth century!

Third and most subtly disturbing, there was the language she heard all around her. It was Greek and not Greek, all at the same time, so she could understand no more than a tantalizing word or phrase in all the buzz and hum, yet one word was repeated over and over, as if in echo of what she'd heard at the Battle of Actium.

Isis. Isis. Isis.

The serpentine sibilance of that name hissed at her from every corner of the shadowed dining room, and it took her a moment to realize why. The name of Isis was being used "in vain." The name of Isis had taken the place of the various names of Jesus and Jehovah in the unthinking blasphemies of casual conversation. It was then that Kate realized that it had not been Mary and Jesus she'd seen carved into the door, but Mother Isis and the infant Horus.

Yes, sure enough. Now that she knew what to look for she easily made out the half-moon headdress on the mother's head and the Ankh pendant that hung from her neck.

Dazed, Kate opened a door at the rear of the dining room and emerged into . . .

Her garden!

There were her familiar poplar trees, there the tangled unpruned grapevines, all in their proper places, except that now they formed a backdrop for a cluster of outdoor tables where strange robed figures spoke some dialect of Greek never heard before and said "Isis" all the time. She felt a surge of unreasoning outrage. What were all these strangers doing in her garden?

Outrage quickly gave way to horror as she realized it was she who was the stranger. William had made good his threat; he and Urizen and Vala had made a world in which Kate Blake had never been born.

She fell into a chair at one of the tables and sat staring at her grapevines until a waiter came walking quickly to her and spoke to her with concern in his voice.

She forced a smile and, seeing he was carrying a menu, reached out for it.

He hesitated, then handed it to her.

She smiled at him again, and he left her to make her selection. Opening the menu she found, without surprise, that it was printed in Greek characters and that she could not understand a word.

A huge jet airliner passed overhead, but Kate was the only one in the garden who looked up at it. Jet airliners were another thing that should not have appeared until the twentieth century, but of course these Londoners did not know that.

Over the top of her menu, Kate studied the crowd.

Some of the women wore crosses . . . but no, not crosses. Crosses with loops on top. The Ankh, Egyptian hieroglyph for eternal life.

The waiter returned. Kate ordered by pointing her finger at the menu. She had no idea what she would get.

As she waited for her lunch, she puzzled over all she had seen since arriving here in 1791, and a pattern began to emerge. This was what England had become as a result of Cleopatra's victory.

She had of course ruled the Roman Empire from her

own capital in Egyptian Alexandria, seat of Hellenistic learning and science, instead of from Rome, seat of mere military power. That explained the advanced technology! There had been no decline and fall of the Roman Empire, no Dark Ages when knowledge slumbered and superstition ruled.

And that explained the carving of Isis and Horus, the Ankh pendants around the women's necks, the casual whispers of the name of Isis. As Alexandria had triumphed over Rome, so had the Great Mother Isis triumphed over the Great Father Jehovah.

And Greek, not Latin, had become the mother of modern languages. This Greeklike tongue she heard around her . . . those who spoke it must believe they were speaking English!

But of course England must now have another name. Kate wondered what it was.

And her garden—she glanced around it, on the verge of tears—her garden had developed the same as if nothing had ever changed. Gardens take no part in politics.

The waiter arrived with her food.

She tasted it. A meat stew of some sort, overly spicy for her, but she ate it anyway. She had become, without noticing it, very hungry indeed. The tableware, in an ornate floral pattern, consisted of knife and spoon, but no fork. A glance at the other tables informed her there was not a fork to be seen. She wondered, *Is the fork a Roman invention?*

Then another thought broke into her consciousness.

This world where a Goddess had displaced God—whose handiwork could it have been? Who would think such a world an improvement? William? No. For all his talk of equality, he liked a world where man ruled woman. Urizen? Urizen would have tried to bring into being some universe ruled by neither god nor goddess, but only pure reason worshipped without benefit of graven image.

No, this was a world created by a woman, for women.

This was the sort of world Mary Wollstonecraft would dream of. This was Mary's feminist utopia! Mary, who somehow must be Vala, had made William and Urizen do her bidding . . . it was she who really ruled the centuries.

Kate thought, *Can I live in a world—in a universe— created by my rival?*

When the waiter approached her with the bill, she vanished.

Language is the great divider; in every society those who easily speak the dominant tongue with the right accent live on top, and those who don't speak it at all live on the bottom, with social rank in between determined largely by linguistic fluency.

Thus Kate sought out the foreigners, the outcasts, in this changed London. She made her search mostly on foot, using her power to slip out of the timestream only when she felt in actual danger, as when a drunk chased her down an alley; when she turned the corner and was out of his sight, she transported herself in a flash to a point some blocks away. She didn't like the place outside of time. The herds of phantoms who roamed there seemed greatly multiplied, and the terrible howling had begun to form words. She wished they could be silent a moment, perhaps elect a spokesman. Then she'd listen to them and be able to understand what they were so urgently trying to tell her.

At first she couldn't understand why the street plan of London was so little changed. Almost all the main avenues followed exactly the same course they had before the change, though the sidestreets were not so predictable. Then she remembered that these main avenues followed roads laid out by the ancient Britons, long before the Roman invasion. William had taught her the history of her nation, along with all the rest, and in her time-voyaging she'd learned far more than any ordinary historian.

She knew, as ordinary historians did not, that before the Roman invaders had called her city Londinium, it had had another name: Lud's Dun. A dun was a fortified hilltop. Lud was a powerful Celtic god, the apotheosis of a war chief who had once actually lived and who had founded a whole chain of cities across the British Isles and the Continent. She knew, as the ordinary historian suspected, that where the Roman milestone called the London Stone stood against the south wall of St. Swithin's on Cannon Street, there had once been a stone of a different sort, where Druids stretched out their victims for a human sacrifice.

Now, in this changed London, she discovered that St. Swithin's had disappeared but the London Stone remained, set apart in a little park in front of an immense temple of Isis. Cannon Street remained in place, and Cheapside, Gracechurch Street, and Fleet Street, though all bore new names she could not read. And London Bridge, though greatly changed in appearance, still crossed the Thames at exactly the same spot.

So different, yet so much the same!

At first she did not understand why, almost without exception, every one of the churches she remembered had been replaced by a temple of Isis on the exact same site. Then she remembered that these sites had all once been Druid holy places: the religion of Isis, like Christianity, had taken care to occupy the locations already made sacred by defeated gods and goddesses, the hubs of a network of magical roads that had once radiated from Stonehenge to the opposite side of the globe.

She wandered all day long, and as night fell she followed some ragged women who seemed to know where they were going, soon finding herself in the neighborhood of what, before the change, had been Westminster Cathedral. Now, not too surprisingly, a rounded and beautifully decorated temple of Isis loomed in the same spot, not so tall as Westminster (it had no steeple) but equally broad. A line formed outside a grimy building next door; Kate joined the ragged, dirty women who stood there waiting.

Her unusual clothing had drawn stares everywhere she had gone in the new London, but here she passed unnoticed in the queue of foreigners and outcasts, the poor people she had sought.

She listened with perverse satisfaction to the low murmur of voices, understanding not a word but able to distinguish at least five different languages, none of which was familiar enough to make sense, but all of which

sounded vaguely like some Near Eastern tongue William
had tried to teach her. One, a clear descendant of ancient
Hebrew, she could translate for whole phrases at a time,
though the rest was mostly gibberish.

The queue began to move.

One by one the waiting women were checked in by a
middle-aged shaven-headed woman in a white robe wearing a steel Ankh pendant. Kate guessed she must be a nun
of Isis. The woman's bald pate glistened in the yellow
light of an unshaded bulb in the hall behind her.

When Kate reached the woman, she handed Kate a
ticket with something written on it in Greek characters and
spoke to Kate in a calm, kindly voice. All Kate could
make out was the part where the nun pointed to herself and
said, "Ahthehifee Boadicea." Ahthehifee was recogniz-
ably the Greek word for sister; Boadicea was an ancient
Celtic name. A Queen Boadicea, in Kate's home universe,
had led a revolt against the Roman invaders of Britain.
Now Kate was sure she was a nun.

Kate stood in line at a battered counter to receive a tray
of food; bread and vegetable soup with some kind of pill
which was contained in a shotglass alongside the soupbowl.
She sat with the others at one of many long narrow
wooden tables and ate. The food was simple but tasty, and
Kate swallowed the pill without resistance when she saw
the others do it.

That night Kate slept well, in the lowest bunk of a
four-decker. The four-deckers were arranged in long straight
tiers in a room as large as a city block. Even though all the
women, including Kate, had passed through a hot shower
before bedtime, the smell of bodies was heavy on the air
and the snores of the healthy and moans of the unhealthy
made an awful din; still Kate slept.

With the dawn most of the "guests" departed, but a few
remained after the breakfast of onion soup and black bread.
These few, Kate gathered by watching them, were volunteering to work in exchange for bed and board. Kate joined
them and spent the day mopping floors.

The second day Kate peeled onions and potatoes.

The third day she washed dishes.

The fourth day Kate volunteered again, not understanding what she was volunteering for, and found herself in a classroom, with Sister Boadicea lecturing.

Though she still could understand only a few words here and there, Kate soon got the drift of what the elderly nun said. This was a class in religion, the religion of Isis, and the graduates, as Kate understood it, would have the opportunity to become nuns. Kate did not really want to become a worshiper of any upstart pagan goddess; the gentle Jesus had been good enough for her father and was good enough for her. Yet she could not pass up this opportunity to learn something, in particular to learn how to speak and write the native tongue.

The maps on the wall taught her something, though she could not read the print on them. The patterns of color told her Great Britain was part of an empire that included all of Europe and most of the Middle East, but there were other empires and nations in the world.

The pictures on the walls taught her more: the religion of Isis had a rich history, with saints and martyrs and kings and queens, the same as in the home universe, but women figured far more largely here than there. Over half the figures shown in the pictures were women, whereas in the home universe the overwhelming majority of important religious figures had been men.

And the flag she saluted told her yet another thing. This banner, which hung above the blackboard in the front of the classroom, was blue except for a white dove in the upper left hand corner. The dove, Kate recalled, was the sacred bird of Isis. Was it also a symbol of peace? Was this new world she found herself in a world of peace? She hoped so.

Kate settled into the routine of the place.

She studied in the classroom before breakfast, worked in the kitchen or bunkroom or laundry for about eight hours, then, after supper, would attend a simple religious service in a small chapel connecting with the main temple of Isis. All the students attended this service and some of the transients, though the transients were more spectators than participants. Kate, for her part, quickly learned to mouth

the right syllables at the right times, though she had only a
dim idea what she was saying. She wore the same white
robes as the nuns, but did not shave her head or wear an
Ankh. If she became an actual nun, she thought, then she
would get her haircut and her pendant and would consider
it a great honor.

The service, oddly moving even when only half-compre-
hended, contained an entrance processional timed to the
tolling of a deep, sonorous gong, some music for harp and
flute and little bells mounted on a silver rod, some singing
of simple folklike songs by the congregation, led by Sister
Boadicea, prayers recited with arms upraised, a slow and
stately dance by some of the nuns accompanied by flute
and bells, and finally a place where a mirror was passed
from hand to hand through the congregation and each
woman, looking into the mirror, whispered "Isis." This
last, always conducted with an air of awesome mystery,
Kate found somewhat disturbing. When she looked into
the mirror it was not always her own face she saw looking
back at her; but perhaps that was a trick of the light. The
whole ceremony took place in semi-darkness, the only
light coming from a bank of flickering candles on the altar.

Once a week, on Monday, or the day of the Moon, the
nuns would fast until sundown, then would eat nothing at
suppertime but a small white candy in the shape of a dove.

A month passed thus, one day flowing into the next as
in a dream, and little by little the alchemy of translation
began to take place in Kate's mind. When Sister Boadicea
spoke to her in her native language, Kate's consciousness
transformed the words into something very like the King's
English.

One morning, as the nuns and novices filed out of the
classroom to begin their day, Sister Boadicea touched Kate
on the arm and drew her off to one side.

"You do well in your lessons," said the nun, speaking
slowly and carefully.

Kate struggled with the words. "Thank . . . thank you,
Sister." She still could not quite form all the sounds in the
alien language.

"Better than the others, my daughter."

"Thank you."

Kate was relieved. She was being kept after class to be praised, not criticized. Usually it was the other way around. Kate had witnessed many a tongue-lashing in this room, though she had yet to be on the receiving end.

"Do you have any questions?" asked the nun.

"Yes."

"Ask me then. I will answer if I can."

Kate hesitated, then said, "What is the name of this city?"

Her teacher was surprised, but answered with a smile, "Lud's Dun."

"Lud's Dun. That's a very old Celtic name."

Sister Boadicea was still more surprised. "How did you know that, my dear?"

"I learned it . . . at home."

Sister Boadicea studied Kate's face intently but did not ask where home was, only replied quietly, "You are right. When the Alexandrian Empire expanded to include our nation, their soldiers brought with them scholars from the Alexandrian Library. Thanks to these devoted men and women, dedicated servants of Mother Isis, nearly all the old place names were preserved as they had been in the ancient centuries of Druid superstition."

Kate asked, still struggling with the language, "And what is the name of this nation?"

"Albion, of course. How is it that you know so much and so little at the same time? You must have strange schools in your homeland."

"I never went to school. My husband taught me."

"As best he could, I suppose. By the Holy Dove of Isis, I should get over being surprised at the odd things in the heads of those refugees who seek asylum in our green islands." She toyed with her Ankh. "Where is your husband now?"

"I don't know."

"Dead?"

"I don't think so." Kate thought, *It is I who am dead, here in this world my husband made, where I never was born.*

"Did he abandon you?"

Kate could not answer. The image of William as he had once been, the good William, forbade it.

The Sister sighed and nodded. "I understand."

Kate thought, *But how can she understand? Only a Zoa could.* Still, Sister Boadicea seemed so gentle, so wise, perhaps . . .

"Where do you come from?" the nun asked.

"Not from Albion. Not from this world at all."

The Sister showed no suprise. "Of course. None of us is born in this world. You have learned your lessons well. The body is born in this world. The Ba, your true self, is neither born nor dies." She smiled sweetly. "As a Ba you come into this world from Isis; as a Ba you return to Her."

Kate was speechless. The Sister would take everything that was said to her and translate it into Bas and Isis; Kate could see that now.

Sister Boadicea continued, "You cannot know how pleased I am to hear you speak in such a spiritual way. You must realize, since you're obviously a bright woman, that our Order teaches you how to speak, not as an end in itself, but so that you may learn and one day teach the truths of our faith. We teach you to read, speak, and write the language of Albion so you may read the holy scrolls of Isis and write them on your heart."

"No, Sister . . ." Kate thought, *I must tell her I am a Christian. I must be honest.*

"Many learn the language here, but few the path of Isis. I think you are one of the few. Yes, I've been watching you toil at your humble tasks. To mop a floor may not be noble, but to mop a floor for Isis is better than ruling a nation. We are a teaching order, my daughter, but we seek not to press knowledge in from outside, but, like the saintly Socrates, to draw forgotten knowledge forth from the inside. We seek to awaken the slumbering Ba, to turn it to its Mother. In you I believe I see a Ba that slumbers lightly. If you let us help you, you can become what I am, one of the loving hands of the Goddess." She laid a gentle fingertip on Kate's arm. "Whatever you may have been before, here you can find a new and better life. The poor and ignorant have need of us, young Kate. We can help them. As Isis raised her husband Osiris from the dead, we can here resurrect those women who are dead to hope and joy, who without us would die in the streets of Lud's Dun, hungry, sick, helpless, cut off from the mercy of Isis.''

Kate made a decision. ''I'm sorry, Sister. I cannot ever be one of you.''

''Oh Kate, once I said those same words, but now look at me!'' Her tone was urgent, serious.

''I am a Christian.'' said Kate.

The older woman stared at her, uncomprehending. ''A Christian? What's that?''

''Jesus Christ died in Jerusalem. He rose again. If we have faith in Him . . .''

The nun continued to stare. ''I have heard of many strange cults, but . . .''

''You never heard of Christianity?''

''Never, my child.''

''Never heard of Jesus Christ, the Savior?''

''Never.''

After a long silence Kate said in a strangled whisper, ''I have to have time to think.''

''Of course,'' said the Sister soothingly, and dismissed her with a tolerant nod.

Kate began spending her evenings in the library. Sister Boadicea excused her from the services. Sister Boadicea understood that she had inner conflicts that must be worked out. It was all right.

Kate forced herself to learn to read, driven by a kind of panic. She had not been unduly alarmed to find herself in a world where she had never been born, but to find herself in a world in which God Himself had never been born . . . that seemed impossible. It would have been easy enough to simply leap into the place outside of time, to go back to the Battle of Actium, forward to Golgonooza, even back to the birth of Christ.

But that was exactly the problem.

What if there had been no birth of Christ?

Then Christ was not really God. At most He was God of

one timestream, one timestream among an infinite number of possible timestreams. He was not Lord of All. He was not Almighty. If the river of time changed its bed, flowed down another channel, the Gentle Jesus would be left high and dry.

The history books told the story.

After Cleopatra won the Battle of Actium, she lent her support to her friend Herod in ruling Judea, but the rule had been marked by the same humane respect for religious differences that characterized the rule of Alexandria. The hatred that had developed between the Jews and the Romans had not developed between the Jews and the Alexandrians, and thus the climate of opinion that demands saviors had not developed either.

The Temple at Jerusalem had been built by Herod, but it had never been destroyed by the Romans. It existed to this day, one of the so-called Twelve Wonders of the World. The Jews had never been driven from their homeland, had never even suffered serious persecution, but Judaism had never developed the synagogue system, never spread out to become a world religion. It had instead become a small local religion of the Eastern Mediterranean, with only a handful of small temples elsewhere, all in large cities within the Alexandrian Empire.

The name of Jesus was not the only one she sought in vain. Mohammed too had vanished from the pages of history. In his place Kate found other unfamiliar names. Buddha was still there. He had lived before the fateful battle between Octavian and Cleopatra. The history of Buddhism even in recent times was, in the main, quite similar to what it had been in the home universe. In both worlds Buddha dominated the East while the West fell to his rival; in the one universe Jesus, in the other Isis.

Also still standing was the library of Alexandria. Today it boasted the largest collection of books in the world, and a collection of antique scrolls that included the works of Plato, Aristotle, and Sophocles in the handwriting of the authors. And also still standing was the great Alexandrian lighthouse, though now it was surmounted by an electric beacon.

Each night Kate would reluctantly close the book she'd been reading and shuffle in a daze to her bunk, sometimes after midnight, and there she would lie in the darkness and pray silently, the only Christian in the world.

"Jesus, help me. Jesus, if you're here, give me a sign. Show me you're here. Jesus, show me you're here. That's all I ask. Please. Please. Please."

She had rarely asked Jesus for anything, had only thanked Him for blessings already received. Indeed she'd had the general notion that God knew better than she did what was good for her. But now she asked, and asked, and asked, always for the same thing.

And always only silence answered her.

Gradually the contrast between the two universes became more and more clear to her. The universe of Isis was one of continuous progress, unbroken by any "Dark Ages." It was one marked by centuries of unbroken peace, at least in the Western world, where the Alexandrian Empire had continuously maintained the technological advantage that prevented any serious victories by the surrounding barbarians. It was one totally free of religious warfare. The urbane Alexandrians had always preferred to talk rather than fight, and they were, as talkers, invincible.

One night she said aloud the thought that had long been struggling to express itself.

"The birth of Jesus may have been the greatest disaster in history."

The following day she stayed in bed.

She told the others she was sick, but her body was not sick. She had another kind of sickness. She could think of nothing worth getting up for.

She stared at the lower surface of the bunk above her, her eyes dull, her jaw slack, her mind full of vague images of ashes, dunes of drifting ashes under a gray overcast, without a hint of green.

On the second day a bunkmate brought her soup and bread. She did not eat it. Instead she slept. Sleeping was easy, and so much better than being awake.

She didn't pray.

What was the use?

On the third day she awoke to find Sister Boadicea standing over her, gazing down with concern. It was, according to the clock on the wall, midafternoon. The two women were alone together in the vast sleeping room.

"Are you troubled, Kate?"

"Yes." Kate's voice was lifeless.

"Can I help?"

"No. Nobody can."

"Isis can."

"Perhaps Isis can help you."

"But not you?"

"Not me."

The older woman laid a hand on Kate's arm. "Those who come here are often troubled, my child. They are often abandoned by husbands, family . . ."

"By God?"

"Abandoned by God? I see you come from a homeland where the diety wears a masculine face. Oothoon perhaps." Oothoon was the red man's nation across the Atlantic, occupying the continent which, in the home universe, had been occupied by the American Colonies.

"No, not Oothoon."

"Remember, child, the ceremony we celebrate every evening?"

"Yes."

"Remember the mirror?"

"Yes."

"What do you see in the mirror?"

"My own face."

"And yet as you look into your own eyes, you whisper the name of Isis."

"Yes."

"Why do you suppose that is?"

"I don't know."

"It's because Isis wears your face. Whoever you are, Isis wears your face. In the world you are Isis. You are Her hands, Her eyes, Her voice. You are Her face. Through you She experiences the world. Through you She acts upon the world. Through you She cares for all Her poor suffering children. Do you understand what I'm saying?"

"I suppose so, but . . ."

"Listen, my child. If a man looked into the mirror, what would he see?"

"A man's face, I suppose."

"The Mirror of Isis never lies, my child."

The nun turned and walked away.

"Wake up!"

The urgent voice was accompanied by an even more urgent hand shaking Kate by the shoulder. She opened her eyes to stare up into the anxious face of one of her bunkmates.

"What's wrong?" Kate blurted, still not fully awake.

"An accident. They need us at the hospital."

Kate sat up, threw off her covers, and reached for her shift. All around her the other women were dressing in frenzied haste and hurrying past Kate's bunk toward the rear of the great room. Kate noticed they were putting on raincapes and rainboots, so she did likewise. Her depression had vanished. Someone needed her. That gave her reason enough to get up. She felt almost grateful for the disaster whose nature she did not yet know.

Quickly, though in general disorder, the women mounted the steep narrow staircase to the roof. Kate, carried along with the rest in the stumbling rush, emerged into the night.

A light rain pelted her face, making her squint. Ahead of her a large helicopter, as big as a bus, slammed its side doors. In the blaze of the lights surrounding the landing pad Kate could see the machine was painted green with white insignia, a dove on the side of the nose and, along the fuselage, a number and the name of the hospital in Greek characters. With a throbbing fluttering roar the chopper lifted off straight up and was lost in the darkness and rain.

Instantly another helicopter, the near-twin of the first, descended, two bright spotlights blazing down to illuminate the landing area. It landed with a thump that shook the building, rolled a few inches, then came to a stop, its rotors slowing so she could see the blades, but not stopping altogether.

"This way," called Sister Boadicea, beckoning.

Kate obeyed, together with a clump of other novices.

The doors in the side of the helicopter opened with a metallic bang and a short flight of steps dropped into place. Kate was the third woman to enter the craft. The light inside, after the bright illumination of the landing pad, was so dim she had to grope her way to her seat.

"Strap down, ladies," came the voice of Sister Boadicea from somewhere up front, carrying above the excited chatter of the women and the rumble of the engine. The elderly nun emerged from the gloom, grim and determined, checking the seatbelts. Kate had trouble with hers and the Sister had to help her.

"May the Goddess be with you," said Sister Boadicea to Kate.

Without a second thought, Kate replied, "May God be with you, Sister." Several heads turned to look at Kate with surprise, but Sister Boadicea only laughed and patted Kate on the arm.

"Remember the mirror," said Sister Boadicea.

"You remember the mirror," Kate replied tartly.

She could not be sure her words were heard, for at that moment the motors began to roar with a steadily rising din. The Sister vanished toward the rear. The doors banged shut. With a sickening lurch they were airborne.

Kate, who had a window seat, peered out at the brightly lit platform dripping away below. Rain, driven in strange directions by the rotor wash, formed oddly beautiful patterns on the glass for a moment, then there was only darkness.

Kate sat back in her seat with a sigh. She had flown before, but not in an aircraft. Though she knew she was in no danger, the noise and the violent pitching and rolling of the craft intimidated her.

Then abruptly, they burst through the clouds and rose above the overcast. The moon, almost full, made the clouds look like a vast polar icefield, white and cold, yet soft. The city made its presence known only by a red glow from below, but the glow had a pattern. Kate could trace the winding path of darkness that corresponded to the

Thames. In the distance another helicopter rose into view, following them.

Kate was startled to hear Sister Boadicea's voice in her ear. The Sister, it seemed, had taken the seat directly behind her.

"I used to think it was very important whether the deity was male or female. Our church, you know, sends missionaries to other countries to persuade them of that very thing. To Oothoon, to Africa. . . . There are so many gods."

"There is only one God," said Kate.

"I agree. Does that surprise you? One god who sometimes turns to us his male face, sometimes turns to us her female face. You will see."

"I will see?" Kate was puzzled.

"Tonight men and women will turn their faces to you in need, and in each face you will see Isis, and in each face you will see that male god you worship."

"Jesus."

"Jesus, then. I will see Jesus too tonight."

Kate twisted around to stare into the woman's calm face, barely visible in the moonlight, and with a sudden rush of gratitude Kate cried out softly, "Yes. Yes, I think you will."

The helicopter tilted forward sharply and began to descend.

Most of the novices had at least a little training in nursing; all but Kate knew some first aid. Even Kate, however, could follow instructions, and the Sisters, particularly Sister Boadicea, knew how to give those instructions in a calm, clear way in the midst of chaos. The nuns of Isis were not quite doctors, but they had been trained to deal with medical emergencies and had been called in many times before when, due to some unforeseen disaster, there had not been enough doctors to go around.

Sister Boadicea knew Kate's lack of training and set her to carrying stretchers, making trip after trip in the elevators to the heliport on the hospital roof where helicopters came and went in an endless stream, disgorging injured people of both sexes, none younger than their twenties or older than their fifties, most suffering from burns and smoke inhalation.

The rain slacked off toward morning and so did the flow of patients. All the beds in the hospital had been filled when Kate first arrived, and now the spaces between the beds were also filled with moaning victims, and lines of mats in the halls made passage difficult. One of the resident doctors had assigned Sister Boadicea the job of temporary head nurse of a ward that consisted of the main hallway on the third floor, so it was to this area that Kate returned when she was told no more wounded were expected.

Kate had stood, dazed, only a moment before Sister Boadicea spotted her.

"Kate, are you free?"

"Yes, Sister."

"Hold this."

The Sister thrust a glass bottle of clear intravenous solution into Kate's weary hand. A plastic tube led from the bottle to the arm of a bandaged woman at Kate's feet. The woman, muttering something, stared up at Kate with pain-glazed eyes. Kate could not understand her over the din of the makeshift ward, but saw her lips move under the bright blueish glare of the ceiling lights.

"I can't hear you," said Kate.

The woman raised her voice. "Warn someone!"

"Warn someone about what?"

"The germs!"

"The germs?"

"The rockets!"

"What rockets?"

The woman tried to answer, but the effort cost her dearly and, her lips still moving, she lost consciousness.

"Sister Boadicea!" Kate called.

The older woman picked her way through the maze of mats and knelt to take the woman's pulse. "Let her sleep, Kate. She needs the rest."

"She said something about germs and rockets."

Sister Boadicea gave Kate a worried glance. "Forget about it."

"Forget about what? I don't know anything."

"Good. And if you do find out anything, keep it to yourself."

Kate, still holding the i.v. bottle, stared at the nun's retreating back, totally bewildered.

Kate worked at the hospital for two days, mostly in Sister Boadicea's hallway domain, catching what sleep she could during lulls, stretching out on a mat on the floor like the patients, a mat still warm from the previous occupant. Some of the patients died. Some were transferred. The hallway became less crowded. The frantic pace of the work slowed.

Kate was allowed to sleep a full eight hours.

One of her bunkmates woke her, saying in a low voice, "Sister Boadicea wants to say goodbye."

Kate rubbed her eyes and sat up. "Goodbye?"

She had been sleeping in her white robe, the same garment she had worn day and night since her arrival at the hospital, though it was by now stained with blood and sweat and badly soiled. She stood up. The ward was unnaturally silent and all eyes were turned toward the far end of the hall where, framed in a T intersection, Sister Boadicea stood side by side with some other nun Kate did not recognize.

Sister Boadicea began, her voice shaking, "You have done well, my daughters. Through you Isis has done Her work. I'm proud of you all. I know you will do equally well under the command of my successor, Sister Ragan." She indicated the stranger who stood beside her, a thin, severe woman with a thin, pinched little mouth. A chorus of protests went up, but Sister Boadicea silenced them with a gesture. "We go where the Goddess sends us, you know, and I have my marching papers. If I do not see any of you again, remember . . ." She hesitated. ". . . remember how things have been, no matter how much things change."

"We will," came a broken chorus of voices. "We'll remember."

"Goodbye."

"Goodbye, Sister Boadicea," came the sad chorus.

Sister Boadicea turned to leave, but first, almost as an afterthought, beckoned to Kate and said, "You, Kate. Will you accompany me to the airport?"

"Certainly, Sister Boadicea," Kate replied, conscious of the honor, conscious of the envy in the eyes of her bunkmates. Sister Boadicea led the way to the elevator and pressed the "up" button.

"I hope you enjoy your new duty," said Kate, with a feeling of saying the wrong thing.

"I have no new duty."

"I don't understand."

"I am retiring."

"Then I hope you enjoy your retirement."

"It is a forced retirement."

Kate was at a loss for words. The elevator doors slid open. They entered. The doors closed. The elevator started upward, the two women its only passengers.

Sister Boadicea, when she spoke, seemed bitter but resigned. "You don't keep up on politics, do you, Kate?"

"Not very much."

"Did you know that Oothoon has been deporting nuns and monks of Isis?"

"I've heard talk . . ."

"And not just nuns and monks. White men and women in general. Oothoon is for the red peoples only, according to the religion of the Sun God. Whites born there, whites whose parents and grandparents were born there, have been deported, at the command of the High Priest of Quetzalcoatl, the Winged Serpent of Azteca. There are very few of us left on the other side of the Atlantic."

"But what has that to do with you?"

The nun sighed. "I have told you Isis can wear a man's face. Some in our church have always denied that, and now that a male deity challenges Isis, a male deity who, according to his priests, cannot wear a woman's face, we have reacted. A new dogma has been adopted. I, and all those who took the opposite position, am no longer welcome."

The elevator doors opened. The women energed into

bright sunlight, so bright Kate had to squint and shade her eyes. A small green helicopter with the white dove insignia awaited them, rotor slowly turning. Sister Boadicea climbed the metal steps, Kate close behind. They settled in and strapped down, side by side. The engine revved up. The helicopter lifted off.

Kate studied the nun's weary, kindly face, and thought of the pinched little mouth of the woman who would take her place. All over the country, no doubt, a similar changing of the guard was taking place.

"Kate, I must warn you."

"About what?"

"This male deity of yours, this Jesus. You must never again mention his name."

"But you said . . ."

"What I said no longer matters. Today perhaps no harm will come to you, but tomorrow . . . tomorrow the mention of a male deity may cost you your life. Politics cannot change the nature of the Goddess, but politics can change the nature of Her children, Her poor foolish mortal children, limited creatures like you and me. Isis does not know how to hate, but we do. She weeps when Her babies fight, but She is no tyrant. She has left us free, free even to be fools, to be beasts, to be worse than beasts. She has left us free to murder each other. We are all Her hands, but the left hand can slash the right, or the right hand slash the left. She feels the pain, but She will not stop us." She took Kate's hand. "Promise me, Kate. Promise me you won't speak the name of Jesus aloud."

"I . . . I can't."

"I will be safe enough on some farm somewhere. They won't bother an old woman who has given good service, but you . . . you'll be in danger. I won't be content knowing that. Promise me."

"If I asked you never to speak the name of Isis, would you promise me that?"

The Sister laughed raggedly and settled back in her seat. "We would both slit our throats with our tongues over a matter of a name. It doesn't matter to Isis. It doesn't matter to Jesus."

"But it matters to us," said Kate quietly.

"So it does. But look. We're coming to the airport."
She nodded toward the window. A row of huge jet transport planes had come into view along a broad runway, and
a little farther on, hangars and a glassed-in administration
building and control tower.

The nun said, "May Jesus be with you, Kate."

Kate said, "May Isis be with you, Sister."

The helicopter landed near one of the giant aircraft. The
two women climbed down the little ladder and stood a
moment, the wind whipping their white but soiled robes,
not looking at each other; then, abruptly, they embraced
without a word, and Sister Boadicea hurried away. Kate
watched her go and thought, *Now I have no friend in this
world.*

Two men in uniform met Sister Boadicea near the crowd
of passengers waiting to board the big jet. The men wore
weapons; even at a distance Kate could see that, so they
were not monks of Isis.

In sudden fear Kate turned and clambered back into the
helicopter that had brought her. She realized that she had
started to think of this world as home, that she had begun
to adjust, to relate to people, to think as these people
thought. She had begun to like it here.

But now everything was changing.

Why did everything always have to change?

Kate continued to work in the hospital, though under
more normal conditions. She worked only eight hours a
day, ate three good meals a day, and had a change of
garments every morning. The new Sister in charge was
distant, but Kate did as she was told and avoided trouble.
As more patients were transferred, Kate had more time for
individuals.

She struck up quite a friendship with the woman who
had babbled to her about germs and rockets, but avoided
bringing up the subjects. People say many things when
hysterical that they'd rather forget.

The woman's name was Hathor, after a minor Egyptian
goddess usually treated, Kate found with a few careful

questions to her bunkmates, as one of many incarnations of Isis. After a week Kate was able to promote a wheelchair for her favorite patient and wheel her down the hall, past the remaining mats and their occupants, to a small balcony overlooking a tree-lined street.

Hathor immediately glanced around to make sure they were alone, then said in an anxious voice, "Can we be overheard here?"

Kate shook her head. "No, I'm sure not."

Hathor closed her eyes and sighed with relief. "You didn't report me, did you?"

"Report you? For what?"

"No, you couldn't have reported me. Nobody has come to arrest me."

"Why would they do that?"

"I talked about things I shouldn't."

"The germs and the rockets?"

Hathor nodded. "So you remember."

"Never mind. I won't tell. . . ."

The woman leaned forward, wincing from the pain of her burns. "But I want you to tell. I want you to tell the newspapers, the radio, the television."

"Tell them what?"

"Haven't you noticed? The media haven't mentioned the accident. Not a word anywhere! All these people hurt, all these people killed, and for all anyone knows it might never have happened."

"You want me to tell reporters about the accident?"

"That's only the beginning. By the Dove of Isis, that's only the beginning. There was a rocket fuel explosion. A careless match, a spark . . . who knows? And suddenly we were knocked flat by the blast and covered with blazing debris. Hundreds of people! But the government doesn't want anyone to know because that rocket fuel is not supposed to exist. It's a military secret! For a month I and everyone else who worked there had been confined to the base, virtual prisoners, so we wouldn't talk to anyone. If the explosion hadn't happened, I'd be there yet."

Kate leaned against the iron railing and gazed out over

the sun-drenched lawns of the hospital grounds. How peaceful everything looked! How deceptively peaceful.

Hathor continued in a low intense voice, ''The accident is only a temporary setback. The rockets were unharmed. The germs were unharmed. Someone has to stop them before it's too late.''

''Stop who?''

''The army. If the people knew what the army is doing, they'd stop them. If the High Priestess of Isis in Alexandria knew what the army is doing, *she'd* stop them. After all these centuries of peace, nobody wants war, not even the majority of the army, but there's a special branch called the Sons of Dis, composed of former citizens of Oothoon who have been deported from their native land. This faction has gained more and more power, quietly and behind the scenes. They have made incredible fortunes in stock speculations and just plain gambling, and in politics they make all the right moves, as if they could predict the future. They're led by three strangers . . .''

''Three strangers?''

''Two men and a woman. The woman is their leader. I've heard she wears a long crimson gown . . .''

Kate felt ill. Vala! Vala had taken command, apparently, leading both the cold-blooded Urizen and the impulsive William around like slaves. Vala had changed the world by making Cleopatra victorious in the Ancient Roman Empire, and now had reappeared to rule the world she'd created. Today Vala might only be a leader of a small minority of exiles, but with the power of time-voyaging she could eventually triumph over all opposition and make herself, if she liked, Empress, displacing the dynasty of the Ptolemys as easily as she had established it.

Hathor continued, ''The Sons of Dis, with the secret backing of a rival branch of the Royal Family, have built huge rockets that stand one upon another until they loom taller than Albion's tallest buildings, rockets that can cross the Atlantic Ocean.''

''Does the Empress know?''

''About the rockets? Yes, I'm sure she does, but not

that they're carrying . . ." The woman hesitated, as if
what she had to say were beyond human belief.

Kate touched her hand reassuringly, then prompted her.

"Carrying troops? Explosives?"

"If it were only that! Carrying germs, nothing but germs.
An artificial plague!"

Kate thought, *William. Gentle William, you wouldn't* . . .

Hathor pleaded, "Can you do something, Kate? Can
you do something?"

Kate answered softly, "Yes, Hathor, I think I can."

Kate went to the Sisters' Common Room.

There was a map of Albion there which, she thought,
was complete and accurate enough so that, drawing on her
memory of England in her home universe, she could figure
out the location of the rocket base from the description
Hathor had given her.

The other sisters were gathered before the large television set at the other end of the room as Kate entered; they
paid no attention to her. Sister Ragan, finger to lips, cut
into their gossip. "Shh. The Empress is about to speak."

Kate glanced at the screen and saw a face she'd come to
recognize as Berenice V, direct descendant of Caesarean,
the first fruit of Cleopatra Ptolemy's marriage (her second)
to Julius Caesar. The lean sad features and large protuberant nose were unmistakable, a kind of caricature of the
ancient royal visage. Centuries of brother-sister marriages
had produced a monarch who did not look quite human; it
was said all her children were "bleeders," several idiots,
one a homicidal maniac.

The Empress Berenice waited patiently for the applause
to subside, then began calmly, "What is Oothoon? A
willful disobedient child, testing its parent to see how far it
can go?"

Kate turned her back to the screen and studied the map,
which took up the better part of the wall. Yes, there it
was. The rocket base was helpfully designated by a gray
featureless rectangle labeled "Military Area." Kate was
about to leave when someone touched her arm. It was one
of the lesser sisters, a pleasant woman named Sister Gonorill.

"Kate," she said in a worried undertone, "you shouldn't turn your back on the screen when the Empress is speaking. It's not polite, it's not patriotic. In these times, my dear, it may not even be safe."

"I was just leaving, Sister," said Kate in a low voice.

"Oh no, Kate. Walk out on the Empress? Are you insane? And after the Empress, we'll hear the High Priestess speaking from the Holy City in Alexandria."

The Empress droned on. "The monks and nuns of Isis, in all faith and love, have taught the red men of Oothoon for centuries, in hopes that one day Oothoon could become a full member of the Empire. Thanks to us, they have been raised from the level of naked savages, preying upon each other in endless little wars, to a level of technology and prosperity almost equal to our own. How then can Albion and the other nations who recognize the authority of the Holy Church of Isis stand by and do nothing when the red men of Oothoon threaten to drive the white people from their continent, deport our monks and nuns, burn our temples, and revive the barbaric worship of the Sun God, the Feathered Serpent, a *male* deity!" She pronounced "male" as if it were a dirty word.

Sister Gonorill nodded agreement to everything the Empress said.

Kate whispered, "How do you know the deity is female?"

The Sister replied without hesitation, "The female brings forth life, not the male. Can a man have a baby?"

The other nuns had turned to look at her, frowning, but Kate was still determined to leave. "Thank you, Sister Gonorill, but I really must be going."

"You don't agree with what I said?"

"I don't agree with hate, with prejudice."

"History will vindicate us," said the nun smugly.

"You don't know what history will say," Kate flared.

"Only Isis can know the future," she agreed hesitantly, but then added, with more firmness, "*you* certainly can't!"

Kate smiled.

A moment later Kate stood in the hallway outside the Commons Room. She had walked out on them, on their Empress, on their war. She thought wistfully that, for a while, this strange land of Albion, this strange city of Lud's Dun, had seemed like home, but it was home no longer. Perhaps she had no home anywhere at all.

She steeled herself for the howling of the hordes of the dead she knew would greet her the instant she entered the place outside of time, soaring toward the future.

A statue of Vala (or was it Mary Wollstonecraft?) draped in classical robes stood on the bank of the river overlooking the vast city of Lud's Dun, longtime capital of Albion and now capital of the World. No building stood taller than Vala's head, and many of the newer buildings were more than a hundred stories tall. Under Vala's right foot, writhing in its death agonies, was a winged serpent, symbol of the Sun God, symbol of the red men of Oothoon.

A green helicopter with a white dove insignia approached from the west with a fluttering roar, a small machine but heavily armed. In the passenger seat directly behind the pilot sat a brooding William Blake, his tunic bedecked with medals. The statue of Vala, now swinging into view up ahead, was certainly a faithful reproduction of William's original design, which in turn had been modeled from life, but somehow on this titanic scale it looked different, more pompous, somehow even absurd. William decided he didn't like the thing, not anymore. The High Priestess of Alexandria didn't like it either and had said so. She had even used the words "blasphemous pretensions."

But her words no longer carried much weight.

"To the palace, Little Eagle," William commanded.

"Yes, sir," replied the red slave, tilting the control column.

The helicopter crossed the river and descended.

Chief Running Water, also a slave, snapped to attention, an impressive sight in his feathered headdress and warpaint. "Announcing my lord William Blake, Prince Consort of Albion," he intoned in a deep, dignified voice.

Urizen, the Prime Minister, looked up from the inlaid ivory chessboard, smiling. "We can finish our game later,

Vala,'' he said to the beautiful woman sitting opposite him, clad in yards and yards of red silk.

"Mate in five moves," she answered lightly, moving a bejeweled pawn, then sprang to her feet and ran across the multicolored geometrical mosaic floor of the immense throne room, her bare soles slapping against the hard little tiles, her silks swirling behind her like the tail of some fantastic tropical fish.

"My William!" she cried out with delight.

William, grinning, stood in the tall doorway where the massive bronze doors stood ajar, his arms outspread to receive her. He was clad in the latest style, neo-archaic, with tunic, cloak, and sandals all in gold-trimmed white, his red hair neatly cut so it hung no lower than his earlobes.

Chief Running Water watched the two embrace and kiss. The red man was impassive, perhaps a little bored.

"Come, darling, talk to me," Vala said, leading William toward the slightly-raised platform where Urizen, reclining on white velvet cushions, awaited them.

Urizen, no slave to fashion, wore no clothes.

As William and Vala settled into the cushions, Vala demanded, "What news from my empire?" Between themselves the three spoke the English of their home universe so no one else could understand.

"The empire . . ." William chose his words carefully. ". . . is imperfect."

Urizen put in placidly, "For the moment perhaps, but since my plan is perfect, the result of my plan will also be perfect."

"But when?" asked William, turning toward him.

Urizen was unperturbed. "All has gone well so far, has it not? We set the world to uniting itself under a single capital, then, when that world capital in due time came into being, we were in exactly the right position to take over that capital for ourselves. Vala the Empress, you and I the powers behind the Throne! That was my plan—a simple one really—and here we are, exactly where I expected we'd be. Politics is like farming, my friends; you plant a seed, then wait." He spoke like the very personification of Reason.

William said bleakly, "I've flown over Oothoon."

Vala prompted him, "And you found?"

"A land of death eternal. Nothing human lives over there, not on the northern continent nor on the southern. I saw trees, animals, but . . ."

Urizen leaned forward. "What do you want? A world split in half? A world like the one in the home universe where the United States and Russia stood facing each other with drawn knives for a hundred years? If we want one world, we must have one power, not two or ten or a hundred . . . one power with the means and the nerve to exterminate all rivals."

William glanced at Chief Running Water. "Not everyone would agree."

Urizen said, "Are you speaking of the Chief there? Believe me, he is only too glad we captured him in the early stages of the war, before the plague infected him. Here, it's true, we make rather a clown of him, forcing him to parade around for our amusement in the costume of his savage ancestors, though we know well enough that before the war he dressed the same as any good citizen of Albion." Urizen turned to the Chief and called out, "Hey there, boy! What were you before the war?"

The answer came without hesitation. "A college professor, my lord."

"And tell me, Chief, where would you rather be? Back there before the war, teaching college, or here, as you are?"

"Here, my lord."

"You see?" Urizen returned his attention to his two friends. He had addressed his question to the red man in the language of Albion, but he now reverted to English.

William said sullenly, "What other answer could he give and live?"

"You're so sour," Vala said, pouting. "You should stay here with me, not go bouncing around the world so. It isn't good for you."

"I am Prince Consort," William reminded her crisply. "Someone must go about and see that things are as they ought to be."

Urizen said languidly, "You sound as if you have still more complaints to make."

William nodded. "I do. I find unrest in high places and low. The officials in the temple complain that we have no priestess of Isis at court."

Urizen chuckled and said, "Well, Vala, would you like to declare yourself a priestess?"

"You swine," she cooed affectionately.

William went on, "Also, the nobility complains that we fail to give proper respect to the old royal family."

"Proper respect?" said Urizen. "If you two had not opposed me, I would have had the whole Ptolemaic clan exterminated. As for the nobility, they must be aware by now that we only preserve them as one preserves the last examples of an endangered species, for the amusement of the zoo-going public."

"And there are riots," William continued doggedly. "Not only in distant parts of the world, but in the very streets of Lud's Dun itself. The young roam the city like packs of wolves and every wall is covered with obscene scrawls. Lud's Dun was to be like Golgonooza, a city of art . . ."

Urizen said soothingly, "William, William, William, it will be a city of art. Patience. We have sampled the future. We know these dark times will pass. A perfect world awaits us uptime from here, a world of art triumphant. It's there, William, the prize that makes it all worthwhile."

"But . . ."

Vala touched his lips with her fingertips. "Hush now, darling. Don't be so serious."

William sighed and muttered, "I suppose you're right."

Vala took his hand, saying, "You're home. That's the important thing. It's almost suppertime. Let's go on down to the dining room and see if we can guess, by sniffing the air, what the cook, Old Naguma, has in store for us." She stood up and pulled William to his feet. She added playfully, "Let's make this a celebration, not a wake. A celebration of your safe return, darling."

The way to the dining room led across a long stone bridge that spanned the gulf between the southern and northern wings of the palace. The bridge was roofed but open at the sides so they could look down into the court-yard twenty floors below, or off across the landscape toward the river. William, tagging along behind Vala and Urizen, glanced toward the giant statue of Vala that domi-nated the skyline, the statue of Vala trampling the serpent-god underfoot. There it stood, a dark silhouette against the afterglow of early evening. He thought, *The High Priest-ess is right. The damn thing really is too big.* And yet it was a perfect symbol of all that Vala stood for, the bound-less vanity beyond the understanding of ordinary humans, but for which ordinary humans by the millions were ex-pected to give their lives. Once Urizen had spoken of freedom, of human rights. Once Vala had spoken of equal-ity, but now . . .

William's thoughts were interrupted when he almost bumped into Urizen and Vala, who had stopped abruptly.

"What's wrong?" William asked, annoyed, then fol-lowed his companions' line of vision.

Someone stood in the shadows at the end of the bridge, waiting for them . . . a woman in a loose white robe.

A familiar voice called, "Mr. Blake?"

"Kate!" William breathed, and then he could say no more.

Urizen, however, was not so tongue-tied. In a voice devoid of any trace of emotion, he said, "You shouldn't have come, Mrs. Blake."

Vala agreed, "No, my dear, you really shouldn't have come."

Chief Running Water came crisply to attention, thump-ing the butt of his spear against the mosaic tile floor, as Urizen and Vala passed him, dragging Kate behind them by the wrists into the throne room. William followed, his features pale and masklike.

"Shut the doors!" Vala commanded.

"Yes, my lord." The Chief shut them with a boom.

As the echo of the boom died away, Kate shouted, "Let go of my wrists!"

"Save your breath, Kate," Vala told her grimly.

"You can't hold me like this!" Kate exclaimed. "A bit of concentration and I can pop a hundred years into the future or a hundred years into the past, where you'll never find me."

Vala said quietly, "Try it, my dear."

She tried. Nothing happened.

"I don't understand," she said, suddenly afraid.

Urizen said, "Remember when I first took you and William to Golgonooza? I held you by the hands, and my power communicated itself to you. I have power, Mrs. Blake, over everything I touch."

"I have power, too," Kate objected. "I've been practicing. It wouldn't surprise me if I was every bit as good at controlling time as you are."

Urizen smiled. "You may be as good as I am alone, but not as good as Vala and I together. Believe me, my dear, Vala and I together can cancel out anything you might be planning to do."

Vala said, "You scared me, standing in the shadows like that, particularly since I honestly never expected to see you again. Kate dear, that was naughty of you!"

"You thought you'd murdered me, good and proper!" Kate was furious.

"Murdered you?" Vala said with mock astonishment. "There is no murder without a corpus delicti. We simply arranged things so you wouldn't be born."

"You murdered me," Kate insisted. "And you murdered all the others, too . . . the people who would have been born if you hadn't changed things."

Urizen was amused. "Is it murder every time a man passes up an opportunity to get a woman pregnant?"

"Let me go!" shouted Kate, struggling with all her strength. Urizen and Vala held her fast.

Urizen went on, unperturbed, "We took life from some, yes, but only to give it to others. That's what it means to be a ruler. You must take the responsibility for saying, 'This one will live, that one will die.' "

"And you never ask yourself, do you, Mr. Urizen, if it's your right to decide that. You never think there might be a higher court." When Urizen did not answer this, Kate went on with more conviction, "Ah, I see I've got you there, sir. You do have doubts!"

"Only at around three in the morning," admitted Urizen, but his tone was ironic. "But now it's my turn to ask a question . . . a simple one at that. What do you want here, Mrs. Blake?"

"I want my husband," she said firmly.

"I can't believe this," said Vala, rolling her eyes.

"Do you know what you're doing, Mrs. Blake?" Urizen asked in all seriousness.

Kate held her head high. "I'm doing nothing more than any good Englishwoman would do, nothing more than my mother's done many a time. When my dad fell in with bad company, with drinking men and loose women, she went right down to whatever tavern or bawdyhouse he was in and dragged him home by the ear, she did."

Vala laughed out loud. Urizen only said mildly, "And why did she do that?"

Kate looked at him as if he were feeble-minded. "She loved him, you silly man!"

"Let her go," put in William softly. He had not spoken for a long time, so Vala and Urizen looked at him sharply.

"I'd like to," Vala told him. "But I can't. She's a Zoa. She has power. The moment we let go of her wrists there's no telling what she might do, and Urizen and I have better things to do than stand here holding her."

"If she promised . . ." William began.

"Could we believe her?" Vala demanded. "No, darling, I sympathize with you, but at the same time I ask you to remember the greatness of our cause. The Plan comes first, above any considerations of sentiment."

"What are you saying?" William was bewildered.

"That we must kill her."

"No!"

"We have no choice, but you may leave the room if you like."

Vala and William faced each other warily, silently.

"Mr. Blake!" cried Kate with dismay. She thought, *Will he simply stand there and do nothing?*

Vala smiled and said softly, "You made your choice long ago, William."

Urizen glanced toward the red man. "Chief, do you have your spear?"

"In my hand, my lord," answered the chief, stepping forward.

Urizen's voice was cold, emotionless. "Then run her through, but try to make it quick and as painless as possible."

"Yes, my lord!"

Kate closed her eyes and waited.

"Am I dead?"

Kate had to shout to hear her own voice above the howling of the clouds of swirling specters.

"No, Mrs. Blake." William's voice sounded deep and gentle in her ear as they fell through the void, spinning head over heels through a maze of vague images that formed and disintegrated before they could be really seen . . . buildings, animals, human faces, machines, unfamiliar landscapes.

"I don't understand!" she cried.

He chuckled.

She was amazed. She'd never heard him laugh before. He'd always been so serious, so unsmiling. "I saved you," he told her with an unfamiliar hint of glee in his voice. How he'd changed! Was he still the same man? He continued, "I threw myself on you and tore you free of Urizen and Vala, then brought you with me here, outside the timestream."

They reentered the timesteam on a summer hillside in Albion, under a cloudless afternoon sky, in the days before Vala's palace was built. The skyline of Lud's Dun in the distance showed no trace of Vala's towering statue.

"I like it much more now." William gestured toward the city.

"Without the statue?"

"Without Vala on the throne."

William sighed and settled himself with his back against

a tree, then looked up at Kate, who had remained standing. "Sit with me, Mrs. Blake," he said softly.

"No, no, I can't."

"Sit with me."

"I thank you for saving my life, but I can't forget you wanted me dead. I can't forget that you plotted with that woman to make a world in which I never was born. Am I now to forget all that and sit down with you as if nothing had happened?"

"It was you who rescued me, from my own madness. You came for me. You sought me out. Now you've found me."

"So I have."

Kate looked down at him. He looked weak, like a child, and his eyes pleaded with her for forgiveness. Her feelings drew her to him, as if he were a little boy who had been lost and now was found, but her mind told her coldly, *If he betrayed you once, he can betray you again.*

She had searched the years for him, had desperately wanted to see him, but now her impulse was to flee, to hide herself from him where he could never find her. She steadied herself. "I believe in marriage, I do," she said slowly, thoughtfully, measuring her words, "but you don't."

"Yes, I do!" he protested.

"No, you write against it and you abandon me and plot with your friends against my life. That's not marriage. You never will be married the way other folk are."

"I am married to you, Kate." It startled her to hear him call her by her first name. "I know that now. Even if you decide you can't forgive me . . . and I wouldn't blame you for that . . . I am your husband now and I always will be. Even if you leave me, I will still be your husband."

"What about Vala?" The thought of her made Kate dizzy.

"I'm finished with her. I've made my choice."

"How nice for you. And I'm to be pleased that you like me better than a murderess?"

"I hope you are."

There was a long silence. Then she said, her voice shaking, "You never were a husband to me. Not really.

But you have been a friend, once, before Urizen came into our lives. I do need a friend.''

''A husband!'' William corrected her.

''No, a friend. An ally. Let's see how you do as a friend.''

''Are you putting me on probation?'' He was dismayed.

''I'm not putting you on anything. You can go back to Vala this minute if you like. Maybe that would be best. Yes, maybe you'd be happy with her. I don't want it on my conscience that I stood between you and your happiness.''

''I'll never go back to her. I only want to be with you, to be happy with you.'' He hesitated, then added, ''I know you love me.''

''God help me, yes I do!''

''And I love you, and I think you know it.''

''Yes, you do. I knew that even when you didn't.''

''So we'll find a way. Somehow, someday, we'll grope our way to a kind of happiness. . . .''

She found within her a new coldness, a coldness that let her say, ''I don't want happiness, Mr. Blake. I fancy I'll never see happiness again. What I need is someone to join me in a war. Two nations don't have to love each other to be on the same side in a war, do they? All they need is a common enemy. Are you with me against Urizen?''

''I'm with you,'' he whispered.

''And against Vala?''

He hesitated, and his hesitation hurt Kate more than anything he had said, then answered, ''Against Vala, too.''

Kate said grimly, ''Then it's even, two against two, and we've got a chance. Urizen will regret he taught us all his tricks.''

''Not all of them, Kate,'' William warned.

''Enough of them, William.'' And to speak William's first name to him, right out loud, took more courage than to face the murderous Urizen and Vala in the heart of Vala's citadel.

As they stepped from the brightly-lit printseller's shop into the darkness of the Lud's Dun street, Kate said,

"Thank you kindly, Mr. Blake, for buying me this map of Avalon."

"You need never thank me for anything again," he replied. "I owe you a debt I'll spend the rest of my life paying."

"You owe me nothing at all."

"My sins . . ."

"You're a Christian gentleman. Forgive! Forgive even yourself." She didn't want him starting in on his damn sins again.

"If you could forgive me . . ."

"I've forgiven you already, Mr. Blake. First comes contrition, and I see you're contrite enough. Then comes forgiveness, and I do forgive you, as Jesus does too, I'm sure. But now comes the hard part. Reform!"

"I have reformed!"

"Maybe. Maybe not. Only time will tell. You're just a man. My mum told me a hundred times, 'A man may be strong in body, but it's up to the woman to supply the moral backbone of the family.' "

Though the day had been clear, a thick fog had started to form around sundown, and now they could see less than a block ahead of them. At least they were in no danger of being run over. Here in Lud's Dun, unlike the London of her home universe, only foot traffic was allowed on the streets of the central business district.

Helicopters had taken the place not only of ambulances but of trucks and buses as well. Now and again one of the noisy monsters would pass overhead with a fluttering roar, or settle briefly on some rooftop heliport. Kate could hear them, but because of the fog could not see more of them than an occasional blinking light. William had become a featureless black shape by her side except when they passed under a streetlamp where she could glimpse his drawn features.

"I hope you know where we're going," he said.

"I know this area well, Mr. Blake. I worked at a hospital right down at the end of this street. I want to talk to Hathor."

"Hathor?"

"She was one of my patients. Ah, there's the hospital now!" The building loomed darkly ahead of them, little halos of light around the few windows that remained lit. They entered a tree-lined street that led to the entrance, passing the broad well-kept lawns of the hospital grounds. Using their power, they transposed themselves through the walls, reappearing at the end of a corridor that had been made into a makeshift ward. Kate knew it well: Sister Boadicea's hallway domain. At the far end a woman in white was just leaving.

"That woman . . . it's you!" whispered William.

"Hush now."

The other Kate passed out of view around a corner. Kate smiled, remembering. Then she led William down the aisle between the mats where patients lay sleeping, finally stopping near the foot of one of them.

"Hello, Hathor," said Kate softly.

Hathor looked up with surprise. "Why, hello. Back again?" She frowned. "You look different. And that man . . ."

"My husband," said Kate softly.

"Did you forget something?" asked Hathor.

"Yes, yes, I did." Kate began opening up the map William had bought her. "I want you to point out on this map the rocket base you were talking about . . ."

Hathor cut in, "Not here!"

Kate whispered, "Everyone's asleep. Please. . . ."

Hathor glanced around fearfully, but it did appear that everyone within earshot was indeed sleeping. "All right." She raised herself on her left elbow, wincing with pain, then pointed with her right forefinger. "The one I was at is there." She indicated the military area Kate had noticed on the map in the Sisters' common room. "There's another there." She pointed to a place farther up the coast. "And there." A place in a wilderness area in what, in the home universe, would have been Wales.

William asked softly, "Three bases. Are you sure there are no more?"

The woman shook her head firmly. "Just three. I've

worked at all of them at one time or another. If there were others I'd have heard of them."

Kate began folding up the map. "Thank you, Hathor. Thank you so much."

Hathor smiled with rekindled hope. "Can you stop them?" Her tone was half grateful, half pleading.

"We can try," Kate answered.

"Isis be praised."

"Isis be praised," Kate echoed, remembering Sister Boadicea.

"Let's go someplace quiet and rest before . . ." William began as they left.

Kate cut him off. "No, I want to get it over with."

Yet she too felt the fatigue she saw in her husband's eyes and heard in his voice. How long had it been since she'd slept? She tried to calculate the hours, but her mind refused to function. She grasped William's wrist and they vanished together.

They appeared atop a featureless administration building, shivering in a damp fog and oppressive darkness.

"Are you sure this is the right place, Mrs. Blake?"

They had materialized in the wrong place four times that night, but Kate had kept doggedly on, determined to complete her task before allowing herself the luxury of sleep.

"I don't see any rockets," William added.

"Well . . . we must look for them then, mustn't we?" She started off and he followed.

Sure enough, there they were, lying on their sides in a long line like cigars in a box, hidden from passing aircraft under vast tentlike camouflage nets. She could see only the closest ones at first, but a quick tour of the area revealed around a hundred.

"Multi-stage," William whispered, indicating the three segments into which each missile was divided. "But no warheads."

William had become, Kate reflected, quite an expert on weapons under Urizen's tutelage.

"They're overconfident," William continued. "They

should know better than to put all the rockets so close together."

"Let's explode them," said Kate.

William's gloomy voice came out of the darkness. "We can't do that. I told you, they have no warheads." A spot check revealed they had no fuel on board either.

"They're not as stupid as I thought," William admitted ruefully.

For a moment the two stood baffled, gazing in frustration at the nearest rocket. The thing's nose and tail were hidden by a fog that seemed to shroud her very brain.

At last Kate spoke. "If there's no fuel on board now, there will be."

"When?" William didn't sound very hopeful.

"When it takes off, you silly man!"

A little over a month later, on a sunny afternoon, the countdown was completed and the first of the trans-oceanic rockets lifted off from its launching pad with a satisfying roar and a stream of billowing fire and smoke. In a nearby concrete bunker, tense scientists began, tentatively, to smile. "All systems go" was the best translation for what came over the public address speaker.

On its side the missile bore, ironically, the insignia of the dove, symbol of peace.

Then one of the scientists shouted and pointed skyward, but his voice was drowned out by the thunder of the rocket. All the same, the others looked where he pointed.

A man and a woman had appeared, gliding swiftly through the air. The woman wore the robe of a nun of Isis; the man, a redhead, wore tunic and sandals and a cloak that swirled in the wind. They banked in purposefully from either side of the rocket, which was still rising quite slowly, and put their hands on it. The rocket, together with the man and the woman, vanished.

In the sudden silence that followed, one of the scientists could be heard, weeping.

The rocket reappeared a little over a month earlier, moving at a different angle, skipping on its side over the ground through darkness and fog. An instant later it rammed into the central segment of another rocket (or was it the same rocket at an earlier time?) with an immense crash, then kept on going, passing through one rocket after another until, almost at the last one, it exploded in a great rolling ball of flame and a deep thump of concussion that broke windows fifty miles away.

High above, their faces illuminated by the flames, the Blakes embraced and laughed hysterically.

"How's that for a firecracker, Mrs. Blake?"

"Capital, Mr. Blake!"

Before dawn the two other bases were also masses of roaring flame, and the attack on Oothoon definitively postponed, perhaps permanently.

Kate and William, soaring upward hand in hand into the brightening sky, gazed down at the white overcast and at the glowing spot in the clouds that marked the site of one of the burning bases.

"A nasty surprise for Mr. Urizen, I dare say," Kate remarked with unconcealed malice.

But William's mood was more somber. "Surprise Urizen? Is that possible? Actually it is I who am surprised . . . that Urizen has done nothing to stop us."

"What are you saying?" Kate too suddenly felt she had made some dreadful mistake. She was so tired. . . .

"I'm saying that before we celebrate our victory, we should go uptime a way and examine the results of this night's work."

A gray overcast hung over Lud's Dun.

Rain fell without cease on Kate's garden, which now grew even more wild than it had when this city had been called London and this nation England. The grapevines had crept forward to reclaim the area where the tearoom tables had stood, where Kate had tried and failed to read the menu. The table where she'd sat, like everything else, was overgrown with serpentine vines and translucent green fruit, and there was no sound but the steady hiss of the rain. The chairs, some still upright, some overturned, were iron under their chipped paint and had begun to rust.

A yellowed skeleton lay face down in the garden, almost hidden by roses, the rain drumming on the skull with a curiously hollow sound.

Kate and William stood in the back doorway of the tearoom for a long time, watching.

Finally Kate spoke. "The skeleton . . . do you suppose that's the chap who waited on me?"

William answered softly, "Perhaps."

Absentmindedly she scratched herself with slender fingers. Fleas thronged everywhere inside the tearoom. They thrived in the dust that lay thickly on all the furniture, here in the comparatively dry interior.

They had walked the streets for hours before finally ending up here. Nowhere had they seen a living human being, though corpses were numerous enough.

She spoke again. "It's like this all over Lud's Dun, isn't it?"

William's large blue eyes turned toward her. "All over Albion, I expect. Probably all over the continent as well . . . and it's our fault."

"Our fault?"

"We exploded the germ warfare rockets here in Albion. We had literally all the time in the world, but we had to hurry, had to rush in and make our silly blunder. We should have known that we'd be spreading here the plague intended for Oothoon! We saved the redmen, but sacrificed Albion to do it."

She thought of Sister Boadicea. She and William had been to the Mission of the Daughters of Albion, but had found no trace of anyone. She thought of poor Hathor. They'd found bones in the hospital that could have been Hathor's . . . or anyone else's. Hathor had been so eager to have the rocket attack stopped! All, all dead.

"Let's leave here," said Kate, and her voice was hushed as if she were in church. "Let's go back downtime to before all this happened, to before Urizen came to Albion."

William shook his head heavily. "No, Kate."

She turned on him angrily. "What's that? Do you like it here?"

He laid his hand on her shoulder. "We must try to learn to like it. It will be our home from now on."

She swept his hand away with an impatient gesture. "Our home? Are you daft? We can go anywhere we like . . . the present, the past, the future!"

He sighed. "No more. Here we are and here we stay."

"No; I won't have it!"

"We've caught the plague, Kate."

For a moment she was stunned, then she snapped, "You're joking! How could we . . ."

"We've been very foolish. You can't walk the streets of a plague city without getting the plague, but I didn't think of that until we'd been here for more than half an hour. Now, you see, we can't leave because we'd take the plague with us; we'd infect any age we visited. Those fleas that have been biting us . . . every one of them must be a plague carrier."

In a moment of panic she slapped and rubbed herself with impotent frenzy, trying to get rid of the fleas that, she now was horribly aware, were crawling all over her.

"Hush now," William said soothingly. "That will do no good. We'll have some time together, I think, before the fever comes on. Urizen told me how it goes. A few days. Maybe a week. Let's make as good use of it as we can."

She stopped slapping and scratching and said with ill-suppressed fury, "You knew for hours and you didn't tell me!"

His large eyes were full of pain. "I couldn't think of any gentle way to say it."

"Look, Kate, the rain has stopped."

She awoke and rolled over on the pile of rotting table-cloths and towels on the floor that served her as a bed. The back doorway, lacking a door, revealed her garden, fresh and bright in the morning sunshine, the grape leaves wet and dripping, the trunks of the poplar trees glistening with moisture, the red and pink roses nodding in the breeze.

With the rain her suffering seemed to have passed as well. The fever had departed, not to be replaced by chills,

as before, but by a curious feeling of great peace. Her
makeshift bed was clammy with old sweat, and she raised
herself slowly into a sitting position, fighting against waves
of dizziness and nausea that threatened to destroy her
strange joy.

William, she saw, sat nearby on the floor, leaning against
the wall. His reddish beard had grown long, dirty, and
tangled. His skin was pale, his eyes bloodshot and his
body pitifully thin.

He spoke with gentle concern. "Can I get you something to eat? I found some cans of food in the kitchen."

"Thank you kindly, Mr. Blake, but I'm not a bit hungry. I'll eat later perhaps. I feel much better."

"You look better, too. I've never seen you more beautiful." His voice, she noticed, was not strong, and had a
quaver in it. They'd taken turns nursing each other, and
that had seemed to work quite well until last night when,
for hours at a time, neither of them had been altogether
sane.

He said, "I thought perhaps, it being such a fine morning, you and I can go for a walk."

"A walk?" It sounded like such an insane suggestion
she wondered if he was in a fever again, but no . . . fever
gives a certain high quickness to a man's voice, and he
sounded perfectly normal. A walk? Why not? People went
for walks all the time.

"Down to the river," he added. "That's not far."

Was he joking? No, he was slowly, painfully, dragging
himself to his feet. For a moment he stood there swaying
and blinking, then, with shuffling sandaled feet, he came
over and extended his hand to help her up.

Could she stand up? Yes, much to her own surprise, she
could.

Very slowly, pausing every few steps to gather strength,
they made their way to the front doorway and out into the
street. Several times Kate felt as if her legs would give
way under her, but each time William held her up, kept
her from falling.

"You're a good man," she whispered. "I always knew
it."

He did not answer. Perhaps the effort of walking and holding her up took all his energy.

As they reached an intersection a pack of gaunt dogs appeared around a corner and, seeing them, came forward slowly. One, who seemed to be the leader, showed his teeth and let out a low growl.

"Go on! Shoo! Skat!" shouted William, bending over to pick up a rock from the cobblestone street. When he raised the rock as if to throw it, the pack fled, but nor far, and when William and Kate continued on their way, the dogs followed at a safe distance.

"They want to eat us," Kate said softly.

"Nonsense. They're just overfriendly." William's voice lacked conviction.

Kate did not believe him. She had heard that growl. But she was not afraid. It seemed right and good that the dogs should eat her. Nature was like that.

As she looked around she saw birds everywhere, more than she'd ever seen before in one place, and other animals, too. Squirrels. Chipmunks. And an occasional huge rat that did not flee as rats used to do, but stood its ground in the middle of the street and watched them with fearless little eyes, so they had to detour around. In every yard the weeds had grown into a small jungle, and in each jungle eyes peered out.

She would die today. She knew it, and all the dogs and birds and squirrels and chipmunks and rats would eat her, because her man would die too and there would be no one to stop them, and that was all right. That was exactly as it should be.

A breeze toyed with her tangled hair, a welcome breeze, because either the day had become suddenly very hot or the effort of walking had become too much for her.

"The fever's coming on again," she whispered.

"We'll be at the river soon. We can rest there." His voice was strained, desperate. Was he getting a fever, too?

They paused to rest.

The dogs settled themselves on their haunches, tails wagging, tongues hanging, intelligent eyes fixed on the Blakes with a calculating gaze. They'd gotten closer.

But the sun was so warm. Everything was so quiet. The birds sang. The insects hummed. The cobblestones glistened, already beginning to dry. She couldn't remember a more perfect day.

Then, without warning, William fell.

She bent over him, concerned yet somehow detached. "Are you all right, Mr. Blake?"

He rolled over to look up at her. "Yes, yes. A little dizzy, that's all. I'll be on my feet in a minute."

But he found he could not stand, and she did not have the strength to lift him.

"Damned nuisance," he muttered, and began to crawl on his hands and knees. The dogs came a few steps closer. She tottered along beside him.

"If we can reach the Thames," he panted, so softly she could barely hear him, "we can find a boat and float . . . float out of here."

"Yes, Mr. Blake."

Her thoughts grew vague.

When they cleared she found herself on the bridge, alone, leaning against the cement railing. Puzzled, she looked around. Where was William?

Ah, there he was!

About a block behind her he came inching along on his belly toward her. The dogs followed him, only a few yards away from him.

"Go away! Go away!" she screamed at the dogs in her high, cracked fever voice. The pack paid no attention, and the leader showed his teeth as if in a triumphant grin.

"Go away! Leave Mr. Blake alone!"

The leader advanced to sniff William's ankle.

"No!" cried Kate. It was no longer a beautiful day. It was horrible. Hot. Moist.

Every cobblestone in the street stood out with a supernatural clarity. Every separate hair on the dogs' pelts stood out so she could have counted them.

"William!" She tried to run toward him, but instead fell to her knees, painfully.

A great roaring rushing sound filled her universe.

She raised her head, looked up.

The last thing she saw before losing consciousness was a large brown helicopter hovering overhead.

The small brown man gazed down at her calmly. His long black hair was braided. He wore clean white coveralls and a small metallic gold winged serpent pin. His teeth, when he smiled at her, were white too, with a glint of gold.

"I see you're awake," he said pleasantly.

"Yes, I think so." Kate found it difficult to speak. "Where's . . . William?"

"William? The man who was with you? He's in the men's ward."

"Ward? Is this a hospital?"

"Yes, fortunately for you both. You and . . . what did you say the man's name was?"

"Mr. William Blake. I'm his wife, Catherine Blake."

"You two should recover in a few weeks. The military police helicopter brought you in for inoculation before the disease reached the terminal phase."

Kate tried to sit up in bed but failed. Her gaze swung from the brown man's face to an unfamiliar object hanging on the wall. At first she took it for a caduceus, symbol of the medical profession in her home universe, then she realized it showed one serpent, not two, and no staff. "What's that thing on the wall?"

"That thing, as you call it, is the symbol of Almighty Quetzalcoatl, the Winged Serpent of Oothoon, the only True God." His tone was suddenly cold, patronizing, as if Kate were a child who had failed to learn her lessons.

"I didn't know . . ." she said contritely.

"I will teach you."

"Are you my doctor?"

"Not of your body. I am your Road Chief. My name is Aztlan."

"Road Chief?"

"I will guide your mind and spirit to the right road."

After Aztlan had left, Kate fell asleep looking at Quetzalcoatl, thinking, *The red men won the war . . . thanks to us.*

*   *   *

All the "Road Chiefs" were men, as were not only all the doctors, but all the nurses. During her first week in the hospital Kate glimpsed only one woman, and her briefly and at a distance. The woman was on her knees around midnight, scrubbing the floor at the far end of a corridor.

Most of the time Kate was alone in her room. She assumed other women were in the other rooms, but she never saw them. When she was able, Kate got up and tried her door, and was not surprised to find it locked.

At intervals through the day and night male nurses came in to see to her needs, but they never spoke to her.

Every afternoon one of the nurses would come with a wheelchair to take her out to the sunporch, saying nothing to her, only silently gesturing.

On the sunporch William, also in a wheelchair, would be waiting for her, in the company of Aztlan. Aztlan addressed most of his remarks to William and, though he never said so in so many words, she got the impression that he did not like to speak to women. From his conversation with William, however, she soon pieced together a picture of the situation.

She and William were the only white people in the hospital. Here, as everywhere else in the world, the red men ruled. The hospital stood on a hill in the south of Gallica (or France as it would have been called in the home universe) near the Mediterranean Sea, so sunny days were many, and the afternoon discussions interesting, in spite of Aztlan's apparent rudeness. Aztlan never left them alone, so to speak together at all they had to resort to speaking English, and Aztlan never allowed them to do that for long. Still, on the third day the Blakes were able to pass the following remarks back and forth.

Kate said, "We aren't carrying . . . plague any more, are we?"

William answered, "I don't think so."

"Then why don't we leave?"

"Where would we go?"

"I don't know, Mr. Blake."

At that point Aztlan interrupted and began to talk again,

always more to William than to Kate, and Kate decided that, indeed, there was no particular time or place she would rather go to than these peaceful sunny afternoons of lazy conversation, always in the language of Albion.

One afternoon, as William and Kate lay in deckchairs clad in bathrobes and sunglasses and Aztlan sat on a stool facing them, William asked him, "Can the nurses and doctors speak the language of Albion?"

Aztlan smiled, teeth very white against dark skin. "Of course. It is the only language all the thousand tribes of Oothoon have in common. Most of us speak two languages: the historic tongue of our ancestors, and the tongue of our former white rulers."

"Then why don't they speak to us?"

Aztlan sighed. "How can I explain? Partly it is guilt. No winner is ever free of guilt. Partly it is resentment. The older ones remember how you treated us before the war, how you ruled us with an all-too-heavy hand." He addressed the Blakes, as he had done often before, as if they represented the entire white race.

William pressed him. "Sometimes they seem afraid of us."

"Afraid?" Aztlan smiled stiffly. "Yes, some of them may fear you, the more uneducated and superstitious of them. You are, to them . . ." He paused, searching for a word. ". . . holy."

"Holy?"

The redman nodded, leaning forward, elbows on knees. "Our religion teaches us that white is the skin color of the gods. That is why the red man was so long content to bow under the white man's domination. Our scripture foretold your coming to Oothoon, foretold that we would be your servants for a while, learning from you until we became your equals, then, when you destroyed yourselves, the scripture foretold that we would inherit the world. All has happened as our god Quetzalcoatl promised." He lowered his voice in reverence as he spoke his deity's name. "And perhaps some of us fear you simply because we have never seen a white man before."

William said uneasily, "I know there are no other whites in this hospital, but somewhere else . . ."

Aztlan shook his head slowly. "No."

"Not even in Oothoon?"

"No. Your race is almost extinct. A few of you survive in the priestly orders. Indeed your skin color could help you attain high rank there, but of all your millions who once swarmed the earth there remain around twenty or twenty-five individuals at most. Twelve of them inhabit a little village on the east coast of Oothoon where they keep alive the ancient folkways of their nations for the benefit of tourists. Perhaps, when you regain your health, you will go there and live with them."

Kate shuddered. "I don't think I'd fancy that."

Aztlan ignored her and addressed William. "They would welcome you, you and your squaw."

"I don't think . . ." William began.

"Then you must study for the priesthood."

"That doesn't much appeal to me, either. I've never loved priests . . ." William glanced doubtfully at Kate.

"There is no third choice," said the Road Chief with great dignity.

After a long silence William said, "Then we shall study."

Lapsing into English, Kate sprang to her feet. "We shall not! You're a Christian gentleman, Mr. Blake, and don't you forget it." Even as she spoke she realized that she, too, had compromised in a similar situation, when she had reluctantly served Isis. What did that word "Christian" mean, here where Christ had never been born? Yet always the thoughts came to her unbidden of the church she'd been married in, that she'd faithfully attended as a child, that she would attend still if she could.

Aztlan gave her a pained look, then said to William, "Can't you restrain her? These unseemly outbursts . . ."

William said, "She and I come from another world."

"The white man's world. Of course. But even there . . ." He drew himself up. "The Isis heresy is dead, sir. Bid your squaw keep silent when men are conversing."

William continued doggedly. "We come from a world

where neither Isis nor Quetzalcoatl has even one worshipper, a world where history turned out differently, where . . ."

Aztlan interrupted. "Impossible! History could not turn out differently. Everything that happens reflects the will of Quetzalcoatl, all events he has planned from before the beginning of time. He created the world, and he created the red men to rule it, and he wrote our holy scripture to show us our future, to ready us for our role as his chosen people!" At this point the Road Chief realized he had raised his voice. Speaking more calmly, he added, "But you will learn all this when you study for the priesthood."

"No, thank you just the same," said William. "On second thought the tourist business sounds more promising."

Aztlan looked at him with pity. "Still clinging to your superstitious faith in Isis?"

William said coldly, "I never did believe in Isis. Isis isn't the real God."

The redman nodded agreement. "Of course not. A real god is someone you can see, like Quetzalcoatl."

William raised an eyebrow. "You can *see* Quetzalcoatl?"

The redman stood up. "Of course. But now I must go and begin the process of deportation. Tomorrow or the day after you and your squaw will be on your way to the white reservation in Oothoon."

Kate stared in wonderment at the little man's retreating back. What did he mean when he said he could see Quetzalcoatl? She thought of things she'd heard about that god in the home universe, things about human sacrifice, about hearts cut out of living bodies.

What if, in this world, Quetzalcoatl was somehow *real*?

The jet transport made the transatlantic flight during the night. At dawn the coast of Oothoon appeared on the horizon, at first only an irregular dark line hardly distinguishable from the gray cloudbank behind it, then, as the sky grew brighter, Oothoon became unquestionably land. Kate stared at it with weary, sleepless eyes through the oval plastic window, brooding, chin in hand.

Next to her, his seat tilted back, William slept fitfully, occasionally snoring. In the aisle seat, quietly alert, sat their guard, a muscular dark young man with a name Kate had been unable to pronounce, let alone remember. Kate had nodded off from time to time during the night, but whenever she had awakened, the man's glittering black eyes had been on her.

He wore fringed leather pants and a fringed leather jacket, both decorated by small tasteful patches of bright-colored beadwork, and high-heeled boots polished to a slick, waxy finish, as if covered with a thin layer of glass. At his belt hung a holster containing a very large pistol.

She leaned over the sleeping William to whisper, "How long before we land?"

The red man did not reply.

After a moment she demanded, "Why don't you answer?"

He said reasonably, "Because I do not know the answer."

She settled back in her seat. Yes, she'd noticed that before. If these red men did not have an answer to a question, they did not say, "I don't know." They simply said nothing at all. Somehow little things like this, which were only natural mannerisms and not meant to offend, disconcerted her more than anything about the red men, more even than their calling her a "squaw," more even than their habit of talking to William and not to her. Indeed, in this respect the red men were comfortably similar to the normal Englishmen of her home universe.

She resumed her study of the approaching coastline, and soon made out the shape of a broad flat island bounded on two sides by rivers and stretching far out to sea. It was covered with tall, rectangular buildings, all glassed in on the side facing the south and windowless on the northern wall. Even in their architecture the red men worshiped the sun, never losing their sense of relationship to nature in the most gigantic structures. As she drew closer still she saw the buildings were interspersed with broad green parks and here and there a lake too regular in shape to be natural.

The plane banked steeply and began to descend.

The warning light snapped on. Kate shook William

awake and began putting on her safety belt. The other passengers stirred too, making ready to disembark.

Stewards, maintaining their balance with ease in the steeply tilting aircraft, made their way up and down the aisles, helping those who had difficulty with their buckles, murmuring encouragements to those who showed signs of uneasiness.

The aircraft swung back out to sea, but not before Kate got a good look at the suburbs, endless patterns of homes partially hidden by trees and connected by elevated railways. The plane banked again, dropping so low she could see the white crests of the waves, then its shadow came rushing up to meet it and it touched down on the runway with a squeal of tires.

As they taxied toward the hangars and administration building, the guard unsmilingly inspected his pistol and, finding it in good order, returned it to its holster.

He did not need to speak. Kate understood him perfectly.

A transparent-canopied monorail, magnetically suspended and propelled at speeds that made the passing trees and buildings blend into a nervous blur, carried the Blakes and their ever-watchful guard away from the metropolis, then away from the suburbs. They had boarded without paying any fare; the guard, when William had questioned him, had informed them that public transportation was free.

By noon they were hurtling past farms, then pine forests, curving upward through the foothills of a distant mountain range. The stops became fewer and and farther between, the landscape wilder, with hardly a trace of human habitation.

"Where are we going?" William asked the guard.

"Whitestown," the man replied without emotion.

The train glided gently to a stop.

"Here's where we get off," said the guard. He carefully followed them as they stepped off onto the railway platform. The sun was brighter than she had expected, and she had to shield her eyes with her hand. Apparently the train's canopy had been unobtrusively filtering out the worst of the glare. With a whispering rush the train departed and snaked off to lose itself behind a clump of pines.

The platform was wood. It echoed hollowly under their footsteps. The nearby buildings were wood, too. In fact everything seemed to be wooden, and rather crude at that, hardly more than log cabins.

A somewhat undisciplined squad of uniformed red men stood waiting for them next to what Kate took to be the railroad station.

"Here they are," said the guard.

"We'll take them from here," answered the leader of the squad.

The guard walked away, apparently to wait for a train back to the city.

The leader introduced himself. "I am Wynono of the Bureau of White Affairs. On behalf of the government and people of the United Tribes of Oothoon let me welcome you to Whitestown. I'm sure you'll be happy here among your own kind, but if you should have any complaints you can take it up with your mayor, Jane Wentworth, or, if she fails to give you satisfaction, you can always appeal directly to me. As you can see, we attempt to preserve here the ancient folkways of the white race, even to the extent of allowing, within the boundaries of the reservation, the worship of your goddess Isis. In fact we actually encourage it, since it brings in much-needed tourist trade from all over Oothoon. People come from as far away as the west coast just to watch your religious services and take pictures."

William answered, "My name is William Blake and this is my wife Catherine." He extended his hand, but the red man only stared at it with distaste.

"You are provided with room and board at government expense, plus a small weekly allowance you can spend however you please," Wynono continued. "Here in the station building we have a general store that supplies all sort of luxuries, reasonably priced. Radios. Television sets. That sort of thing. And it also serves as an outlet for white handicrafts which the tourists buy as souvenirs.

Now, William, if you'll go along with my friend the doctor, there's a little formality. . . .''

"I'll be right back," William told Kate reassuringly as he stepped forward to meet a small dark man in white coveralls. Kate watched the two of them walk off toward a nearby building that looked somewhat more modern than the rest.

Wynono turned his attention to Kate. "And now, Mrs. Blake, do you by any chance know any songs?"

"Songs, Mr. Wynono?"

"Yes, hymns to Isis, old folktunes, white popular songs, that sort of thing. A researcher from the Bureau of Anthropology lives here, sharing your life patterns almost as if he were a white. If you know any songs or can recite any poems or stories, he'll want to make some recordings of you. Someday some student of history may want to know what the white race was really like." To Kate he seemed to regard the white race as already dead and in danger of being totally forgotten. She recoiled from the thought. Could an entire branch of the human family actually become extinct?

"I think I know a few," she said uncertainly. "Hymns . . . but not to Isis."

"They have to be to Isis. Otherwise they wouldn't be accepted as authentic."

"I'm sorry. I don't know any others."

"Well, sing them anyway. The anthropologist will fit them in somehow." An older man, balding and somewhat overweight, stepped forward, thrusting a microphone into her face.

"Not now," Kate objected.

"Let her alone," said Wynono.

"I want to get at least a sample before she talks to the others. They could teach her things and I wouldn't get a pure . . .''

The men fell to arguing while Kate looked first at them, then at the building where William had gone. After a while the door of the building opened and William emerged, looking pale, followed by the doctor.

Wynono said cheerfully, "Now you can go and join the

other whites.'' He gestured toward a large log cabin set back among the pines. "I think they'll still have some lunch for you."

Kate and William left the red men and walked toward the cabin.

"What happened to you?" Kate whispered, though there was nobody but William within earshot.

"A little operation," William answered offhandedly.

"An operation?" Kate was horrified.

"It's called a vasectomy. It keeps me from fathering any children. They don't want us whites propagating, you know."

"You can't have any children?"

"No."

"Mr. Blake, how could you let them do that to you? And why didn't you discuss it with me?"

He frowned. "I don't see any harm in it. Actually, it's a relief. There's one thing at least that we won't have to worry about."

"But you can still . . . make love? Like a natural man?"

"Oh yes. There will be some swelling for a few days around my groin, but an icebag will keep it down. After that you won't be able to tell the difference."

But she thought, *If you do make love to me, William, I will know the difference. If you do make love to me after all these years.*

The Blakes pulled open a screen door and let it bang shut behind them.

The mess hall, for that was what it was, seemed made for a great deal larger group than actually inhabited it. Most of the tables stood empty except for two of them at the opposite end of the long rectangular room, and there a small cluster of men and women, all white, turned to glare at the newcomers.

"Mr. Wynono told us to come here," William announced lamely.

The whites were, Kate realized, all old. Not a one of them could have been under sixty.

"We're Mr. and Mrs. Blake," said Kate.

A fat, gray-haired woman in the white robes of a nun of Isis separated herself from the group and shuffled forward, squinting in the sunlight that streamed in from the door behind the Blakes to illuminate a portion of the dark and gloomy interior.

"I'm Mayor Jane Wentworth," said the woman. "You're white?"

"Yes," said William nervously.

"Really white?"

"Yes," he said.

She reached out to touch his arm as if she couldn't believe her eyes. "You are. Yes, you are. And you're young. You could have children. . . ."

"No, I'm sorry," said William.

"They had you fixed?" Her tone had turned angry.

"Yes," he said.

"The redskinned bastards," the mayor muttered, turning away. "Then there's no hope. No hope for us at all. When we die, that's the end, and we won't last long. Without hope, you don't last long." She had her back to the Blakes and was waddling back to her friends.

William called out, "Can we have something to eat, Mrs. Wentworth?"

Not looking at them, the mayor replied, "Help yourselves to whatever is left in the pot, and if there's nothing there, you can contain your soul in patience until suppertime."

William and Kate did as she told them, and did indeed find a little stew at the bottom of the pot on a nearby table. When they had finished they saw that Mrs. Wentworth was about to deal a hand of cards.

"Can we join you?" Kate asked.

"Well, we have enough people for cards already."

"We could clean up," said William. "Wash dishes, sweep . . ."

"The government man will do that," said the woman.

"I understand you make handicrafts for the tourists," said Kate. "We could help with that."

Mrs. Wentworth sniffed. "We don't make things any

more. We just sell them. They're mass-produced in Japan much cheaper than we could make them ourselves.''

"What do you do, then?" Kate demanded.

"Nothing," came the answer, and Mrs. Wentworth dealt the cards.

I don't think I'm going to like it here, thought Kate bleakly. Then William took her hand and she glanced at him, surprised. He looked at her with a warmth she had not seen before. She thought, *Or maybe I will.*

William spent the rest of the week in his bunk in the communal bunkhouse. Many cabins stood vacant around the bunkhouse, but the little colony preferred to huddle together where, if one of them had a medical emergency, the others would be able to help or to summon Mr. Wynono. The swelling in William's groin never did become more than a nuisance, and soon Kate was able to break through some of the reserve of the other colonists and engage all but the sullen mayor in conversation.

With one little old lady Kate discussed the mayor.

"Is Mrs. Wentworth really a missis?" Kate asked. "I mean, is she really married?"

"I don't know," was the hesitant reply. "Whites don't always exactly get married. They sort of just pair off."

"But she wears the robe of a nun. Can a nun get married?"

"I don't know if she's really a nun. She does act the part for the tourists. It's just for the tourists, you know."

"For the tourists? Doesn't she believe in Isis?"

"Nobody really believes in Isis. I mean, if Isis was a real goddess, we would have won the war. Isn't that so?"

"I don't see the logic of that."

"Besides, Isis isn't real. Quetzalcoatl is real."

"How do you mean?"

"I've seen him with my own eyes."

"Where?"

"On television," said the little old lady, as if speaking to an idiot child. "You'll see him, too."

"I will?" Kate was more baffled than ever. "When?"

"When he has his next special."

The woman had become so convinced of Kate's stupidity that she didn't dare question her further, but she did tactfully raise the subject of Quetzalcoatl's reality with some of the others. All had, they claimed, seen the deity at one time or another on television, and one claimed to have seen him in the flesh, in a parade.

On Sunday morning the woman stopped Kate on the way to breakfast and said offhandedly, "You can see Quetzalcoatl tonight."

"On television?" Kate asked.

"Of course. Did you think he'd waste his time visiting the likes of us in person?"

"I suppose not."

"We'll all gather in the mess hall to watch it together. Mrs. Wentworth is having the big screen set up. I envy you in a way, if you really haven't ever seen the Quetzalcoatl Specials before."

"I haven't. They didn't show them where I came from."

The woman looked at her oddly. "A very strange place you must have come from." Then she shrugged and went on. "To see the Quetzalcoatl Special for the first time! Yes, I do envy you. You must be excited! He'll have singers, dancers, clowns . . . the biggest stars."

"I wouldn't miss it for anything."

"Tonight at eight-thirty. Don't be late! You wouldn't want to miss a minute of it. I really envy you."

"Yes, yes, I know. I won't be late."

As the woman walked away, Kate turned to William and said, "What do you think of that?"

He stood, arms crossed and head cocked to one side, his face unreadable. "I have my suspicions."

"Tell me! Tell me!"

"No, it's just a hunch. We'll see."

And she could get nothing more out of him, though she needled him again and again through the day. She had always hated the way he kept his thoughts to himself, so that after all these years he still seemed almost a stranger to her. She would far rather have listened to the most outrageous nonsense, or have endured the most violent argument, than have him always keep his secrets.

In the afternoon the sun shone out of a cloudless sky, and she took him for a walk in the forest, along the monorail track. As they trudged along, they heard animals moving in the underbrush, but except for a circling hawk, they didn't see any. She said wistfully, "We could leave."

"Yes, I don't think anyone would stop us from boarding the train, but where would we go?"

"We don't need trains, Mr. Blake."

"No, I suppose not." He nodded moodily. "But the same question still stands. Where would we go?"

"Uptime, downtime, back to Albion. We're immune to the plague now, you know."

"I want to stay just a little longer. I want to see the Quetzalcoatl Special."

"What difference can it make?"

"Perhaps none, perhaps a great deal. We may have to make a few more changes in history."

Kate drew back in alarm. "No, Mr. Blake! Haven't you had enough of that?"

He looked at her sadly. "The only way we can avoid changing history is to avoid time-voyaging. Whenever we make a jump, we change things, like it or not. Some changes are bigger than others, that's all."

"We don't have to wait for tonight at least. That's such a little jump. The others will simply think we've been walking all afternoon."

"Even a little jump . . . oh all right." They joined hands.

Suddenly it was evening, and they were walking toward the mess hall. They had scarcely glimpsed the place outside of time. As they entered the hall Mrs. Wentworth greeted them out of the gloom with, "Well, you two missed supper." She seemed to take some sort of obscure satisfaction in this, as if she had caught them in a particularly embarrassing breach of etiquette. The television set on the front table hummed and crackled as an image formed. The little group of old people fell silent, eyes on the screen.

William inquired in a low voice, "Mrs. Wentworth, is Quetzalcoatl white?"

She answered him crossly, "Just as was foretold in the Aztec scriptures. Everyone knows that."

He persisted, "And does he have long white hair and a long white beard?"

"Yes, he does, just as the scriptures describe."

The television camera tilted skyward, as if searching for something. The announcer spoke, voice over. "And here he comes, the god you've all been waiting for, the omnipotent, omniscient, just and loving father of us all. Yes, here he comes, ladies and gentlemen. Look, up in the sky! Here's . . . *Quetzalcoatl!*"

A winged figure circled downward out of the blue, naked and muscular, and with a showy thrashing of wings, alighted in front of the camera while a symphony orchestra, playing in the background, was almost drowned out by the thunderous applause. The figure raised his hand and the crowd fell silent.

"Blessings on you all, my children," said Urizen.

William grasped Kate roughly by the hand and whispered, "Come along, Mrs. Blake. It's just as I feared. We've got work to do downtime."

Nobody noticed the Blakes slipping out quietly through the screen door, closing it carefully behind them, and tiptoeing down the front steps into the twilight. All eyes remained on the screen, as if everyone were hypnotized, as perhaps they were. Kate glanced around at the peaceful forest and wished for a moment that, in spite of everything, she could stay here. She felt suddenly so very tired, so weary of change, even change for the better.

But William tugged at her hand and said, "Now, Mrs. Blake."

She let him tow her into the swirling vortex, closing her eyes to avoid seeing the stream of howling phantoms that rushed by them.

"Awake, O Bacchus, immortal God of Wine," Cleopatra called from the entrance to Antony's tent.

Antony groaned but remained sprawled face down on the bunk, one arm dangling to the dirt floor, his nude,

hairy body more that of an aging wrestler than of a poten-
tial god-emperor of the known world.

She sniffed. The air in the tent stank of vomit and stale
spilled wine. She stepped inside, letting the tentflap fall
shut behind her, plunging the interior into darkness. "Wake
up, Antony darling. Battle time."

He rolled over onto his back, eyes still closed. "Leave
me alone, bitch," he mumbled thickly.

"Antony dear, the enemy awaits."

"Let'um wait."

"Someone has to lead your fleet into battle, darling."

"You lead it."

"Antony!" she shouted, but he had slipped back into
unconsciousness.

She stepped forward to shake him, but though she was
so rough she almost dragged him out of his bunk, his only
answer was the beginning of a ragged snore. Panting, she
stood up very straight and considered the situation a moment before turning on her heel and, muttering obscenities, pushing her way out through the tentflap into the dim,
predawn light.

A young bearded soldier in armor, tunic, helmet, and
cloak snapped to attention, thumped his breast with his
fist, and gave her a straight-arm salute. She knew the man,
a native Egyptian with a dark African skin, one of Antony's
trusted freedmen. It was this lowborn fool who passed on
Antony's commands to the army.

The soldier's crisp voice interrupted her speculations.
"Is the general awake, Your Majesty?"

"More or less."

"Does he have any orders for us, Your Majesty?"

"Yes . . . as a matter of fact." An ironic smile played
across her lips. "He ordered that he be carried in his cot
on board his flagship."

"Carried, Your Majesty?"

"You heard me, soldier. Then he told me to tell you,
you must sail out and engage the enemy." *That will be a
sobering experience,* she thought with malice, *to wake up
in the middle of a sea battle . . . with a hangover.*

"Is that all, Your Majesty?" The soldier had turned quite pale.

"One thing more. When I asked him who would lead the fleet into battle, he confidently placed the responsibility in my hands."

"But . . ."

"But I'm a mere woman? My own Egyptian troops would not question that, as you well know, but of course the Romans have their blustering masculine pride. Very well, I shall give the commands and you will pass them on, but as far as the troops know, Antony, the great general Antony, has spoken. Do you understand?"

He hesitated, then murmured, "Yes, Your Majesty."

"Dismissed!"

He again thumped his breastplate, gave her a straight arm salute, then hurried off to do her bidding.

She strode through the camp, so deep in thought she hardly saw the soldiers who leaped to attention and saluted her. She squinted at the sky, thinking, *A beautiful clear morning, fine weather for a battle*. Octavian's fleet, she knew, waited out beyond the mouth of the channel. Octavian had lighter ships than hers, faster and more maneuverable, and better-trained, more seasoned troops, the cream of the Roman legions. She had Antony's Romans, but also a mixed bag of slaves and freedmen, Egyptian palace guards, the private armies of various allied minor kings, and a scraggly mob of local peasants pressed into service. Nevertheless, she calculated, she could win.

She must at all costs avoid hand-to-hand combat, where Octavian's legionaries would butcher her irregulars, and instead ram his fleet head-on when, as it always did, the wind picked up around noon, blowing his ships so they'd bunch up and show their vulnerable sides to her. Her stronger heavier ships would smash his light ones to splinters!

Antony, as usual, had laid his camp out in a perfect square, his own tent exactly at the center where the two main roads crossed at right angles. She had set her own camp, somewhat smaller but equally square, a little apart, with its own log walls and its own embankments and trenches. To reach it, she had to pass briefly through a grove of pines that hid her from the view of the sentries from either camp.

It was here she had her vision.

Suddenly, so suddenly she leaped back with a gasp, there appeared before her a man and a woman floating through the air. The man, stocky and red-haired, wore a short tunic. The woman, slender and light brown-haired, wore a long white robe.

Kate spoke first, raising her hand so her sleeve hung down like a wing. "Cleopatra Ptolemy!" Her Greek had an accent Cleopatra had never heard before.

"We bring you a message," boomed William. His Greek was better.

"From whom?" Cleopatra demanded, standing her ground unafraid.

"From the gods!" William announced pompously.

The queen drew herself up proudly. "There are no gods save those within us! All others are theater."

She saw the flying man had not expected such an answer, not realizing perhaps that a Queen of Egypt would be schooled in philosophy and the secrets of nature by the wise teachers of the Alexandrian library, the most skeptical men on earth. He said uncertainly, "But you believe yourself to be the goddess Isis . . . ."

She smiled. "I do not believe, I know it, but I also know what a goddess is. Religion's too important to rest on mere belief!"

"But look!" The man sounded desperate. "We're flying!"

She laughed openly. "Mirrors! Wires! Back home in Alexandria we have magicians who can make an elephant seem to fly." Though her voice showed no trace of fear, her glance flicked nervously about. Was this a trap? Had Octavian sent assassins? Seeing no obvious danger, she took a step forward. "Speak and be gone! I have men to kill today."

"I can't . . ." He sounded flustered, frustrated.

The woman with him spoke to him in some unknown tongue. "Yes, Kate," he answered doubtfully.

"Well?" prompted the queen.

He said haltingly, "We've come to warn you."

"Warn me?" Her tone was almost pitying.

He had regained his composure and now spoke with a deep and somber voice. "The spirits of the dead gather here, my queen. They want you to rule the Western Land, to rule Amenti, Kingdom of the Dead."

Still she answered mockingly: "And you, I suppose, have come to offer me a crown?"

"Not a crown, my queen. A sword. And not now but later today, when the battle begins. I will come flying to you over the waves, and with me will be a woman in red robes and a man with a white beard. The man will offer you a sword, saying it is the sword of Octavian, but it is not! It is the Sword of Amenti, and if you accept it you will lead no more living men into battle, but only specters. Do not accept that sword, if you love life, but flee."

"Flee from a battle I expect to win? Impossible!"

"Then stay and die."

Cleopatra laughed again, this time with unconcealed contempt. "The gods did not send you. The dead did not send you. That sick weakling Octavian sent you!"

Kate spoke up then. "The dead sent us, and we can prove it." The two darted forward. Kate grasped Cleopatra's right wrist and William the left, quickly, giving the queen no chance to struggle.

"This is the proof," said William.

Suddenly Cleopatra saw the world she knew, the world of pines and brightening sky, vanish. Instead a cloud of moaning spirits swirled toward her out of a gray nothingness that had no up or down, images of the past and future appeared and faded, and everything seemed bathed in a fitful gray-green light that she seemed to see more with her mind than her eyes. She screamed as she fell through the nothingness, clutched at the wrists that held her wrists, and, at last, believed.

The soldier looked up from his work of supervising the loading of the ships to see Queen Cleopatra running toward him. He was surprised, so surprised he neglected to salute her. Cleopatra never ran, she strode, with queenly dignity, yet here she came, pale, panting, with her hair in wild disarray.

"Antony is loaded, Your Majesty," he blurted. "I mean . . . he's safely on board."

She half-sat on a barrel of water and, gasping for air, commanded, "Load . . . the sails and the rigging."

Taken aback, he answered with sweet reason, "But we need no sails in battle, only oars!"

"Fool!" she screeched, kicking him in the shins. "We make ready not to fight, but to flee!"

"Yes, Your Majesty. Whatever you say, Your Majesty."

With intense relief she watched the man carry out her orders. She knew that when the wind came, she would use it to escape Octavian. He, with his sails and rigging left behind on shore, out of the way of the battle, would never be able to catch her. She would change course and never even see that sword from Hell. What she did not know was that she would also change the course of history, swing it back to what it would have been if the sword had never been offered to her.

"We threw a scare into her, didn't we?" Kate exclaimed delightedly as she and William drifted through the gray-green place outside of time, watching the wave of change rushing on into the future, making everything once again "the way it ought to be."

As the wave moved off into the infinite distances, the clouds of ghosts faded, except for one figure that floated toward them.

"Robert!" called William.

"William," answered his brother.

"What happened to all the spirits?" William asked him. "I saw multitudes of them when the missis and I came back from that future where the red men ruled the world. Now where have they gone?"

"To be born," answered the transparent Robert.

"But couldn't they be born before?"

"You changed things," said the spirit. "The bodies meant for them were not brought into being."

William protested, "Not the same bodies perhaps, but

there were bodies in the red man's world, and in Vala's world. Who was . . . wearing them?''

Robert shifted uneasily. "Other spirits, spirits never intended for human form. When Urizen diverts the timestream, these unhuman things seize the opportunity to invade the human universe, to take on human form. Thank God you two managed to return the timestream to its proper channel.''

"So all's well now?'' William asked hopefully.

Robert shook his head. "Urizen, as you well know, will not give up so easily. He'll try again, I'm sure, to make some universe he can rule, in which he can realize his dream of false perfection. Next time he may go farther back in time to make his change, draw more of the unhuman beings into the human universe. The other Zoas no longer restrain him or correct his changes. No one can stop him but you two now.''

"But you'll help us, Robert,'' Kate put in hopefully.

"I can do so little,'' the spirit sighed. "I have no physical body, but I can warn you when Urizen makes a change. We spirits know it here in the place outside of time before the chain of cause and effect reaches you within the timestream. We can see his changes coming, like a line of falling dominoes.''

"Warn us then, Robert,'' said William seriously. "Promise to warn us.''

"I promise,'' said Robert, fading away.

Kate said, "And we, Robert, promise to do what we can.''

Albion was gone, and Oothoon was gone, and Lud's Dun.

Instead it was 1791 in Lambeth, across the Thames from metropolitan London, the evening of the day Kate had left in search of William. The sky was still clear, the moon and stars plainly visible.

Kate stood at her back door and gazed into her garden, contemplating the familiar wild untrimmed grapevines, the tall poplar trees.

She murmured, "When everything else changed, my garden stayed the same."

William lightly slipped his arm around her shoulders. "There could be other changes, changes that even your garden, though it is uncommonly hardy, could not resist," he said grimly.

"Don't say that, Mr. Blake!"

"Why not? It's the truth."

She sighed. Of course he was right. The garden seemed so alive, so eternal, so indestructible, but there was an infinite number of ways it could be changed or utterly obliterated. The birds she heard could cease to sing. The aroma of her plants and flowers could turn to poisonous fumes. The cool night breeze could change to the airlessness of outer space. Impulsively she reached out to caress the moist surface of a dewy grape leaf.

Softly, so softly not even William could hear, she said three words. "While we may."

Then she took William by the hand and led him into the garden.

Robert, drifting in the place outside of time, could see the years 1791, 1792, 1793, and 1794 all at once, in a single glance . . . peaceful years, almost uneventful. He turned his spectral head, looked downtime.

So distant he could hardly see it, a wave of change appeared, rushing toward him, a wave of change more profound than Robert had believed possible.

"I must warn William!" cried the spirit, wheeling and darting toward 1794.

7

THE PRECEDING YEAR WILLIAM BLAKE had printed and distributed among his friends and neighbors the following curious document:

Prospectus, to the Public.
The labors of the artist, the poet, the musician, have been proverbially attended by poverty and obscurity. This was never the fault of the public, but was owing to a neglect of means to propagate such works as wholly absorbed the Man of Genius. Even Milton and Shakespeare could not publish their own works.

The "Prospectus" went on to tell how William had invented a process for overcoming this problem, and ended by stating, "I have been able to bring before the public works (I am not afraid to say) of equal magnitude and consequence with the productions of any age or country."

There followed a list of eight illuminated books and two historical engravings.

In Blake's coterie all eyes were upon the recent books by other members of the Johnson group: Mary Wollstonecraft's feminist *Vindication of the Rights of Woman* had aroused a storm of controversy, and now it was joined by William Godwin's anarchist *Political Justice* as a subject for scandal and argument, not only in London, but throughout the world. With the execution of Louis XVI and the declaration of war between England and France, the pros and cons of freedom became the only topic deemed worthy of polite or impolite conversation, and thus nobody, except the faithful Thomas Butts, paid the slightest attention to William's venture into self-publication.

All the time, William spent most of his time after the announcement working on the promised books which, when completed, bore such titles as *The First Book of Urizen, Visions of the Daughters of Albion*, and *America, A Prophecy*. He prepared, but did not print even one copy of *The Book of Vala*. Kate, on seeing the title, had asked him, "When will you write a *Book of Kate*?"

He hastily changed the title to *The Four Zoas* but then lost interest in it.

The books, tiny things, displayed on every page images from William's adventures as a time-voyager through alternative worlds, and recounted tales from those worlds, all in poetry.

The public ignored them.

Since Thomas Butts was his only customer, William began to cheerfully refer to him as "my employer."

Kate cut the engravings that put food on the table. Though some of the publishers began to suspect who the real artist was, as her style, against her will, began to take on a character quite distinct from the stiff formal style of her husband, they did no more than exchange winks when she delivered, always before the deadline, her unsigned masterpieces of commercial art. She specialized in sentimental glimpses of children at play; though she had no children of her own, her engravings, by their lifelike rendering, moved many a matron to tears.

She worked in the same room with William, sharing his tools, but with an altogether different method. He worked very slowly, sometimes copying or tracing things line for line from other artists' work. (DaVinci supplied the model for many of his designs.) His slogan was "The Bad Artist seems to copy a great deal: the Good Artist really does."

She, on the other hand, pressed by financial considerations, worked with harrowing speed, without preliminary sketches, finishing a plate in a single evening in a clean, uncluttered style that omitted the fine detail that darkened the pictures of her competitors, implying things rather than stating them. (They might well take a week on a similar assignment.)

Sometimes, as she worked, she broke her intense concentration long enough to look up and see William staring moodily at her, but she would pause to throw him a smile and instantly return to her task. She loved her home and her garden and could not by any means keep them on what he got from poor old Butts.

William had resumed the habit of reading aloud to her after supper, but he no longer sang. His writing had become too long-winded and heavy to be set to music. Though she knew who Urizen, Vala, and the Daughters of Albion were, she often could not understand what he was talking about, and so couldn't help but wonder how the general public could ever figure it out.

She liked one of his verses, part of his *Songs of Experience*.

The Tiger

Tiger, tiger, burning bright
In the forests of the night,
What immortal hand or eye
Could frame thy fearful symmetry?

In what distant deeps or skies
Burnt the fire of thine eyes?
On what wings did he aspire?
What the hand dare seize the fire?

And what shoulder and what art
Could twist the sinews of thy heart?
And, when thy heart began to beat
What dread hand forged thy dread feet?

What the hammer? What the chain?
In what furnace was thy brain?
What the anvil? What dread grasp
Dare its deadly terrors clasp?

When the stars threw down their spears
And watered heaven with their tears,
Did He smile His work to see?
Did He who made the Lamb make thee?

When she first heard it, she remarked, "Very pretty, Mr. Blake. I like to see you getting back to animal poems. Much more wholesome!"

He glared at her across the kitchen table, his large eyes glowing in the candlelight. "Animal poems?"

"Did I offend you, Mr. Genius? Seems to me I hear an animal or two in there somewhere." She went on sharpening her graver on a small oilstone.

"The tiger is Urizen! I want to show how Urizen must have come from some other universe, how he must have been created by some other god."

"There's just one God. You know that, I hope."

"For this universe perhaps, but . . ."

"For any universe. I've come to think He may wear a different face someplace else, even a woman's face, but He's the same old God for all that. I take the poem in a different way, I do. I don't see no Urizen in it at all. I see this beautiful tiger, walking proudly along in the jungle moonlight, and someone says, 'Upon my word, that's a pretty kitty, a credit to his Maker.' "

"No, no, no!"

She shook her engraver at him. "You'll see. That's the way the public will read it too, if they ever look at it at all."

"Future ages will view it as I do," he growled, almost as if he were a tiger himself.

"Will future ages pay for it?"

She instantly regretted her words as she saw the pain in his face. *He's home,* she thought in a wave of guilt. *Am I going to drive him away again?*

They had done no more time-voyaging since returning from Actium. Robert spoke to them now and then, as they sat before the fire of an evening, but otherwise their lives had become quite normal, even—as William sometimes put it—"bovine."

William would say to him, "Robert, do you see any danger from Urizen?"

And his brother, a half-visible shadow in the glowing coals, would answer, "Not yet."

But the warning did come at last, in broad daylight, as Kate threw on her shawl to go out shopping. Robert appeared, smokelike, in the dust motes that drifted in a beam of sunlight from the window. His hissing windy voice seemed to come from far away, but with unmistakable urgency. "Get out of the timestream! Now!"

She grabbed William's wrist and together they leaped into the place outside of time.

And saw the wave of change—or did they feel it—rushing toward them out of the distant past.

Oh Lord, thought Kate, half-praying. *What now?*

Among the swirling clouds of faces, she could see some not human, some that were leering, lizardlike, and the screams of the multitude formed a monstrous discordant harmony, as if some mad organist had laid his arm from wrist to elbow upon the keys and would not let up.

The wave passed.

With a shared sigh of relief, the Blakes reentered the timestream at the same point they'd left it.

Kate's garden had vanished, along with her home. Instead she saw, looming over her, an immense silent building of dull green stone, its lines not straight and rectangular as in a normal structure, but disquietingly curvilinear; in fact she could not find one straight line in it. Even in the hot bright sunlight, it seemed oppressively dark and forbidding, as if the smooth stone somehow sucked in light, creating a halo of blackness around it.

William spoke softly. "Careful."

She had already begun to walk slowly around it. Alien as it seemed, it reminded her of something, some half-forgotten vision seen in the glowing coals of her fireplace. Into its walls were carved, in undulating lines, the characters of some unknown language, different from anything she'd seen before, yet irrationally, she felt she might be able to read it, if only she concentrated hard enough.

She came to a broad staircase which wound upward to a

round cavelike entrance near the top of the building. She knelt and touched the stone. How cold! It seemed to draw the warmth of life out of not only her hand but her whole body. Hastily she drew back and shook the hand to restore normal feeling. It had gone numb, as if frozen. The steps looked worn as if by centuries of use, and were high, disturbingly high, as if designed for creatures far taller than humans. With difficulty she managed to mount to the first step. She could feel the cold through the soles of her shoes, but it was not unbearable.

"Where is everyone?" she whispered, afraid to break the sepulchral stillness.

"I don't know, Mrs. Blake." He too spoke in a low voice.

He followed her up as, step by arduous step, she ascended. Halfway to the top, she paused to rest, turning to gaze out over the city.

The skyline still vaguely reminded her of London, and there, unchanged, wound the familiar River Thames, but the block after block of various-sized dull green structures stretching to the horizon were crafted according to some insane non-Euclidian geometry never meant for human understanding.

She whispered, "The streets, the buildings, everything is in curves."

"I noticed that."

"And I see no windows anywhere, no windows at all."

"And no people. I shouldn't wonder if everyone's asleep."

"Asleep?"

"Well, they wouldn't need windows, would they, if they slept all day and only came out at night?"

On that note he recommenced the climb, taking the lead, and she followed. At the head of the stairs they paused again, panting and sweating. No breath of wind stirred to relieve the moist heat of the air and give them relief, so she felt almost thankful for the unnatural coldness of the stone. The building had tapered inward, much narrower than at the base, and leveled off into an irregular platform around the dark doorless entrance.

She took William's hand and said, "Let's not go inside. Not yet."

William nodded.

They began to explore the platform, a moment later turning a corner and coming in sight of where they might have expected to discover downtown London.

Kate gasped, pointing. "Look!"

On the opposite bank of the Thames, dwarfing all other structures, stood a gigantic statue of Urizen.

"He did it again," William groaned, but then added, more cheerfully, "But he used my design. He must have liked it to go to all the trouble of including it in this reality."

She saw he had actually begun to smile; he smiled easily now, particularly when something tickled his vanity, but, Kate reflected, that vanity could prove to be a handle Urizen could grasp him by, as had happened before, and this frightened her more than even the strangeness of her surroundings. A man who could change sides once could change sides again! And then what would she do?

They continued around the platform until they arrived once again at the cavernous entrance. In all this time they had not seen a single sign of life or heard a single sound except their own footsteps and anxiously whispering voices, but now, as they stood before this opening that gaped from the building's head like the empty eyesocket of a blinded cyclops, they heard, from deep within, something stirring.

"Footsteps," Kat murmered.

"Yes, I think so," William confirmed.

They sprang silently back around the corner of the building and waited. The footsteps, unmistakable now, came closer, but she realized all too well they could not be human footsteps. Humans didn't have claws that clicked and scraped on the stone floor. Humans didn't—Good God, what was that sound?—have tails that slithered along with a faint frightful rustle. And humans . . . humans did not chat in birdlike chirps and sibilant hisses, or smell—Good God, that smell!—like decaying roses on some rainsoaked grave.

She peeped around the corner.

And saw them!

Two of them, twice as tall as men, emerged into the sunlight, heavy lids closing to protect huge, black, glistening reptilian eyes, gaunt clawed bejeweled fingers drawing heavy dark-green capes around brownish-green lizardlike bodies, broad fanged mouths grimacing in evident distaste for the light.

They paused, raising cowls to shield scaly heads, then continued on down the stairs, tails flicking nervously from side to side.

Kate watched the two in frozen fascination as, reaching the foot of the stairs, they bumped snouts and parted to stride with quick, delicate steps in opposite directions.

"Ugly things," muttered William, his normally ruddy features quite pale.

"I never liked reptiles," Kate answered absently.

"What will we do?"

"Go inside," she said, and seeing him hang back, she added, "Well, we have to learn what this is all about, don't we?"

They made their way into the shadowed interior.

Because her eyes took a second to adjust to the gloom, she almost tripped over a sleeping lizard. William caught her arm not a moment too soon.

"What's he doing here?" she demanded in a whisper, more indignant than frightened.

"Look at his cape," William answered. The cape was worn and dirty. "He's poor."

Kate glanced around, then said with surprise, "There's more of them!" Indeed the stone floor was strewn with sleeping lizards, all with worn and dirty capes wrapped around them.

An odd idea struck her. "The Daughters of Albion . . ."

"What? That was a different timestream."

"I mean, this is like the place they maintained for the outcasts of their world. We're in some sort of sanctuary, I wager. And this building is so much larger than the others in the neighborhood. Do you suppose it's a temple?"

William answered grimly, "I wouldn't be surprised. If

so, I hope we aren't trespassing on holy ground. Our scaly friends might take that badly."

The Blakes soon passed the last of the lizards and entered a high-ceilinged corridor that sloped gently downward. The walls curved inward slightly, lined with columns that, because of their subtle tapering, suggested ribs, as if they were proceeding deeper and deeper into the stomach of some gigantic beast. She could see it all only too clearly, thanks to a dim shadowless green glow from walls, ceiling, and even floor.

The cold increased steadily as they went, and a faint breeze blew in their faces, assaulting Kate's nostrils with occasional waves of lizard-scent, fetid and sickening. She almost wished she could see the beasts. That would have been better than knowing they were around, but not knowing where.

"Maybe we should turn back now," William suggested in an undertone.

Kate reassured him. "We're in no danger."

The passageway opened out into a cavern where both roof and floor were so distant they were lost in the gloom. A narrow stone bridge, without railings, spanned the gulf. (Here the stench grew all but unbearable.)

Kate, somewhat giddy from the height, crouched down on the bridge, holding her shawl over her nose, for all the good that did. Below, all along the walls of the chasm, she could make out dim white objects which she at first did not recognize.

Then she did.

"Mr. Blake," she whispered in horror.

He laid his hand on her shoulder. "I know, Kate. I can see them too."

Skulls. Bones. Rotting corpses.

She stood up and turned to him, clutching his reassuringly hard forearms, saying, "So . . . so many."

"I'd say these are just the few that got stuck on the way down. There's many more at the bottom, I wager."

"What are they?"

"Some sort of sacrificial victims, I'd guess."

"How inhuman!"

He smiled wryly. "No, I'd say it makes them more like human beings than I would have expected. Don't try to tell me our species hasn't done this sort of thing, and more than once in history, too."

Kate and William, as they crossed the bridge, were careful not to walk too near the edge.

Beyond the bridge they entered a narrow passage, made a sharp turn to the right and entered a vast arched room that reminded Kate irresistibly of the interior of some medieval cathedral. The light shone brighter here, thanks to what appeared to be an airshaft or skylight on the opposite end of the room, behind what could only be an altar.

Between her and the altar stretched a wide expanse of open floor, sloping downward, then a long, vaguely oblong or perhaps oval pool of water with steps leading down into it. On the other end of the pool the steps emerged again to lead up to a raised platform, almost a stage. Behind the stage, silhouetted against the sunlight that filtered down the airshaft, a huge lizard statue knelt, arms outstretched, reptilian head thrown back. Was the creature praying?

In front of the statue stood two chairs . . . or were they thrones? If they were thrones, then those must be jewels glittering in the chair arms and the high, ornately-carved back.

Though the thrones were in the shadow of the statue, Kate, shuffling forward in the semi-darkness, could see the suggestion of a figure sitting in one of them, the one on the left. The pool reflected the figure, the muscular body, the long white hair, the white beard.

"It's a statue of Urizen," she breathed.

Yes, it was Urizen all right, seated, motionless, elbow on knee and bearded chin on palm, in an attitude of deep thought.

After a moment William agreed. "Yes, I believe you're right."

Then the statue moved.

"No, William, she's wrong. I'm not a statue," said

Urizen, his mocking voice echoing in the huge empty room.

Urizen made no attempt to harm them, but only remained in his place on the throne on the other side of the pool, talking in a light, ironic, sometimes almost loving voice to them, trying, it would seem, to put them at their ease.

"Sorry I can't offer you a chair, my friends. My worshippers are generally content to stand in my presence. And there's always the factor of efficiency to consider. You may never have thought about this, but I think you can see one can crowd more than twice as many worshippers into a given area standing as you can sitting." Urizen leaned back, enjoying the comfort of his throne. "I have a place for you, William, right here by my side." He gestured toward the other throne.

"I've no use for thrones," William answered stiffly.

"Once you did. Admit it." Urizen's voice was full of scornful amusement.

"I made a mistake," said William.

"The mistake you made was turning against me," said Urizen. "Is it Christian to do evil to someone who does only good to you? I created a world for you and Vala and me to rule together, and now it's gone, thanks to you. Lud's Dun, Albion, Oothoon, Gallica. All gone." His tone had become quite somber, but now he brightened, actually chuckled. "I must say, though, that was clever, the way you handled Cleopatra. As your teacher I take as much pride in your victories as I do in my own, even if they're won at my expense."

"I hope you enjoy it when I put an end to this world, too." William indicated that room around him. Kate felt proud of him at last, more proud than ever before.

"Not this one," said Urizen confidently. "I have, as it were, put a lock on this one."

William was unimpressed. "I can still change it."

"You're welcome to try." The very blandness of the man's voice worried Kate.

She broke in. "Mr. Urizen, I don't understand you."

"But actually I'm such a simple fellow, under it all, Mrs. Blake."

"Are you now? Then give me a simple explanation of why you had to put this big heap of stone right on top of my garden."

Urizen stroked his beard. "I wanted to be where you would find me."

An idea had begun to form in Kate's mind, but it had not yet become clear, perhaps because it was a painful idea, perhaps because she didn't want to believe it. "I still don't understand, Mr. Urizen. You seem to take such a great interest in us, more interest than you do in all the billions of folk whose lives you snuff out in an instant. Why is that? Will you tell me?"

"Actually, my good lady, I'm not interested in you at all. It's your husband who engages my attention, but unfortunately you seem to come along with him. Once I bought a fine racehorse, but a lot of fleas come along with it. It's the same thing."

"Is it?" Kate was angry now. "And why, of all the men ever born on Earth, should William be so very special?"

"You don't want to know the answer to that, madam," Urizen said gently.

"We'd both like to know it!" William spoke up. "If you'll not leave me alone, at least tell me why!"

After a long pause, Urizen sighed deeply. Finally he said, "Yes, the time has come for truth. I see that only truth can end this foolish war between us." He regarded William gravely. "Look at me. Don't you recognize me?"

"No, but I've always thought you looked somehow familiar," said William, puzzled.

"Imagine me younger. Imagine me clean-shaven." Urizen stood up. "Imagine me with a weak, thin body."

Kate saw it first. "Urizen . . . you're William Godwin."

The naked man nodded slowly. "I used that name when I lived in London in the home universe, when I sat at table with you at the literary evenings at Joseph Johnson's, I championing reason while you championed madness. In my own subjective time that was centuries ago. I have learned the secrets of immortality uptime, the secrets of eternal health and more-than-human strength, and I had planned to teach these secrets to you, William, along with much else that you can hardly imagine now."

William said softly, "Yes, William Godwin, I recognize you now."

Kate said, keeping her voice steady with effort, "And Vala . . . she is Mary Wollstonecraft, just as she appears to be."

Urizen bowed slightly in her direction. "Of course."

But her husband still did not understand. "But that doesn't explain why you should be so interested in me."

Urizen smiled. "I think Mrs. Blake has guessed it all, but let me show you how it goes, step by step." He spoke as if to a retarded child.

"All right. . . ." His square features were knotted with bafflement.

Urizen went on. "I am William Godwin. Vala is Mary Wollstonecraft. Think, man, think! What is the relationship between Vala and me?"

"I don't know. . . ." William, thought Kate, could be so stupid at times. Vala herself had told him, long ago in Golgonooza.

"Vala is my mother," said Urizen, patiently.

"Your mother?" William echoed incredulously.

"Think, William." Urizen took a step forward. "If Vala is my mother and you are Vala's lover, what are you to me? It's simple logic, like mathematics. *You, William Blake, are my father!*"

The Blakes had sat for a long time together on the broad ovoid roof of Urizen's temple, gazing in silence out over the plains of fog below them that gleamed white under the full moon like banks of slowly undulating snow, staring at the only other structure tall enough to rise above the overcast, the statue of Urizen; now she turned toward William, studying his grim profile, his stocky body clad in rumpled kneepants, suitcoat, unbuttoned shirt, and buckled shoes. Who was this man? Who was this man she thought she knew so well? His shadowed face revealed nothing.

With a shudder she drew her shawl tight around her,

though the temperature was mild. Her first words were hesitant. "You could have told me."

"I didn't know." His voice, deep and resonant, was so much like Urizen's, yet she'd never noticed, like Urizen's but unlike the abrasive voice Urizen had had in his role as William Godwin, back in the home universe. The science that had changed Godwin into Urizen physically had changed his voice as well, and that had fooled her, though now the resemblance was obvious. The nose alone, so big and protuberant, told the tale.

"That Urizen was your son? How can that be?"

"When we were together, we never . . . we never . . ."

"You never made love?"

"No, never. She was already pregnant."

"You made her so, William, before, in the home universe, when she was Mary Wollstonecraft. You didn't connect Vala and Mary because you didn't want to. You didn't want to see what you'd done. The Bible puts a name to it. Adultery!"

William lowered his eyes, unable to meet her steady gaze. "Do you love me, Kate?"

She gave a broken little laugh. "Love you? Once I did indeed. Once I could look the facts in the eye and still say to myself, 'Mr. Blake ain't like other men. He's some kind of bloody saint who has risen above the Things of the Flesh,' as you put it."

"If you really loved me, you'd rejoice that I'd finally overcome my problem, that I'd at last been able to be a man. Why, if you loved me you'd pick out two women for me, a blond and a brunette, and sit on a riverbank out in the woods watching to see which one I'd take."

For a moment this image rendered her speechless, then, "Problem? Problem? What problem?"

He looked away, his voice so low and thick she had to lean toward him to understand what he said. "I don't know why it is, but I can't seem to be a man with a woman I really love. I can't be a man with a woman unless . . ." He seemed unable to go on.

Kate almost shrieked. "Tell me, for God's sake!"

" . . . unless *she's cruel to me*," he finished miserably.

As she heard it she knew it was the truth. It was another of those things one knows and does not know at the same time. She'd known and not known it from the very first, the day they'd met, when he'd talked of how Polly Wood tortured him, his wide madman's eyes gleaming, when he'd pleaded for pity. She'd known and not known it when he'd tormented and provoked her, trying to force her to torment him in return. She thought, *How can I condemn him for that? I knew what he was, but I married him anyway.*

He murmured sadly, "If you'd been a little harsher with me . . ."

She thought about that for a while, then said, "I am what I am. To be cruel to a man, to me own dear husband . . . that's not the way of a Christian lady." She had no anger left, only an overwhelming sense of relief, and a touch of guilt. She thought, *It's Polly he should have married. Polly would have made him a Hell where he'd feel right at home.*

"Well," he said uncertainly, "now it's all in the open, maybe I can change."

This time she refused to not know the truth. "No, you are what you are, too."

In the long silence that followed, an aircraft passed slowly overhead, leaving a white trail against the stars, so high it seemed to make no sound.

William said softly, "All the same, I am your friend."

Kate sighed and took his big hand in her little one. "I'm your friend, too, Mr. Blake. A good friendship's a rare thing, worth a dozen of the kind of marriages most folks have. How strange, though, that we can change everything in the universe but the one thing that matters . . . ourselves."

Later Kate and William went down into the temple to watch the ceremony where the lizard people worked themselves into a frenzy and hurled themselves off the bridge into the chasm. Kate listened to the shuffling and slithering of the dancing, the drumbeating, the chanting, and the ecstatic reptilian screaming, but her eyes never strayed from William's face. How his large eyes gleamed and his moist lips hung open as he followed with his gaze one after the other of the holy suicides. He looked somehow reptilian himself, and she clutched his thick arm firmly, on the chance he might, on impulse, leap off the bridge with the others.

Urizen, too, looked vaguely reptilian the following day as he strolled with the Blakes along the banks of what once, in a different reality, had been the Thames. The windowless buildings stood silent, looming over them on their left, under a swiftly moving gray overcast; the lizards, except for a few "day-watchmen," slept.

It puzzled Kate, that touch of green in his skin, that faint suggestion of scales, but perhaps it was a trick of the light. She stopped a moment to carefully inspect her reflection in the water. Long dark skirt; white blouse, shawl . . . and a disturbing greenish cast to her skin. Did she imagine it, or had her hands changed ever so little since yesterday, grown longer in the fingers, more clawlike?

William had been complaining about being Urizen's prisoner, but Kate had paid little attention until Urizen remarked, "On the contrary, my dear William, it is I who am your prisoner."

Kate picked up her skirts and ran a few steps to catch up with the men. "What do you mean, Mr. Urizen?"

"Simple," the bearded man replied with a smile. "You outnumber me two to one. Your combined energy fields could easily cancel mine out, if you both took hold of me at once. Why, you could, if you liked, snatch me out of the timestream, even kill me. Now is your chance, while Vala is away and can't help me."

Kate asked suspiciously, "Would that change everything back like it was?"

Urizen laughed. "Who can say? It would be an interesting experiment, of course, since it was I who, as it were, created this universe. Can the Creation continue without its Creator? I suspect it can. I doubt if killing me would change a thing. The world you see around you is the real world now, quite able to go on without me. To change it, you would have to go back in time, as you did when you frightened poor Cleopatra so! But now you would have to go back even farther to make things, as you might say, the way they're supposed to be. Frankly, I don't think you could do it."

"Why not?" William demanded.

Urizen bent over, picked up a smooth flat stone, and pitched it expertly out over the river; it skipped three times before sinking. "To make things they way they're supposed to be, you have to know how they're supposed to be. I'll give you a hint. Let us say I made my change before the dawn of history, before any era you've visited, so far in the past that science can only guess what conditions were like. I have had a chance to study the chain of cause and effect that produced the world as it was. You will not have that chance, since that chain no longer exists. You cannot bring back your old world, and you must not kill me, because I am the only person who can."

"Then do it, Mr. Urizen!" Kate reached out impulsively to touch his arm. "This isn't the perfect world you dreamed of, is it?"

Urizen frowned, but answered firmly. "Not yet."

"It never will be!" exclaimed Kate. "You dreamed of a world of human beings, not talking lizards!"

"Define your terms," Urizen snapped. "I say these so-called lizards are as human as you or I. So what if they have a different skin color . . ."

"They're not human inside, either," Kate said urgently. "Their spirits come from somewhere else, they're inhuman spirits . . . and while we live in this changed universe, they can enter our bodies, change us, absorb us."

"Nonsense," Urizen said, but with a trace of doubt in his voice at last. He forced a smile.

And Kate could have sworn his teeth had grown smaller since yesterday, and sharper.

She thought, *He won't ever admit that things are happening here he does not understand, that things are actually completely out of control!*

Kate studied her hand. The lengthening of the fingers was subtle but unmistakable.

"We must leave," she told William.

"Urizen expects us for supper. Vala is returning."

He sat on his cot in the room Urizen had given them in the temple, looking up at her like a pouting child. The glow from the torch stuck in the wall illuminated his squarecut features in a flickering light, glittered in his large eyes.

"Still," she insisted, "we must leave."

She could not help but notice that he seemed stupid, not like his old self. The lizards were stupid, she knew, in that same way. They could talk, but Urizen had given them all the science and technology they had. They never invented anything.

She coughed in the acrid smoke from the torch. Why didn't Urizen teach the beasts how to make lights: Gaslights if not electric? But they didn't like light, these nocturnal monsters.

For a moment she became stupid herself, her own mind vague and unfocused. She knew she must leave, but she'd forgotten why. It didn't matter why. She leaned over, grasped William's hand. How rough and dry it was! She dropped it with a shudder.

"Come," she pleaded. "Please."

He stared at her, eyes dull and mindless. She grasped his unresisting wrist and bounded into the place outside of time, dragging him along.

And found chaos!

Flocks of human ghosts and lizard ghosts swirled screaming around her, locked in desperate combat. As she glanced around, startled, she saw a battle raging as far as she could see in all directions. Impulsively she reached out her hand to try to help a passing human ghost, then remembered she could not touch these beings. Some passed right through her body with no more effect than a brief, sudden chill. The familiar gray-green shadowless light had been replaced by a dull glowering red, like a fire in her fireplace, and there was a hole in space . . . she knew not how else to describe it. There was sky, and in the middle of the sky a sort of jagged rip through which she could see another sky, different, redder. The rip grew steadily larger, and out of the other sky poured an endless stream of lizard ghosts.

The humans were putting up a valiant fight, but they were losing.

Can a ghost be killed? she wondered.

Perhaps not, but a ghost could be overpowered, if outnumbered. A ghost could be dragged away through the rip in space.

For an instant she caught a glimpse of a giant Kate and a giant William, seated in rocking chairs and gazing at her intently. *Am I in my own fireplace?* she thought wildly.

Robert swooped past, shouting, "Go downtime!" His voice wailed like the whistle of a passing train.

With her clouded mind she took an instant to understand, then she grasped William's arm with both her hands and drew him, a dead weight in her fingers, back toward the past.

The red light faded, the battle sounds died away. She could not see a single ghost, human or lizard. They had, she decided, all gone uptime to join in the battle.

Her mind rapidly cleared.

She could focus on the blurred images from the time-stream as they flashed by, see a tree growing backward and vanishing into the ground, the sun coming and going with the effect of a strobe light she had once seen in the twentieth century of the home universe.

The light had returned to a normal gray, and she could hear no sound but a steady familiar rushing.

She looked at William. His face was normal, with no trace of greenness or scales, and her hands, she saw with relief, had lost their clawlike appearance.

"Feel better, Mr. Blake?"

"Much better! It's like a fog has lifted off my mind."

She wondered about Urizen. Was something happening to Urizen's mind, too?

On impulse she said, "Let's stop here."

They reentered the timestream.

Low, flower-spread hills stretched to the bent river. (Kate still thought of it as the Thames.) On the horizon, bright in the noonday sun, moved tall billowing white clouds. Clumps of poplar trees grew to her right and, turning her head, she found a genuine forest beginning not far behind her, amid a thick tangle of wild grapevines. Nowhere could she spy a house, or any trace of human or lizard habitation.

A warm, daisy-scented breeze stirred her curly light-brown hair, rustled her long skirts, and set her dangling shawl swaying. With awe she murmured, "Mr. Blake, do you recognize this place?"

"Can't say as I do."

"This is my garden."

She took his hand and led him toward the forest. The poplar trees were short, younger than she remembered them, but their peculiar spacing remained the same, and the way the grapevines clustered around them.

"Why, so it is!" There was surprise and a dawning delight in his voice as he picked his way through tall grass that reached to his kneebreeches.

"The grapes are ripe." She picked one and ate it, spitting out the seeds. "Open your mouth." She gave the second grape to her husband.

"We should name this place," William said thoughtfully, talking with his mouth full.

"Name it? Yes, I suppose it's not really London anymore," she said wistfully.

"Or Lud's Dun, or Golgonooza. Let's call it Eden."

She giggled like a child, then said seriously, "Nothing so grand as that, please. New Lambeth will do well enough."

"New Lambeth." He tried the name on for size. She could see he would rather have called it Eden, but he nodded. "Yes, New Lambeth."

"Home," Kate whispered.

That afternoon they flew in slow circles over New Lambeth, surveying their domain. Passing birds screamed at them and fled.

She banked steeply, her shawl streaming behind her. "We could live here," she called to William.

"Perhaps so," he called back.

"We'll have plenty of wild fruit, fish, and small game." She loved the rush of the wind on her face.

William's normally serious face broke into a smile.

"And with no neighbors to summon the law we can take a bit of sun with nothing on but the bodies the good Lord gave us."

She frowned but let that pass. Perhaps he was right. Perhaps a new world called for new ways.

But even here, she decided, one must draw the line somewhere.

"Look there!" William pointed earthward.

"I see."

She did indeed see the moving figures on the riverbank, some miles distant. Were there humans down there?

"Let's go in for a closer look," he called.

A moment later she called back. "Only lizards."

She tried, without success, to hide her disappointment.

The lizard-people, it seemed, had built a village of crude huts with straw roofs and walls of mud and rock. In spite of the sunlight, a few of them waded in the shallows, fishing with spears, and as the Blakes glided overhead, the lizards broke into a panic, screeching and hurling spears skyward that came nowhere near Kate and William.

"How crude," Kate said, puzzled, as they rose to a safer altitude. "I didn't think we'd come that far downtime."

"We haven't, Mrs. Blake. Don't forget. Urizen told us he taught the lizard-people all their science and technology. It wouldn't take long to transform this level of civilization to a higher one with Urizen as teacher, but as of today, I'll wager, the lessons have not yet begun."

"Well, Mr. Blake, this ain't quite the Eden you thought it was," she said bleakly.

"What would Eden be without its proper reptiles? And we've nothing to fear from them. We can fly, you know, and we have our temporal energy fields to protect us, and the power of time-voyaging, with all that implies. Why, we could, if we liked, take Urizen's place here as the gods and culture-bringers of the lizard-people."

Kate shuddered. "No, thank you just the same."

At sunset they landed at New Lambeth.

"Nightfall," William said, studying the red sky. "We'd better head downtime."

"Why?" she challenged him.

"To find where Urizen started the change that made this world." He gestured at the fields and trees around them. "How else can we change things back?"

"Are you sure you want to change things back?"

"What are you saying?" William stared at her in amazement.

"It's very nice here, Mr. Blake."

"Well, yes, I suppose so," he admitted reluctantly.

"And I'm very tired. Aren't you tired, too?"

"Maybe so, but if we stay the night here, we'll have to take turns standing watch. You know how those lizards love darkness."

"I don't mind."

For a long time they stared at each other in silence as the red sky gradually turned purple and the stars became visible, then William said gruffly, "Help me build a lean-to, in case it rains."

As she sprang to the task of gathering branches, she began to hum a lively little tune her mother had taught her.

Dawn came during Kate's watch.

She sat huddled against one of her beloved poplars, watching the eastern sky turn pale pearly gray. She had not slept well, even during William's watch; the night had turned bitter cold and the ground had been hard. Her bones ached, and her flesh was covered with goosebumps.

Yet she felt content and at peace.

New Lambeth was hers: no landlord would come and ask her for rent, or evict her if she didn't have the money. The vast flocks of birds who now sang a discordant fanfare to the sun, the rabbits who peeked at her from the tall grass, the squirrels who wiggled their noses and chattered at her from the trees, the fish she could hear, even at this distance, leaping for insects and falling back into the rivers with a plop and a splash: all were hers . . . and William's too, of course.

She glanced over at William, who lay under the lean-to on a bed of weeds, snoring softly. How young he looked! Like a huge overgrown baby. She smiled.

Through the stillness came the plop of another leaping fish. She thought, *Breakfast.*

First she looked around carefully for any sign of danger, then she spread her arms and soared skyward, circling the area a few times to be doubly sure, then she glided toward the river.

From directly above she could see all the way to the bottom, see the fish darting to and fro, see when one was rising to make a jump. She missed the first one, but the second she managed to strike with the flat of her palm and slap onto the shore.

With flint from William's pocket she started a small fire on a hollow in the top of a rock, and when William awoke it was to the mouth-watering aroma of fish and the brilliant light of a sun already some distance above the horizon.

"You are indeed a wonder, Mrs. Blake." He yawned, stretched, and rubbed his eyes, staring at her with unconcealed admiration.

"Thank you, Mr. Blake." Carefully she turned over the fish impaled on the end of her stick.

Breakfast eaten, the Blakes reclined at leisure and swatted at insects, she with her back against the tree, he with his head in her lap.

"We'll have to raid the lizard village for some tools," he mused. "We need an ax to cut down trees—not your special trees, of course—to build a log cabin. This lean-to won't give us enough protection when the weather turns nasty."

"I suppose you're right, but . . . ."

"The lizard axes are probably made of stone, but that will do the job."

"Stealing's not right. Maybe we can trade something."

"They're not human beings, Kate!"

"All the same. . . . I could trade them my shawl." She took it off and looked at it wistfully. She hated to part with it but had nothing else she could spare.

He sat up, frowning. "We have our own needs to think of. How will you keep warm without it?"

"It will be worth something to be able to live in peace with our neighbors," she pointed out.

William, she saw, was getting angry. "I can't talk to you, Kate. You're too soft. There are times when one must be hard!"

Kate responded with an unaccustomed sharpness. "If you wanted someone like that, you should have stayed with Vala!" She instantly regretted her words, but once again Kate's mouth was acting as if it had a mind of its own.

William sprang to his feet. "Now you're talking sense, woman! Vala, at least, faced life as it is. Vala was a realist!"

"Then why didn't you marry her?"

"Well, after a fashion I suppose I did. Who is more my real wife, the woman who's bound to me by a slip of paper or the woman who's the mother of my child?"

With a cry of fury, Kate scrambled to her feet. "Swine! Swine! Swine!" Like a cat striking at a bird, she lashed out and slashed his left cheek with her fingernails.

"Kate!" His anger had vanished. His voice was soft now, almost pleading.

"Swine!" She kicked him in the shins. Lines of blood appeared on his cheek where she'd clawed him. At the sight of the blood a ghastly glee welled up inside her. *I owed you that, Mr. Blake,* she thought triumphantly. *And a lot more!*

She raised her hand to claw him again.

He caught hold of her wrist.

He was strong, stronger than she would have believed, but she went on struggling, even when, through vision blurred with tears, she saw his face grow rigid and strange, saw beads of sweat appear on his forehead and his large eyes become opaque and staring.

He tried to kiss her lips, but she bit him, and as he jerked back with a curse, she kicked him twice in the shins with all her strength. He was so strong! Now he held both her wrists in one powerful hand, panting, grinning fixedly. Where was his other hand?

She felt him clutch her skirt, heard the sound of cloth ripping. . . .

Later, as they lay breathing heavily side by side among

the crushed weeds, not touching each other, she remembered the operation William had had in Oothoon. At the time it had not seemed important, since she and William never made love anyway. Now it was important. In fact she hated him far more for what he had let the red men do to him, long ago in another universe, than she did for what he had just done to her a few minutes ago.

She thought, *Even now Vala is here, laughing at me, telling me I will never be the mother of a child of William's.*

William began apologetically, "Kate . . ."

Her voice had never before been so utterly cold. "You bastard. You God damned dirty bastard."

The Blakes lived at New Lambeth for a week and a half, fighting, making love, and building.

William had, in spite of Kate's objections, swooped down on one of the lizards and snatched a stone ax, which proved surprisingly effective at chopping down and trimming trees that were not too thick. Little by little a small, one-room cabin took shape.

The first rain came before the roof was quite finished and they had a bad night of it, but managed to remain dry if not warm by huddling together in one corner; their fire, contained in a crude fireplace made of piled stones, could not heat the place so long as a portion of the roof was missing.

They stared in silence at the dying embers, teeth chattering, bodies shivering.

William spoke first. "You know, we need never go time-voyaging again. You like it here, don't you?"

"Yes, it spite of everything."

"We could live out our lives here in New Lambeth."

"If Urizen and that whore Vala let us."

"Urizen won't even try to find us. He has all time to search through, and other things to do besides hunt for us. Of course we're not comfortable here yet, but soon we'll have our cabin built, perhaps a dog or two trained. I've seen wild dogs around."

She nodded. "We'll make it, if your slut leaves us alone."

"Vala is nowhere around."

"She isn't? Then why do I feel her presence? Why do I think I see her out of the corner of my eye, and when I turn she's gone? Why do I hear her voice in the distance, laughing at me?"

"Imagination, Kate. Just imagination."

"But Mr. Blake, 'twas you who taught me reality is made by the imagination. 'Twas you who taught me that anything possible to be imagined is a shadow of the truth."

"Oh Kate, damn it. Don't use my words against me."

Kate opened her mouth to reply, but froze. A dim, vague shape was indeed forming in the smoke from the smoldering fire. A human shape!

"Look!" she screamed. "Vala!"

The shape took on a more definite form. It was Robert. Kate felt a wave of relief. Only the good old ghost of William's brother. She never would have believed she would be so happy to see a ghost.

Robert's voice came to her as if from a great distance. "So here you are. I thought I'd never see you again."

"Never see me again?" said William. "Why?"

"The lizard-spirits are driving the human spirits out. They almost got me too. I tell you, William, the battle is going against us uptime." The transparent face had become translucent. She could see the moving lips, the pain-filled eyes.

"Stay here with us," Kate invited.

Robert shook his head. "That I cannot do. The lizard-spirits will track me here by the wake I leave through the grayness. If they catch up to me they'll drag me away, and they may harm you, too. No, you must not stay here, either. This is a lizard's universe now. Humans cannot stay human here. You'll change, become cruel, without humanity's feeling, consideration, intelligence. The lizards have a whole different range of emotions, a love of destruction for destruction's sake. They love to kill so much they find their greatest pleasure in killing themselves. Suicide is, for them, a dark ecstasy, the only action in which one can be absolute aggressor and absolute victim at the same time."

"We won't change," William told him firmly.

Kate turned in his arms to look at him. The firelight flickered on his face, but she had to accept the truth . . . it was not entirely his face. She said, "We will change. Yes, we will. It has already begun." She was thinking of the way William made love. Each time, it seemed, he was a little more brutal, took a little more pleasure in hurting her. She thought, not for the first time, *Someday William will kill me.*

"Nonsense!" William snapped, a bit too quickly. Had he noticed the changes too, but kept them to himself? *And,* Kate wondered, *am I changing, and would I know it if I was?*

Robert continued urgently, "It's worst uptime, near the battle. Urizen is changing. Vala is changing. I've looked into their future, into the future of their civilization. Nothing awaits them but an orgy of destruction. Everything Urizen and Vala have built up will be joyously torn down by those who call themselves his worshippers, and Urizen himself will be so changed he'll call it progress. And there will be progress, of a sort. The science of destruction will move ahead at a steadily-increasing rate. They'll build bombs more violent than exploding volcanos and rockets to carry those bombs to any part of the globe, and as an afterthought they'll send a lizard to the moon. The air and water will be full of poison and the food without nourishment. There will be no new symphonies, no new operas, no new ballets; just noise so loud it makes you deaf, but lizards like it that way. There will be no more painting, just smears of meaningless color and pictures pasted together from the fragments of other pictures, no beauty in architecture, just big and little boxes, all drab and featureless. Even chemistry will become chiefly an instrument for making bearable the unbearable. And Urizen and Vala will not know they're becoming lizards! That's the worst of it."

William remained unconvinced. "But all that is far in the future. It doesn't effect New Lambeth. Kate and I can be happy here, at least for a while."

"At times you will sense what is happening to you,"

said Robert, his image dimmer, his voice fainter. "Will you be happy then?"

"Wait, Robert!" William called, but Robert had faded out altogether.

Neither of the Blakes spoke for several minutes. The fire glowed feebly. The rain fell with a steady hiss. There was no wind.

Kate sighed and broke the silence. "Robert's right, you know."

"I suppose so."

"One more night here, Mr. Blake?"

"If you like."

"Then we head downtime to the source of this lizard universe, but of course if we change things then, we'll have to change them to something where there is no New Lambeth."

"There will be something else."

"There is always something else." She raised her lips to be kissed.

This time William was not cruel.

They found the place outside of time deserted and silent. A dim red glow filtered down from uptime, and the images from within the timestream, as they flowed by, seemed distorted and sluggish.

"I feel as if reality itself was dying," Kate commented uneasily. "Not just this universe, but all possible universes."

William, drifting at her side, nodded.

They had come far downtime from New Lambeth, and the glimpses they caught of the lizard-people revealed steadily more debased levels of culture. No huts. No stone axes. The lizards had become indistinguishable from any other wild animals.

Then came an abrupt change.

The Thames overflowed its banks. The water, in the strobelike flickering light, flowed uphill, higher, ever higher.

Suddenly she saw darkness and rain, endless rain.

No dry land at all remained, only wildly swirling sea fitfully illuminated by lightning flashes. In the place outside of time Kate and William could see, though unclearly, all that happened, but could hear nothing, feel nothing.

Kate thought, *The Deluge! Just like in the Bible*.

They flew eastward, searching for some place that rose above the titanic waves, not daring to enter the timestream for fear the storm would prove too violent for their protective shields of temporal energy.

"Look there," said William.

Ahead she could make out islands, and, an instant later, a dark jagged coastline.

"That can only be the Himalayan Mountains," he said. "The world's highest. Perhaps we can locate some survivors there."

The coastline passed beneath them. They no longer moved backward in time, and thus everything seemed more normal, free of the strobe-effect and the curious double-images and fadeouts that made vision so difficult in the place outside of time.

William grasped Kate's elbow and whispered one startled word.

"Human!"

On the hillsides, inland from the coastal range, human corpses lay strewn in small groups, a few here, a few there.

"Freshly killed," William commented grimly. "No decay."

Kate added, "And they aren't no savages, either. Look at the fine robes they're wearing and the workmanship on the swords in their hands. I wonder what killed them. The storm?"

"I don't think so." William's face was pale in the gray light. "You don't fight a storm with swords. I'd say they've been torn apart by some kind of animal."

Kate shuddered, but as they dipped down for a closer look, she had to admit William was right. "Let's nip into the timestream a bit, Mr. Blake. I think our energy shields will hold off this much storm."

"All right. There's a mystery here, right enough."

The howling wind and driving rain exploded around them, but their shields held off the rain and wind. They landed near what appeared to be a family—father, mother, three children, and a horse—all frightfully mutilated. A few yards away was the brink of a steep cliff overlooking a gorge through which thundered cascades of white water studded with branches and debris.

Kate knelt beside the mother. Was it the rain that made it seem the blood in the woman's gown was still wet?

Shouting to make himself heard above the gale, William called, "No animal did this!" She looked up, saw him beckon to her.

Moving quickly to his side, she looked where he pointed. And saw tracks, but not animal tracks. Once, with Urizen, she and William had visited Europe during the First World War, and there they had seen just such tracks as these, the tracks left by a heavy armored tank. Even half submerged in muddy puddles, the broad segmented ruts were unmistakable.

"A tank?" she shouted into the wind, unable to believe her eyes.

William nodded, the rain against his energy field forming a halo of mist around his troubled face. "The tracks are fresh. The tank must be close by."

At that moment, without warning, there was a violent explosion. It was so close that without their energy shields they would certainly have been killed. As it was, it threw them both to the ground, Kate face-down in the mud, William flat on his back.

Rolling over, Kate looked up and saw, through the sheets of rain, a vast black shape lumbering into position on a ridge above her. It was a tank, all right, but a tank unlike any she'd ever seen in World War One. Instead of cannon, it carried banks of rockets, and from its sides jutted long metal arms with tiny clawlike hands. A flare of flame briefly illuminated the tank, and Kate watched as if hypnotized as a bright-tailed rocket rushed toward her.

This second explosion came closer than the first, but Kate had strengthened her shield against it. *You can't hurt me,* she thought triumphantly.

Then she realized the blast had broken loose the cliff on

which she lay. With a great grinding rumbling roar, the cliff began to slide down into the foaming flood.

Airborne an instant before the cliff hit the water, Kate and William soared upward toward the tank, she on its right, and he on its left. As they swooped in on it, it raised its metal arms, its tiny hands opening and closing convulsively. Kate's fingers closed on the cold wet metal of the rocket launchers on its side. She waited. William shouted, "Now!"

And they, with the tank between them, broke though into the place outside of time, adrift in a universe where there was no gravity. The tank continued to struggle, its curiously human hands trying to catch them, its caterpillar treads spinning helplessly, but the Blakes avoided its defenses and approached it from the bottom.

"Look," called out William. "A door!"

He clutched the handle and wrenched it open.

"Nobody inside!" he exclaimed, astonished.

Kate crowded in alongside him. Sure enough, she could certainly see the narrow interior full of electronic equipment studded with many-colored blinking lights, but no sign of a driver.

"It is—what do they call it?—radio-controlled?" asked Kate.

"No, it still functions here outside the timestream. It must think for itself, as it were, with some sort of on-board computer." He scrambled inside and began ripping out wires at random. With a flash of arcing electricity, a puff of ozone-scented smoke, and a brief crackling sound the tank's struggle came to an abrupt halt.

"Programmed to kill," he mused grimly as he clambered out.

"But who would do such a thing?"

Wordlessly he showed her a stamped metal emblem next to the door. There, in low relief, she saw the familiar form of William's statue of Urizen.

They had dragged twenty tanks into the place outside of time before they realized the futility of it. There were too many of the tanks . . . hundreds, perhaps thousands of them, patrolling the Himalayan continent and killing every human they could hunt down, and with their complex electronic senses, they were very good hunters indeed.

Kate and William flew out to sea, only to glimpse, below the waves, dark long moving shapes.

"Robot submarines," William shouted above the howling wind.

"What for?"

He smiled grimly. "To sink Noah's ark."

Again they left the timestream and William explained. "This natural disaster is Urizen's opportunity. The flood kills off most of the human race, except for a few who have managed to build some sort of ships or to flee to the highest mountaintops. Then Urizen's robots hunt down and exterminate these few, putting an end to humanity. Urizen has a clean slate to write on; his precious lizards can evolve without fear of human competition."

"So it's here, then, where he has made the big change."

William shook his head. "Not here. Earlier. This is only part of his plan, and a late part at that. He must have entered the timestream at least far enough downtime from here to have been able to build up his huge army of computerized killers."

"But all the same, Mr. Blake, perhaps here we can switch things back."

William sighed and took her hand. "I wish it was that easy, but Urizen was right when he said we can't make the correct changes unless we know what we're doing. We could create an even worse future than the one Urizen made!"

The dull apathy in his voice frightened her. She gripped his arm and said, "But we must do something!"

"Must we?" He sounded so tired, so lifeless. "Maybe Urizen is in the right. After all, lizards are living creatures too. Who's to say lizards aren't as good as men? Or better?"

She shook him. "Now you sound like those Zoas, ready to give up, ready to slip away into a garden of dreams, because you're not as fanatic as Urizen, because you're not as insane as he is! Come along now, we've things to do!"

He looked at her with something very like pity. "What things, for instance?"

"We can explore, investigate. Urizen must have a weak spot, but we shan't find it without looking for it!"

"You look for it, Kate. If you find it, let me know."

With that Kate finally lost her temper. "Mr. Blake! You damn fool! Come along!"

He did follow her back into the timestream and the storm, but unwillingly.

In spite of concealing pools and radical erosion, the Blakes found they could follow the tank tracks from the air, and they soon determined that each and every track radiated from a common source. Kate guessed the source before she actually saw it.

"Mount Everest!"

"I think you have it, Mrs. Blake."

They flew swiftly along the face of a mountain range as Kate thought, *Of course. What better location for Urizen's stronghold than the peak of the world's highest mountain?*

The separate tank tracks became rutted roadways, and they in turn became broad paved highways cut into mountainsides, tunneling here and there, crossing gorges on fantastic suspension bridges that even this world holocaust had left undamaged.

Urizen's kingdom must have flourished up here for centuries, perhaps completely unknown to the humans to the east and west, the humans in the valley nations now lost beneath the sea. And the citizens of Urizen's kingdom had had nothing to say to the outside world . . . they were mindless machines, every one.

Below two roads met to become one in a Y intersection, near the crest of a mountain. Kate could see it clearly; the rain had slackened and the sun, low in the western sky, came in under the overcast, over the turbulent waves that now completely covered India, and illuminated the sheer west face of towering Mount Everest with a hot red glow.

The glow faded as quickly as it had come. Kate realized

they must reach their destination within the next few minutes, or lose it in the fast-falling darkness, but she felt no urgency. A simple leap backward in time would bring them once again in sight of the setting sun.

No backward leap was needed.

Ahead, where she knew the peak of the mountain loomed unseen, a light appeared. As she watched a huge door opened, vertically like a mouth, and a bright bluewhite light blazed forth. Kate and William soared toward it.

They glimpsed a broad highway leading out of the mouthlike door, covered with the mingled tracks of many vehicles, then, trusting to their temporal shields for protection, they darted inside.

The door reversed its motion and closed behind them with a metallic, echoing boom.

Kate bit her lip anxiously. Perhaps they should not have rushed in so eagerly. Perhaps they had carelessly fallen into Urizen's trap. But William had led the way, apparently unafraid, and she had followed without really thinking. Could he be overestimating the immunity resulting from their Zoa training?

"Mr. Blake, did those doors open just for us?"

"It would seem so. I expect at any moment to find Urizen waiting for us. Otherwise he would have made some move to stop us."

"He's so sure of himself!"

They had traversed a vast empty hall, and now the passage narrowed. They landed and proceeded on foot. Glancing around, Kate noticed that, though the bright shining bluewhite walls of some glasslike material seemed clear and smooth as if brand new, the floor lay concealed under a thick layer of dust that rose in choking clouds as their feet disturbed it. She wondered, *How old is this place? How many centuries?*

They passed dark rooms full of the hulking forms of immense motionless silent machines. These machines, Kate guessed, must have built the robot army.

But now the passage widened again, opening into a round room with a high domed ceiling, a room with a disquieting echo. Indeed, this echo of their footsteps and whispering voices was the only sound; the storm outside could not be heard at all.

In the exact center of the floor squatted a low raised platform, oval in shape, and on the platform stood what appeared to be an open coffin of the same glasslike material as the walls. A carved inscription decorated its side, framed in an ornate serpentine border, and above it, at an angle, tilted a full-length mirror.

The Blakes stepped closer to read the inscription.

The language was English, the letters Roman capitals.

AHEAD OF YOU ALWAYS.

William frowned in puzzlement. "I don't understand."

Kate glanced up into the mirror. "Look! Urizen!"

In the mirror they could see a dust-covered Urizen in the coffin, eyes closed, a faint smile on his lips.

"Is he dead?" The echo repeated her question.

William sprang up on the oval platform and peered into the coffin. "He's not here!"

Kate joined William beside the coffin, thrust her hand inside it and felt around. In the mirror it appeared as if she put her hand inside Urizen's body, but she could feel nothing but the cool soft smoothness of the white silk lining. "Is it some kind of stage magician's trick? A mirror illusion?"

William sat down dejectedly on the edge of the platform. "Not exactly. Urizen told me about this once, though he never showed me how to do it. He's in that coffin, right enough, but a fraction of a second in the future. We can see the light that bounced off him as he passed . . . that's his reflection in the mirror. But we can't see him."

"Can't we nip ahead and catch up with him?"

"Not a chance. It's like Zeno's paradox. As he says in the inscription, he'll always be ahead of us. By the time we reach the fraction of a second he's in, he'll have bounced ahead to another one. And he's not dead, either, but only in a special kind of suspended animation."

Kate rested her elbows on the rim of the coffin and gazed disconsolately up at Urizen's reflection. Paradox! Everything about time-voyaging was paradox. For example, was Urizen really in the future? Or was he in the past?

He was certainly in the past in one sense. He had been there, and gone.

She sighed. "He's teasing us, putting himself barely out of reach, so we can see him but are helpless to do anything."

"Right. He can't be very far ahead, just far enough so the light has time to strike his body, pop up to the mirror, and bounce down to our eyes."

She examined Urizen's bearded features, his muscular naked body. Urizen held something rectangular in his arms. "What's he got there?"

William answered, "I recognize it. It's the bronze book Urizen has inscribed with the laws for his perfect world. I am beginning to understand what he meant when he said he'd put a lock on the universe. Here he is, safe, and outside his robots are setting everything up for him. He talked about this many times, when he and I ruled Albion."

"But what can we do?"

"Nothing."

"I won't accept that, Mr. Blake. There's always something a person can do."

He shrugged. "We can head downtime. We might find something."

"We *will* find something!"

They plunged into the world outside of time.

Before the flood they found a world of men, and land where they expected water and water where they expected land, and they found giants, and visitors called the Sons of God who loved and taught the Daughters of Men, all in a time forgotten or but a whisper of legend, bits and threads of truth torn from a vast lost fabric.

They saw men fight giant lizards and win.

They saw empires, and a man who owned the world and everyone and everything on it, and they saw cities rise and fall. They saw people with strange visions and people with stranger blindness. They saw jewels full of power and grains of sand full of knowledge.

They saw continents sink and continents rise from the sea, and billions of books written and billions of songs sung and billions of battles lost and won, and much evil and cruelty and glory and pride.

Once or twice they saw a moment of real love.

Through it all, Urizen slept in the mountain.

Finally they saw only sea, except for one lone island, and inside that island, the only dry land on the planet, Urizen slept. Under endless clouds moved sluggish seas where life flickered and glowed in unending night, with no moon, no stars, no living thing that walked on land or flew in the air.

A vast and horrible peace.

Water boiled in the heat of an unseen sun, and boneless monsters lived in the boiling water, eating invisible energy.

Above the boiling water and drifting fleshy giants, above slow-moving clouds of steam, hovered Kate and William Blake, she in torn and tattered long skirt, clutching the remains of a shawl; he in battered, filthy knee-breeches.

"Where is Urizen's mountain?" she asked.

"Over there, that dark area where none of the monsters are glowing."

They glided slowly toward the darkness.

Kate screamed.

Something had reached up from the water and grasped her ankle. She pulled free, with William's help.

Feeling her ankle with anxious fingertips, she discovered a wetness. She thought, *Is that the sea, or slime from the creature, or my own blood?*

There was no way to be sure.

They alighted on hot, dry stone and groped around through the darkness. A long time later—she had no way of knowing how long—she located a crack, straight as a ruler line. "William, I think I've found the door to Urizen's stronghold."

She followed the crack with her fingertips to a right angle turn. She was certain now. There are no right angles in nature.

"He must still be in there," William said wearily.

"We must go downtime still more. It can't be much farther. We must reach the point before Urizen's first change."

"What if there is no beginning, Kate? What if Urizen was *always* there?"

"No! No, I won't believe that. Urizen's not God!" She fumbled in the darkness, found William's sweating hand. "Come. Just a little farther," she pleaded.

Even the place outside of time was dark.

"We've passed it!" Kate could no longer feel the crack in the rock.

"Are you sure?"

"It was here. Now it's gone. Let's go uptime a little, to when Urizen first arrived from the future, before he began to build his hiding place."

The moment they got outside the timestream, they saw a light, like a tiny star at first, then larger and brighter. "Here he comes," whispered Kate.

The light did indeed come from uptime, from the far future, and from the odd angle at which it traveled, she got the impression it came from a *different future*. But of course. It would be coming from the home universe, from Golgonooza at the end of time, in the future of the world before the change.

From here, at the mathematical point from which the two futures branched, she could see along both branches. An idea began to form in her mind, a flicker of hope . . . but it was driven away by the rushing arrival of The Ship, fat, monstrous, blazing with lights. Urizen's insignia, the picture of William's Urizen statue, was embossed on the hull, painted in glistening metallic paint.

She and William had to move quickly to get out of the behemoth's path as it rushed past them and entered the timestream. They followed it.

From a distance, hovering in the steamy air, they watched the timeship open its doors and disgorge a horde of quick, insectlike machines. The machines instantly set to work digging into the side of the island's only hill. Kate recognized the style of the devices. They had come from the very distant future, from the time when Luvah would be a galatic emperor, a time when technology would reach a height it would never afterward surpass.

"We attack now," whispered Kate.

But it was already too late.

Urizen and Vala had just emerged from the forward hatchway . . . a surprisingly young Urizen and a young Vala. No one could fail to recognize their previous identities as William Godwin and Mary Wollstonecraft.

Urizen raised a microphone to his lips and spoke. The voice, greatly amplified, drifted up to Kate across the steaming water. "Mr. and Mrs. Blake? Is that you my radar has picked up? But of course! How nice of you to drop by to help me celebrate the grand opening of my new universe! Come on down here and join us in a spot of tea."

William whispered, "Let's get out of here."

But Kate answered, with a peculiar hardness to her voice, "No, I want to talk to them."

"Why?"

"I want to try and find out some things from them that can help us."

"I'll go with you."

"No. No use risking us both."

"I won't let you . . ."

"Yes you will!" Her sudden fury cowed him, and he watched anxiously as she drifted downward into the camp of the enemy.

Kate felt more comfortable here, near the looming bulk of the immense timeship. The ship generated some sort of energy-field that drove off the steam, and on-board air-conditioners puffed a cool, normal atmosphere into the resulting bubble. Two beetlelike machines about the size of cats had brought out a card table and set it up; another similar machine had provided three chairs; yet another had appeared carrying a tray with teapot, cups, dishes, and silverware.

Vala eyed Kate with distaste. "You look awful, my dear. In this new future, have you abandoned such conventionalities as baths and clean clothing?"

Kate did not reply, but only sank gratefully into one of the chairs, only too well aware of how she must look. If she looked half as bad as she felt . . .

Vala and Urizen also seated themselves. Urizen poured tea. "Sugar? Cream?" he asked politely.

"You must taste the cookies. I baked them myself," added Vala, taking one herself as if to prove they weren't poisoned.

"Sugar and cream both, thank you," Kate answered. She tried the cookies and found them delicious. It was all she could do to keep from wolfing down the whole plateful.

Urizen clucked his tongue sympathetically and said, "Won't you let us give you a bath and the loan of some fresh clothing?"

"If you wouldn't be inconvenienced . . ." said Kate.

"Not at all," said Urizen smoothly, between cautious sips of the hot liquid.

"But," Kate went on guardedly, "I never knew you to give anyone anything for nothing. What do you want in return?"

Urizen answered with a smile, "A little information, that's all. Tell me, how does the world turn out, the one I'm about to create?"

"Yes, tell us," prompted Vala, coolly beautiful in her flowing red robes.

"It's a Hell you're creating, not a world," Kate told them without hesitation.

Urizen raised an eyebrow. "A Hell? Why do you say that?"

Kate thought, *It doesn't have to happen. I can talk them out of it.* She blurted, "There are no people uptime, just giant lizards."

"Excellent!" Urizen exclaimed with satisfaction. "Just as I'd planned. We're tired of humans, Vala and I. Humans are so unmanageable, not to mention ungrateful. We can't have utopia with humans, can we, Vala?"

Vala said grimly, "I once thought so. But then I met a man in France, an American, who talked a wonderful utopia, but who sent me on a wild goose chase to Norway while he set up housekeeping with a woman who called herself, as such women sometimes do, an actress. Then this man had the cheek to preach to me about freedom.

No, lizards may be a bit stupid, but otherwise they're much better. Less hypocritical and easier to control.''

"If you like lizards so well," Kate challenged, "are you prepared to *become* one?"

Vala said broodingly, "What nonsense are you talking now?"

Kate said, "That's what will happen. The new future you're creating doesn't like humans. If you linger too long in it, it will change you, change you into something that . . . fits in.''

"Interesting," Urizen said, then sipped his tea. "To turn into a lizard. That would be a novel experience." He gazed off into space.

Vala shuddered. "Really, Urizen dear!"

Now Urizen spoke blandly, though his words were far from polite. "Shut up, mother." He turned to Kate and added, "You women have no stomach for projects that are really grand. Power isn't power unless you use it! That's what I always say."

Vala looked at him oddly for a moment before saying to Kate, "If you've finished your snack, we could see about that bath and those clothes." She stood up. "I'll give you something for William, too. For old time's sake."

She led Kate through the hatchway into the ship.

As soon as they were out of earshot of Urizen, Kate caught Vala by the arm and said urgently, "Are you really determined to go through with this, Mary?"

"Yes, I am, and don't call me Mary."

"I call you that because as Mary Wollstonecraft you were my friend."

"I'm not your enemy now, but I have not been Mary Wollstonecraft for a long, long time. She was an idealistic fool, your Mary. She thought a little education would cure everything. Ever since Mr. Blake took me with him up-time, I haven't quite been able to bring myself to believe that.''

"William took you uptime?"

"Yes. Did you think our relationship was merely sexual?"

"Did he take you uptime . . . before me?"

"I learned how to do it easily. For you it was harder, I suppose."

The pain of this new revelation was almost too much for Kate, but all she said was, "Yes, for me it was very hard, very hard."

Mary patted Kate's hand. "Never mind. William is really an idiot."

Kate answered with instant anger. "William is a genius!"

Mary laughed. "What misplaced loyalty! Would he defend you that quickly?"

"I think so."

"You know as well as I do he would not. He's a man! That says it all."

"Mary, once you wrote to defend the rights of men."

"When I was an idiot myself."

"Once you wrote to defend the rights of the poor."

"Be kind enough not to remind me."

"Once you wrote to defend the rights of women, and your words helped, really helped, millions of women back in the home universe, down through the ages that followed. Women believed in you, Mary Wollstonecraft! Women took courage from your words and your example."

Mary hesitated, then said in a low voice, "I suppose they did."

"Somewhere behind that mask you call Vala you are Mary Wollstonecraft still. Somewhere behind that mask is the woman who would not side with the oppressors of women."

Mary took Kate's hand in her own and said in a low voice, "If I were indeed Mary Wollstonecraft behind a mask—I don't admit that's true—what would you ask of me? That I abandon this experiment? Remember, Urizen wants it, and I am Urizen's mother. That is all I have left. I am Urizen's mother."

"Then you have more than me."

"Ah, so William still plays the monk with you?"

"No, worse than that. In Oothoon William had an operation. He can be a husband now. Indeed he frightens me with his lust. But he cannot be a father."

"But what is that to me?"

"I do not ask you to abandon your so-called experiment. William is weary of fighting you. I think I am weary, too. We want only to find a quiet place in this universe you are creating where we can live out our lives in as normal a fashion as possible. Will you grant us that?"

"It is not in my power to grant or withold."

"It is! With the science in this ship"—Kate gestured at the banks of machines they were passing—"you could let me have what you have . . . a child."

Mary was silent for a long time, then said, "Luvah taught me a way to make a woman pregnant with an electric spark. The child will be female, an exact duplicate of yourself."

"No, then we would not be even. William must be the father of my child as he is of yours."

Mary's voice was filled with genuine compassion. "I understand. We have another way. We will need a bit of William's flesh. It doesn't matter what part of of his body we get it from, so long as it contains his inheritance."

"His inheritance?"

"Never mind. I can't explain it to you. But when, at the proper time, we put that inheritance into you, the effect will be the same as if you and William had made love. You will get pregnant, and William will be the father."

"I don't understand."

"Trust me." Trust Vala? Her rival and enemy? Yet she remembered that this was also Mary, her friend, Mary, the defender of women.

"Yes, Mary, I do trust you."

"Then come. We shall fly uptime. You will show me where I can find William asleep, and I will cut him . . . such a small cut he will not even notice."

Together the two women bounded into the place outside of time.

Kate remembered a day when she had left William alone for a few minutes just before dawn, back in New Lambeth. William had been very tired that morning and had slept late, sprawled on their makeshift bed. It was to this moment that Kate took Vala.

The women drifted toward the sleeping man like ghosts, their feet not touching the floor for fear of making a noise. They could hear William snoring, and the cries of the birds welcoming the day, and their own heartbeats, nothing more.

Finger to lips, Vala floated close to him, her red gown swirling slowly about her as if she were underwater. From a leather bag slung around her neck, Vala took a metal helmet and gently, gently placed it on William's head; then she spoke, in a normal conversational tone. "He won't wake up now, no matter what we do. He's in electrosleep."

Kate nodded but said nothing, not understanding this magical-seeming device, not quite trusting it.

Vala rummaged around in her bag again and came up with a short steel cylinder and a glass tube. "A laser knife," she explained, but Kate was none the wiser for her explanation. "And a bioculture tube." One more mystery.

Vala settled on her knees next to William and clicked a switch on the laser knife. At last Kate broke her silence to whisper, "Don't hurt him, Mary."

"He won't feel a thing," Vala reassured her, and touched his arm with the thing. Sure enough, he did not move. Vala opened the stopper on the glass tube and put something in it, then closed the tube again. "The deed is done, Kate!"

"Is that all there is to it?"

"That's all. Now be quiet a moment."

Vala levitated a few inches and, with infinite care, removed the electrosleep helmet from William's head. William frowned and changed position, but did not awaken, though his snoring stopped abruptly. Kate became aware of the sound of footsteps coming through the weeds from the direction of the river, then recognized the sound of her own voice humming softly an old folksong. Vala clutched Kate's wrist and the two drifted to the ceiling.

William called out, "Kate? Is that you?"

The answer came from outside the cabin. "I'm right here, Mr. Blake!"

Kate and Vala faded out of the timestream an instant before William opened his eyes.

Kate and Vala reentered the timestream two years uptime from where they had left Urizen and William. Kate glanced around in surprise, then remarked, "Are we in the timeship, Mary?"

"Yes."

"It's changed."

"The robots have been working on it, making it larger, tunneling into the rock."

"But where is Urizen?"

"In suspended animation in the room down the hall. I should be in suspended animation in the room next to it. We have a long sleep ahead of us, Urizen and I. But come along to the operating room."

"I don't know . . ."

"You want to have a child by William, don't you?"

"Yes, of course."

"Don't worry. You'll lie down on the table, put on the electrosleep helmet, and when you wake up, you'll be expecting." She pronounced this last word with a mocking irony that made Kate distinctly uneasy, but nevertheless she did as she was told.

Everything went exactly as Vala had promised, and when Kate awoke on the table she sat up and demanded, "When are you going to operate?"

"I already finished, my dear."

"But I felt nothing at all."

"Of course." Vala had her back to Kate, putting gleaming glass and chrome instruments into a cabinet. This done, she slid shut the cabinet door and stripped off the thin rubber gloves on her hands. "Congratulations. Hail Kate, full of grace. Blessed are you among women!"

"I will have a child?"

"You will have a child. A son."

"A son? How can you tell?"

"I have arranged it that way. We are to be equal, are we not? I had a son, so you must have a son, too." She threw her gloves through a small oval hole in the wall. "But now you think you are clever, don't you?"

Kate had swung her feet off the table, but now she hesitated. "Clever? What do you mean?"

"You will have a son uptime, after Urizen and I have exterminated the remains of humanity. With a little tasteful incest you and William and your offspring will breed a new human race to spoil all Urizen's beautiful plans, to compete with his precious lizards for world domination. I know what you're thinking."

"I wasn't thinking of that at all," said Kate, quite truthfully. "I only wanted a home, a family, a little peace." She paused, then added, "But if what you say is true, you may have saved the human race by what you have just done. In spite of yourself, you are still Mary Wollstonecraft, the friend of humanity, not Vala. Not Vala, the . . . the . . ."

"Vala, the evil destroyer of humanity? Is that what you want to say? Go ahead and say it. I don't mind. But so you won't have one more illusion to add to your vast collection, let me tell you I have made you and William a new Eve and Adam for my own reasons, not because I have the smallest feeling for that plague upon the earth you call humanity." Vala's eyes gleamed. Cold, reptilian eyes. "Nor would I have you think I did what I did because I felt sorry for you, or felt some faint echo of the friendship we shared, you and I, long ago in another universe. No, no, my dear, nothing like that."

To Kate it seemed Vala was changing from moment to moment, her voice growing colder and more unfeeling, her skin showing the faintest trace of green. Or was this the way Vala had always been, secretly, even back when she had called herself Mary and presented herself to the world as a lover of freedom and defender of women's rights? No, Kate would have noticed. It was this place, this universe. It changed people.

Kate said softly, "Why, then? Why did you do it?"

"Didn't you hear him? Urizen told me to shut up!" Then Vala chuckled, and Kate could not associate that particular chuckle with any human emotion at all. It seemed to bespeak a whole spectrum of feelings altogether outside the experience of men and women, feelings that had never been shared and thus never had been named.

But now Vala composed herself, her face becoming an enigmatic mask. "Come, Mrs. Blake. You have what you want. I have what I want. Let us join the gentlemen downtime." She took Kate's hand. "We will return to the moment following the moment we left. No one will know we've been gone. Aren't we clever?" She chuckled again. Kate shuddered and tried to pull away as if she had been groping in the dark and touched a huge hairy spider, but Vala dragged her with a jerk into the place outside of time.

When Vala released her, Kate was standing in the passageway where Vala had just said, " . . . such a small cut he will not even notice." Indeed, the last trace of the echo of her words still hung on the air.

Vala said, "Ah, where were we? Oh yes, I was going to give you a bath." At a snap of her fingers, two of the beetle-robots wheeled forward. In a daze Kate docilely allowed the machines to wash her and dress her in a flowing white linen tunic that made her look like an ancient Greek.

It was either during the fish course or the meat course or perhaps during dessert that Urizen explained to Kate that he would go through with his "little experiment," come what may. He ended by saying, almost sadly, "And there's nothing you can do about it."

Before going into suspended animation, Urizen gave a lecture in a dry, overbearing manner that strongly suggested his old self, William Godwin, the longwinded philosopher.

"Because I am here, slightly out of phase in the timestream, there will be a powerful locking effect for several miles in all directions. You won't be able to pull anything with you out of the timestream on this island, or on the mountaintop this island will become, nor will you be able to use temporal energy to move any of my toys here." He glanced at a line of beetle-robots. "At the proper moment uptime the mountaintop will open and send out a flying robot to capture dinosaur specimens and later, during the second flood, it will again open to release the robot army that will exterminate the last of mankind. Both those times Vala and I will patrol the area to see that you and William, Mrs. Blake, don't do anything naughty. So go in peace! I will not harm you, because there is nothing you can do to harm me.''

He actually went so far as to kiss Kate lightly on the cheek. Kate was amazed. The usually cold Urizen displayed genuine warmth . . . but then he could afford to.

He was winning.

Urizen lay down in his white coffin and vanished.

Kate could still see him in the mirror above the coffin.

She walked with Vala to the next room, where an identical coffin awaited.

Vala said, ''I will not go uptime to preview the results of what we do here, nor of what we have already done.'' She gave Kate a knowing glance. ''That would be like reading the last chapter first in a novel. I want to be surprised. Will you surprise me, dear?''

''I don't see how,'' Kate answered bleakly.

''You have surprised me before. You know, I hope you do.'' She too favored Kate with a peck on the cheek, then climbed into her box and vanished.

Kate went outside and called to William.

He landed next to her.

''We're safe,'' she told him tonelessly. ''I'll get you some clean clothes, food, and a bath.'' She led him inside the timeship, relating all that had happened except Vala taking her uptime and performing the operation on her. This was Kate's secret. Some other time she would tell him. Some other place.

When she told him about the time lock, he tried to move some of the beetle-robots, but the machines ignored him. Urizen had been telling the truth.

As William ate, the robots worked, and by the time he'd finished the timeship was half buried. Within hours, Kate realized, the craft would be completely underground, with nothing to show its location but the cracks in the stone that marked its main doorway.

She gave William the clothing Urizen had left for him: a Greek tunic, cloak, and sandals. (Urizen had called this "the only rational clothing style in history.") In a gesture perhaps of contempt, Urizen had left William a Roman shortsword and scabbard.

When he had dressed, Kate said, "We'd best be on our way."

"Where to?" He sounded as if he hadn't slept for a week.

"Uptime, I think, to New Lambeth."

She too felt weary, but her secret gave her a wild joy she did not reveal by the slightest outward sign.

The winter rains had fallen without cease for three days, but Kate and William, snug in the one-room log cabin they had built with their own hands, bided their time in comfort and fed logs to their great stone fireplace. The first months in New Lambeth had been hard. Though there remained a great deal of work, now and then in the evenings they could afford the luxury of sitting, warm and dry, and watching visions in the fire.

The Greek-style clothing, Vala's gift, was worn and torn, but still Kate wore it night and day under the deerskin dress William had made for her. Deerskin kept you warm, but linen felt better on the skin.

She turned from the fire and, stretched full-length on her belly, chin resting in palm, elbow on floor, contemplated William's bearded features in the firelight. He seemed older. His beard showed traces of gray. His clothing— jacket, pants, boots, floppy cap—was made from animal skins. He sat on the floor, his back against one of the pillars that supported the roof, his scraggly chin resting on his knees. His Roman shortsword lay nearby. He always kept it within easy reach.

"What are you thinking about?" she asked him softly.

"About despair." He spoke in the calm deep voice of the man she'd married in another universe.

"Despair?"

"I've come to rather like it. When you have no hope at all, not a speck, you begin to feel a special peace that, all

things considered, satisfies the soul more than victory.
There's contentment in despair, and freedom, the freedom
to think of other things." He sighed and smiled. "You
know what I mean?" He raised his head expectantly.

Kate sat up and said primly, "No, I don't, because I
have not despaired."

William's head swung slowly, heavily, from side to
side. "Then you're a fool, Kate." He did not sound bitter,
just tired. "Why put yourself through the tortures of Hell?
Yes, Hell, for of all torments, hope hurts the most. And
it's all for nothing. Urizen has won, and there's an end to
it."

"William, you underestimate the uncertainty of life.
You can't count on anything, not even disaster." Listening
to her own words, she realized how much she sometimes
sounded like Urizen, like Vala. Perhaps at long last she
was learning the wisdom of the Zoas, becoming a real Zoa
in her heart.

"If we have any hope at all, it's for making a home for
ourselves here in New Lambeth," he said.

"Sometimes I think the same. Yes I do. But then I think
of Urizen and I know we've got unfinished business."

"Forget Urizen."

"Never!"

Should she tell him now? Should she tell him what gave
her hope? No, not yet.

She felt something move in her belly.

Neutrality had proven impossible.

The lizards were capable of hostility or worship, but not
peaceful coexistence. Thus the Blakes faced a strange
choice: apotheosis or war. War, once started, would have
lasted forever, so, reluctantly, they accepted the duties of
godhood.

How quickly it happened, thought Kate, as she stood by
the door to her cabin and watched a procession of lizards
march toward her in single file in the spring afternoon
sunshine. With the end of the winter rains, lizard emissar-
ies had presented themselves at her door, expressing ado-
ration with eloquent obsequious pantomime. William had,

with equally eloquent and comically imperious pantomime, accepted their offer. (William had made the choice without consulting her, but she had not protested.)

So now here they came, green scaly tails swishing, vast toothy mouths grinning, carrying a pair of makeshift sedan chairs which, if Kate understood them aright, would serve to transport the Blakes to some sort of evening ceremonies in the village where Kate and Willim would, as it were, take their vows as goddess and god.

She had fraternized with the creatures for little more than two weeks, but already she understood some of their language, could actually speak a few words of it. She listened to the hissing, chirping, and birdlike twittering that passed for song among them. They sang about her! About how she could fly, about her omnipotent power, about how she would help their crops to grow. She frowned. She could certainly help them, teach them many things, but only a real God could make crops grow. Somehow she would have to make that clear to them.

"Mr. Blake," she called, as the procession halted before her.

William emerged from the cabin doorway, clad in the Greek tunic, cloak, and sandals Vala had left for him, grinning like a gleeful boy. Unlike Kate, he had put his gifts away, as if he knew just such an occasion would arise. Did he know? Had he gone uptime without telling her? She thrust the thought away. Now, in beard and long hair, he looked disturbingly like Urizen. Kate thought, *Like son, like father*.

"Rather fancy becoming a god, do you not?" she demanded sharply.

His grin vanished. "Why no, not at all, but we must do it, you know."

"Only temporarily, and don't you forget it. As soon as we can, we'll explain things to them. Promise?"

He frowned, but said, "I promise. Upon my word, what do you take me for?"

Before she could frame an apt reply, two of the lizards flung themselves face down on the ground and came creeping forward on their bellies. The others bowed deeply.

William led Kate to one of the sedan chairs, helped her into it, then settled himself in the other, checking his shortsword.

At a bouncy, jouncy trot, the procession started for the village. As she lurched from side to side, forward and back, Kate reflected that she could have flown, or even walked, much more comfortably, but of course she didn't want to hurt the lizards' feelings.

They arrived at sunset, and in the gathering darkness a bright bonfire on the riverbank supplied ample light, together with not a little greasy black smoke. In the flickering firelight at the edge of a large cleared space a dozen or so lizard drummers listlessly thumped drums of various sizes and shapes with no detectable rhythm. Other lizards peered wide-eyed from the doorways of their rude thatched huts, while others fell in behind the procession that now conveyed the Blakes into the heart of the village.

When the sedan chairs had been gently set down on the ground, a particularly tall lizard raised a conch shell and blew an earsplitting discordant honk. All around her Kate heard the rustle of tails, the shuffle of clawed feet, the excited yet subdued sibilance of the serpentine language. She stood up slowly, with all the dignity she could muster, and stepped from the sedan chair. William joined her, touching her reassuringly on the elbow.

The lizards fell silent and backed away, clearing an aisle through the crowd. Kate noted uneasily that many of the creatures bore stone axes and long spears. Out of the corner of her eye she could see William rest his palm on the pommel of his shortsword while she, just to be on the safe side, concentrated a moment and brought into being her shield of temporal energy.

A fat lizard with one eye missing waddled forward, looming over the Blakes, and bowed low. This one wore brightly colored feathers in a long cape over his shoulders, and on his head carried the skull of a wild boar.

"He wants us to follow him," William said in a low voice.

"Then follow him we shall." Kate stepped forward.

The fat lizard led them to a low platform on which stood

two crude stone chairs as the murmuring crowd closed in behind them.

"Thrones," William whispered.

Kate nodded and followed him as he took his place in one of them. When she too sat down, the fat lizard signaled the drummers with a theatrical gesture of his claw.

The music began: a low, slow, steady, hypnotic thumping punctuated by occasional birdlike warbles and cries from the tribe. The lizards began to dance, with a boneless grace no human could hope to equal. No human could balance for half an hour on one foot, moving his arms at a rate of a few inches a minute, so the motion could hardly be detected. No human could send ripples pulsing through his body, first fast, then slow, but always perfectly controlled. No human had jaws that opened wide enough to completely conceal his face, or a tail that could at one instant stick out straight as a rod behind him, at another whistle through the air and crack like a whip. Kate could discern no planned step or choreography, yet at any given moment all the dancing lizards seemed to form a perfectly-balanced, intricate, interwoven design; a scaly green living arabesque that lazily, languorously, luxuriously undulated in the shifting shadows.

Her vision blurred, the edges softened, the colors blended. It seemed to her a healing, soothing, relaxing warmth had begun to creep over her, starting at her toes and gently advancing through her instep, her heels, her ankles, whispering to her to release, relax and let go, murmuring to her of a perfect peace that awaited her down, down, down in the womb of the deepest darkness. The feeling continued its stealthy progress through her calves, through her knees, through her upper legs, into her pelvis. It seemed to say that all these organs functioned perfectly well without her supervision. Why not just let go, and drift, and sleep?

The stomach did its work, quietly and unobtrusively, supplying the body with everything it needed and everything it wanted. No need to pay attention to that. The lungs went on breathing all by themselves, gently, constantly breathing out the past and breathing in the future.

The heart went on beating at exactly the right rate, with
exactly the right pressure, as it had done all her life, as it
had done for her mother, her grandmother, her great-
grandmother, for all her ancestors to the beginning of
humanity. Why not just drift off and sleep?

The feeling crept through her shoulders, as if some
infinitely gentle fingers rubbed her with warm oil, mas-
saged each and every muscle. The feeling crept down her
arms. Her hands fell open, letting go of the past and
remaining open for all the good things coming toward her
from the future.

The feeling oozed up through her neck. Her jaw slackened. Her mouth opened. The feeling entered her mouth,
reconciling her to everything she'd ever said. It entered her
nose, reconciling her to everything she'd ever smelled. It
entered her eyes, reconciling her to everything she'd ever
seen. It entered her ears, reconciling her to everything
she'd ever heard. It moved upward again, smoothing out
her forehead, relaxing even her scalp, relaxing the very
roots of her hair. All tension seemed to drain away like a
receding tide. All caution, all worry, all care went out to
join the sea.

And then the warmth entered her mind.

Her thoughts slowed.

Why not just watch this beautiful dance forever?

Forever. Forever.

The word echoed away to the farthest stars.

Her eyelids had become so very, very heavy. Slowly,
gently, they began to close.

William's powerful fingers dug into her arm, hurting
her. He shook her, called to her, but his voice came from
far, far away. "Kate! Don't let them get to you!"

Her eyes opened. Her vision sharpened. Her mind speeded
up.

She noticed for the first time all of the bright gleaming
serpent eyes fixed upon her. Every one of the dancers
watched her as it danced, watched expectantly.

"Tricky rascals," William muttered angrily. "Don't
look at them for more than a few seconds at a time."

Kate blinked, dazed. "Yes . . . I understand . . . all right."

The lizards seemed disappointed, but the dance continued, the tempo gradually accelerating, the volume gradually growing louder, but Kate did not look at the dancers again. She leaned toward William and said, loud enough to be heard over the din, "I wonder if I have to die to become a goddess."

William gave her hand a squeeze.

The music mounted to a thundering crescendo, then stopped.

A lizard guard of honor advanced, bearing a cup of some dark liquid, a wooden cup with crude but complex floral patterns carved in it. The village had become so silent she could hear the tread of the creatures' claws, even the chirping of crickets, and the crackle of the fire which had now dwindled away to red glowing embers that popped from time to time, sending sparks arcing into the surrounding darkness.

Kate made out some of the words in the serpent language as the monster spoke to her, holding out the cup to her. "Sacred drink," he hissed. The other words she could not understand.

He thrust it toward her, right under her nose.

She hesitated a moment, then pushed it away.

She pointed at the creature and in its own language said, "You."

The lizard drew back, then tried again. "No, you," it said, and she could hear a hint of fear in the alien voice.

"You!" she repeated, rising to her feet.

The other lizards looked to the fat one with the wild boar skull. The fat one gestured. The crowd moved in around the one with the cup, swiftly, silently.

As Kate looked on in frozen horror, his comrades forced the drink down his throat.

He fell to the earth, writhing in agony, his tail thrashing and whipping, screaming and hissing and clutching at his throat. He still showed some signs of life when the tribesmen threw him on the fire to cook.

If Kate had not known they weren't human, she could have sworn they were laughing.

Later, as dawn began to brighten the eastern horizon, Kate and William rode in their sedan chairs out of the village toward their cabin in New Lambeth.

The lizard guard of honor seemed subdued, depressed.

Kate turned and called back to William, "Am I a goddess now?"

He shrugged. "How should I know?"

She rode a while in silence, putting together a simple sentence in the unfamiliar language of the lizard-people. After practicing it a few times under her breath she leaned out of the sedan chair and addressed her question to one of the guards that trotted alongside. "Am I a goddess?"

At first the creature failed to understand, but when she repeated her query, it answered with a caw and a hiss. "Yes, Sky Queen." Then, after a pause, it added, "You passed the tests."

He was handsome, as monsters go.

Twice as tall as a man, with muscular hind legs, a long elegant tail, and a full set of arrowhead-like pearly white teeth, he strode up to Kate's cabin door one fine morning and in that blunt way the lizards had, he informed her, "I am yours."

"Thank you," she replied, at a loss for any better reply.

"My full name is Morr Droon Fahra Rahoor Thee Ahh Oh Thahrr Noh Grooh Rahhr. You may call me Grooh for short."

She smiled at him.

He smiled at her.

In the month since the Blakes had "passed the tests," a relationship had sprung up between humans and reptiles, something a little like friendship (though the lizard language contained no word for "friendship") and a lot like symbiosis. The lizards could not speak any human language, but the humans, with more agile tongues and brains, quickly learned the lizard language, with its very small vocabulary, though with an unavoidable "human" accent.

So she did not fear Grooh, and in a few days felt

perfectly at ease when Grooh accompanied her on an afternoon expedition to the forest to gather wild grapes and berries. His claws were too large to pick fruit, but he seemed to enjoy the role of Protector of the Goddess, and conversed freely with her as she plucked grapes from the vines in the bright afternoon sunshine.

She asked him, "Did the tribe send you to me?"

"No, I came on my own."

"To worship me?" She wondered if the time had come to set him straight.

"No, I know you are not a goddess."

"You do?" That surprised her.

"You are some kind of strange creature, nothing more. You will live with us a while, grow old, and die. Then, if I have good memories of you and your mate, I may call you goddess and god seriously. Until then, I pretend. Until then, I learn from you."

She pondered this a while, placing some of the grapes in her mouth instead of in the crude deerskin sack on the ground beside her. "And you're not . . . afraid of us?"

"One male of your species would not frighten me. One female would not frighten me. A male and a female together would not frighten me, unless they brought children."

Without looking at him she asked uneasily, "What difference would that make?"

"Without children you will live a while with us, then die and be honored. With children you would breed another race that would fight us for land, for water, for food. Children would mean war between your kind and mine."

She felt something move within her. She felt dizzy and swayed a moment. His gray claw darted out to steady her. "You are so small and weak, and the sun is so hot. Let me carry your sack."

"Thank you, Grooh. You're very kind."

He shouldered the load. Still a little giddy, she seated herself on a stump, one of many left behind when William had cut the logs for the cabin.

She looked up into the strange toothy grinning face, into the glittering black reptile eyes, and said softly, "Why, you're almost human."

He stood so that his shadow fell over her, protecting her from the sunlight. "I think. Yes, I think, and so few of my tribe do. They all believe you are a real goddess and fear you. They're so stupid. Before the flood we were a great race, but now each generation is more stupid than the last. Someday we will forget how to speak."

"No, that can't be!" Kate's sympathies were easily aroused.

"When brother mates with sister, or even with cousin, it can be, and when the tribes are so small . . ." The monster broke off his sentence with something very like a sigh.

"Sit with me, Grooh," she said, gesturing toward the open patch of long grass next to her stump.

Obediently Grooh crouched on his haunches. "I will sit, little female creature. It is good to talk."

"Some day your tribes will grow larger. Then brother will no longer have to mate with sister."

But Grooh replied gloomily, "The taint is there. When the few become many, the taint will remain."

"But why?" She had become almost angry now at his bleak attitude.

"All my people descend from one couple. One couple and only one couple survived the flood, and that couple . . ." He sighed deeply. ". . . had the taint."

Kate wondered, *Did Urizen, without knowing it, preserve a pair of feeble-minded lizards?* That could explain their lack of progress, and that streak of unreasoning violence in their nature.

Again something moved within her. Her secret!

She had not told William. She had been afraid to, afraid he would change, grow hostile and resentful. Nor had she told anyone else.

Perhaps she could confide in Grooh!

She turned toward him, opened her lips to speak.

But no! She could not tell Grooh. Least of all Grooh!

"Troubles?" He was remarkably perceptive. She sometimes felt he understood her better than William did.

"No, it's nothing." She spoke softly, but Grooh, she knew, could hear her anyway. He had better hearing than any human. Better eyesight, too, even in daylight, though he much preferred the darkness. He pointed skyward. "Your mate is coming," he told her gently.

She strained her eyes, shielding them with her hand and squinting, but several moments passed before she found the dot that was William gliding toward her. In a few moments more she could see his deerskin tunic and cape, then his beard and long hair twisting in the wind, then she could hear him laughing with delight, and Mr. Blake was not a man who laughed often.

He landed lightly between Kate and Grooh, crying excitedly, "Oh, Mrs. Blake, what a hunt! You've no idea! With me in the air to spot deer herds for them, our lizard friends bring home more venison than they ever dreamed possible!"

Grooh perked up at this. The mention of food revived his spirits like nothing else. "You're a useful little thing."

William extended a hand to help Kate to her feet, but no sooner did she rise than she fell back again, dizzy, nauseous. "Come now," scolded William. "Our lizard friends await us. Tonight we feast!"

"You go," she told him weakly. "I'm not hungry."

Suddenly William was all concern. "Upon my word, have you picked up a touch of sunstroke?"

"No," she whispered.

"Something you ate?" coaxed her husband, leaning over her.

"Not that either," she said.

"Then what's wrong?"

She tried to think of something, but her mind seemed numb. *Don't guess, William*, she thought desperately. *Don't guess.*

The answer, when it came to him, came with the force of a certainty. "Kate," he said with wonder, "you're pregnant."

She looked at Grooh.

The giant lizard rose stiffly and said with reptilian coldness, "How nice for you."

The lizard witch doctor would not treat Kate, nor would the lizard midwife. Grooh and his people came no more to

New Lambeth. To them the Blakes had changed from gods into devils.

William, however, revealed a gentleness in his nature that bordered on the feminine, acting as doctor and midwife and nurse all in one.

In the last month of Kate's pregnancy, the Blakes chose a name for their child. They called him (Kate believed Vala had determined the child's sex) Orc, a name that in the lizard tongue meant "revolutionary." Orc, together with other later children, would lead the human revolution against Urizen and the lizards. Or so Kate planned. She knew she could not make things as they had been before the change, but at least humanity would have a chance!

On the last afternoon of her pregnancy, Kate lay on her crude but comfortable bed near the fireplace in the cabin, half awake and half asleep, listening to the singing of the birds outside and dreaming of the new race she would mother, and it seemed to her in her drowsy reverie that her swelling abdomen contained, not one child, but multitudes, vast armies of unborn men and women who would rise from her womb to reclaim the planet, snatch it back by superior wit and courage from the serpentine usurpers.

When Urizen awakes, she thought, *he will find a human, not a lizard world.* Too bad for Urizen! Kate chuckled softly to herself.

Suddenly, without warning, a sharp pain jolted her into full awareness. *Is it beginning?* she wondered anxiously.

She waited a long time for a second pain, and had almost decided nothing would happen when the pain came, harder than before. When it passed she sat up, drawing her deerskin cover to her chin, and shouted, "William!"

No answer.

"Mr. Blake!"

Silence.

Wrapping the deerskin cover around her naked body, she stumbled to the cabin door and peered out.

She saw the poplar trees and wild grapevines of her familiar garden, and there, in the distance, wound the familiar river. She saw the usual long grass, and weeds, heard the usual humming bees and twittering birds. No pastoral painter could have imagined a more peaceful sun-lit landscape.

But where was William?

She felt the pain come on again, and she turned and threw herself on the bed.

"Mr. Blake!"

The pain was bad this time, but the fear was worse. Could she bring little Orc into the world alone, by herself, without aid? What if, at some critical moment, she fainted?

"Mr. Blake!"

The pain faded.

In spite of the coolness of the room, Kate found herself drenched with sweat. With the back of her wrist she wiped her damp forehead, brushed the unruly hair back out of her eyes.

"Mr. Blake!" she screamed.

Then she heard footsteps approaching, a rustling in the high weeds outside the cabin. With a great sigh of relief she closed her eyes and fell back, relaxed, on her fur-covered pillow.

"Thank God you've come, Mr. Blake!"

Kate waited for William to say something, make some excuse for not being with her when she needed him.

"Mr. Blake?" she called uncertainly.

Why did he stand there saying nothing? What was wrong?

She opened her eyes and looked toward the door. A pair of glittering reptilian eyes gazed in at her. A huge green scaly head grinned at her, framed in the open doorway.

"Grooh!"

The lizard did not reply.

"You are Grooh, aren't you?" She slid back in her bed until her shoulders pressed against the wall.

"Yes, I am Grooh." He spoke slowly, so she understood every hiss and click.

In his own language she demanded, "What . . . what are you doing here?"

"I heard you scream. Are you having your baby?" He spoke with a flat, emotionless tone.

Kate thought, *Why does he want to know that? Is he here . . . to kill the child?*

"No," she said.

"You lie."

After a long tense silence, Grooh added, "Do not fear me. I am yours."

"What?"

"Once I told you I was yours, and I am yours." The huge creature hunched over and thrust his snout inside the cabin. "To me you are no evil demon, as you are to my people, but a helpless little being who wants to live and give life, like any other animal. Like me! I stayed away because the chief commanded it, but I passed close by every day, keeping out of your sight, watching that no harm should come to you."

She did not know why, but she believed him instantly. "Grooh, Grooh, you're right. I did lie to you. I am having my baby. My cramps have begun and Mr. Blake is nowhere in sight. Can you help me?"

"I have helped at many birthings," said Grooh. "My people hatch from eggs, but we keep dogs, horses, cattle, cats . . . I have helped them. I know how to help creatures who give birth to live young." Eagerly he tried to enter the cabin, but quickly gave up. "I can't get through the door. It's too low and narrow for me!"

Kate felt the contractions begin again. She rolled over with a despairing groan. The huge reptile hissed in frustration and tried once more, without success, to thrust himself through the doorway.

"Grooh!" she cried. The room seemed to spin around her. The pain became unbearable. She reached out toward him. "Grooh!" she screamed.

Grooh gripped the sides of the doorway in his powerful front claws, braced his hind legs against the cabin's stone foundation, and, with a muffled grunt of effort, pulled. Through her agony she heard a long drawn-out creak as the wood bent, then a loud sharp crack as it broke. A major portion of the front of the house splintered and crumpled as it came loose in his hands.

A moment later he loomed at her side, leaning over her.

Was it his presence, or simply the natural progress of the cycle? Whichever it was, the pain drained away as she clutched Grooh's heavy claw in her small sweating hands. She whispered, "Oh thank you, Grooh. Thank you. Thank you."

She looked up, past Grooh's shoulder, out through the gaping hole in the side of the cabin, and caught sight of a dot in the sky, growing larger. She smiled. "It's all right now, Grooh. Here comes Mr. Blake."

It was indeed Mr. Blake. She could see him clearly, clad in his animal skins, his beard and long hair streaming in the wind. Then she frowned, puzzled. William was drawing his shortsword from its scabbard. Why was he doing that?

Then, in a horrified flash, she understood. "No, Mr. Blake!" she shrieked. "Don't!"

With the full force of his flying momentum, William rammed his sword to the hilt into Grooh's unprotected throat.

As the great beast fell, Kate saw his glittering eyes turn toward her with mute incomprehension before they went stiff and opaque, like smooth round black stones. His tail thrashed a few times, making kindling of some of the crude furniture in the cabin, then went limp. The blood spurted from his neck once, twice, three times, then, as the monster's huge heart stopped beating, the flow slowed to a steady oozing.

Kate turned her gaze to William. "My God, Mr. Blake, do you know what you've done?"

"He tried to kill you."

"No, no, he tried to help me! And he could have helped me, too! Go back in time, William. Go back and undo this terrible thing."

But William's jaw was set. "No. It was a trick. He tricked you!" She gazed at William with anguished frustration. *He won't admit he made a mistake*, she realized. *He'll never admit it.* But she needed this man now. Whatever he'd done, she needed him.

"Mr. Blake . . ." The pain started again.

William, still carrying the blood-wet sword, stepped over the half-coiled tail of Grooh's corpse and knelt at her bedside.

"Help me," she moaned, eyes closed, and felt his strong arms encircle her.

The sword, as it turned out, came in handy for cutting the umbilical cord.

Orc was a human baby the first day.

On the second day he began to change.

On the third day she felt teeth against her nipple as the baby sucked and, holding him away from her, she forced open his tiny mouth.

He had teeth all right, but not human teeth. There were too many of them and they were too small and sharp. Orc began to cry. She put him back on the breast. His teeth didn't really hurt her, at least not yet.

She did not mention the teeth to William.

On the fourth day Orc hissed at her.

Still she said nothing to William.

On the fifth day she caught Orc staring at her intently as he lay bundled up in his furs in his makeshift crib. She stared back.

And she began to understand.

"Are you Grooh?" she asked the chubby, strangely silent child. A five-day-old baby should not be able to focus his eyes like that.

Orc said nothing.

"Are you Grooh?" she repeated. "Give me some sign."

He smiled, ever-so-slightly, and she saw his teeth had grown. They looked more reptilian than ever.

On the sixth day Orc's skin took on a faint tinge of grayish green.

William inquired, "What's wrong with him?"

Kate replied lightly, "It's just a phase."

She laughed in a forced way that made William glance at her with suspicion. *Have to be careful,* she thought.

William wouldn't understand. William wasn't a mother.

On the seventh day, when the nub of a tail appeared at the base of Orc's spine it was impossible for her to know it and not know it at the same time.

On the eighth day she awoke to find William standing at her bedside in the dim light of morning, a naked Orc in his arms, examining the nub of a tail. William was gentle; Orc, eyes closed, hissed faintly with contentment. She sat up quickly, trying to meet her husband's accusing gaze.

"I'm sorry," she said, her eyes on the nub. "It's not my fault."

"You didn't tell me. Did you think I wouldn't notice?" The supressed anger in his voice frightened her.

"At first. Then he got worse." She stretched out her arms. "Give me my baby."

She took the child and put him to her breast. William watched grimly, hand on the pommel of his shortsword. Kate thought, *Poor little thing. Mama will protect you.* But the tiny teeth had begun to really hurt her nipple.

"We can't keep him," William said softly.

"I won't let you kill him!" She turned to the wall, shielding Orc with her body, looking at William over her shoulder.

"He's not human, Kate."

"He is! What does that mean, 'human'? When he gets older he'll be all right."

"You know better. He started as a human, and he's half lizard already. In a matter of days he'll be all lizard." How she hated the calmness, the unemotional reasonableness of his voice. It was William who was not human!

"Leave us alone!"

William sat down on the edge of the bed and laid a warm hand on Kate's bare back. "I won't kill him, but . . . but you can't ask me to accept that thing as my son."

"You never wanted to have any child at all with me! I was never right for you. I was never clever . . . like Vala. Why don't you go to Vala and leave Orc and me alone? She's the only one you think is worthy to be the mother of your child."

"Kate, I . . ."

"Go to Vala, damn you. Orc and I will be all right. We don't need you. I'm not helpless. I'm a Zoa. I have powers. I . . ."

"Kate, listen. . . ."

"We won't kill him but we won't keep him either. What will we do with him then, I'd like to know?"

William considered her question, brows knit, great eyes full of pain. At last he said, "I want to give him to Urizen."

"Give him to Urizen? You're insane, you are!"

"He belongs to Urizen."

"He belongs to me!"

"We live in Urizen's universe. Everything in it belongs to Urizen. You belong to Urizen. I belong to Urizen. So Orc belongs to Urizen, too." He reached for the child.

"No!" She retreated across the fur-strewn bed. "Urizen don't know how to care for no baby."

"Vala does."

"Vala!" Her cry was like that of a wounded animal. "Vala! No, no, not Vala. Anyone but Vala!" Cornered now, she cowered back into the place where the side and rear walls of the room joined.

"Don't you see, Kate? If Orc were human we might have had a chance. He's not. He's a . . . a monster."

"No!"

"And you and I, we'll be monsters too. Urizen will be a monster. Vala will be a monster. You and I, we've lost, don't you see? And with us humanity has lost, too. The fight's over and we've lost." He leaned over and roughly wrenched Orc from her arms. Oh, why did he have to be so much stronger?

As he stood up she sprang forward and snatched the shortsword from his scabbard. They faced each other in the center of the room, he with the baby, she with the sword. Orc looked first at one, then at the other, eyes glowing with unnatural concentration.

"I have my energy shield down, Kate," William said gently. "You can kill me if you want to. I won't stop you. Will you really kill me?"

Kate hefted the weapon, getting the feel of its weight and balance. She asked herself silently, *Well, will I?*

They stood motionless for at least a full minute, face to face, breathing. Finally Kate said, in an almost inaudible voice, "Not you."

"Who then?"

"Urizen!"

As she leaped into the place outside of time, William followed close behind her, still carrying Orc in his arms.

Clouds of spirits swirled around them in the vortex of fading, brightening, shifting images, none human, all lizard. Lizards! Lizards! Lizards! As she soared uptime they whirled around her, green and transparent like emeralds, hissing and whispering like waves on an ocean beach. They paid no attention to her, occasionally even passing through her body with a sensation like a cold wind. Was the battle over here, too? Had the lizards won, once and for all?

Ahead she sighted the rip in the universe, the gap that led into . . . somewhere else. It had almost completely closed. Here and there the last few humans struggled in vain against an overwhelming reptilian force. Was that Robert being dragged through the opening by a half-dozen opponents? At this distance she could not tell for certain. Even if she'd known it was Robert, she could do nothing to help him.

The red light faded as the rip closed, but the new light blazed much brighter and greener than the one she remembered. A reptilian green!

She changed course, cutting through space as well as time. Spain passed beneath her, then the Mediterranean. Egypt came in sight, and that great gash that marked the valley of the Dead Sea. The Himalayan mountains appeared on the eastern horizon.

She squinted, searching for Mount Everest.

She thought, *There will be a moment, when Urizen wakes, when he will fade back into common time. He'll lie there in his white coffin, dazed, vulnerable, with his shields not yet up. At that moment I will strike!* Would that bring back the world she longed for? She no longer cared.

She sighted Urizen's mountain and circled it, planning.

The stronghold will be sealed when Urizen awakes, but a little later it will have to open to let him out . . . in fact, when he's out of the coffin the locking effect will be off. I'll slip in then, go downtime, and when he opens his eyes, the first thing and the last thing he will see will be me.

She headed uptime, rushing through the weeks, the months, the years.

The stronghold opened. The mouthlike entrance gaped wide. Urizen and Vala emerged. Vala carried something in her arms but Kate, at this distance, could not tell what it was.

Before the entrance closed again, Kate passed through, unseen. She drifted down the great hall where Urizen's white coffin lay, now really empty; then, still outside the timestream, she hurtled backwards in time.

In a blur of reversed motion she recognized herself, William, Vala . . . and Urizen! Urizen alive! Did that mean Kate's mission would fail? No, she decided, just that her intervention had not yet generated a new future.

Now she saw Urizen in the mirror but not in the coffin.

She entered the timestream.

In the awesome silence of the stronghold, she floated toward the coffin, her forcefield stirring up a cloud of age-old dust beneath her. Gently, gently she touched down, feeling the cold stone under the carpet of dust with her bare feet. She looked first down into the empty coffin, then up into the mirror where Urizen slept, just out of reach. She thought, *Am I too early?*

As if in answer to her unvoiced question, Urizen moved, ever so slightly. In the coffin the dust stirred. A cloud of dust motes arose, outlining a figure, still invisible, lying there.

Kate raised her shortsword. Her hands shook only a little, both left and right firmly gripping the weapon.

Urizen gradually became transparent, then translucent.

Kate thought, with dreamlike detachment, *One second more.*

And then Urizen was there, breathing gently, but the dust that covered him made him seem hardly human. His eyes remained closed. Hardly human. Hardly alive. How easy now to drive home the blade!

But that same dust that made Urizen seem less than human also obscured his identity. For one instant Kate had the ghastly impression that not Urizen, but William, lay there under the dust. She hesitated.

Urizen's eyes opened.

Kate stabbed downward.

The blade shattered in Urizen's forcefield.

"Too late, Mrs. Blake," Urizen said, smiling and sitting up.

Kate had no idea how long she had sat on the platform near the foot of the coffin, weeping hysterically. She could hear William and Urizen speaking to her with concern, but their voices were so similar she could not tell them apart. She could hear Vala's voice too, and the rustle of Vala's long robes.

Vala's voice was full of pity. "There, there, my dear. There, there. Don't cry. Everything will be all right." Kate had never heard Polly Wood's voice, but she had imagined it many times, sounding just like that.

"Leave me alone!" Kate screamed.

"But, Kate dear . . ." Vala's cool hand rested on Kate's shoulder. She shrugged it off.

Urizen had been speaking to William while Vala tried to calm her. For a moment Urizen's words came through clearly. ". . . amazing woman, William. There was a chink in my armor that I didn't know about, and she found it. She could have killed me if she'd had it in her to kill anyone." Kate's consciousness blurred.

Looking up, a little later, Kate saw William handing Orc to Vala, saying, "Take care of him for us."

Vala looked down at the half-human infant with a false smile. "Of course, William. You can come and visit him when Kate feels better."

"Good of you," William said.

"Not at all," Vala said.

"Think nothing of it," Urizen said.

Kate sprang up. "No! No! You can't have him!" She tried to reach Vala, who backed away a few steps, but William and Urizen blocked the way. Kate slapped William's face, then kicked Urizen in the shins. They hardly seemed to notice. They were so strong, so hard. When she tried to scratch them with her fingernails, they caught her by the wrists.

Fragments of words and sentences came to her through the sound of her own shrieking. ". . . she's in no condition to . . ." ". . . of course . . ." ". . . obviously in no condition . . ." ". . . rest . . ." ". . . a long rest . . ."

The room tilted, spun around. She thought with determination, *I absolutely won't faint.*

She fainted.

The long fever had passed.

Kate opened her eyes and looked around, finding herself in her cabin at New Lambeth with no clear idea how she had gotten there. Through the doorless doorway she could see a low, slow-moving overcast. And rain, a light drizzle. She thought, *William fixed the wall.*

"Mr. Blake?" she called weakly.

"Yes?" William emerged from the shadows to stand, looking down at her. His face was lined with weariness, and his beard and hair had turned more gray than red. His fur cloak was wet and filthy.

She asked him, without emotion, "Where's Orc?"

"Uptime, with Urizen."

"With Vala, you mean."

"With Vala, if you want to put it that way."

"We must go . . ." She sat up in bed, but fell back almost instantly. Her body, it seemed, would not obey her.

"We'll go," William said, sitting down on the edge of the bed, then added, "When we're ready."

"When I get well, will we go?"

"It isn't that." Something in his tone alarmed her.

"What then?"

He smiled faintly, and she saw his teeth, small and sharp, not human. "We must wait until we've become . . . like Orc."

"You're changing!" She inched away from him.

He nodded slowly. "Yes." The S drew out unnaturally long. He reached out to take her hand.

"Don't touch me!"

"Look at your own hand, Kate."

She looked at her . . . claw. "Oh my God," she whispered.

William said gently, "Soon we'll all be together, a family."

When she did not speak for a long time, he asked, "What are you thinking about?"

"I'm praying," she murmured, eyes closed.

He stood up with a sigh and shuffled over to toss another log on the fire. She listened to the pop and sizzle of the flames, fragments of half-remembered prayers mixing in her mind with a disjointed, incoherent pleading.

Kate slept badly that night, by fits and starts. A little before dawn, after hovering for some time between waking and sleeping, she suddenly understood.

She rolled over, grasped the sleeping William by the shoulder, and shook him. "Wake up, wake up!"

With an uncomprehending groan, he raised up on one elbow and stared at her.

"Listen, Mr. Blake, I've found the way out!"

"Out of what?" he said stupidly, rubbing his eyes with his fist like a child.

"This universe!" She sat up, her enthusiasm overcoming her weakness. "There is a way out, and it has been in front of us all this time without our seeing it."

"What are you talking about?"

"Time! There is time in the place outside of time!"

"What?" His face, in the dim predawn light, was a blob of sullen incomprehension.

"Don't you see? If you want to get out of the stream of normal time, you go into what we've been calling the place outside of time, but it's not really outside of time! There's another kind of time there. Things happen. Things like the battle between the lizard and human spirits begin, go on a while, then end."

"So what?"

"Aren't you awake yet? Don't you realize what this means? Just as we can, by concentration, get out of the normal timestream into the so-called place outside of time, so must we be able, by concentration, to get out of the place outside of time and into some other place that's *really* outside of time."

"No, impossible. We would have seen it. . . ."

"But we did see it! Remember when we went downtime to Urizen's island and saw his timeship come rushing toward us out of the future?"

"I remember, but . . ."

"That timeship didn't come from this future we live in, but from the other future, before the change. From where we stood we could see both futures at once. Both futures still existed! So there must have been some kind of time common to them both. It's clear as day, Mr. Blake. And when Urizen shot his own earlier self, where did the old self go? And where did the lizards drag all the human spirits to in that battle, and where did all those lizard spirits come from in the first place? Answer me that if you can."

"Urizen would have figured out . . ."

"No, Urizen didn't figure it out! I did! But it's got to be true all the same. There is another place outside of time, a place where all the different futures exist together."

"If there were, we couldn't find it."

"Yes, we can." She grasped his hand. "Come!"

New Lambeth vanished.

Occasional lizard spirits rushed past heedlessly on urgent but unguessable errands. No trace remained of the battle uptime and the rip had healed over without leaving a trace. The light glowed an even shadowless green. The images had lost vividness and life, and here and there Kate could see peculiar crumpling effects, as if the very fabric of spacetime might collapse under some unthinkably mighty stress.

Kate glanced at William. He had a tail.

A small tail, but a tail nonetheless.

Kate reached behind herself and found she had one too.

She said firmly, "Concentrate, Mr. Blake, while you still have a mind that can."

They concentrated.

She did not know what to look for, and almost ignored the effect when it first appeared.

She had an impression of distance, nothing more.

Her impulse was to say, "That's not it."

But then she realized that she was seeing, more with her mind than with her eyes, both the world inside the timestream and the world outside of time, superimposed, neither more sharp than the other.

"Here it comes," she told William excitedly, and grasped his hand.

Quite suddenly, with a rush, she fell back away from her vision. Everything shrank rapidly. Other things came into view, too far away to see clearly. The light grew brighter, taking on a brilliant bluewhite color.

She glanced to her right. William, still holding her hand, looked so bewildered she had to smile.

"You see?" she cried. "You see?"

She laughed out loud from sheer exhilaration.

The place they had come from was shrinking to a point.

A point is that which has position but no magnitude. William had taught her that, along with so much else. A point has neither length nor breadth nor depth, yet it exists.

And now she saw that the place they had come from was part of a thin glowing line.

A line is the course of a moving point, having length but no other dimension. In each line lay an infinite number of points.

Infinite!

Kate had heard William pronounce that word so many times. She'd thought she understood it, but she hadn't . . . not until now!

The line they had come from was one of many. It branched and branched and branched again, and from each branch grew other branches, and from them yet others. It was like a tree, or better yet, a fan. It stretched out endlessly into the haze of distance, an infinite fan-shaped plane.

A plane is a surface such that a straight line joining any two of its points lies wholly within the surface.

Her mind struggled to understand.

The point she'd come from was a point in spacetime. That point was part of a single timeline, the timeline of the lizards, but the timeline of the lizards branched again and again. There was an infinite number of lizard timelines, and all the lizard timelines, taken together, were a branch of yet another timeline. *And where am I?* she thought. *Am I really finally outside of time?*

No. Events still happened to her one after the other, in ordered sequence. Even here, above the fan of time, above the infinite different branches of time, time continued to flow relentlessly.

She saw more.

The fan could rotate. It could describe a vast cone . . . a cone! But what lay outside the cone? As if in answer to her question she began to see another cone, completely within the first cone, *yet branching off from it at a right angle*.

William screamed.

She saw him cover his eyes with his right hand, his left clinging to her hand so tightly it hurt her. She closed her eyes a moment, only to find that she could still see the impossible thing.

She remembered, oddly, a line William had recited to her from his *Marriage of Heaven and Hell*.

"If the doors of perception were cleansed, everything would appear to man as it is, infinite."

She said soothingly, "There, there, Mr. Blake. Don't take on so. You've nothing to fear. Why, everything is really just the way you always knew it was."

His large eyes fixed on her, filled with more madness than she'd ever seen before. "There's a limit!"

"A limit to what?"

"You know!"

"The universe?"

"No! *My mind.*"

She turned away from him to look again at the cone. And the cone within the cone. And the cone within the cone within the cone. There could be no mistake. The bluewhite light was very bright. It hurt her eyes.

Light blazed all around her. It moved and undulated like smoke, like the northern lights on a freezing night, like a waterfall that sparkled in the sunlight, like a swarm of fireflies, yet it was somehow solid. Was it made of colored glass? She tried to touch it, but could not.

And it seemed to her she could somehow not only see the light, but hear it, and the sound was like a vast billion-toned chord on a cathedral organ, a chord that changed constantly yet always remained the same, and she could feel the chord on her skin, like sunshine.

And in light and sound she could sense . . . *consciousness*.

Wordlessly, something or someone seemed to speak to her in her mind, something or someone ancient and wise beyond any hope of human understanding.

Kate was dimly aware of William weeping at her side.

She herself felt neither terror nor confusion. The presence that now spoke to her without speaking was familiar, had been near her all her life. She could call it God. She could call it Jehovah. She could call it Isis. She could call it Quetzalcoatl. Any name would do, but no name at all was best. Any face at all would do, even her own, but no face was best.

And it loved her. It cared about her. It watched out for her.

And it guided her.

A third time she looked at the cone. Of all the timelines, one seemed to stand out, to beckon to her, to call her, as if it were stronger and brighter than the others, though it was not, and of all the points on that brighter line, one stood out as if it were a spot of pure white flame, though it was not.

Still without words, *something* directed her toward that flame, guiding her gently, patiently, tenderly.

Something spoke a wordless word in her mind.

Home.

"Come along, Mr. Blake," she said firmly.

The cone hurtled toward her.

Only when the rain hit her skin did she realize her nakedness and William's. In the dim early morning light she looked at her hand. She had a human hand, not a claw.

She looked at William. He had no tail.

She looked around her.

She stood, she realized, in the middle of the street, facing a house, and with mingled shock and relief she recognized it as her own home, 13 Hercules Buildings, Lambeth, Surrey, London, England, one of a row of terrace houses of eight or ten rooms each, surrounded by gardens, trees, and bushes.

Something told her the year, 1794. Something told her she would find no giant talking lizards in this universe, no temples of Isis or Quetzalcoatl, no Albion, no Oothoon, no Lud's Dun, no New Lambeth.

William turned toward her, dumbfounded.

"Mrs. Blake, what . . ."

"We'd best go inside, Mr. Blake. Think of the scandal if the neighbors should see us bare as the Good Lord made us."

She opened the unlocked front door.

Inside William remarked, dazed, "Not a speck of dust, and we've been gone so long."

"No, we haven't. We left here yesterday afternoon . . . to go shopping. Remember? I suppose we have to go shopping today instead, but you shave first. You look a sight!"

She slipped on her robe after drying herself with a towel, then stood at the back window watching the rain fall gently on her wild grape vines and her poplar trees.

Soon William joined her, saying, "How do I look?"

"Much better, without the beard."

"Kate! You've been crying!"

She nodded, lowering her eyes. "Yes, I suppose I have."

"But we've come home! Everything's back the way it was!"

"Yes, I know, but . . ."

"Is it Orc?" he asked softly.

She nodded. "Yes, it's Orc. I miss him, I do. He was a dear thing, in spite of his . . . bad complexion."

"Perhaps I can go back, get him away from Urizen. Perhaps if I bring him here he'll change, become like other little boys."

Something told her the process of change, when it had gone beyond a certain point, was irreversible.

She shook her head. "No . . . but thank you for offering." Here she broke down and cried for a long time while William held her close and soothed her.

That afternoon, though she felt weak, she went shopping and William got a haircut.

The Blakes sat in their rockers before the fire.

"No more time-voyaging," said William with no regret, only a vast, weary relief.

"One more trip," Kate corrected him, gazing into the glowing embers. She had given the matter a great deal of thought, and made up her mind. William could hear the firmness in her voice and offered no arguments.

He only said, "Where will we go?"

"Not we, Mr. Blake. This time I travel alone."

"You need me to protect . . ."

She broke in with an ironic laugh. "And who will protect me from you? No, I am a Zoa. I have power of my own. I may never use it again, but I will always know I have it. This time I go alone."

"Where?" She could tell her remarks had cut him deeply, but he could not deny the truth in them. His tone gave him away, the sadness, the pain, the guilt.

"I want to visit Vala," said Kate quietly.

"Vala?"

"Or Mary Wollstonecraft, as she calls herself here."

"Mary went to Paris."

"She will return, and I will go uptime to see her." She stood up. "Do you want to stop me?"

"No, but why . . ."

"Don't worry. I mean her no harm. Your darling is safe, I assure you. She did me a kindness, William, when she helped me to conceive Orc. In a universe where no one could help me, not even you, she helped me. Now I will help her."

Without waiting for his reply, Kate stepped out of the timestream.

Mary Wollstonecraft looked up from her desk where she sat, quill in hand, writing a letter, as Kate materialized out of the dust motes in a beam of sunlight that streamed in an open window.

"Hello, Kate. I see William has taught you the trick."

Kate took a hesitant step forward. Now, face to face with her rival, some of her confidence slipped away. "May I sit down, Mary?"

"Of course." Mary gestured toward an overstuffed sofa.

Kate sat down with a sigh. "I know about William and you."

"I assumed as much when you made your grand entrance just now. But didn't you always know?"

"I mean I know you are William Godwin's mother, and that William Godwin is Urizen . . . all that."

"You don't know everything, my dear. William Godwin and I have married."

Kate was stunned. "You can't . . . A mother can't marry her own son!"

Mary shook her head sadly. "You are not a Zoa yet, after all. You're still a prisoner of the prejudices of the age. You must really try to transcend your background, take a broader view; but don't worry, I am Mrs. Godwin in name only. Urizen and I occupy separate dwellings and separate beds, though we maintain the appearance of marriage, of a great romance in fact, for the sake of the child."

"The child?"

"I am going to have another baby."

"And the father?"

"You can go anywhere, see anything. How could I conceal it from you? The father is your husband, of course. He doesn't know. I hope he doesn't find out, but he is a Zoa too." She looked toward the window, a wistful expression on her delicate features. "He is a Zoa, and he taught me to be a Zoa, too."

Kate sat a while, composing herself. *I am a Zoa, too,* she thought. *I do not need to see things through the eyes of a poor ignorant farm girl. I am a Zoa and I have seen things no explorer in this universe has seen. I am a Zoa and I know things no university professor in this universe knows.*

Finally Kate said, "You and Urizen are experimenting."

"I don't deny it."

"You are changing time."

"Yes."

"I want to tell you where these experiments can lead." And with that, slowly at first, and then faster, and finally in a great torrent of words, Kate blurted out all that had happened. The sun had set by the time she finished, and the two women sat a while in silence, unable to see each other's face in the darkness.

Then Mary Wollstonecraft spoke, very gently. "You are my friend, Kate. I see that now. I know you have told me the truth, and I promise you we will make no more of what you call experiments."

There was something in the other woman's voice that made Kate uneasy. "Mary, are you already doing an experiment?"

Mary laughed. "So you read minds as well! You're more powerful than I am!"

"What is it, Mary? What is it this time?"

"Don't fight me on this one, Kate."

"I can't promise."

"You'll find out anyway, so I'll tell you. But think about it before you try to block me. Don't fight me just because you're against these experiments on principle. Don't fight me just because you see me as your rival. Can you promise that? Can you promise to judge this little game on its own merits?"

"Yes, yes, that much I can promise."

"Then I tell you, the seed of this future lies within my womb. Within my womb grows the best tomorrow of them all." She leaned toward Kate in the darkness, voice husky with excitement. "I carry a child who combines William Blake's unbounded imagination with Mary Wollstonecraft's social consciousness, and who will be raised in the discipline of William Godwin's scientific rationalism. Los, Vala, and Urizen! All three in dynamic balance within one brilliant mind!"

"What will he do, this wonder child?"

"Did you say 'he'? My child will be a female. My child

will show the world what a female can do! Yes, my child, named Mary after me, will write a book.''

"What kind of book?" Kate heard the madness in Mary's voice, a madness she'd heard before in Urizen's voice, in William Blake's voice.

"A novel," said Mary softly. "A simple tale of horror, fit only to frighten children on Halloween, some will say, but it will give birth to a whole new genre of literature. I have been uptime, Kate. I can tell you the title of the book."

"Tell me then."

"*Frankenstein, A Modern Prometheus*!"

"But a simple novel . . ." To Mary a novel was a silly fiction whose only purpose was to waste the time of some rich and lazy woman.

"My daughter's book will open the door for others. My daughter's book will show how to combine the rationalism of a Godwin with the imagination of a Blake. Other authors will imitate it. A few at first, then more and more. At first the genre will be part of a literary movement called Romanticism and the stories will be called Scientific Romances, then when Romanticism dies the genre will change name and go on. It will be called Scientifiction, then Science Fiction, always balancing the principle of Los against the principle of Urizen. Slowly, through the nineteenth century, through the twentieth century, the spirit of Frankenstein will seep into the consciousness of the masses. Finally, by the end of the twentieth century, this genre will dominate all the others, this genre will be the voice of the age, and those things its writers have only imagined will become realities. And my spirit will be there too, the spirit of Vala, of Mary Wollstonecraft, the spirit of social change, the voice that always compares what is with what might be and finds reality wanting. Not only will men walk on the moon, but women will vote. Not only will pictures move and voices traverse the planet in seconds, but slaves will be freed and kings lose their power."

"All this because of your daughter's book?"

"All this because of my daughter's book. Armies of authors will follow her lead, creating thousands upon thousands of alternative realities. Don't you see what it will lead to?''

"No, I . . .''

"In the twenty-first century all humankind will develop the kind of consciousness only a Zoa has now. All humankind will see, as your husband sees, a world in a grain of sand, and Heaven in a wild flower; hold Infinity in the palm of the hand, and Eternity in an hour. All humankind will have the doors of perception cleansed and will see the universe as it is, infinite! Oh, Kate, tell me you won't fight me this time. Tell me you'll let it happen.''

Kate sat in the darkness, considering. Then she said, "I envy you.''

"Don't envy me. Let me do it, Kate Blake. It's a good vision. It's the good part of your husband's vision, after the sickness and weakness in him is burned away. Let it happen, for his sake.''

"I will let it happen. Yes, I will. Not for William's sake, but for yours. You were kind to me, Mary. You were my friend. But I am not Zoa enough to rise above envying you the joy of raising such a child.''

"I will not raise her.'' Mary Wollstonecraft's voice was suddenly bitter.

"Why not?'' Again Kate had been thrown off balance.

"Didn't I tell you, my dear?'' said Mary Wollstonecraft. "I will die in childbirth.''

8

THE BLAKES WERE OLD. Kate was still vigorous, but William had, for several years, been suffering from recurring attacks of what he called "shivering fits," each worse than the last, and lately from jaundice as well, both symptoms of gallstones, the disease that would eventually cause his death.

They no longer lived in comfortable Lambeth, though Kate occasionally walked past their old home and paused a moment to look at it. Now they rented two small rooms on the ground floor at No. 3 Fountain Court. In one of them he lay, bed laden with well-thumbed books in French, Latin, Italian, Greek, and Hebrew, reading, writing, and drawing by turns, whenever his weakness permitted. Most of all he read the Bible; his copy had been all but destroyed by constant use.

Their house stood in a narrow slit between the Strand and the River Thames. His long engraver's table was placed under the room's one window so he could, while working, gaze out across the squalid yard and see this river, as he said, "like a bar of gold." In all the universes he had visited, this river had been the same, though all else changed. The fireplace occupied the corner opposite the window. It would have warmed him if he'd sat there. A pile of portfolios and drawings he could have consulted lay on the right hand end of the table, near the room's only cupboard, and on what would have been his left was a pile of books placed one upon another. He had no bookcase. Just two pictures hung on his walls: a print of an illustration by Giulio Romano of Ovid's *Metamorphoses* and, close by the engraving table, Albert Dürer's *Melancholy, the Mother of Invention*.

The bed, like everything else in the room, faced the window, as if the window were a theater stage on which the seasons performed an endless, enigmatic and somewhat boring play.

The other room, though it served as a showroom for his art, was much darker and somewhat smaller. Though this place was not so grand as the Lambeth place, William did not complain. Here the landlord never pressed them if the rent was late; he was a certain kindly Mr. Baines, Kate's brother-in-law.

So here William lay, not like an invalid, but like a languorous Roman emperor reclining on a royal dais, his bald forehead rising majestically above an oddly shrunken face, clean-shaven, calm, and dignified. His eyes had not changed: they shone as large and strange as ever, but everything else about him seemed in some way paler, smaller, more shrunken . . . the ruddy color of his skin had been replaced by an alarming yellowish tinge. Yet he remained an emperor for all that, his toga a linen nightshirt worn but white with the whiteness of many washings.

He sighed, squinting out the window at a beautiful bright August morning, at the white clouds piled above the familiar skyline of Lambeth across the Thames. Then he heard the front door open and close gently, heard whispers, the rustle of clothing.

"Kate, is that you?" His voice was not strong.

"Yes, Mr. Blake. Me and a neighbor lady that's giving me a hand with things."

He turned his head as Kate came quickly to his bedside. She wore a white muslin blouse with slightly puffed sleeves; her skirt, also of white muslin, hung almost to the floor. The clothing did not fit her well, as it was a hand-me-down from "the other Kate," William's sister. The neighbor lady hung back in the doorway, fidgeting.

"Can we talk?" asked William.

Kate shot a meaningful glance at the neighbor lady, who

said, in a sickroom whisper, "If you need anything more . . ."

Kate told her, "Not now, but thank you so much. You've been such a comfort."

The woman left, obviously grateful to escape from the presence of disease. Kate doffed her broad-brimmed straw hat and tossed it on the table, not looking at William. "So much to do. . . ."

"Can we talk?" William repeated.

Kate perched on the edge of the bed. "I've heard some of the most dreadful gossip next door. Would you believe . . ."

He silenced her with an impatient gesture. "Today is the day."

She understood instantly. Today was the day of his death.

"When?" she asked softly.

"Sometime after six this evening. I jumped uptime—I know we agreed not to do that—and I saw my corpse, here in the bed, and you bending over me. The grandfather clock chimed seven. I fell back into present-time before I could see anything more."

"Can't you hang on a bit longer? We have so much unfinished work. That engraving. Mr. Cumberland's bookplate . . ."

"You'll have to finish them without me."

"No, I can't!"

"You can, and you must. We've worked together so many, many years. All our best work we've done together. I have the grand ideas, yes, but you have the skillful fingers. On these jobs the grand thinking's done."

"But we have other commissions. Business is finally taking a turn for the better."

"Do the best you can, Kate."

"I'll do perfectly rotten! Alone I do such trivial things, though I can do them quick and well enough to please the customers. Tell me true, if it was you could you go on working without me?"

"I suppose not." He closed his eyes. "But since we're telling the truth today, let me say I never was a real artist.

I never could give life to the things in my mind. Ah, but when we worked together . . . my rough clumsy sketches and your fantastic finished cuts. When we worked together we made pictures that could have come from the hand of Raphael or daVinci. All the prophetic books, all the books about the things we did in other universes . . . we did them together, Kate!"

"The books aren't finished either. What about *The Book of Kate*? That was to be your gift to me, the master key that unlocks all the rest!"

He shook his head wearily. "Too late. Too late. Forgive me."

After a pause she said, "Perhaps we've done enough already, Mr. Blake. Robert told me . . ."

"You saw Robert?"

"He came to me in a dream last night, to comfort me, I suppose. He says all the human spirits have come back to our own timeline. He says the lizard timeline is dying."

Surprised, William asked, "How can a timeline die?"

"Timelines rest on human will. Human will fades."

He took her hand. "I see, I see. The lizard world is Urizen's dream isn't it? Something must be happening to Urizen. Perhaps he's dying, too."

Kate shuddered. "Don't use that word 'dying.' "

"Remember what I said last year when our old friend Flaxman died?"

"You said you thought you should have gone first."

"And I said I could not think of death as more than the going out of one room into another. That's what it is, too. Who knows better than we?"

"Yes, yes, you're right, of course."

"What else did Robert say?"

"Don't ask me to tell you."

"I do ask, and now is the time for truth."

"Urizen is all lizard now, his proud intelligence gone. Robert thinks he realized, too late, what was happening to him. At any rate he went insane and tore Vala and poor Orc to bits, and now he wanders from universe to universe, howling with anguish and fury. The Zoas, Luvah and Tharmas, have gone searching for him to take him to

Golgonooza, to Vala's Garden of Dreams. Only there will Urizen find peace."

"Another question, Mrs. Blake." His voice was weaker. "The truth, now."

"The truth, Mr. Blake."

"Why did you never leave me? The way I treated you . . ."

She touched his cheek. "Ah, William, at the very beginning, when I realized how crazy you really were, I almost did. I almost went home to me mum." She chuckled, remembering. "But then I saw that if I lived with my mum, I would be like my mum, and even then I knew she lived in a very small world while you lived in a very large one. Even you didn't know how large then. I didn't want to live like her, shackled with prejudice, protected but at the same time imprisoned by walls made of local, temporary ideas she took for universal, eternal truths. I saw in you a way to grow . . . though if I'd known the price . . . But never mind. In the years since we stopped time-voyaging, I do believe I've found what it really means to be a Zoa. All those magic powers don't mean a thing. It's something else, something simpler."

"What is it?"

"We both know, don't we? To be a Zoa is simply a way of looking at things. A Zoa doesn't live in one time and place, but in all times and places, equally at home in them all, equally a stranger in them all, past, present, and future, real or imaginary. I never left you because, even at your worst, you taught me, and you let others teach me. Urizen. Vala. Sister Boadicea. A poor lizard named Grooh who was the wisest of all. I went with you and never abandoned you because, I see now as I look back, you helped me become what I am."

"You have succeeded?"

"Yes. I am a Zoa at last."

"I wish I could say the same," sighed William.

He dozed off for a while, then awoke a little before six. He began to sing hymns.

Kate could see he was trying to cheer her up.

She joined in, as did the neighbor lady and a friend of

William's who had dropped in, a young fellow named George Richmond. The woman and Mr. Richmond wept as they sang, but Kate and William were dry-eyed.

The singing continued for several seconds after William fell silent.

William Blake was buried in Bunhill Fields on August 17, 1827, near where other members of his family were buried. An orthodox clergyman of the Church of England performed the orthodox service. The widow, together with three of William's friends, were the only mourners present.

The clergyman noted with a raised eyebrow that Kate did not give way to tears, but instead consoled the others and generally managed things so all went off without a hitch.

She looked quite handsome in black, in spite of her age, though the clergyman felt she should at least look a little upset, for the sake of appearances.

He was further scandalized over the matter of the tombstone.

Kate refused to buy one.

"A waste of money," she announced flatly.

If it had been anyone else who took this position, William's friends would have raised the accusation of hard-heartedness, but since they knew how devoted Kate had been to her William, they could only shake their heads in puzzlement.

Obituary notices appeared in a few journals, some making much of William's "spirituality" and "unworldliness."

The decay that had begun in the lizard universe spread. One timetrack after another faded out. The main timeline was the last to go. William's dream, and Kate's.

The year 1828 winked out of existence in the home universe, unnoticed by anyone in 1829 because of the false memories that remained intact.

Alone, bewildered, confused, the dragon Urizen wandered the fading gray-green shadowland outside of time. Around him vast glowing cones and planes crumbled and disappeared.

Suddenly he made out a familiar figure drifting toward him.

Kate!

He bared his teeth and let out a low growl.

"William Godwin," she called.

He paused. Once, he thought, he had answered to that name.

"Mr. Godwin, do you know who I am?"

The lizard hesitated before nodding.

"I won't hurt you," she told him gently. "I want to lead you to safety. You're not safe here. This whole reality is falling apart. Will you come with me?" She held out her hand.

Slowly the creature extended a quivering claw.

Her grip was firm, her warmth communicated itself to his cold reptilian blood, reviving him, bringing back dim shadows of a past when his touch too had been warm and soft and moist.

She headed uptime, drawing him unresisting behind her. Around them the flowing images stopped decaying, grew clearer, sharper. They were outrunning the wave of change.

A cloud of frightened souls swirled around them for an instant, then swarmed away downtime.

Faster, faster she drew him on.

Abruptly he found himself in a hall lined with stained glass windows. In one he saw himself (for the window was at last complete) hand in hand with Kate. Except for the slight stylization, it could have been a mirror image of what was actually happening.

She led him to a gateway. "This is the Gate of Dark Urthona, in Golgonooza, the City of Art," she said. "Beyond lies the Garden of Vala." Vala? He thought he had heard that name sometime, long, long ago. A vision of a frightfully mangled corpse flashed into his mind, but he pushed it vigorously away.

Through the gateway he saw an unearthly dreamlike landscape, restlessly transforming itself with a fluid, oozing motion under a sullen red sun.

"You'll be safe here," she said softly, letting go of his hand.

The kindness in her voice reassured him somewhat, but still he paused, afraid.

"Luvah! Tharmas!" she called.

The two Zoas stepped out from among the slowly writhing trees.

"Urizen!" They came forward, arms outstretched to welcome him, and only then did he dare to pass through into the garden.

Behind him he heard, "Goodbye, William Godwin." He did not look back. "Goodbye, Urizen." At this he turned, his great jaws open in an idiot smile, like a panting friendly dog, but he could see nobody. The voice seemed to come out of empty air. He grunted out a bewildered, wordless farewell as the Zoas flanked him.

The beautiful Luvah spoke. "Stay with us, brother. Be one of us. It's better . . . better than being real."

King Tharmas, the Atlantian, added, "The Garden of Vala is the true place outside of time. Here there is no memory, and thus no time, only an endless, meaningless dream. Vala's Garden is the perfect trap, removing the desire to escape, removing even the memory that escape is possible. Even *our* minds, schooled in the disciplines of the Zoa, are slowly melting. I think someone called Buddha once searched for this place but never found it . . . or perhaps he did. I don't remember anymore."

Luvah asked, "Urizen, can you understand what has happened to you?"

Urizen's reptilian eyes stared at him with an opaque incomprehension.

Luvah said, "You love change, don't you?"

Urizen's eyes glowed feebly, and the huge gargoyle head nodded.

Luvah said, "Here there is nothing but change." He gestured toward the ceaseless metamorphosis surrounding them. The red sunlight waxed and waned like an irregular heartbeat.

Looking around, Urizen felt the last of his lifelong discontent drain away. There was so much to see here, always something new. He'd need an eternity to see it all. For a moment he remembered someone . . . a woman.

Kate Blake.

And a man, William . . . He couldn't recall the last name.

When one awakes, dreams die quickly. To remember dreams one must force oneself to scribble them down as soon as one opens one's eyes. Few of us take the trouble. Is there anything in dreams worth saving?

Urizen slowly shook his head.

The three Zoas strolled to where a hill had begun to grow. They stood on the hill and let the ground raise them slowly above the level of the surrounding forest.

Again the image of the woman passed before Urizen's inner eye, a woman now nameless, faceless. He remembered only a white dress drifting in emptiness, and even this fragment was overwhelmed in his mind by the majesty of the panorama stretching out below him as the hill became a mountain.

But then in his mind all the light he saw around him began to stream together. He watched it and watched it and watched it. Finally all the light that existed seemed to concentrate in a single point, infinite energy in an infinitely small space.

He wondered what would happen if it exploded.

Outside the entrance to the Garden Kate felt the temperature rapidly rising. The earth shook and rumbled, first softly, then more loudly.

The supernova, Kate thought, and leaped downtime as the Earth became a ball of flame. No one remained in the hall to see the gateway to Vala's Garden glow red, then white, then soften and melt. No one remained to glance through the portal in those last seconds to see the undisturbed mountain within where the three Zoas stood meditating.

In the October of 1831 cold rain fell on London.

Shaking water from overcoats and umbrellas, Frederick Tatham and his wife came stomping and sniffling into the hallway of Kate's rooms at Cirencester Place. William's sister greeted them in a hushed voice and ushered them into the sickroom.

Kate lay quietly in a huge four-poster bed, reading William's dog-eared and underlined old Bible. She looked up, smiled, and laid the book aside.

The embarrassed silence was broken only by the drumming of the rain on the windowpane.

"You're looking well," said Frederick hesitantly.

Kate answered with an amused little smile, "No need to lie. I know I'm dying."

"Don't say that, madam!" He was shocked. "You don't know what the future holds."

Kate sighed. "Are you sure of that, Mr. Tatham?"

"Oh, yes indeed. We have all heard of cases of miraculous recoveries from the most serious of illnesses."

Kate patted the bedcovers at her side. "Come. Sit with me. There are matters we must discuss this morning."

"Surely they can wait until . . ." He approached her bedside.

"No, no." She waved aside his objections with a frail bony hand. "This afternoon I will not be here."

Mrs. Tatham and William's sister hung back, trying not to cry, as Frederick seated himself on the bed.

Frederick said, "Of course, I place myself completely at your service." His voice shook only slightly. Frederick Tatham prided himself on his composure in difficult situations.

Speaking slowly and gravely, Kate said, "William chose you to receive his legacy, such as it is. You're a good man. I know you'll do the right things with it, and you've been very kind to me since William passed on. There's not much. Some books, some manuscripts, some plates ready for printing."

"You two never were rich. I couldn't expect . . ."

"But there are no debts. Mr. Blake and I don't hold with going into debt." For a moment Kate's voice lifted with pride.

"I know, but . . ."

"You remember how William was buried?"

"Well . . . yes."

"That's the way I want to be buried, in Bunhill Fields, close by him, with a regular Church of England service. I've always tried to be a good Christian."

"And you have been, Mrs. Blake! Everyone says so!"

The two women, over by the door, hastened to agree.

Kate continued, calm and unperturbed. "I'll not have a lot of strangers staring at me. You three—that's all right— but you put me in my box and nail down the lid. No pawing me over and making me pretty, you understand."

"Of course, if that's what you want."

"Indeed it is, and I'd be much obliged if, before nailing me in, you'd dump a bushel of slaked lime in the box with me."

Frederick had turned quite pale. "Whatever you say, madam."

Kate frowned. "We make too much fuss over a corpse in this country, Mr. Tatham. This isn't ancient Egypt, you know. It's the soul that matters here, or it ought to be."

"Quite right, of course." Frederick's voice had faded to hardly more than a whisper.

"Hmm. Now let's see. Have I taken care of everything? Yes. Yes, I believe so. Now if you don't mind . . ." She gestured for her visitors to leave.

With what dignity he could muster, Frederick stood up and walked unsteadily toward the door. Mrs. Tatham and William's sister waited, as if uncertain whether to leave or stay.

"Miss Blake?" called Kate.

"Yes?" answered William's sister, suppressing a sob.

"I know you and your family never liked me, never thought I was good enough for your William."

William's sister protested, "That's not so!"

Kate nodded slowly. "Yes, it is so. And it's all the more reason why I want to thank you for taking care of me now."

The two women could contain themselves no longer, and fled, weeping openly, into the hall. Frederick followed them out. When the door had been carefully closed, Kate lay back with a sigh and picked up her Bible.

*   *   *

Mr. and Mrs. Tatham and Miss Blake stood vigil in the hall, listening to Kate's weak voice reciting fragments of scripture, singing snatches of hymns, muttering things in unfamiliar languages, and repeatedly calling out, "Don't fuss, William. I'm coming. It won't be long now!"

A little over two hours later she abruptly fell silent.

Mrs. Tatham cried, "No!" and ran into the bedroom.

Frederick entered at a more dignified pace. Mrs. Tatham was holding Kate in her arms and rocking slowly back and forth, sobbing. Kate was obviously dead.

Then Frederick frowned, noticing something.

There was a smile on Kate's face.

"She spoke . . ." Mrs. Tatham blurted out between sobs.

"Good heavens, woman," Frederick said impatiently. "Get a grip on yourself. What did she say?"

"It was only a whisper."

"Come along there. Let's have it."

"It—it sounded like 'William,' as though she were greeting him."

"Well, and there you are, Mr. Blake!"

William saw that Kate was as transparent as he. "What's this, Kate?"

"Aren't you glad to see me? I just died uptime and came down to join you. It was the oddest thing . . . I closed my eyes and the universe vanished."

All around them the last of the timestream was fading, crumbling.

"So it's all over then." A note of wistfulness had come into his voice. "Urizen's little experiment, and everything else."

Her large strange eyes glowed with suppressed excitement. She took his hand. "Not over, Mr. Blake. Just beginning."

She led him swiftly forward out of the deepening darkness toward a distant light.

9

IN EIGHTEENTH CENTURY LONDON a redheaded, blue-eyed boy screamed and ran to his window.

He didn't know exactly why, but he had expected to glimpse a naked, bearded, winged man rise into the night and pass across the face of the moon.

There was no figure, only silent empty darkness.

Little William was disappointed.

He had a feeling that somehow, somewhere, this had happened before, but the other time it had been different, more exciting. He shuffled back to his bed, frowning, and climbed under the blankets.

He thought, *Anyway, I can still pretend.*

He closed his eyes and imagined a beautiful green dragon living eternally in a magic garden of dreams.

Urizen the Dragon grinned in the Garden of Vala as the vast vortex of stars and dust we call the Milky Way Galaxy revolved once, twice, three times . . .

While he is safe, we are safe.

POUL ANDERSON
Winner of 7 Hugos and 3 Nebulas

HERALDING.....

Avalon to Camelot, a widely praised and handsomely produced illustrated quarterly magazine. Prominent writers and scholars explore the Arthurian legend from the Dark Ages to the present in features and columns including the arts, literature, the quest for the historical Arthur and more. Articles, news, reviews.

- Illustrated quarterly
- 48 pages
- 8½"x 11"
- Acid-free stock

I do very much appreciate you sending me copies of the first two numbers of *Avalon to Camelot*. I have found both to be full of interesting and useful articles, handsomely laid out and beautifully printed.

William W. Kibler — *Translator; Lancelot, or The Knight of the Cart*

I enjoyed perusing the recent issues of *A to C* and appreciated their remarkably charming eclectic appeal. If only I had the soul of an Arthurian . . . life would be better. I just know it.

Bill Zehme — *National magazine writer*

As a new subscriber, I'd like to thank you for putting out such a wonderful magazine. Your offer of the back issues was irresistible.

Abigail W. Turowski — *Woodlawn, MD*

CLIP AND SEND TO: *Avalon to Camelot*, 2126 W. Wilson, Box TR, Chicago, IL 60625

- -

☐ Please send a year's subscription:

☐ Please send a gift subscription in my name to:

Name _____

Address _____

City _____ State _____ Zip _____

☐ Enclosed is a check or M.O. for $15, payable to:
Avalon to Camelot, 2126 W. Wilson Ave., Box TR, Chicago, IL 60625
ALLOW 6 WEEKS FOR DELIVERY